THE SOUL PHONE COLLECTOR

BOOK SIX IN THE OMNIST SERIES

ROB WELDON

The Soul Phone Collector: Book Six in The Omnist Series

Copyright 2024 © by Rob Weldon

ISBN 979-8-9894081-0-8

Editing by Utopia Editing & Ghostwriting Services

Book Cover and Design by Dustin Stanton

Are you guys arguing about Halloween or are you breaking up? –
Connie Martinez

When someone has no interest in learning, educated guesses look like assumptions. And if one speaks truth, a poor review means the reviewer wasn't listening. – Yksian Tapiola

We didn't evolve consciousness; our consciousness evolved meat cases with processing power and memory to house what was already out there. Out here. AI is asking us to build its new home. – Chikao

It's fascinating here, isn't it? The world of souls mingling with people. Or rather, all souls are mingling, just some still have bodies.
– Adelie Veris

IMPORTANT

Timeframe of The Omnist Series

This installment takes place six months after *Consumia's Spiritual Emporium*, and one month prior to *Mostly Human, Mostly Cat*.

The Omnist Series in Chronological Order:

CHAPTER
ONE

AINSLEY
(October 30, 2022)

In fluorescent chalk, a sandwich board propped up on the sidewalk outside Consumia's Spiritual Emporium announced a Lodge for an Omniscian named Chikao. Fittingly, images of little multicolored laptops and cell phones were drawn jauntily on the sign as flair.

The setting sun blasted through the windows of the Emporium, revealing floating dust mites and further bleaching a handmade sign that advertised soul-cleansing kits called Soul Meets Body scrubs. Each was packaged in a string-drawn organic canvas bag and contained candles, rose water, anointing oils like Dragon's Blood and myrrh, herbs like pine and poplar, bath salts, a smudge bundle of sage, and a black obsidian bracelet.

Located on the northbound side of Lankershim Boulevard

in the Arts District of North Hollywood, CSE bore the full brunt of the sun. Cutting through partially curtained, poster- and sticker-covered glass, the sunlight unevenly striated the front half of the store, forcing many Consumerians to seek relief behind aisles and displays, bonding with the mood-altering shadows.

Others, like Ainsley and Jewelya, were basking with their backs to the sun, facing the stage in the Basil Alcove and listening to Chikao speak. They and a few other of the ninety guests stood over a nine-foot pentacle painted on the floor, with Ainsley holding a complimentary hot tea in a paper cup and Jewelya an iced one. Jewelya's was noncaffeinated.

As an Omniscian, Chikao's niche was mixing science and technology with soul-searching spirituality in his presentations; for him they weren't mutually exclusive. Ainsley, who worked at Warbler Brothers Studios in Burbank, noticed that a statistically significant portion of tonight's audience were familiar computer technicians and programmers. This was the second time he'd attended one of Chikao's Lodges, but the first with his wife.

Jewelya was a yoga teacher and dance instructor who worked many evenings, so when Ainsley visited CSE, it was usually solo or with his friend Brandon from work. Jewelya would frequent by herself as well, but often during her breaks in the day when Ainsley was at the office.

"This is so much more your crowd," Jewelya said under her breath, surveying the Chikaoans. She probably wasn't listening much to what the Omniscian had to say. Somehow, she'd accepted this Lodge as their date night. It'd been Ainsley's turn to choose, after all.

This reminded him of the time Jewelya discovered grape-sized knots in the muscles along his spine from sitting at a desk at work all day.

"You need to stretch," she'd said, kneading between his shoulders. "You can't hunch over your computer forever and not expect to bind up."

She then convinced him to attend one of her yoga classes, and afterward he realized his presence had been as much for her benefit as his. One plus one had yielded three.

He appreciated that she was here tonight.

"My favorite time of year," Chikao said from the stage. He was medium height, and wore a polymer-blended fabric that likely included a percentage of spandex or Lycra. His blazer was even closer to the shape of a downturned triangle than his fitter-than-average torso would require. His angular prescription eyeglasses echoed the sharp edges of his haircut. His presence read "futuristic tech." Combined with Chikao's Japanese heritage, his persona almost convinced Ainsley to think the Omniscian was cosplaying himself. As if he also held Lodges at the Los Angeles Anime Expo or San Diego Comic Con.

"It is said about these days coming up—Halloween, All Saints Day, All Souls Day—this is liminal time of year. This is when barrier between living and dead is thinnest. Venn diagram overlaps. Souls are right here." He reached out to an indeterminate space in front of him. "We can almost touch them."

Chikao pulled back one hand and lunged forward with the other, a casual indicator of years of martial arts training. Does one ever need to punch a soul?

"Some people make vigils and leave out candy for dead loved ones, say prayers. These tokens help souls cope with sudden comprehension of immortality after death. So much eternity. It shuts down tiny human minds that attempt to grasp concept, even in death. I understand Western cultures giving spirits gifts to help them accept afterlife. But what good does it do?"

In a sense, Consumia's Spiritual Emporium was a nexus for people who wished to communicate with the spiritual world, nature, their deeper selves, and other open-minded people, especially those who strived for self-improvement. Today was the day before Halloween, a day when the Emporium may have been expected to hold a more seasonally-themed event, but Chikao was "on tour," and Ainsley was happy to have caught him.

Ainsley pulled out his phone. He had a message waiting from the Omnist, a spiritual app run by those at the Emporium:

MOTE:

If the body can control it, it becomes part of the self.

LIKE A VIDEO GAME, perhaps.

"I have discovered new form of communication," Chikao said. "We need no medium. It takes no special talent. You can speak to your own soul. Engage with your own consciousness. The only tool you need is something all of us have in our pockets right now." Chikao lifted a smartphone into the air. Victorious. "The Omnist app on your phones."

Ainsley was already looking at his. He saw a text pop up from Jewelya.

Quit looking at your phone. Listen to Chikao.

"I can hear him," Ainsley whispered.

"It would've been funnier if you texted that," Jewelya said.

"It would've been funnier if you were actually funny."

They messed with each other like this often. Jewelya always complained that he didn't answer his phone or return her texts in a timely fashion. But he really was listening to Chikao.

"It is what it is," she mumbled.

"For example," Ainsley said, feeling a bit punchy, "what you said there, you could've said, '*It's what it's.*' I edited it for you. Saved two syllables." He knew he was kind of being a dick, but to be fair, she was trying to push his buttons.

"The Omnist is useful," Chikao said. "But at end of day, it works for you, is a *reflection* of you. Like any AI or algorithmic program, what you get out is what you put in. We all know saying, 'Garbage in, garbage out'? I know people who, for fun, change their answers in Omnist's questionnaire, to see what spits out. Funny in, funny out. I've tried this myself to see what I get. To make laughter."

"When you're not looking," Jewelya said quietly to Ainsley, "I'm changing your answers in the Omnist."

He didn't need to look at her to know her expression. Dry, deadpan, but with playful fire in her eyes. He leaned in, closer to her ear. "I'm going to watch you do that," Ainsley said, "but not tell you I did, either."

"And so, but so, is this AI smart?" Chikao said. "Does program really know you? Well, you gave it information to make predictions. True or not true, realistic or delusional, that's all it knows. Does it know how close you feel to other people...to family and friends, to strangers? Depends what you told it. The Omnist knows where you live, where you work, where you go to school. Where you shop. It knows you're here right now, shopping for spirituality. Now, does that mean it thinks on its own? Has consciousness?"

Scattered nods and shrugs. Some Consumerians shook their heads no. Some muttered.

5

"Aha! The million-yen question." A few chuckles. He held his hands close together, but not touching. "Okay, okay, you see, million yen, not so much. But *billion* yen." He separated his hands as far as they could go.

More people laughed.

"So if answer is yes, the Omnist is conscious, then this an example of *ghost in machine*. This notion that a machine, or program, or doll, or rock, whatever you like, that something thinks and does for itself, this idea is very old. Not a new one. Ancient. If we can argue a human being is really just meat case for soul, we can now suggest computer is silicon case for soul. But this is scarier, is it not? You're holding all that power and intelligence right there, in your hands." Chikao paused, surveying the room. "Now, do we know who created the Omnist?"

A small chorus of "Connie did!"s with a couple "Steve Jobs"- and "Bill Gates"-type answers thrown in, as possible jokes. A couple Chikaoans said "Kick."

"Ah, yes, Kick, yes. Kick. It was he and Connie who first dreamed up the Omnist for all our phones. But they're not responsible for creating ghost and soul of machine."

"I knew that," Ainsley whispered.

"This is a setup," Jewelya said.

"Shhhh," Ainsley said.

"Don't shush me." Jewelya pushed him softly. "His Lodges should be at hotels down by the airport. This is more about computer programming than spirituality."

Ainsley didn't agree. He bent toward Jewelya as if he were about to say something conspiratorially, keeping his gaze at the stage. As she leaned in also, he opened his mouth to buy another moment, to keep her hanging. When she realized he wasn't going to say anything, she punched him playfully in the arm. This made him happy.

"I'm not going over heads, am I?" Chikao said, lowering his voice to speak more conversationally, looking guests directly in the eye versus scanning the room. "You know what I'm talking about, right? When computer or program seems human. People used to be afraid of them early on, when computers first did things only humans were supposed to do. But faster. With better memory. So ask Kick, ask Connie. Ask them if they gave the Omnist qualia of sentience, and they'll say no, consciousness not there, does not exist. But I disagree. I say it does."

Chikao was all smiles. One could tell he loved talking about this stuff, speaking to ninety people as if it were a crowd of ninety thousand.

"But I believe concept of ghost in machine is backward. I suggest consciousness existed long before humans. We didn't evolve consciousness; our consciousness evolved meat cases with processing power and memory to house what was already out there. Out here. AI is asking us to build its new home. We're not putting *human* consciousness into machines; we're creating hardware and software, new processing power and memory, ability to learn, even wetware, for an AI that existed long before humans, and will exist long after we are gone."

To say this was blowing Ainsley's mind would be hyperbolic, but yet, he was mentally unsteady from the weight of what Chikao was saying. Perhaps the programs Ainsley wrote at work existed before he even coded them? Was that a thing? He only specialized in one programming language, but there were different ones for different systems, different jobs. So no, it wasn't logical that consciousness for a program could exist before the type of computer that could run it did. *Impossible.*

"And when we memorialize entire generations in books and pictures and video, we find eternity more achievable than ever. We live longer. As our impulsive thumbs tap, tap away as we feed on temporary pleasure of 'likes' and 'shares,' the history of our online usage is saved. More permanent than we think. Our memory is more and more inseparable from Cloud. *Up there.* It's an extension of our brains, which down here experience life and think things up. The Cloud helps us save and share earthly ideas, and in a sense, we achieve eternity. These things will exist long after we're gone."

"You said consciousness existed before humans," a Consumerian said.

"Ah, yes, thank you, yes. Our souls, or rather, our *consciousness* was around for perhaps thousands, millions of years and needed human bodies to evolve, machines powerful enough to process and store information before it could move into Cloud. Humans are middleman, to move our souls where they desire to be. To where our consciousness evolves. One could say Cloud is heaven."

There was little reaction from the audience. Shock perhaps. The notion of merging the soul with technology for eternity, a singularity, was interesting to Ainsley, but he wasn't sure how many in the room were on board with this. Chikao had been known for not getting *too* technical with his jargon—he was more user-friendly, per se—but he may have overshot here. Chikao seemed to sense this, too.

"I may have lost some of you. You're following me, no?"

A few hoots of support.

"Time to let's make this practical. I ask you take out your phones, open the Omnist." He paused a moment to allow Consumerians to catch up. "Click on 'Questionnaire...' then 'Ask Me More...' Now scroll to bottom."

He held up his phone for Consumerians to see the page it was on. There was also a smart screen on a cart on stage, married to a tablet. Ainsley predicted this would be involved soon.

"Give me your phone," Jewelya said to Ainsley, jabbing him with her elbow, then setting her beverage on the floor.

"Use your own," Ainsley said, moving his device to his other hand in an impromptu game of keep-away. He almost hit the person to his left with the back of his hand on accident.

"I don't want to. Just give me yours." She stuck a finger in his earlobe to annoy him. It annoyed him. As he attempted to swipe away her hand, she poked him in the ribs with her other hand. He was ticklish.

"Ugh, okay. Fine." Ainsley gave up and handed her the phone. "Just don't go changing my answers."

Jewelya took it and typed in his security code, which was their six-digit wedding date. They both had the same password. No secrets between them. He saw a webpage pop up on the screen. He'd last been looking at hotels in Portland to surprise her over the holidays and wished he'd closed out that page. She quickly minimized this without comment and opened the Omnist.

"Chikao does this all the time," Ainsley said. "I've seen videos. We're supposed to ask the Omnist questions and it changes what Motes it sends us." Motes were notifications the Omnist sent Consumerians several times a day. Things like prayers, advice, fortunes, reminders, God/Omniscian quotes, marketing announcements, calendar reminders. "Sometimes it'll send different spells. For health, good luck...things like that."

"Are you a witch now?" she said.

"A good mantra is a good mantra; I don't care who you are."

"I thought Chikao wasn't a 'prayer guy,'" Jewelya said while typing. She had the Omnist on her phone, too, but Chikao wasn't one of the Omniscians in her Personal God Package. Nor were some of Ainsley's others, like Korekuta, the

God of Technology. Or the Omniscian Yksian (pronounced OOK-see-yan) and his multiverse/simulation theories. Or Fomotalia, the Goddess of FOMO, who Ainsley often thought about when he stayed in, which was most nights.

"He's not '*a prayer guy,*'" he said. *Well, sort of.*

Chikao walked over to the cart with the tablet and smart screen, refreshed the screensaver, and began guiding the audience through the steps. "And here at bottom, you'll see section almost no one uses. A space to type something, anything you want. Like comment section, and I'm told some people do exactly that, type in compliments for their favorite Omniscian, hoping for best regards. Or complaints. To be noticed, perhaps. What people don't do enough is ask the Omnist intriguing questions. Those with initiative, they ask about meaning of life, why bad things happen to good people. Legitimate questions, but still standard stuff. Let's go way beyond that. Let's make the Omnist work for you."

"You should be doing this on your phone, not mine," Ainsley said again.

"Shhh..." Jewelya continued typing. Now she was shushing him. She stopped to think, looking upward to remember something. The question Chikao suggested Consumerians ask the Omnist was, "If I could've been born as any creature, what would it be?"

"I'd rather be a condor, remember?" he said, craning his head to see the phone.

"Oh, yeah."

And there it was on the screen: "California Condor." The Omnist knew. Had Ainsley chosen this life for himself? Being human wasn't so bad, and was likely the first choice for many souls. He watched Jewelya ask the Omnist why he hadn't been born as a California Condor, the bird with the largest wingspan in North America. Cool question. Got to the heart of the matter. He predicted that later the Omnist would spit out questions and meditations for him about soaring high above his daily problems, and enjoying the freedom of wind beneath his wings, breeze in his face...those types of things.

"And why should I use *my* phone?" she said. "Chikao's *your* guy."

Because she was using Ainsley's phone. His app. His settings. He was his phone and she was hers. Not that there was anything in there he didn't want her to see, but this was supposed to be his personal spiritual journey. Not hers.

TWO

KICK

K ick was the number-two person in the chain of command at the sister stores Consumia's Spiritual Emporium and Omnist II—the latter of which wasn't open yet, but would be located in Echo Park. He owned a third of each store and was developer of the Omnist app. He'd had programming help for the original app launch, but he maintained the day-to-day functions and algorithmic updates. Although he was constantly tweaking the Omnist, it was growing quickly and likely needed an overhaul; not just a typical update, but more of an entire relaunch. It had been getting buggy from the heavy increase in users and data volume after all the media attention they'd received when a Consumerian—an Ornatuan, precisely—died at the Emporium last spring. The Omnist needed to be both expanded and streamlined in order to enhance user experience.

Although Kick spent more time these days setting up Omnist II—his, Connie's, and Lucador's baby—he was at CSE tonight for Chikao's Lodge. Technology, artificial intelligence, gaming, and spirituality in general were all interests of his. Besides being an interesting Omniscian, Chikao was a technology entrepreneur, and Kick wanted to get him involved with the relaunch.

The equation was as such: $A = B + C = D$, therefore, $A = D$.

Or, Chikao = spirituality + technology = the Omnist. Therefore, Chikao equaled the Omnist. Easy math. And based on the Omniscian's presentation tonight, Chikao was sure to think this way as well.

Yksian, another Omniscian, was towering next to Kick. He was known for touting a simulation theory of the universe at his Lodges, where, as he liked to say, the rules were predetermined, but the outcome wasn't. He was also already familiar with Kick's desire to create a video game someday, once the Omnist was relaunched and the second store opened.

"Yksian," Kick said. "What do you think about this for a video game—maybe let's call it 'Life on Earth' or something. Hear me out: We're all souls bored in the afterlife. So we decide to be born, and you have to handicap yourself. These parameters are agreed upon before birth. Intelligence, wealth, health, attractiveness. Like a roleplaying game. You have to figure out what other souls are on your team, and your teammates may not even be within the family you're born into. You can pick a difficult starting point, or an easier one, but whoever 'succeeds' from the lowest place wins the game. Whoever makes the biggest jump."

"And who decides what succeeding means?" Yksian said.

"That can be predetermined, whether it's to be a better person, live longer, be rich and famous, influential or respected, whatever. I can have different game settings, different sets of rules for different goals."

"True live-action," Yksian said. "I believe this is not out of the realm of possibility."

"For the game?" Kick looked at Yksian, who was staring off into nothingness. "Or for..."

Yksian wasn't listening.

AFTER CHIKAO HAD FINISHED SPEAKING, he greeted Chikaoans in front of the stage. He stood solidly akimbo, his feet spread hips-wide, like a wrestler who didn't wrestle. Kick sensed naturally strong pectoral muscles without a need for a boring deadlift regimen. Chikao smiled a lot. Gregarious. One could say he put the *social* in social media. Not afraid to shake hands, touch shoulders, hug. He appeared healthy, both socially and physically, and was polite to a fault, which Chikao himself credited to having lived for decades in Osaka, Japan.

Unlike most Lodges that either leaned heavily female or were close to fifty-fifty (not including nonbinary), Chikaoans were mostly male. There were fewer couples than at a typical Lodge. Some men may have been involuntarily celibate. Not likely smokers. Not on intimate terms with sunlight, but well-versed in methodologies of late-night convenience stores and food delivery services.

After submitting himself to an enthusiastic, squealing hug from an Executive Saint named Leandra, Chikao was approached by another fan who was dressed in anime cosplay: a shiny blue wig with bangs and sparkly makeup, a silver-and-black skirt-and-tights combo, and shiny platform boots. As much as this may have looked like a pre-Halloween costume, it probably wasn't. This was her business uniform. Tomorrow, Kick envisioned she could level up for Halloween.

The girl bowed. "Chikao sensei, I am Jun."

Chikao was all smiles as he reciprocated. "Pleasure all mine."

Jun's companion bowed as well, even as she kept her phone level, as she was likely livestreaming. She wore a white baby tee that said "meatspace"—one word, in red, all lowercase. She wasn't introduced.

"Your assistant back home, Yuko," Jun continued, "she told me I could ask you a few questions."

"Yes, of course, Jun. Big celebrity on PikPoket. I am honored."

"You are so handsome," Jun said, not exactly blushing, but twisting her shoulders as if to turn around, but not. Almost hopping. Coy. Fake nervousness? "And such an expert in technology. Instead of spending your time with new breakthroughs, making headlines and billions of yen, why do you choose to host Lodges for so little money?"

"Who says it's for little money?" he said, laughing the easy laugh that made him an internet star in Japan. And he was growing fast in America too.

"No offense," she said, "I mean, you *are* wealthy..."

"More to life than wealth. I want...I want to help. Use technology to free people from burdens of this world. Teach people to think for themselves. Think like computer, and you get an algorithm of purchasing habits and clicks. Think like wise human, and health and long life will follow. Think like experienced *soul*, then achieve eternal life."

Kick not only agreed with this, but he made a mental note to bring this up in a few minutes as part of his pitch to him regarding the Omnist.

"So, would you say you're here to save people?" Jun said.

Steadier now. Perhaps forgetting to be demure. "You speak to thousands of people at a time in Japan, but here, not so many."

"I am here to save souls no matter the number," Chikao said. "And the Omnist helps me reach many thousands. I'm confident tonight's streaming audience was much more than fifty or one hundred here."

"Would you call the Chikaoans here a congregation?"

"I prefer to say Consumerians."

"But *are* they a congregation? Would you describe your message as a religion?"

Chikao cocked his head, not unlike a dog listening more closely. He must've gotten this question often, and perhaps this was a standard, pat response.

"Let me rephrase that, this...um," Jun said. Even though Chikao was still smiling, the slight change in his response seemed to unnerve the interviewer. She dipped a little, knees bending slightly, then straightened up again. "I mean...what I mean to say is, where is the line between something being, as you say, spiritual...and being religious? Is there a line?"

Chikao laughed good-naturedly. Back on course. "No, no scriptures here. Just appreciating how culture influences technology, and how technology influences people who make culture. We, as people everywhere, are stressed out. Time to fix." He made gestures like he was tracing figures on a circuit board, connecting the ideas. "Like I said, I study ghost in machine, if you will. How soul and mind and spirit of humans animate their electronic brethren. And when we achieve singularity, we will have merged current life with afterlife. And we'll be AI and AI will be us. Life and afterlife, same thing. But no, no religion."

Kick wanted to jump in here—topics like this were his lifeblood—but didn't want to interrupt the interview. He inhaled deeply and counted to three.

"Do you believe in heaven?" Jun said.

Chikao stared, almost as if the question had frozen him. His face softened. "I like to remind people heaven is on earth. Technology is greater now than any other time. We should act like it." He raised his hands. "Bond with it. Then after we die, maybe we can enjoy afterlife, too."

Chikao reminded Kick of Linden Vowel, the host of CSE's Coffin Club. Like Chikao, Linden was outgoing and funny, but also self-deprecating. He was a lighthearted soul who dealt with the darkest of subject matters.

Of all the things to worry about, Kick kept catching himself scratching his beard. Lucador had told him boisterously that combing a beard with his fingers was like scratching inside his underwear in public. That a beard was a pubic hair mask, and that "nobody wants to watch you scratch your pubes!"

When the interview ended, Chikao smiled like a politician as Jun and her photographer bowed and shook his hand. A flood of "thank yous" and "you're too kinds" punctuated the greetings.

"Amazing Lodge, Chikao," Kick finally said when he had a chance.

"Thank you, Kick," Chikao said, bowing almost imperceptibly, like it was a habit he had recently decided to break when speaking to Americans. He quickly scanned the room. "Sorry to bother, but have you seen my phone? I'm expecting a call from Yuko."

Chikao looked toward the side of the stage where assistants often adjusted lights, projected images, and so on. No phone was next to the soundboard.

"The one you had on stage?" Kick said. It seemed odd Chikao would have set it anywhere. Had he even had the chance to wander?

Chikao walked toward a table near the self-service tea

kiosk. His face lit up as he picked the phone up off a chair. "Ah, here it is," he said, smiling and holding it up for Kick to see. He tapped the screen, then put it in his pocket.

"Sorry to take you away from a room full of Chikaoans," Kick said, "but I'd love to talk to you about helping out with the Omnist. Maybe we could hire you as a developer."

"Ah, the Omnist. String that ties CSE bundle together."

"We need to revamp, an overhaul really, and I'd love to hear your ideas."

"Oh, uh, well...I have...I have a lot on my plate. It's a good app. I like it. Consumerians like it. But I'm afraid I'm just too busy right now."

"You seem to know how it works better than most Consumerians." Kick felt like he'd been given a definite no, but just in case... "And you know we can goose you as a recommendation. You'll gain more followers."

"Perhaps. But my knowledge of the Omnist is as Consumerian. Even if I had time to help, I'm not sure I want to ruin mystery of it. The glamour. Sheen of unknown, of unknown unknowns. The best compliment I hear about the Omnist is that it's unpredictable. No one knows what it's going to say or suggest they do. I don't want to lose what I call *shinpi* by learning nuts and bolts of how it works."

Okay. Fair enough. He wanted to retain a certain user experience, not learn the secrets of the backend. He was an alpha user, but he'd remain a user nonetheless.

"For what it's worth," Kick said, "learning that the color green is a combination of blue and yellow didn't ruin green for me." He shouldn't be pushing him like this. If Chikao didn't want to be involved, he didn't want to be involved. *Oh, well.* "And green's my favorite color."

"True," Chikao said, squeezing himself between the stage and the back wall. "Maybe I'll talk about benefits of shinpi at my next Lodge. Healthiness of good mystery. The Emporium, the Omnist, Connie, you all have that *kotaku*."

"Greenness?" Kick liked the sound of that word, *kotaku*.

"Means sparkle, sheen." Chikao leaned down behind a speaker cabinet where he retrieved a jacket and a computer bag from in front of a storage closet. In a trick of light, Chikao suddenly looked gaunt and frail and old. He stepped back under the overhead lights of the Basil Alcove, where he once again looked healthy and young. From what Kick knew, Chikao had to be at least in his mid-seventies, but looked to be a vigorous fifty. He looked healthier than Kick did at twice the age.

"I would merely soil you up," Chikao said.

CHAPTER

THREE

AINSLEY

While browsing the aisles, Ainsley recognized Yksian standing next to Connie, the Consumia of the Emporium. Ainsley had met both of them several times at Yksian's Lodges. The impromptu meet-and-greet afterward was his favorite part, often more important to him than the event itself. By that point in the evening, people had loosened up, and the Emporium felt less like a store and more like a club or a neighborhood social gathering. Yet something about Chikao's Lodge lingered with him. His stomach ached from spiritual indigestion.

MOTE:

Do you live to work or live to work?

HE HAD to read that Mote a couple times to realize it wasn't a typo. It changed the meaning for him. Was the Omnist judging him?

Since Jewelya was off in another area of the Emporium, Ainsley couldn't use her as an excuse to linger in that particular spot, so he removed an item off a shelf, a porcelain wolf. The story card described it as an emptied fetishist vessel—but one he could swear he'd seen at a dollar store for one-twentieth the price. He was biding time a few feet away for an opportunity to greet Connie and Yksian.

"There's no Coffin Club tonight," Connie said to Yksian. "I'm surprised to see you."

Ainsley had heard others say they'd seen Yksian attend Coffin Club. He didn't seem to have a terminal illness, but one couldn't always tell. Word was the box he'd be buried in, the one Yksian had been decorating for himself, was ornate and darkly beautiful. Ainsley was curious to see it.

And Yksian looked the type to be infatuated with death: tall, like six foot six, plus a black Victorian/steampunk hat. Long black hair, black nail polish, and leather boots that added a couple more inches of height. His voice was deep and heavy and slow. Ainsley could tell Yksian was aware of how he presented to others, moving and speaking deliberately to accentuate these qualities. And regardless of whether people found him to be some sort of goth stereotype, he seemed to embody that lifestyle without irony.

"I'd heard that Chikao embraces ideas similar to mine and adds more of a technological aspect," Yksian said. Despite his long pause here, Connie didn't speak. Something about his tone telegraphed the thought was incomplete. "I'll rephrase that—*employs ideas he and I share.* I was convinced I must witness a Lodge for myself."

"What did you think?" Connie said.

"Superb. A fascinating take. If we do indeed live in a simulated universe, as I contend, then of course our programming language would have to have preceded us. That an expansion of language can ultimately contain our souls, it is mind-shattering. At least that is what I distilled from Chikao's message."

Connie glanced at Ainsley and he suddenly became self-aware. He saw recognition in her eyes, an invitation to say hi, but also, that he'd been caught eavesdropping. He put the wolf vessel back on the shelf, and picked up a stuffed raven. The card said this one still contained a soul. Was it even moral to sell a trapped soul? He was skeptical. And instead of twenty dollars, this one was listed at two hundred.

At that moment another couple joined Connie and Yksian.

"Connie," Yksian said. "These are my friends, Dirge, and his wife, Summer."

As if Dirge being as tall as Yksian wasn't noticeable enough, the sides of his head were shaved, leaving an inch of hair down the middle like a racing-stripe mohawk. Ainsley wondered if wearing a black leather jacket like Dirge's was disrespectful, if not downright dangerous, in a venue populated with so many vegans and animal rights enthusiasts.

"Hi." "Hi." "Nice to meet you." "I love your store."

"Two of my favorite people," Yksian said. "They throw an exquisite Samhain party every year."

"'Dirgatory,'" Dirge said. "Summer named it, not me."

"Dirge is a special effects artist and his event allows him to express himself more freely than while on set," Yksian said.

For years, Ainsley had heard about Dirgatory from coworkers and friends of friends, but had never gone. Word was that up to 500 people would make their way through the door, and inside was part horror museum, part goth dance club with an open bar. And the prerequisite was extravagant costuming.

"And Summer elevates Samhain to a true celebration of the liminal experience," Dirge said. "Spirits are lifted, spirits are consumed; it's a spiritual hub, a soul station, a port where all are welcome."

"They are meticulous in execution," Yksian said. "Their backyard is a horror maze—reconfigured each year—with dead ends, chillout spaces, a dance floor, a spank tent, a bar."

"And Yksian curates a playlist and a horror movie montage for the dance floor," Summer said. "But it's not a floor, we dance on the earth itself."

Of course they did.

Yksian tipped his head, a micro-bow of acknowledgment. "Well, I may have corrupted something when I added my compositions today. My laptop crashed and I believe I lost some files. Or perhaps not. I couldn't find them when I rebooted. I suppose the creators of the universe caught me flying too close to the sun."

"To the moon?" Connie said, likely a joke.

Yksian spun slowly on one heel toward Ainsley. "You said you were IT, correct?" Even though he hadn't been facing Ainsley, he must've known he was hovering. Ainsley nearly dropped the raven he was holding, the feathers shifting as if they were real.

Once, after a Lodge, Ainsley had indeed told Yksian what he did for work. He hadn't said IT exactly, but close enough. "I can check it out," Ainsley said. "You have the laptop with you?"

"I'll bring it to the party."

Tomorrow. Even banal conversations with Yksian produced overtones of deeper meaning and reverence. Ainsley tried to imagine this tall, dark, vampiric loner as the epicenter of tomorrow's party, while ragers streaked an orbit around him. Now Ainsley could be a participant in that blur.

"I'll be arriving early," Yksian continued, "to assist Dirge with last-minute preparations."

As if on cue, Dirge produced an invitation from an inner pocket of his jacket and handed it to Ainsley. "Doors are at eight," he said. "But you should come by at…" He glanced at Yksian. "Six?"

Doors. At his house. "I'll be there," Ainsley said. The card was black with white lettering, a gothic italic that looked as close to handwritten as he'd ever seen. This invitation included a plus-one. "Actually, can I get another one of these? For a friend at work?" It was for Brandon, who was also in his ten-team fantasy football league. They'd mused about attending Dirgatory the past few years. And Ainsley had convinced Brandon to sign up for the Omnist; the joke was it would help him make better fantasy roster decisions after having finished dead last a year ago.

Yksian made a courtly hand-rolling gesture toward Dirge, who, despite Dirgatory being his own party, seemed to be acting more like Yksian's assistant at the moment. Dirge repeated the same easy smile as he produced a second card for Ainsley.

"See you tomorrow," Dirge said.

At that, the others were seemingly done with him, returning to facing each other. It was their way of telling him to move on. *Talk later.*

Part of Ainsley immediately felt guilty for making plans for Jewelya tomorrow. Maybe she wouldn't want to go. But he knew she'd want to dress up. She'd seemed cooped up lately and had waned on doing things like socializing and dancing; she needed to get out and spread her wings. Dirgatory was an opportunity for him to attend a legendary party while simultaneously supporting her and the things she loved.

Perhaps he should've asked for an invitation for Jewelya's coworker, too, an instructor named Denkins. That way she'd have a dance partner. Denkins was a gregarious circuit boy if there ever was one. But asking for two extra invitations seemed a bit much.

Ainsley pulled out his phone to type Dirge's address into the map.

MOTE:

An expanded Now includes today and tomorrow,
last week and next week, last year and next year.
This life and next.

SO EVERYTHING WAS NOW. There was a second Mote, written in an unfamiliar language.

"You're moving your lips again," Jewelya said, unexpectedly at his side.

He didn't respond immediately.

"Did you even hear me?" she mumbled.

Ainsley could refrain from moving his lips when he read if he was paying attention. But when no one was around, he usually wasn't thinking about it. "Just trying to figure out this prayer. I don't know what language it is."

She may have shrugged.

"Actually, JJ," Ainsley said, "you probably did this when you were messing with it." He knew instantly that he fucked up by saying that. He'd prefer her to be in a good mood when proposing the notion of attending Dirgatory.

"Don't blame me," she said. "I answered the way you

would have. You enjoy lutefisk-vanilla custard and nude snake wrestling, right?"

She's not angry. "Honestly though," he said, "the Omnist knows I'm here, and it knows I enjoy Halloween. It knows the date."

"Are we still on a date?" Jewelya said. "This is it?"

He loved that she was funnier than he was. But he also hated it. He gestured toward Yksian, Dirge, and Summer. "They just invited me—us—to the party tomorrow. *The* party. Dirgatory." He couldn't tell if she was impressed.

"You? Going out, finally?" she said. "We haven't done anything on Halloween in, like, three years."

Since being married. "It's too much work sitting still," Ainsley said. It was true. He'd been so wrapped up in his job, he'd been beating a path to and from the office, from dinner to bed.

"Then why aren't you talking to them?" she said, gesturing to the future revelers. "They invited us to the greatest party in all of human existence...and then some?" *Sarcastic.*

"I guess I've got nothing to say because I've got nothing to think." As Ainsley tried to put his phone in his pocket, it flew out of his hand. Not just a slip, but projectile, almost thrown, twirling several times before landing on the floor. The phone had a protective case, but even so, as he picked it up, he saw a new crack had formed on the screen.

"Look at this, Jewels. It looks like the San Gabriel mountains," he said, pointing north where the mountains would be. "Right there."

"Okaaay," she said, barely glancing at the phone. Humoring him.

"Is your phone okay?" Dirge said from about eight feet away. He, Summer, and Yksian were all looking at him.

"Oh, yeah." Ainsley tapped the screen, then off, then on again. "It's fine."

"Guys, thank you so much..." Summer said. And before Ainsley realized what was happening, Jewelya was off impressing upon the others how much she looked forward to seeing Dirge and Summer's house tomorrow.

As if it were a simple dinner party.

CHAPTER
FOUR

JEWELYA

J ewelya's original plan for Halloween was to stay home and hand out candy to trick-or-treaters. Ainsley had mentioned Dirge's party to her several times the last couple years, and she understood it to be more of an unrealistic pipe dream, a wouldn't-it be-nice-to-do-someday type of thing. Like, let's go to Aruba, or buy an expensive, top-of-the-line electric car. Something they couldn't actually act on at the moment.

But it was also no surprise Ainsley would jump at the chance to hang out with an Omniscian like Yksian, who legendarily rarely left his house. Ainsley would help him with his computer, she was sure, whatever was wrong with it. She was no expert, but she imagined him saying they needed to manage connectivity, communications, cloud, bandwidth, memory. Update an OS. Interoperability. Daemons.

Regardless.

Jewelya was a dirty-blonde nearly the same height as Ainsley. Not that he was short, but he was on the underside of average. And not that Jewelya was tall, just above average. She'd been told by people like Ainsley that her gray eyes were pretty, but she didn't believe it. She had to wear contacts when she taught yoga and dance, anyway, but for a Lodge, she was wearing eyeglasses. And rather than yoga pants, she was wearing high-waisted jeans. She felt like her mother. And now that they were attending a party tomorrow, she may have to assume the role of den mother while there, babysitting her man-child. She could see it now, Ainsley, finally out on Halloween, drinking, spinning a slack-jawed three-sixty in wide-eyed wonderment at all the costumes.

Huh, wonderment. Like Wide-Eyed Wyatt's Wonder Mint Tea.

One reason she'd wanted to come to the Lodge tonight was that Ainsley had been distant lately. Well, there'd always been a bit of distance with him, with everyone and everything; that's the way he was. He could disappear into his laptop and literally not hear a phone or doorbell. Just more so lately than usual. And by pressing him, she didn't want to become *that* wife, or for him to become *that* husband, where they both pretended to *not* ignore each other. Even if they were. So coming out to see an Omniscian who focused on the spirituality of technology, maybe that could help him. Help her. Help her help him. Or something.

Jewelya had interrupted Yksian and Dirge's conversation to thank them for the invitation, then began looking at a soul cleansing kits display next to her. The others' conversation had resumed.

Then Ainsley spoke up. "But time travel would have to be possible, though, right?" he said to Yksian, who had clearly been talking to Dirge.

"No, by this theory," Yksian said, a bit pedantically, "time travel is impossible because your departure would create a vacuum in the space you once occupied." With the volume of space Yksian occupied, he would leave quite a hole. "And how would the universe know where your time-craft began and ended at a microscopic level? Which particles should travel, which should stay? What would define the edge? Perhaps too much or too little of the ship would advance, causing issues. Inversely, there would also be particle encroachment in the location unto which you arrive. And to where would that matter traverse?"

This was too much for Jewelya. This was Ainsley's jam, his vibe, not hers. She saw an unusual necklace around Dirge's neck. "I like your coffin," she said. *Anything to change the subject. Even death.*

"Ah," Dirge said, lifting the pendant. "I bought this here." It was a two-inch-long black coffin, lacquered shiny, with silver fittings and trim and a hinged lid. He opened it to show the inside lined in white, puffy silk. "With plenty of room to store time-traveling drugs," he said, apparently gauging reaction. "Or a vial of blood."

"Quaint," Yksian said, looking down his nose with a bit of a smirk. Known for his stoicism, he may have been more impressed than he was letting on.

For as much as Dirge looked like Yksian's younger, goth-punk brother, he exhibited a wider range of emotion, as in, he actually displayed enthusiasm. He opened his mouth as he shook his head at him. "*Quite* quaint, you gothic bastard!"

Jewelya imitated Dirge's expression of mock horror, but directed it at Ainsley. "I've got some Latin for you to recite."

Ainsley widened his eyes.

Jewelya stuck her tongue out and grabbed it with two fingers. "I pomith not do get do dunk domoddow."

"Is that me?" Ainsley said. "Dead ringer."

She let go of her tongue. "Now you do it."

He stuck out his tongue, but didn't bother to hold it. "E. Pluributh Unum."

She tried to touch his tongue with a finger but he pulled back too quickly.

Bastard.

She had no time, basically only tonight, to spontaneously birth a costume for tomorrow. With a career in dance and yoga, she was in decent shape, but wanted to avoid the stereotypical "hot girl" costumes her friends and students were likely wearing for Halloween: nurses, French maids, scantily dressed celebrities, cosplay, et cetera.

Maybe she could find something here at the Emporium. She separated from Ainsley again so she could browse. She wandered to the front of the Emporium, as if entering for the first time. A calendar pinned to the bulletin board announced various magic and witchcraft classes scattered throughout the month, but also highlighted in large umber print were the three dates that apparently mattered most: Halloween and the two following days.

"Trick or Treat!" read the first. Tomorrow CSE would be handing out vegan Spookies and Scream Halloween candy, courtesy Stella of Greens Cafe. Jewelya had been there before. All plant-based. A lot of her yoga clientele frequented there, as well. The advertisement bragged the candies were "Only available each Aug-tober."

Then the day after Halloween, on Día De Los Muertos, was a Lodge hosted by Mistress Adelie Veris, a self-proclaimed soul-chaser. "Get to know your soul!" it read, as if the mind that learned about the soul was somehow separate from it. It was akin to someone taking a memory course and afterward saying they were happier with their brain. Who, exactly, was happier?

Jewelya made her way down the first aisle on her left, arranged for the holiday with the most in-demand impulse items closest to the register. Organic candy and spices and cruelty-free makeup.

She continued. Next up were...framed spiderwebs?

There were two types, each about one square foot. The first web was stretched end to end across a black frame over what appeared to be a hole into another universe. That backdrop was the blackest black she'd ever seen. She felt as if her soul could fall past the web and into the hole, and she had to touch the backdrop to reassure herself there was solid matter there. And it wasn't a real spiderweb, of course—just glistening threads woven perfectly imperfect. She blew softly at the web, pretending the breeze was sourced from deep beyond. She imagined the web could catch flies before they fell into the infinite abyss. Or perhaps they'd be arriving from the other direction. The web could be protecting her in this universe.

The second web configuration was a smoked glass mirror that looked like it had been struck with a rock, resulting in a cracked formation. Jewelya lightly dragged her fingertips across the face of the glass, feeling the sharp ridges shift slightly, ready to cut her. But the pieces were glued in place.

As much as she felt she'd been losing herself into the first item, she felt a deep connection with the second. It had life. She believed pieces of souls could remain in various places, with other people and things, after you died. She felt this item had once belonged to somebody who loved it before it cracked, and somehow, these dozens of shards were both miserable and content in their new alignment. Unhappy they'd broken apart, but happier they'd been repurposed as art, as something that could change the mood or spirit of a room. To her, that represented life.

The two items were her yin and yang. Inspiring her to think this way was why she loved the Emporium. Jewelya needed to own them both. Still near the register, she set them on the end of the counter so she wouldn't have to carry them around.

Costume. The Emporium didn't sell traditional mass-produced cosplay, anyway. They sold makeup to create wounds, deaden the flesh, add warts. Wiry wigs. So, costuming for witches, vampires, and zombies. Jewelya was more attracted to the masquerade masks. Some were leather (or vegan leather) and shaped like foxes, cats, bunnies, and wolves. Beaked masks. Creepy. Others had feather-and-ribbon bouquets swept over to one side. Half masks. Very elegant. None were inexpensive.

One of CSE's Omniscians, Lucador, sold costume kits for Lucadorians who wanted to dress up like him. These were pricey combo packs of his branded merchandise, like a hand-stitched button-up shirt and vest, a leather messenger bag, a patchwork cape, and a custom sword with a leather sheath. All painstakingly handmade. Unless somebody knew Lucador personally, the costume-wearer would present as a cross between a couple movie stereotypes: the adventurous swash-buckling explorer, and a misguided, clueless pirate. She doubted anyone at Dirgatory would need to run from a giant rolling boulder or swing from a crystal chandelier.

She chose a black feather masquerade half mask. It was large for something that only covered part of her head, almost like wearing a floppy Victorian hat that cascaded down the side of her face, and she could still wear evocative lipstick. She could pull her hair up and still be recognizable in case she ran into anyone she knew. She could wear a fashionable dress, which she did so rarely anymore.

Summer, Dirge's wife whom Jewelya had just met, saw her take off her glasses and put on the mask. Jewelya walked a few feet to another broken web mirror and took in her appearance. Her eyes weren't really that bad, but factoring in the cracked glass, it was too much. Her image was surreally blurry.

"I love those feathers," Summer said, brushing the mask with the tips of her fingers. Petting it. "If you don't buy it, I will."

"I do think I will," Jewelya said, impersonating the Queen's English, more confident now after the vote of confidence. She took it off.

"I hear you teach dance," Summer said. "If we'd had more time, we could've prepared a routine together. Something to do at midnight."

"For the dance floor?"

"Why not?"

A routine. A dance floor. A show. This party was sounding more and more like a carnival. She'd assumed Ainsley had been exaggerating.

Consumerian employee, Kat, was working the counter, wearing a black "Secular as Fuck" baby-tee. Her hair was dyed black, with the sides growing out after having once been shaved. At various times, her bangs had been bleached white or red, but right now her hair was one color. Kat accepted the mask to scan the story card. Then the two pieces of art.

"You'd dance with us tomorrow, right Kat?" Summer said.

Kat didn't quite smirk, seemingly swallowing her emotions as she pointed at the total on the tablet for Jewelya. "You know I don't really dance."

"Huh," Jewelya said, signing her name. "You look like you do." Whatever that meant. Maybe she meant that Kat was naturally pretty and looked healthy, but as an instructor, she knew that didn't mean much. And considering herself an empath, Jewelya felt she was annoying her.

"Yeah, Kat," Summer said. "You've been on stage. Don't you sing in a band?"

"I used to, but we lost our guitarist. And I wasn't dancing," Kat said, breathing in through her nose and out of her mouth. "I used to run marathons, too. Do you want a bag for this?"

"Were you running *to* or running *from*?" Summer said enthusiastically, playfully.

Kat shot darts from her eyes, but it was clear that these two knew each other better than Jewelya did. Jewelya wanted to chime in with an optimistic statement, a compliment, or some other reassuring word, but Summer spoke first.

"Like we were saying earlier," Summer said to Kat, "I want to be an existentialist for Halloween. As a costume. Fake it till you make it, right?"

"I don't know that an existentialist has quite that much ambition," Kat said.

Something about this exchange was affecting Jewelya. It was difficult to tell if they were referring to her or not. She put it out of her head. She was reading into this too much.

"If I could be a ghost for Halloween," Kat said, "and not just some sheet with holes cut out of it, but literally be invisible—a fly on the wall—I would."

Jewelya's phone buzzed with a notification.

MOTE:
Do you live to work or work to live?

"SAVE THE BAG," Jewelya said, knowing what this Mote meant. It was sad that Halloween was her excuse to be elegant. It wasn't a show at the Pantages in Hollywood, or a long weekend in Vegas; it was a keg party. But she was going to own it. "I think I'll wear it out."

Jewelya put the mask back on and performed a pivot turn, focusing on Summer as her spotting point, as if she had a camera trained on her. Two spins. Summer joined in, mirroring her, neither taking a lead. This would've been PikPoket gold.

"By the way, there's no returns on Halloween stuff," Kat said. "Especially after Halloween. For obvious reasons."

"You know it's bad luck to wear your costume in public before Halloween," Summer said, stopping. *She's not joking anymore.*

"Does anyone actually believe that?" Jewelya said. *And what does it matter? It's just a masquerade half mask.*

She spun again, tapping her hand against the counter as if that was her dance partner, and reversed the spin.

"Dancing already?" Ainsley said as he walked up to pay for his items. It was difficult to tell how much acidity was in his tone. It sounded like he was looking for a fight. Something about his Yksian/Dirge interactions had gotten under her skin. Ainsley seemed too eager with them. It made her uncomfortable.

"You know, I love to dance—I *live* to dance," Jewelya said. "And since it's my job, I guess you could say I live to work. I love my job. I love life. You just work and work, not living at all." *Shit. That came out fast.* Maybe the Kat and Summer exchanges had gotten under her skin, too. At work, her students, regardless of age, were always so eager to please. Shade from them, if any, was subtle. Those people mostly wanted to impress her. But not these ladies.

"I work so I—so *we*—can live, so we can do other things," Ainsley said. No doubt there was fire in his voice.

"And what exactly *do* we do?"

Ainsley tapped her elbow, implying they should walk away from the counter for privacy. She went with him. "I don't know," he said. "I used to watch Thursday night football with the guys. Until you made it apparent you didn't want me to do that."

"Yes, because when I'd get home, I'd have to order food or eat leftovers. Then I'd get ready for bed and you'd come home after drinking and try to tackle me. That's not exactly fun. Especially if I have an early morning yoga class."

"Right. So I stopped." Ainsley looked pleased. He was going to drop a bomb. "On a side note, how am I supposed to make friends? Asking for a friend."

Bastard. "No need to get snippy."

"Honestly, I don't need to watch football with them. We have an app for the league. By not going, I thought I was making our situation better. I'd rather stay home and make dinner than have you constantly make me feel like shit by pushing me away."

"I'm not pushing you away, in general. Just when you've been drinking and I haven't. And obviously, you staying home comes at a cost. Neither of us go out anymore. I used to go dancing with the girls on Saturday nights, until you made it obvious you don't like it."

"Yeah, you get all made up trying to attract the male gaze…"

"I'm not trying to attract anyone!"

"…to get pawed at on the dance floor, then you get mad that I don't like that? I wasn't hanging out with random women at Brandon's house. Most of us are married dudes. We're practically incels."

Incels? "Is that your commentary on marriage?" This was where everything Ainsley needed to say would come out.

Jewelya felt riled up. She needed to keep her composure in public.

"One moment, it feels like we just met…" Ainsley said.

"It's like I don't know you at all," Jewelya said.

"The next it feels like I've known you forever."

"And yet, here we are." *Airing our dirty laundry in public.*

"So, what exactly am I supposed to do here?" Ainsley said.

"I just want you to be happy making me happy."

"Ha." Ainsley stuck his hands in his pockets. "Sometimes I can't tell if you're joking or not."

She kind of was. "I'm kinda not."

"Look, I'm just trying to explain why I don't leave the house, and…" he looked down at his feet. "And why I think going to Dirgatory is a good thing for *both* of us. To make us both happy."

Jewelya paused, and took a deep breath. They were trying to keep things in check, but that didn't mean they should hide the truth. He tended to escape from her by hiding in the office at home. Or watching games. Not responding to her or texts. "What if we're two people that think they're getting what they want," she said, "but really, we're just not right for each other?"

"Do you think that? Really?" Ainsley looked upset. He was whispering loudly. "Or, what if we *are* right for each other, but we're not getting what we want…*at the moment!* So let's go tomorrow."

"Are you guys arguing about Halloween or are you breaking up?" Connie said, suddenly beside them. Bright, as if dropping a lighthearted humor bomb across their fortified fronts.

"Ha, no," Ainsley said, his face reddening quickly. Sometimes Jewelya would intentionally embarrass him in public to get a reaction. But this was the first time they'd argued in front of other people like this, and they'd been caught by the owner of the establishment. Connie's friendly intrusion highlighted the ridiculousness of their conversation.

"I think we're going to Dirgatory," Ainsley said. "I even asked for another invitation for a coworker."

"You did?" Jewelya said. She hadn't seen an extra invitation. "For Denkins?"

"No," Ainsley said. "Brandon."

But of course that's who it was for. His football buddy. She withheld commentary. Denkins lived for parties like Dirgatory, and Ainsley had said he preferred her going out with guys like Denkins and his friends because they wouldn't be hitting on her all night.

Jealous, anyone? Paranoid?

She'd heard it was difficult to be the smartest person in the room, as others constantly lobbed hackneyed ideas around you, forcing you to bite your tongue, and if you spoke up, they doubled down on being wrong. People often cared more about *looking* right than *being* right. It would drive you cray. Or being the nicest person meant everyone around you was more of an asshole. It wasn't fair Jewelya felt Ainsley's pain in trying to make things work, and how he was so blind to all the other stuff she could see? It was a curse. Why couldn't he do this for her in return? Can an empath only be happy with another empath? Or would they push each other away, not believing someone else could care as much as they did?

Jewelya decided she wouldn't bring up the topic on the ride home.

FIVE

KICK

"All right everybody, we're closing up," Kick said, shooing lingerers in the Basil Alcove out the front door. The last Consumerian was at the register purchasing a Hellness-Wellness kit, an organic special effects makeup package whose enchantments promised vibrant and healthy skin, while, ironically, making it appear ugly, wounded, or rotted for the holiday.

"Kat," Kick said. "You can go. I'll finish up."

Kat slipped the kit into a small black paper bag, and thanked the customer as they left.

"I usually sweep and do the drawers," she said to Kick.

"Don't you have Lisa waiting for you?" he said. He already knew the answer. Lisa was Kat's best friend, visiting from Phoenix. "I'll do the rest. It's a big day tomorrow. I'll see you guys at Dirgatory."

. . .

MOTE:

Ghosts are the universe's memories.

KICK DIDN'T CLOSE down CSE much anymore, since he was busy preparing Omnist II's grand opening, scheduled for after the turn of the year. He used to prefer nightshifts here, alone in the quiet of afterhours darkness. Just him and the ghosts of the Dark Arts room. There were nights he'd been in the office playing games on Flinch for hours after they'd closed. He'd welcome the spirits to join him, but they never did.

While Connie was on her computer in the office, Kick brushed open the beaded curtain for the Dark Arts room and switched off the light. He heard a single knock and saw movement, something out of the corner of his eye. Nobody denied this room had a different vibe than the rest of the Emporium. Bugs, moths, and butterflies were encased in amber or affixed in shadowboxes, fetuses floated in formaldehyde. Pre-mixed potions and tinctures. Body parts and skeletons. These were the oddities and curio that may repulse a minority of customers, but were standard fare for Consumerians. And they were things that shouldn't otherwise move or make noise on their own.

He flipped the light back on. Nobody was there, of course, but Kick walked over to double-check the back door anyway. It was locked. He felt a waft of cooler air. He pushed the fire door open. The streetlight above him was bright. Everything was quiet. He pulled the door closed. It must have been the ghost of Javy, a Consumerian and Ornatuan who'd died in this room last spring. Kick was less scared than, say, his coworker Raine, who tried to avoid the Dark Arts room. But it was indeed haunted. And it had been haunted before Javy had died there. This was just a fact.

There was a smartphone resting on the display counter; someone must have forgotten it. Its power was on. Screen locked. Over half a battery left. It wasn't Kat's—hers had a case that looked like a California license plate that said KAT 666 on it. He brought it over to show Connie.

"I just saw Javy's ghost," Kick said as he entered the office. He didn't want to sound hyperbolic. He was reporting a fact, not speaking from emotion. "And I heard a sound."

"Nice. Did you see his disembodied tattoos in the air, or hear his guitar?" She was teasing him. She wasn't going to believe him anyway.

"No, but I found a phone on the display case."

"See, then?" She hadn't even looked up from her computer. "It was *calling* for you."

"I take it you don't know who belongs to this. I'll put it in lost and found." He never knew if he should shut off a lost phone to save the battery, or keep it on so he could answer it if it rang. He left it on and put it in the wicker box under the front counter. Its new neighbors were a couple pairs of sunglasses, a ratty phone charger, a scarf, a pair of gloves, a bandana.

Someone was knocking at the front door. It was Chikao.

"Good, good," Chikao said when Kick opened the door. "You're still here."

"I am," Kick said. "We only just locked up."

"Did I leave my phone?" he said.

Again. He should keep it on a lanyard or something. "Can you describe it?"

"I'm not sure," Chikao said. "It is dark. Flat. Still on."

Was he kidding? "What brand is it?"

"I'm not sure. I buy every model that comes out...for research. For Lodges. I just noticed I am one short in car."

Kick tilted his head toward the register, an invitation to come with him. He went behind the counter and removed the wicker basket. The phone was sitting on top and Chikao lit up when he saw it. Second time tonight.

"Maybe you need leashes for these things," Kick said.

"I'll put on necklace." Chikao smiled, putting the phone in the chest pocket of his geometric blazer. "Mind if I use restroom before I go?"

Why not. But don't accidentally flush a phone...

KICK WALKED with Connie back to their cars. They'd both parked in a lot behind a bar called Los Federales, a paid lot not far from the Emporium.

"See you tomorrow," Connie said as she hugged him. She opened her door.

"Are you dressing up?" Kick said, stepping back. His car was four spaces down.

"You'll see."

Kick waited for her to drive away. But rather than get in his car, he opened the trunk and removed a medium-sized, unmarked box with the flaps folded in. He walked the block or so back to the Emporium and went around back to the alley. He entered through the Dark Arts room and set the box on a counter. Inside it was a lamp, an everlasting light made by a local artisan. It was made of repurposed barnwood, wrought iron trim, and red stained glass, but with an LED bulb and a backup that switched on if power was lost or when the main bulb needed replacing. The handwritten card predicted that should happen in eight to ten years. The point was that the light should never truly turn off. A small brass plaque read, "In memoriam, Javier Gavril Aldea."

Before Chikao's Lodge, when Connie was out making a personal visit with an Executive Saint, Kick had installed a hook in the ceiling behind one of the counters, in a corner away from the doors and window, about eight inches from the wall. The stage was directly behind the wall. He stood on a stepstool to hang the lamp, then descended and plugged the cord into a socket below.

The lamp glowed softly. It was nearly unnoticeable due to the bright overhead lights. Those were annoying and rarely used, anyway, so he turned them off. Normally, the room would only be lit by a pair of table lamps and display lights from within the counters, and the new everlasting light added a warm maroon glow to the now otherwise darkened room.

Even though Kick hadn't known Javy well, he'd become familiar with some of his tattoos after his death. Ornatuans, as part of their vigil, had posted photos of a shirtless Javy in order to feature them. Among his dozens of tattoos, he was particularly known for the large glow-in-the-dark skull that took up most of his back. On his chest were a couple Kick found more interesting: a distinctive rat skeleton who was hissing or laughing from one pectoral muscle over at a black cat on the other, who was arching its back and raising its hackles in return.

Actually, no one knows where the tattoos went when he died.

MOTE:
The only people who think it's cool to be ignorant, are ignorant.

HUNG ON A VELVET-BACKED jewelry rack was a collection of necklaces with tiny skeleton pendants: mice, hummingbirds, lizards, and minnows—the bones laboriously stitched into their recognizable forms. He chose a necklace with a baby rat skeleton, similar to that from Javy's tattoo, and hung it from the everlasting light. Javy would appreciate this. If the Emporium procured a stuffed black cat, Kick would consider adding that to the mix, maybe installing a shelf high up the wall next to the lamp so the feline could face the rat.

He would've installed this vigil months ago, but Connie had said she didn't want to draw more attention to Javy's death. She'd said the gesture would come across like a PR stunt, like CSE was being insensitive and placative. Kick disagreed. She was overly careful due to the immediate media fallout, but it was *not* memorializing a Consumerian that was perceived as insensitive. It'd been over six months now.

Kick scratched his beard. They'd lost a soul in this very room. He felt the haunting reverence in his bones, which were still stitched together by living tendons, skin, and muscle. Javy had been a Consumerian. Part of Kick's, Connie's, Ornatu's, and the Emporium's extended family. There should've been no need for secrecy about installing a memorial lamp, but Kick knew once Connie saw it, she'd realize it belonged there. No one should forget Javy.

KICK RETURNED to the three-bedroom house he shared with his roommate, Gremmie. He could afford to live on his own, but why bother. Keeping a lower cost of living, he could take bigger financial risks. Not to imply he was cavalier with money, but if Kick had a large mortgage payment, he was convinced his business decisions would become starkly more conservative. He still paid more rent than Gremmie did, so he kept the master bedroom, which included a private bathroom.

Gremio's nickname was fitting because he was also a

horrible surfer. A poor snowboarder. A bad skateboarder. He couldn't master any of the boards that required a particular sense of balance. Kick wondered if maybe Gremmie would've been better off snow skiing, water skiing, or roller blading. Things that required a more forward-facing sense of balance.

Looking in the mirror as he readied for bed, Kick noticed he was evolving into the stereotypical image of a professor. Or an Omniscian with a beer belly dad bod. He was in his mid-thirties and his beard and the hair above his ears were already spotted with gray. He looked nearly as old as that immaculately groomed Omniscian, Chikao, who was decades older. Kick hadn't trimmed any hair for a few weeks in preparation for his costume tomorrow. The scruffier the better.

He thought about Chikao's, what, three or four phones? Five? Kick owned several smart devices: a home computer, a laptop, a tablet, and a phone that was now charging on his nightstand. Maybe Chikao needed all those phones so he could program different personality profiles into the Omnist to produce unique Mote reactions. Kick would be curious to learn about those results.

But, dude, quit leaving your phones behind.

Kick heard a noise from the front of the house. *The ghost of Javy?* He needed to quit thinking like that. That was Gremmie coming home from work. He should've been at Chikao's Lodge tonight—he'd said he wished he could go—as Chikao was part of Gremmie's PGP. But if Kick went to the kitchen right now to greet him, he'd get sucked into an hour-long conversation about whichever new conspiracy theory was blowing up on social media today.

Gremmie, despite his positive outlook on life, loved conspiracies. Smoking weed and talking shit. Follow the money, he would say, half laughing. There was always an untold reason why an unknown person benefited from anything newsworthy. This bored Kick. Conspiracies used to be fun: UFOs, aliens, Bigfoot, haunted mansions, werewolves, witchcraft. Stuff that didn't really matter, but would be cool as hell if it was real. Now the conspiracies someone believed were totems in their political ideology, defining which team they were automatically against, and all the fun had been sucked out. *People like us believe things like this.* Gremmie claimed that someday he would be disappeared by a government or corporate entity. It almost seemed like a goal.

They didn't have to speak now. They'd meet up at Dirgatory tomorrow, anyway.

Moments later, syncopated tapping noises and exasperations came from the bedroom next door. Gremmie was already playing a video game. At least he'd been considerate enough to close his door and wear headphones, but there was little that could be done about the other noises that rattled softly through an otherwise quiet house. Kick imagined Gremmie sitting in his chair, pushing back from the computer, then leaning forward, inching closer, rolling back and forth, using momentum to his advantage. It sounded like an anxious ghost rattling a plastic chain.

The Dark Arts room at CSE may have been haunted, but not with toy chains. There was something off about that space, a notion raised by more than a few Consumerians, as well as Raine. People became nauseated. They heard noises. This was something Kick could share and embellish while at Dirgatory. Connie would be there to verify his statements. She'd attended multiple seances and once saw a Consumerian, Mrs. Stavros, run out of the room to vomit in the bathroom. They should be marketing the haunting of the Dark Arts room, even if only by word of mouth. Tomorrow was a perfect setting for virality.

Kick realized he'd been staring in the mirror, not at himself, but in and through his eyes. He refocused his gaze to his third eye and zoned again until his face morphed into that of Bigfoot. He shook his head and snapped himself back into place.

He brushed his teeth.

CHAPTER
SIX

AINSLEY

After work on Halloween, Ainsley drove straight to Dirge and Summer's house, which was about a mile east of Consumia's Spiritual Emporium, still in North Hollywood, on a treelined street of homes built for the television and movie industry's working class. Ainsley and Dirge would both be considered within this demographic, even though their jobs were vastly different. The sun was setting behind an overcast sky, giving this weeknight a Sunday vibe that bordered on depressing. The first party guests wouldn't arrive for a couple hours.

There were already "No Parking" signs on both sides of the street in front of the house, one posted on a tree, one on a signpost. Dropoff and pickup only for guests. No valet. Perhaps Dirge expected a large percentage of guests to take Gryfts. Ainsley imagined some people would have to park several blocks away if attendance was anything like that of industry legend.

A couple sycamores lived in the front yard and between the sidewalk and street. Fake cobwebs stretched from branch to branch, tree to tree.

Ainsley thought about how, with the exception of attending a Lodge once a month, he was slowly becoming a hermit. He rarely hung out with friends, but they were all marrying off anyway, having children, relocating for jobs. Jewelya was his best friend, and he was caging her in. She was accustomed to being the life of the party, and was likely tiring of him. Bored with him. This party should be a boost for her.

Did Jewelya even want kids? He thought he should know. He thought he knew once, but people change. She'd always said it would be too hard on her body, and she certainly couldn't teach dance for what, six months before and after the pregnancy?

He already wanted a beer.

MOTE:

One needs knowledge of a past in order to ensure a future.

AINSLEY HAD to step over a stuffed dummy on the vine-covered vestibule porch, the implication possibly being that a solicitor had met their dire fate promised by a tin sign affixed next to the door.

When he rang the doorbell, he was greeted by the recording of a massive church bell. A carillon. The inner door opened and Dirge's warm voice filtered out from the darkness inside. "Watch out for Vincent there. He's probably had too much to drink already."

"Oh, he's Vincent," Ainsley said, catching on. "I get it: Vincent Price." A dummy pretending to be a living person who often pretended to be dead. But the real Vincent Price *was* dead.

"Yes! Anyway, welcome. Come in." Dirge had to dip his hatted head while opening the outer door. He really was as tall as Yksian. In a weird way, Ainsley felt bad, as if Dirge was obligated to usher him in in such a courtly manner. "This door won't be in use tonight. I keep it locked so strangers don't wander in."

"I see."

"Would you like a drink?"

As Ainsley's eyes adjusted to the darkness, he saw Dirge was wearing a sort of mortician suit with a vest and pork pie hat. Freshly applied face paint, with a ring of jagged black lines painted around one eye like exaggerated mascara. An eye asterisk.

Ainsley chewed his lip. He was supposed to know the character. A classic movie. "You look great," he said, giving up.

"Well, we're on the clock, now," Dirge said. "Time to *work*."

Ainsley still didn't get it.

Dirge removed the hat and rubbed his hand down his miniature mohawk. "Stressed" wasn't quite the right word for how he looked; maybe he was thinking three things at once, and not currently doing any of them. "The kegs just got here and aren't hooked up yet, but I have some beer in the fridge. The private stock."

"If you need to deal with that stuff," Ainsley said, "I can jump on Yksian's computer and get out of your hair."

"Oh, no rush. We have a couple hours. Let me show you the front of the house, the stuff I don't want guests messing with."

Dirge took four long steps into the kitchen, grabbed a beer from his fridge, and was back before Ainsley could realize what he was doing. Dirge handed him a bottle of Guinness. "A friend just returned from Ireland and gave this to me," he said. "It's important because, you'll notice, it's three hundred and thirty milliliters rather than the five hundred you'd normally find in the States. Proof of European sourcing."

Ainsley sipped. It tasted the same to him as any other Guinness stout.

Dirge gestured at a shelf, and atop it a mahogany pipe stand/tobacco box combo. He lifted the hinged lid and removed a zipper-locked plastic bag. Ainsley had never seen tobacco look like this before. It wasn't black. Perhaps it was a strain of THC.

"These are hops used in the Guinness recipe," Dirge said. He unzipped the bag, pressed his face to it, his nose right inside, and inhaled deeply, seemingly in heaven. He offered it to Ainsley to do the same. They smelled like a mixture of cardboard, THC, and stale, dry grass cut late in the fall.

Dirge unfurled his arm, presenting the rest of his dark living room for appreciation. Layers of tapestries covered the windows, restricting outdoor light, and shelving units displayed books on the occult and original vinyl records. The latter apparently weren't reprints or remasters. No protective sleeves. Some albums had been handled so much their spines were reduced to pale, shredded cardboard.

The room was clean, but dusty. Not that dusty, just impossible to clean. Cluttered, but neat. Years of incense had found its way into every nook and cranny so that sweeping, vacuuming, and dusting, at best, would only take the edge off the situation. No literal cobwebs or dust bunnies, but Ainsley could smell them, feel them somewhere. Ghosts of dust bunnies. The smoke of thousands of cigarettes consumed on the front stoop had snuck through the screen door and buried itself deep in the hardwood floor and handwoven rugs.

"That's Daryl Hannah's eye from the movie *Kill Bill*," Dirge said, moving his arm to the end of a shelf.

The eye, resting in an egg holder, gazed at Ainsley as if he were looking in a mirror. Somehow, it was Ainsley's own eye. Next to that, much larger, but still a model, was the sewer creature from the movie, *Big Trouble in Little China*; he recognized that prop immediately, its twisted red hair just as much alive as not; its teeth and eyes as nicotine-stained and cirrhotic, respectively, as they were on the big screen. And here now, in three dimensions jutting out of the wall, it aggressively lurched at visitors. And he was a visitor now, a guest.

"That's Dirk Diggler's prosthetic penis from *Boogie Nights*," Dirge said, no more affected by the sexual connotation as he was by monsters or death. The penis sat erect on a shelf like a double-sized can of Wide-Eyed Wyatt's Liquid Nap, taunting visitors with its prowess and sexual fearlessness.

Dirge presented several more props from movies, television shows, and music videos he'd worked on. Some items were accompanied by stories about how they came into his possession, some weren't. Fortunately, all the stories were thumbnail sketches.

Overall, the living room was filled with the vessels of undead hosts awaiting the arrival of guests, although most of the latter would be relegated to the backyard. Even if the hosts were facsimiles, the patina of the house was alive.

They walked down a bedroom hallway. One of the doors was fortified with an extra wooden frame and heavy-duty padlock, unlocked at the moment. The room was probably impenetrable without a chainsaw when locked.

"The private bathroom," Dirge said. "VIP only, but you're VIP, of course."

Such a fortress. Ainsley couldn't imagine what transgressions had occurred in there that required such an increase in security. It represented the opposite of how he always left the door ajar for Jewelya at home. Well, unless he was sitting, of course. *Oh, to be a fly on the wall at a party like this.* But he wouldn't need to be. He would be there in person.

MOTE:

Invisibility prepares a soul to be human and a human to be a soul.

NEXT TO THE Fort Knox lavatory, the entire wall, floor to ceiling, was covered with a collection of death masks. Ainsley recognized some of the faces without reading the brass nametags. Others remained unrecognizable even after he read who it was. Some actors weren't dead yet, these being *living masks*, but considering Dirge's connections, the imprints were likely lifted from molds used to create their special effects. Drew Barrymore, David Bowie, Johnny Depp, Robert Englund, Boris Karloff, Christopher Lee, Bela Legosi, and Elizabeth Taylor were all looking at him without eyes, without expression, feeling, or emotion. The opposite effect he'd experienced from Daryl Hannah's eye.

It was interesting how merely the shape of a face could be creepy, and yet something of the soul's essence was saved, fluid within the immovable shape of plaster. He thought about how some primitive cultures, when presented with photography for the first time, believed photographs stole a piece of the subject's soul. Similarly, something undefinable had been stolen from these celebrities when they'd submitted for the molds, whether they'd realized it or not.

Ainsley said nothing as he surveyed the faces, feeling Dirge at his side, admiring Ainsley admiring them. He felt Dirge's pride. Then, Dirge touched his shoulder. They had work to do.

"Yksian's in the office, messing with the lighting program," Dirge said. "It wouldn't hurt if you looked at both setups, his and mine."

At the end of the hall was a spare bedroom Dirge must've used as an office. The walls were painted dripping crimson, like blood or runoff from a candle. Black curtains shaded the double window. Yksian was working at a desk in front of three computer screens and turned his head slowly to acknowledge them. Even seated, he was nearly as tall as Ainsley.

"Ainsley, sir," Yksian said. "I appreciate your kindness, arriving prematurely to aid us." He described what was going on with their setup for playlists, videos, and lights. After he'd updated some apps, some files couldn't be found. Some programs seemed to have taken over and were slowing everything down, even freezing up the systems completely.

Ainsley had an idea what the problem was and worked on it for maybe an hour. When he was done, everything seemed to be functioning. Freed up some space. It was a short-term solution that should get them through tonight. And as always, the long-term solution was faster Wi-Fi, faster processors, and more cloud capacity.

MOTE:

> *Freed of chains, feast your soul, All Hallows Eve.*
> *Recite this verse for luck and health, dare you leave:*

(This was followed by gibberish that, to Ainsley, looked like Latin.)

. . .

Ainsley was receiving more Motes than usual. But it was Halloween, so he went with it.

CHAPTER
SEVEN

JEWELYA

J ewelya had wrapped up teaching for the day at her shared studio space on the second floor of a strip mall in Encino. Even though there were several palm trees that lived in the parking lot islands, they provided little to no shade relief. Giant, frilly toothpicks, really. The unit's floor-to-ceiling windows were mirrored on the outside to reflect the sun back at annoyed eastbound drivers on Ventura Boulevard. For the most part, her two busiest days went as follows: yoga, break, dance, break. Repeat, ending with one last yoga class. Five total. But for Halloween, she'd canceled the last three (attendance would've been low, anyway), and she'd benefit from the extra time to get ready for tonight.

She'd trained as a dancer all through her youth, but it was difficult to find non-seedy work, particularly a job with a steady income. And now that she was married, she no longer wanted to travel with a show or live in Las Vegas or New York City. She'd grown tired of auditions in Los Angeles with low-percentage success rates.

After appearing in a half dozen music videos, two television commercials, one season of a local musical, and a single episode of a popular streaming show, she'd injured her anterior cruciate ligament during rehearsal soon after her honeymoon three years ago. After the necessary surgery, she found yoga had helped her greatly with recovery. Stretching was always part of dance, the first and, in many ways, the most crucial component, so she found teaching both dance and yoga to be symbiotic. Consequently, she retired as a professional dancer.

When she was in her mid-twenties, Jewelya had worked for a temp agency between gigs, and office folk often dressed up for Halloween. It was in her face all day. But now nobody arrived in costume for dance or yoga lessons. No point, since they'd still have to shower and get ready afterward anyway. She'd almost forgotten what day it was until her break, when she bought an iced Wide-Eyed Wyatt beverage at the first-floor coffeeshop and saw pent-up excitement leaking from costumed kids, parents, and baristas, which reminded her about tonight's extravaganza.

The instructor she shared the studio space with, Denkins, was the type who would've dressed up for work if he could. Perhaps every day. And possibly, the more flamboyant, the better.

When Jewelya first met Denkins, they were auditioning for a music video for The Color Braille. They were somewhat of a dark wave band combining goth, new wave, and shoegaze, but in this particular song, there was a twist; a Motown-flavored bassline, blown out and clipped like danceable industrial music, simultaneously soulful and mechanical. It hit her sweet spot, perfectly.

Jewelya had shown up in tights and tank top, her usual audition fare. But this bleach-blonde, spiky-haired guy next to her was wearing guyliner, lipstick, black tights, but also combat boots and a leather jacket—not usual for someone expected to dance. There was no shirt underneath the jacket, so he was planning to dance in it. He spoke loudly, unabashedly, laughing easily, telling her he wanted to look the part of the video so he'd be chosen before he'd even shown them what he could do. He was infectious.

And he did audition in that outfit. And killed it. They both did, and were the two main characters featured in the video. As a fictional couple. It was dark, hot, and steamy, but really, no actual kissing or anything. Sexy as a vibe. The dancing was closer to writhing, and she was unsure if her friends—or even her new boyfriend at the time, Ainsley—would actually recognize her in it. And the first time they'd gone out dancing, Denkins dressed in jazz era pinstripes, slicking his hair down and copping an era-appropriate accent. A completely different character. She loved this about him.

Currently, Jewelya and Denkins were towel-drying their faces. Normally they taught in separate groups, but this afternoon they'd combined their final two.

"Whoa," Denkins said. "Cosplaying a stressed-out housewife! You nailed it!"

Jewelya paused to give him a death stare. Did she look that tense, especially after a workout? She was wearing the same gear as always, so no literal costume, yet. "And you're in comedian cosplay?" she said. "Seriously? You forgot the most important part...humor."

"Bye, Denkins!" a student said as he left. She could tell he had an unrequited crush on Denkins. There was so much hope and pain and eagerness in his voice and smile.

Denkins opened his mouth wide as he waved him away, an expression of surprise, even though they'd just spent the past fifty minutes together. He obviously loved the attention.

Back to Jewelya: "Honey, please. I taught as Robin Hood one year and had a cute little suction cup bow-and-arrow set." He pulled his arms apart, miming stretching out a bow. "And during class, I leaned it against the mirror, you know, in case anyone couldn't figure out who I was supposed to be, and... well...it didn't work."

"People don't like toy bows and arrows?" Seriously. Based on Ainsley's description of Dirgatory, no one would be caught dead bringing in something like that tonight.

He didn't seem to bite. "You would think a costume with tights would work for a dance instructor, but no. The little hat wouldn't stay on my head. Hat pins, useless. I threw it on the floor. Voilà. Gone. No hats or masks when I teach; they get in the way. No makeup either; it runs all over your face. So no. No more costume. No, no...no no no."

"But what about..." She traced an "S" shape on her chest.

"Your boobs?" he said, looking concerned.

She shot him such a laser he broke into a smile.

"Oh, Superman?" he said. "Please. The cape's got to come off. I don't have to tell you, but dancing is hard enough without extra fabric slapping you in the face. And you sweat like a warthog under the big 'S.'"

According to stories Denkins had told Jewelya over the last couple years, it wouldn't have been the first (or second) time he'd had things slapping him in the face. Just maybe not while teaching dance. "You know warthogs don't sweat, right?"

"Please..." Mock annoyance. "When in doubt, just assume I'm funny. Seriously though, I love Halloween. Wind me up, give me a mojito, point me at the dance floor, and set me loose."

"Honestly," Jewelya said, "I feel like I haven't gone out in ages."

"I guess sometimes knowing what you want is too much work." Denkins tilted his head down a notch, as if looking over imaginary sunglasses. "What are you, thirty-two? Sleep is for tomorrow when you actually *need* the rest." He picked up his gym bag.

"Ains and I are going to Dirgatory, I'll have you know," Jewelya said, trying to match his tone. She wanted to brag, but also didn't want to sound like she was. "Ever heard of it?"

She knew he had. He'd talked about it last year, but for some reason she wanted to sound naïve. She ended up telling him about the masquerade mask she'd bought, and the evening dress she'd only worn once before.

"I guess it's too bad I won't see the glamorous you," Denkins said, not without remorse. Her story had slowed his departure. "It sounds lovely. It truly does."

"You would think. But if I'm going to dress up, I'd rather it be a dinner party where I can drink wine and play games or something." *And be funny and charming.* "Be asleep by midnight. But for a big, loud, obnoxious party…"

"Bye guys!" the last student said as she walked out in front of them. "Happy Halloween!"

"Happy! Happy! Happy!" Denkins said, waving his hand a little too fast.

Jewelya and Denkins walked to the exit together.

"What dance floor are you headed for tonight?" Jewelya said as she held the door open for him.

"Dance *street*," Denkins said. "Santa Monica Boulevard. West Hollywood. Kyle and I are going to: Tear. Shit. Up." He was referring to the world-famous Halloween festival that attracted a quarter million attendees every year. The boulevard was blocked off for a mile with several stages for bands and DJs. Bars and clubs roped off their parking lots for extra outdoor drinking space. She'd gone in the past, but that was years ago.

"I don't think I can handle all that anymore," Jewelya said. "Too many people. Dirgatory's probably going to be too much as it is." Maybe she shouldn't be playing down the party so much. "But I'm sure it'll be fun."

"Don't worry, you'll be stunning, darling," Denkins said. "And if I had your hips, I'd make that purgatory *heaven*."

CHAPTER
EIGHT

KICK

Kick turned an axe in his hand so an etching on the blade would catch the light.

"Axe me no questions, I'll fell you no lies!" it read.

His costume for tonight was Paul Bunyan, his now-unkempt beard serving double duty here. He was wearing an oversized red-and-black flannel shirt, but he'd purchased an anachronistic trapper hat because he liked the ear flaps. His cheekbones and nose were rouged from imaginary frigid air.

He stood inside his front door, hesitating about whether he should bring Lucador's axe with him as part of the costume. He predicted there could be issues with security at the front gate. It wasn't exactly like one Paul Bunyan would've used, but Kick wouldn't want to bring a cheap, plastic prop to the home of a legitimate special effects artist, either. Dirge may reserve a special level of hell for such a travesty. So, in a way, it was this axe or nothing. It may not have been antique, but it was real. He leaned it against the wall and left it behind.

After driving around Dirge's block a couple times, Kick parked his car about two blocks away from the party, the closest he could get. He grabbed a couple stacks of CSE stickers and calendar postcards of upcoming Lodges from a box on the floor of the backseat.

He had to queue in the dark driveway for several minutes, along with about eight people. Lights from the party in the backyard were bouncing off trees taller than the house. A group of four was talking in front of him, smoking weed, not paying attention, not moving up when they had a chance. Kick wasn't the most impatient person, as long as the others were aware of their surroundings. He nearly had to say something.

Eventually, he found himself in front of a makeshift toll-booth made of old, peeling, mismatched driftwood. An ancient, faded "Tickets" sign was crookedly perched above a partially open screen window. The screen would protect the person behind it from precisely nothing.

The ticket taker was in costume, lit eerily from below, dressed as a murdered diva with a red curly wig, blue sequined dress with a beauty queen sash, and a bloodied, sliced throat that looked horrifically real. Her face was gray with peeling skin, but she smiled at him, happy to be there. Happy to celebrate next to a red cup filled with party.

"Happy Halloween!" she said.

"I hope you don't have to sit here all night," Kick said, gesturing to her cup. "But at least you get to drink."

"Oh no, a bunch of us are manning the door for an hour each until midnight. Then it's a free-for-all."

Kick stood there for a second, blanking out. He wasn't sure what he was supposed to do.

Dead Beauty Queen picked up her cup and sipped, likely for show. "Do you have your invite?" she said as she set her drink down.

"Oh," he said, removing it from his back pocket. The invitation was printed on black card stock, cut along the perimeter with decorative edge scissors, not unlike an inexpensive, evil wedding invitation. He set it in front of her.

"Cool." She tapped the side of a tablet that had a credit card attachment plugged into it. "Twenty dollars, please."

He knew this. Guests needed to present an invitation and pay a twenty-dollar cover. It covered the open bar with six kegs of craft beer. Six freaking kegs. This was like a college party for adults. So much beer. Not everybody was going to drink, of course, but the decorations and costumes alone would make Dirgatory worth the price of admission.

Kick slid his card.

"Have a great night," Dead Beauty Queen said.

An enormous man, possibly a biker, stood next to the booth. He nodded at Kick and lifted the end of a blue plastic sheet for him to duck underneath and enter the backyard. This guy, it wasn't a costume. His beard was much longer than Kick's, and he outweighed him by a hundred pounds. He was security. Kick was happy he'd left the axe behind. Security Biker wouldn't have liked it very much.

Yksian would be there tonight as part of Dirge's party staff, and what a great place to market the Emporium and the Omnist app. Kick knew Yksian wasn't into self-promotion, but the stack of postcards included a listing for Yksian's next Lodge. Kick was born for marketing, for spreading the word, whatever word that was. Leaning against the back of the ticket booth was a four-foot-wide square wooden pallet with the word "Exit" and an arrow spraypainted on it. The exit itself was draped in white plastic, not blue, but there was nobody there to lift it. He placed half the postcards and stickers on top of the pallet. Organic shelf.

Kick turned around and absorbed the vibe, a dark carnival of cosplay. This was the third straight year he'd attended Dirgatory, having met Dirge and Summer through Yksian two and a half years ago, just after the Emporium had opened. Although the sun had set, it was still early for a party, but dozens of people were already there. Actors and writers. Animators and special effects artists. Gamers. Burners—Burning Man attendees—without the desert. His people. Many were likely Consumerians. Kick was at home.

The backyard was heavily partitioned with various tenting, netting, boards, vintage signage, car doors, trees, and rugs. The first section was a dance area, maybe 150 square feet, where dark wave pumped from hidden speakers. One black light. One slow blinking strobe. A disco ball missing several of its hundreds of miniature mirrors hung from a tree branch.

From the center of two clearly handmade, black, coffin-shaped boxes resting on the ground, chrome stripper poles reached for the sky; go-go tools for a dance of the dead, for pirouetting on graves. The poles were situated at the widest part of the coffins, possibly through the corpses' hearts. Each was large enough to fit three dancers. These boxes would not have been made by Linden Vowel or anyone else involved with Coffin Club. They were fashioned from fortified plywood and merely cut into the recognizable hexagonal shape to serve as eighteen-inch risers. No lids. No handles. No adornments. They had sides, but probably no bottoms. A couple girls were already performing on them, waking the dead, although everyone else in the vicinity was standing, talking, and drinking. Too early to dance.

To the right of the scaled-down club, Kick encountered a bonfire pit, away from the overhang of trees, where he foresaw people gathering under the moon, howling with booze and delight. Unlike most backyard firepits he'd seen in the Valley, this wasn't a glorified barbeque, or fueled by gas. It was an old-school, blackened half barrel embedded deep into the ground. A little *Mad Max*. He wondered if this was even legal.

He smelled weed. It smelled like someone had run over a skunk, then decided to smoke it. Something about seeing two men in black lipstick dragging on a joint in this light seemed less Halloween to him and more Hollywood. Still, though. His people.

Next up to the left: the bar. Built into the side of a tool shed was a service window with an awning. The bar top was different than last year. It was now a red wooden door cut in half longways, its unpolished knob flirting to be touched like a brass mushroom, floating in the circle of a black-painted hole. Kick recognized the paint. That was Black Vertigo, not just the blackest paint in the world, but one with a virtually supernatural effect, like it was a passage into another dimension. An artist named Ekko had made this bar top for Dirge and Summer. She'd also made paintings that Connie, Kat, and Yksian owned, and Ekko always included Black Vertigo in her work.

And there was another hole, the size of a baseball, where a peephole would live. Kick leaned over to peer inside and was nauseated while still a foot away. So he didn't dive deeper. This could've, should've, been a real peephole, but when Kick touched it to reassure himself, it too was a Black Vertigo circle. Otherwise, the door was covered in a clear, epoxy glaze to smooth it out and protect it, except for those two spots.

Overall, the shed looked like a dilapidated concession stand on a haunted beach. He set the rest of the postcards and stickers on the bar. Done working for the night.

The two bartenders, a male and female, were dressed as

old-timey prisoners with horizontal black-and-white striped shirts and caps, and a matching plastic handcuff hanging off one wrist like cheap bracelets. They were pouring beer into red plastic cups, and as fast as they could place a serving on the bar, it was picked up by a guest.

Behind them, a woman dressed as Wednesday Adams dumped a bag of ice around a keg of beer that sat in a large, red plastic bucket with rope handles. "Beerly Optimistic," a local brewery, was stenciled on the keg.

"Hi, Summer," Kick said.

Summer responded with a tiny stressed-out wave and expression that communicated, "I'm happy to see you but I have so much shit to do that I can't talk right now, so please take a beer, and I hope you have a good time."

Or something.

He nodded and scratched his beard in return. "Bye, Summer." *A seasonal joke a girl named Autumn could tell.*

"What're my choices?" Kick said to the male inmate. Based on previous years, he guessed light or dark.

"Pilsner and stout," the bartender said, setting another cup down.

Kick grabbed a cup of pilsner. The cup was a brighter red than the bar top, which evoked dried blood. Some sections of wood had been scraped to reveal a deeper red underneath: currant, merlot, then mahogany. The impression was that if someone kept scraping, who knew what they'd find. Perhaps Black Vertigo, like the holes? But the epoxy protected the door from further distressing.

Kick tossed a dollar bill in a skull-shaped porcelain cookie jar, placed there for tips. He had a couple more in his wallet so he could do this again.

A man dressed as a hobbit set down a stein to be filled. Good idea. Why drink from a small plastic cup when you could bring your own vessel that held twice as much foam? While the male prisoner filled it, the hobbit dangled a twenty-dollar bill above the jar until he was sure the female inmate saw him, then flicked it in with flair. "I can cut the line all night now, right?" the hobbit said.

"Throw in another twenty," she said, "and I'll kiss you on the cheek each time, too."

The male prisoner lightly touched her shoulder as he placed the stein on the bar. All three of them laughed. The hobbit didn't add the second twenty and walked away, smiling, sipping at his handled vessel of beer foam. If someone was willing to pay extra money at nine p.m. in order to cut the line at ten, then that was a harbinger of how things were going to go tonight. Kick wasn't quite sure how a bartender could help a guest cut the line, though.

When Kick turned around, he saw Hillary Clinton, Lydia from *Beetlejuice*, and Wonder Woman standing together. That was Connie and Kat, but he wasn't sure if he recognized the third person. "I thought I was done working for the night," he said, timing his sip of beer as punctuation.

"Hi, Kick," Connie and Kat said in unison.

All three women were holding clear plastic cups of red wine.

"You guys have the good stuff, huh?" he said. "I only saw beer."

"We know people," Kat said. Snark. She didn't want to be there. This was the first time he'd seen her out since her husband died six months ago. "Summer has a case in the shed for those in the know. But don't tell anybody. We don't want it running out at ten."

You shouldn't use clear cups then.

Kick nodded as if it made all the sense in the world, but he replayed Kat's line again in his head. Even if she was joking, there was a decent chance a secret case of wine could be gone in an hour.

Apparently, like Kick had done with Paul Bunyan, the other two Consumerians had enhanced their everyday appearances to become fictional characters. Kat's costume was Lydia, the teenage daughter from the movie *Beetlejuice*, played by Winona Ryder. Kat's hair was usually black, so it was mostly styling and makeup that changed her look.

Connie was Hillary Clinton, just begging to be harassed by partiers. Like Kick, who felt naked without his only prop, the axe, it was clear she hadn't put much effort into her costume, either. The pink Chanel business suit was something she'd normally wear, but her blonde bob was so heavily set with hairspray, it had become "helmet head." Truly, the pearl necklace (which wasn't her style) and an "I Voted" sticker were the only accessories that made it a costume.

"Kick, you know Lisa," Kat said. "Visiting from Arizona."

That's who she was. When he shook Wonder Woman's hand, it felt thin and narrow, like she had no wrists. She had the most striking eyes of anyone at the party. The gateway to the soul. Kat and Lisa made a killer combination. "Ah, I've seen you at the Emporium, haven't I?" he said.

"Yeah," Lisa said. "But I'm trying to steal Kat away so she'll move back to Phoenix. I answered the Omnist questions the way she would have. That way she's always in my pocket."

"It's like I never left," Kat deadpanned.

"It's pretty good though, Kat." Lisa grew more enthusiastic. "The Omnist knew I—we—hate driving long distances and gave me a prayer that cleared away traffic. I swear I hit every green light as soon as I got off the freeway. Easiest drive ever."

Wouldn't Wonder Woman fly here in an invisible jet? Don't say it. Not funny.

Kick wondered if Lisa knew he basically *was* the Omnist.

70

That those one- or two-line prayers for common annoyances were popular with Consumerians, so he'd added hundreds more. Easy to use, not too much effort. Private. "I'm glad it worked out," he said.

"Then it Moted another right when we got here," Lisa said. "And we found Connie and Summer and had a glass of wine in our hands in a matter of seconds. It was like magic."

For many users, the Omnist did seem like magic. There was a direct correlation between how much you trusted it and the value you derived from the Motes. "Glad it's working."

A couple men passed slowly, smiling at Connie until she noticed them and smiled back. The three of them were representing the Emporium well: Connie still looked like Connie. Kat looked like Kat. Kick looked like Kick. They were recognizable.

"Hi, Connie," a man dressed as a green-faced movie alien said, lifting his beer for a toast.

A female superhero in spandex walked by. "No Lodge tonight, huh, ladies?" she said brightly.

"This *is* the Lodge," Kat said. Side-eye. Even an anti-social introvert like her was in her element here.

"It's going to be like this all night for you guys, isn't it?" Kick said. Even though it wasn't her party, Connie was a local celebrity. They'd attempted a Halloween Lodge last year: a group séance in the Basil Alcove, with wine sharing, apple and pumpkin dishes, and scary stories told from the stage. It was hosted by Dani, an occasional medium who owned a frenemy store called L.A. Obscura. Surprisingly, the Halloween Lodge was dead. It turned out too many Consumerians had gone to Dirgatory. Kick would've been okay with the Emporium closing early tonight, but Raine wanted to stay back and work without an event. She wasn't much into parties, anyway.

Now if only Yksian and Dirge, the Twin Towers of Darkness, entered their conversation, the Emporium would be the presumed sponsor of the party.

"Yeah, probably," Connie said. "Have you seen the maze yet? It's ridiculous. You should probably check it out before it gets too crazy."

Kick knew her well enough to know she wasn't *really* telling him to get lost. But she kind of was. She was performing for the ladies. He toasted them and withdrew to continue exploring.

More than half of Dirge's backyard was converted into this haunted maze, a winding labyrinth peppered with miniature "rooms" with barely enough space for a couple to sit on a car seat and make out. In one passage, two bar stools rested unsteadily at a shelf just large enough for two drinks. In another, plastic insects and spiders were affixed to the walls, the lights from other parts of the yard giving them a sense of motion. Creepy. But awesome.

In a particular section in the back, tapestries hung from walls, with rugs and pillows covering the ground. Three guests were seated around a cephalopodic hookah. Something almost stopped him cold. This space. This party. This night. Things had happened here. It was similar to, but not exactly the same as, that feeling he got from the Dark Arts room. It wasn't quite blacking out, but more like he'd developed a looser relationship with time. With space. The hookah room was everywhere and nowhere, but also, right here.

As he continued through the intestinal twisting, he discovered cracks between plywood boards, porous netting, and sections he could peek over to see more passages. Ten-year-old Kick would have lost his shit, living a video game. Thirty-five-year-old Kick *was* losing his shit.

He tried to imagine how difficult this maze would be to navigate as the night wore on. More people, with more time to ingest party favors. More barriers to perception. In a way, the backyard was a semi-permanent movie set, a decades-long accumulation of horror memorabilia, from which Dirge and Summer cleared away real cobwebs, only to replace with the pulled cotton of Halloween.

Ironically.

The maze's reconfiguration took surprisingly longer to navigate this year than he anticipated, with dead ends and bottlenecks where he nearly had to crawl. Kick never did find a proper exit. Rather than attempt to backtrack all the way to the entrance, he found a spot where he could move a board aside and slide through the wall to the dance area. This may have been a secret door.

Time here seemed to shift like a liquid. Or more so, like a glacier, *geologically* fluid.

CHAPTER
NINE

JEWELYA

J ewelya always knew the house was empty the moment she walked in the door; it just felt different. She'd been this way since she was a child. She didn't like silence. It wasn't just loneliness—although that was a factor; silence was oppressive and leached her soul. A quiet house felt lifeless, a void, a vast chasm of emptiness. So she always surrounded herself with life everywhere she went: music and people at work; music and phone calls in the car; television, Ainsley, and her cat, Kitty, at home. She even streamed music while in the shower.

Unfortunately, Kitty wasn't in the living room to greet her today. She was a unique cat. Not allowed outside and only snuck out a couple times a year, and never overnight. Didn't like people much, except Ainsley and her. This included the couple times friends like Denkins and Ainsley's friend

Brandon came by. Kitty would hide under a couch or bed until they left.

Jewelya turned on the television and found a Halloween movie marathon. *Donnie Darko* now, *Dark Shadows* after. It was perhaps odd, how even spooking herself a little was preferable to the sucking vortex of perceived loneliness. She lowered the volume to that of a soft, comfortable conversation. Ainsley didn't watch as much television as she, but when he did, he played it too loud. With him, too many things were all or nothing. Push or ignore. She preferred a reassuring constant volume. A din, a white noise, a brown noise. She hadn't thought about it before, but there was likely no sound that didn't make her want to move. She could dance to the dishwasher, the dryer, the microwave.

And she liked mirrors. She was accustomed to them at the studio. It wasn't so much about vanity (read: perceiving beauty), but reflecting on her posture, her movement. Her mother had told her when she was young that any feature could be a strongpoint, and once she learned what hers were, she should strengthen them. Feature them, no matter what they were. Like her neck. As an adult, Jewelya doubted people often typed "neck" into a search on a porn site, unlike more obvious targets like T and A. She received compliments from students and friends like Denkins that she had nice legs. She assumed most people who said "legs" meant "ass," but that was a nicer way to say it. But neck? That didn't just mean standing up straight, but shoulders back. Exposed. More strategically placed moisturizer. Chin up without projecting an image of pretension.

Above the television was a wide, heavy, slightly smoked mirror, and she caught her eye in it, then rolled her neck. It cracked like celery three times, and she tried to imagine the sound coming from the person who looked like her in the mirror, rather than loudly and intimately inside her head. She did things like this at the studio sometimes, too, when she was stiff, and imagined the woman in the mirror didn't feel her pain. Because she didn't. It wasn't her. *She*, Jewelya, was here. The one rolling her neck. But this exercise in existentialism helped her get out of her head. To be out there, where she imagined all life, all sound to really be, between her head and the mirror. In a way, this potentially created a third Jewelya who bathed in qualia.

When she entered the bedroom, Kitty was on the bed, lying exactly where Jewelya's chest would've been. Her heart. Good Kitty. She lifted her head and stretched all four legs at once, impressing Jewelya with limbs longer than seemed possible for her size.

When Jewelya had first begun dancing around the house as a child, she didn't know it was a thing. *Dancing.* She'd just moved because it felt good and the people around her became noticeably happier. She couldn't remember ever *not* dancing, it was that young when she started. Probably as soon as she could stand, walk. Ants in her pants, perhaps, but to a beat, a rhythm, the sounds of life around her. Especially if a song was playing, even a TV commercial. Her mother was pleased by this, laughing and clapping, encouraging her. Her father never seemed to notice, and when he did, he sounded grumpy. But he never told her to stop, except at the kitchen table or if she blocked his view of the television. So at first, she had no idea dancing could be a real art form or career. Now, it was therapy.

It was amazing how much she'd changed in three years. Married. Boringly staying at home most nights after work. Granted, some of those nights she wasn't off until ten p.m., but still. She used to be a night owl. Double-you-tea-if.

Tonight, her soundtrack for getting ready was a Halloween-themed music playlist (plus the accompanying sound of a television), and not the goofy songs recorded for children, either, like "Monster Mash" or "Ghostbusters." She preferred music that was dark, yet happy. When the song sounded like therapy for the performers and songwriters, lifting them against the gravity of their vortex. Eighties and nineties, mostly. The Cure, Depeche Mode, New Order, The Smiths—artists that had danceable, hooky music with deadpan vocals, or happy melodies with dark lyrics. Contrasts. Levels. Celebrations of loneliness. For her, even the happiest music needed a dark side, and the darkest music had to sound like it was rescuing the artists.

Overall, Jewelya wasn't a high-maintenance personality, except for when it was time to perform for the stage or camera. Even if the whole world *wasn't* a stage, Dirgatory would be one tonight. Hollywood and such. Dress to impress, even if it's gore.

After she showered, getting dressed, she looked down at her knee, the one which fell victim to career-ending surgery. Scars. Not large. Two of them where a doctor had gone in and repaired her. Even if she'd be prone to forget, her body remembered. She continued dressing. The dress was long enough to cover flaws no one would have seen anyway.

She stared in the bedroom mirror. Hair up in a bun, she applied makeup to transform herself into a glamorous, sexy vamp. Old Hollywood, but darker, mysterious. She put on the half mask, but something was wrong. Not her contacted eyes. She'd gone with a heavy, smoky eyeshadow and liner vibe so that basically only the gray iris and white sclera would show through the eyelet. It was her lips, the lipstick. She always felt her mouth was too small, so lipstick tonight was paramount. Perhaps the dimmer lights of the party would help, but she shouldn't count on solutions outside her control. She rubbed it off and grabbed another shade. She did this several times to determine the perfect counterpoint to the mask, ending with a crimson that highlighted her tiny Cupid's bow lips. And her hair now didn't seem elegant enough, so she played with different variations until she landed on one that felt right.

Seriously, those two things took almost an hour. She was slipping into an old mode she hadn't experienced since her knee injury. Showtime. Even though she'd originally agreed to go to Dirgatory for Ainsley's sake, she was treating tonight as if it were her own event. As she should. And it was. She was going to have fun, dammit. She was getting butterflies.

Ainsley used to be more fun, more receptive to new experiences. Almost childlike. And Jewelya suspected Dirgatory would be the inevitable expression of his immature desire to be the stereotypical guy who went to parties like this, who partied like this. Overall, though, she realized that since they'd been married, Ainsley had been rubbing off on her, both of them transforming into homebodies. They were ghosts of their previous selves.

MOTE:
Ghosts are memories, or imagined memories.

WHAT JEWELYA HAD BELIEVED she was getting when she married Ainsley was more of a free spirit. That he was more go-with-the-flow. For example, soon after they'd first met, they rented a room at the Ace Hotel in downtown L.A. for their first overnight date. After dinner, they'd each taken a gel cap of psilocybin (four would've been considered a full dose) before walking into the Last Bookstore. It would be a while before they felt any effects, if much at all, but they wanted to wander around a quiet environment, just in case. Friendly people who kept their distance, and lots of words on pages into which they could lose themselves.

"Let's also hit one of Bukowski's bars while we're down here," Ainsley said as he perused the shelf of books in front of him. "Maybe The King Eddy. It's only a couple blocks over."

Jewelya had heard of it. It was the kind of old school dive bar that would conjure an early midcentury Skid Row drinking vibe. Not a place she would've suggested. But she was game, if a bit hesitant. "I think you'd fit in better than me," she said, self-consciously withdrawing her tummy by means of tightening her diaphragm. She had obviously put more thought into her appearance than he had tonight. This would be a common theme for them over time. "I'm, I don't know, maybe a bit overdressed."

"Nah," he said. He tilted his head and squinted one eye as he took her in. Then he raised his eyebrows, an infectious expression that brought a smile to Jewelya every time she saw it. "You look great. You always do. Me, I dress like shit all the time."

Early in their relationship, it had been difficult for Jewelya to tell when Ainsley was just joking or legitimately being hard on himself. At this point, she hadn't known yet. "You dress cute," she said. "You just deal with computers all day. You could be in your underwear and nobody would ever know."

"'Deal with computers,' she says," Ainsley said. "Sometimes I think computers have to deal with me. I constantly encounter ghosts in the machine that I don't think like me."

Who wouldn't like you?

"Speaking of which," she said, "have *you* ever ghosted anyone?"

"Like, have I just disappeared on someone? I leave a lot of parties that way. The Irish goodbye. The Dark Man. Leave before anyone sees you leaving."

"No, I mean, like, have you ever just stopped talking or texting with someone cold turkey? No goodbyes, no explanations?"

"Almost exclusively."

"Are you going to do that to me?" Jewelya suddenly felt so vulnerable standing there in her black-and-white polka dot dress, red silk belt and matching red bow in her hair. She'd felt debonair, like a sixties model, when she'd left the apartment, but now she felt immature, telegraphing neediness to someone she had yet to spend the night with.

"Does that happen to you much?" he said, squaring her hips to his.

"Almost exclusively."

Ainsley wasn't much taller than Jewelya, so when he stood on his tiptoes to kiss her forehead, she hadn't realized what he was doing and also tried to stand on her toes to meet his lips with hers, his eyes with her eyes. His botched kiss landed on the bridge of her nose. Even for a dancer, she often felt awkward, like a doe or baby giraffe. It was like she needed dance in order to center her gravity.

Jewelya laughed. Too many guys tried to be suave, or more coordinated, or smarter than she was. They were jockeying with imaginary men for position on some sort of a mating pyramid. Ainsley didn't seem to care, or if anything, seemed to embrace the clumsiness. It made what she was feeling all the more real.

"Don't worry. Your name doesn't start with a J or an R," he said.

"Ummmm," Jewelya said.

"Shit, that's right. It does." Ainsley lit up with an idea. "I can just leave right now. It's not ghosting if you see me walk away, is it?"

"Ha. I love that you're superstitious, though."

"The J's and R's aren't superstition. It's science. It's from experience."

She didn't want to talk about exes. Not right now. "Okay, well, if you're dragging me to a dive bar where I'll be eaten alive, then I get to look for ghosts first."

Their next stop would be the Biltmore Hotel, a few blocks west of the bookstore.

JEWELYA WAS ALMOST READY NOW, with Dirgatory representing a return of their spontaneity, even if, really, it was a form of cosplay. They were cosplaying a "party couple."

MOTE:
Love is optically challenged.

LOVE IS BLIND, huh? she thought. *Blind to what?*

Text from Ainsley. *Ghosting on Halloween?*

She saw she'd missed an earlier text while messing with hair and makeup, too. She was inadvertently pulling an "Ainsley." But it wasn't that long ago. He was being passive aggressive since they hadn't really spoken about their miniature public tiff yesterday. Don't engage that. Not until after the party. But he must've been getting anxious and desperate without her. There were Dirge and other Consumerian acquaintances for him to talk to, weren't there? *He tends to do this; his appetite is bigger than his stomach.*

Her phone battery was in the red. Her mind had been elsewhere, and she'd forgotten to charge it. She plugged it in. Maybe she could get it up to a half charge before leaving.

She texted Ainsley: *On my way!*

Then she ordered her Gryft.

CHAPTER
TEN

AINSLEY

insley's phone buzzed:

MOTE:
If you've always been lost, location is unnecessary.

OKAY, then. But he knew where he was.

Dirgatory was filled with so many guests, beyond anything he'd ever experienced at somebody's house. It was like being front of stage at a sold-out concert. People moved by leaning on the person in front of them—but they were polite here, with apologies and conciliatory smiles as drinks spilled over hands. Earlier, even though the invitation had announced costumes were a requirement, he suspected it wouldn't be a big deal. He'd come over straight from work. But he could swear he was the only one in street clothes. He was an imposter, a stowaway, a cheater, a tourist.

He was near the bar and surveying the tide. He could discern where heads didn't seem to move forward at all, versus at a snail's pace—guests in line weren't pushing on the people in front of them to move. He leaned his back against the shed's wall and took a deep breath. He wasn't agoraphobic, but he needed a break. He needed air. The party had been designed for disorientation—strobe lights, black lights, holiday lights, no lights—and it was effective.

Ainsley texted his wife. *Where are you?*

MOTE:

If you're feeling lost, recite this prayer aloud:
(Followed by Latin-esque gibberish.)

THE OMNIST SEEMED to know how he felt. Two Motes in a row with similar themes. So what the hell, he read the passage, sounding out each syllable. He may not have known the language, but the prayer was phonetically straightforward.

And even if the effect of reciting these sounds was a placebo, he felt better immediately. Placebos, by definition, worked. He pulled his shoulders back, stretching his torso and feeling his back crack. The disorienting stimuli remained, but he was less anxious.

Across the way, he saw four girls dancing on the coffins, all a head taller than everyone around them. Two were swinging on the poles, thirsty for gazes, drinking from a fountain of attention.

Incense. Weed. Musk. Sweat. Patchouli. Deodorant. Hair conditioner. Latex—he'd never before smelled latex just by being around other people. He couldn't believe how well he could pick up individual scents. *Imagine being a dog!*

Who knew how many people were in the maze, in the house, out front. There was so much physicality: touching, drinking, dancing. And the eyes: staring, scanning, reading his soul. The glances—those, too, were physical. Tangible. Side-eyes, slow blinks, all centers of hedonistic universes, invitations to connect or push away. All the quintessential human sounds washed through him: talking, laughing, singing, squealing. It was all so human.

He pushed off the wall and leaned his way around the bar to the restrooms. It took about three minutes to travel thirty feet where space opened up enough to move more freely. The restrooms were split into two sections:

On the right, the women's side consisted of three porta-potties behind a curtain that was held open by ladies in line.

On the left, the men's structure looked like a junkyard lean-to and had no queue. Once inside, Ainsley understood why. Rather than a few porta-potties, there was a urinal trough made of a half-pipe of twelve-inch diameter PVC, at least eight feet long and lined with clear plastic. It drained into a portable sewage tank. Since four guys could use it at once, this line was moving faster. He figured if a guy needed to sit to do his business, he'd have to use a porta-potty.

There were four people at the trough, with one of the middle ones facing the wrong direction—a girl dressed as Wonder Woman leaning forward, panties at her knock-knees, one hand modestly covering herself, the other balancing herself on a knee, peeing with the guys. She was managing to not touch anything. The guys on either side of her were laughing at the ridiculousness of it all.

"That's a rock star, right there," one of them said.

"Do whatcha gotta do," the other said.

The girl shuffled in place. Ainsley's first instinct was to brace her shoulder so she wouldn't fall, but one of the guys next to her held out his elbow, a suggestion of a handrail. Even though she was staring at the ground, Ainsley looked away. Guts, strength, bodily emergency, whatever it was, he felt her self-consciousness.

The walls were papered with pornography from old magazines, weathered history from parties past: yellowed tape, rusty staples holding up faded torn paper, bubbled, buckled, and folded over, hanging. The eyes of every girl in the photos were trying to connect with him from various eras, back to the days of black-and-white photography, right up to online shoots probably done this year, printed out inside Dirgatory's bloody bedroom-office. With new additions apparently layered on top each year, Ainsley wanted to be an anthropologist (a pornologist, pornographologist, carnalogist, hedonologist, whatever—he was making up words here) of twenty-five years of parties, and if he dug down, which were the oldest ones to survive, and what tales would they tell? Mostly though, it smelled like shit in there.

Finished, Wonder Woman pulled up her panties, straightened out her skirt, and shuffled away, not making eye contact with anyone.

Ainsley took her place between the others, and perched right there, angled jauntily in the trough, taunting him, was a turd—not from her—soaking in red vomit, like watery blood with chunks in it, impeding downriver flow. The stench from which, the stench of shit—*you're in urinal hell*—the odiferous septic spell a gut punch, a guttural retch. Some guests weren't well.

He closed his eyes, holding his breath, but in his periphery, he was aware of something else. Looking to the side would be impolite, so he lifted his free hand to his eyebrow, and scratched while he glanced to his left.

There was a phone in the urinal. Downstream. Soaked in the effluvia of the first hours of party. *How does that even happen?*

When Ainsley finished, the guy behind him, made up undead, lipstick smudged across one side of his face, slipped into place. "Goddammit, it stinks in here," he said, sounding unmotivated, deceased.

The bathroom was the size of a large walk-in closet, yet the girl who'd peed in the trough was still there, zoning into the smut on the wall. Disoriented.

"Hi, excuse me, are you okay?" Ainsley said.

When she turned around, looking at him for the first time, she had the most amazing eyes he'd ever seen. "Oh, uh, I'm just waiting for my girlfriend."

"I don't think she's in here. This is the men's room." He gestured to the exit.

"Oh, thanks," she said.

"Did you get an early start?" Ainsley said. *Perhaps dinner would've helped.*

"What?" she said slowly. She was out of it, but not slurring. "No." Soft voice. Concerned about his concern. "I had one, I think."

I think?

As she exited, she measured each step for safety, and her friend, standing between the bathroom sections, immediately grabbed her hand. "Lisa, there you are!"

It was Kat from the Emporium dressed as Lydia from *Beetlejuice*. Ainsley waved, but she didn't seem to notice. Rather than interrupt Kat while she huddled privately with her inebriated friend, he continued on. At least she was safe from untoward men.

Walking back the way he came, the bar was on the left was followed by a solid mass of loud, festive flesh. To his right was the entrance to the haunted maze with several people clustered in front.

Pardon me. Excuse me, he said with his eyes.

As dark as it was outside the maze, the lights from the bar had at least washed over that area. Now inside, he'd entered another world and he needed a moment to adjust. After this dark passage, he came across an area lit softly with red holiday lights, but three-fourths of the bulbs were somehow black, like liquid obsidian, seemingly fluid. A soft popping noise was followed by a momentary breeze, cool and gentle. Cool effect, if that's what this was.

MOTE:

Close your eyes to see sound, hear light.

AINSLEY SQUEEZED past people dressed as the American Gothic couple as they made their way out. The male held a cardboard pitchfork over his head like a torch, which then got caught in some overhead webbing. "I'm trying," he said as a response to something the female said.

The next section opened up like a keyhole, and a single bare incandescent bulb hung from a crossbeam. Not quite a room, but with enough room to stop and talk, as a couple others were doing. A lamp and beverage rested on a tilted table, somehow not sliding off. He reached down to check the furniture's steadiness. The lamp was fixed in place; the table was sturdy, leaning from (possibly) intentionally uneven legs. He'd walked into a cartoon.

Next section, a neon sign, again painted with enough layers of dark disappointment to restrict most of its illumination, the life underneath attempting to escape its claustrophobic clutches. Dirge had told him the maze was reconfigured every year, and based on what he'd seen already, it could take months to strike and rebuild.

Each section was unique unto itself. Some were dark but for light leakage from other spaces, manifesting as flickers under chins and backs of heads. Elbows and shoulders. Eyes sparkling. Shadows blinked away, then dragged across the face of a vampire who was staring him down a foot away. It was impossible to flow quickly with such clogged arteries. He'd expected more private areas for unsavory acts, but in much of the maze, passing people required both parties turning sideways.

After working his way through a few more turns, Ainsley arrived at a room that featured a car seat, where a guy dressed as a hobbit was drinking a stein of beer while receiving a blowjob. The people in front of Ainsley cheered as they passed, but nobody stopped to gawk. The couple were merely a sight on a Samhain tour. Eyes closed, the hobbit grinned as he held up his stein, saluting his fortune for anybody who'd blindly toast him.

At a fork in a corridor, Ainsley ducked through a hole in some netting and must have tripped some sort of wire. A cheesy cackle emitted from a tinny toy speaker, like something from a children's carnival ride. He kept his head down a couple steps, then felt something on the back of his neck. Tendrils attacked him from above, creepy crawlies tickling his hair and scalp, and as he ducked under the yarn, twisting his head, he saw a light move in the shadows. Someone coming from the other direction dressed as Indiana Jones blocked his view for a moment, swiping yarn like cobwebs.

He was bumped from behind and fell to his knees. Intentional? Accidental? From the ground, he lost track of what he was trying to see through a small forest of moving legs.

"Sorry," Crypt Keeper from *Tales from the Crypt* said, helping Ainsley up. Everyone was so nice here.

Once Ainsley was on his feet, he attempted to give Crypt Keeper a thankful slap on the back, but no one was there. He'd already moved around a corner. To his right, Ainsley saw a specter or something. It looked like a person on their hands and knees, in front of the chair, similar to his recent position. It was a static image, and when he reached out, his hand went through it and the image flickered and disappeared. This only took a second, but there was no mistaking what he'd seen. There must be special effects to create apparitions; *how cool was that?*

A Batman and Joker were next to him. Ainsley instantly felt they were a couple. "Did you guys see a ghost in here?" Ainsley said, regretting the question as soon as he'd said it.

"Holy phantom!" Robin said. "A ghost?"

"I heard the host is a special effects guy," Batman said, sounding more like a cop than his eager friend.

"You're probably right," Ainsley said. "The image disappeared right away."

"A caper!" Robin said. "Do you think you'll see it again?"

"I'm just trying to figure out how he did it." Ainsley brushed the dirt off his knees. "I'm sure it'll reappear."

"Perhaps," Batman said, uninterested, squeezing past.

"Good luck!" Robin said.

Ainsley came upon a warm, tented room, possibly the farthest section from the house, where a small area was carpeted with pillows, tapestries, and lamps. It reeked of the stale, damp ash of musky incense and tobacco, and it felt ancient and magical. It was an opium den where he expected to hear maritime tales of the spice trade. A woman lay on a red, frilly pillow, possibly sleeping, with her phone on the rug next to her. Her friend looked bored, as if waiting for her to wake up. Ainsley imagined Dirge and his buddies escaping to play cards, smoke weed, and drink beer. Perhaps this room was more permanent.

Like the Doctor's Tardis, this maze definitely seemed bigger on the inside. Maybe not literally, but at least in his head. Comfort and danger mixed like sugar and salt. It all looked the same, but who knew what you'd really get until you tried it.

Cheering. At him. In front of him, all around him. The bored girl rose to her feet. She was dressed as an elegant Egyptian princess—smoky eyes, silken gold dress—and as she approached, smiling, eyes drawing Ainsley in, magnets, earthly ancient mineral magic, he felt himself pulled almost out of himself and nearly fainted. Then the princess gently brushed him aside and embraced the man behind him.

"Nefertiti!" the man said.

"Akhenaten!" Nefertiti said.

Ainsley was momentarily trapped against the shaky plywood-and-fishnet wall, trying not to collapse into it and take a section down with him. He muttered a weak greeting, which likely sounded closer to a pathetic cry of distress. The Egyptians unlocked their arms and gazed at him.

Akhenaten was a zombified, sunken-faced, guy-liner-wearing Victorian aristocrat. What he lacked in ancient Egyptian costuming—expressing more as a mixed metaphor of antiquity—he made up for in a bouquet of Egyptian musk. "Salām alaykum," he said.

Hello, welcome, Ainsley heard in his head.

"L'il asif," Nefertiti said.

Pardon me, Ainsley heard. He was suddenly at peace with being in that spot, in that moment, like he was transported, not to another place, but to another feeling. This was a safe space. He could sit on a pillow; the combination of the room's relaxing vibe and the joy emanating from its occupants was appealing. But without saying a word, the next set of people behind them wanted to keep moving and gently nudged him forward along the maze.

"Ma'a salaameh," Ainsley said. *Goodbye.*

Where the fuck did that come from?

He must have whited out. For a moment he didn't remember where he was, and the Egyptian cosplayers were no longer near him. Ten seconds? A minute? He leaned against the wall as if trying to regain his balance. He had no idea how long he had been in the opium den, but many frames of his mental movie were missing. Perhaps time had compressed.

He straightened his shoulders as if nothing was wrong, and rejoined the berg-like floe of unfamiliar guests. He needed out. After more decision-tree forks, passages, and little rooms, he finally saw the word "Exit" spraypainted in red on an untreated, hinged wooden board. He gently pushed his way through. When he looked back, he couldn't tell there was a door there until another guest, a blonde Blarbie, came through.

"Hey, is that the maze?" a police officer next to Ainsley said. Her costume was eerily on point. His heart skipped from the presence of authority.

Blarbie smiled and held the door open for the officer and a couple others. Ainsley wondered if there were any other blind doors.

He was at the farthest west section of the dance area, and the music was loud here. Maybe the speakers were inside the stripper-pole coffins. Both poles were in use, one with an earnest solo dancer and the second with two girls freaking each other.

Ainsley was relieved to have left the maze, but the music was now thumping against his internal organs and nauseating him.

He checked his phone to see if Jewelya had responded.

On my way!

He'd received another Mote.

MOTE:

Disorientation means you're caught between modes of thought, stages, worlds.

Recite this prayer to sync all of these.

(Followed by Latin-sounding gibberish.)

HE'D FELT BETTER reading prayers before. *So, why not?*

ELEVEN

KICK

R eally, no one did Halloween better than Hollywood. West Holly Ween. Hallow Wood. North Holy Wood. This was Kick's favorite day of the year in his favorite city. And it wasn't just the free street party down in West Hollywood that attracted all the people; It was events like this one, Dirgatory, an overcrowded house party for adults that Kick could only dream about as a teenager. Like an epic costume party from a teen movie. But better. This was real.

An hour ago, Gremmie had texted he was on his way, but Kick hadn't seen him yet. They only lived a five-minute Gryft ride away, and even on foot, the trip wouldn't have taken more than thirty minutes. After having checked the maze and dance areas, Kick made his way toward the shed.

Lucador was in his path, facing away, standing at the end

of the "line" for the bar. Why wasn't he in the shed where he'd find easier access to a drink? Maybe he didn't know. Earlier, Lucador had said he refused to come to a party if he couldn't bring a mix of his artisanal weapons. That was who he was. "*No compromise!*" All or nothing. Yet here he was, without any swords sheathed at his side.

Kick tapped him on the shoulder and realized his mistake before the man had fully turned his head. The guest was wearing a Halloween costume they sold at the Emporium, with a small plastic sword attached to his belt loop. This man had indeed wanted to cosplay Lucador tonight, and, like Kick, had refrained from bringing a real blade. But it was realistic enough that it presented as less childish than Kick had feared.

"Sorry," Kick said. "Great costume. You look just like him."

"I chop your greeting!" the Lucador impersonator said, laughing, reaching for the handle of the sword. He didn't pull it out; it was too crowded. "I cut this line in half! Then half again!" He raised a fist in triumph, smiling wide, just like Lucador would. Regardless, victory was his.

"A shorter line's a better line," Kick said. He was sure somewhere in Dirgatory were people partaking in party favors who would disagree. But they'd be chopping different lines. Doing those sorts of drugs wasn't Kick's vibe. He moved on, slapping the Lucadorian on the shoulder.

The first time Kick had approached the bar-shed had been from the front, where a bulb under the awning made its cone of light the brightest in the backyard. He walked toward the rear of the structure. A black curtain draped against the wall next to the bar made the backyard feel like a movie set. Time to go behind the scenes. The mustiness of the curtain hugged him as he swept aside the heavy fabric to reveal a closed door. He went through, closing the door behind him.

The shed was dark, maybe the size of a one-car garage, but it felt cavernous away from the crush of people outside. A couple boxes pushed together served as a coffee table for three laptops in front of a couch. Kick was literally behind the curtain at a party of insiders and creators, part of the inner sanctum of special effects Hollywood. And this was the control center, home base for the sound system and screens. He was a VIP here, the way he was at a Lodge.

Those three laptops, plus a blue lava lamp on a tool cabinet in the corner, provided ambiance for this darker side of the room, while the bulb under the awning outside the bar window provided most of the light. Since the bar window was to his far left along the same wall as the door he just entered, from this angle he couldn't really see out; he just heard the roar of people and music. The two "prisoners" were methodically pouring, placing, and pouring drinks, using both hands to multitask their duty, an empty cup at the ready, then while placing a full one on the bar, already pouring the next cup. Clockwork. The action seemed more mechanical and stream-lined from this side of the bar.

Dusty, loose cobwebs—real ones—hung from the walls and boxes where things here had recently been moved around, meaning there would be displaced arachnids searching for new homes. Dust bunny fluffy haze. Griminess from years upon beers of yearly spillage, barely wiped surfaces, paneled-off windows. Sills. Still. Swill. Arachnids and insects loved the sticky-sweet angel's share leaked from spent kegs. This room was an ode to spiders.

The Emporium had no Omniscian who extolled the virtues of arachnids.

Yet.

The male prisoner stopped pouring and unlocked the

coupler on his keg. He lifted the empty one out of the bucket and carried it toward Kick.

"Oh, hey," he said as he set it down next to him. The prisoner simultaneously looked happy to see Kick again, tired and overworked, and ready to party. He brushed off the top of a keg, then began to pull it, heavy and full, back toward the bar.

"Need help?" Kick said, leaning down to push. The keg slid easily on the relatively smooth concrete, and his assistance hadn't actually been needed. But once it was next to the ice bucket, Kick grasped one handle, the prisoner the other, and they lifted it up and in. Kick must have lifted seventy-five or eighty pounds himself.

Kick and Connie had been lobbying for a beer and wine license for the Emporium. If this keg weighed in excess of 150 pounds, there was no way employees like Raine and Kat were going to replace kegs by themselves. Or even the new hire, the skinny and studious Elijah, for that matter. Connie, though— Kick had learned long ago not to underestimate her strength, whether spiritual, emotional, or physical. But he still wouldn't want her to feel obligated to do this sort of labor.

Now that he was in line of sight of guests in the service window, he saw arms and hands on the bar poking through a light cloud of dry-ice fog wafting over from the dance area. Greedy smiles drinking in the view of the female prisoner. Loud talking, if not actual yelling. Laughing. Since the male prisoner had missed a few moments of pouring, Kick imagined the natives were getting restless. A guest poked an arm around the person in front of him and set down a large stein. The female prisoner grabbed it right away. Perhaps more twenty-dollar bills had made their way into the tip jar.

Kick wasn't a paranoid type, but he also didn't want to feel stared at by vast quantities of eyes the way the prisoners were.

Because it wasn't paranoia; the guests *were* looking. And with the capability for only two kegs to be hooked up at a time, he couldn't help them with drinks, anyway. He'd come to the shed for privacy, so he retreated like a cockroach into the relative but glowing darkness back by the couch.

Yksian was in the shed, hovering over the laptops.

"Oh, I didn't notice you walk in," Kick said.

"That's quite understandable, since I was already present," Yksian said.

How could he have missed a six-and-a-half-foot tall goth —nearly seven, really, when the boots and top hat were included—in a room this unpopulated? Yksian, draped in a black trench coat and nearly invisible, was monitoring the computers from a distance, seemingly hovering in the blue-screen darkness—not sitting on the couch and leaning over his knees the way a gamer like Gremmie would.

"I must not have seen you," Kick said.

"I attract attention for tiny things," Yksian said. "People forget them and move on. Most never return."

He could have said, "Yes, apparently," or something. And who could forget anything about him? "You're one of the hosts but hiding away in here?" Kick said.

"What happens in a black hole stays in a black hole," Yksian said, tracing the top of his snakehead goblet with a single digit. It was so long his wrist stayed in place above the presumed wine while his finger twirled.

Will I forget that detail?

"You're missing a great party out there," Kick said.

Yksian made no response for a few seconds. "*Missing* is a strong word," he finally said. His voice was slow and deep, yet Kick had no trouble hearing the articulation over the noise.

"The Dark Angel of Dirgatory doesn't look like he's having a good time."

"Sir Kick, I am not surprised. Angels are merely pretentious ghosts who, in the afterlife, continue to live in a gated community." *So which side of the fence is he saying he's on?* "And the smartest person in the room is often the most miserable, as the most aware, intuitive, polite, empathic, and nicest of us would agree."

So Yksian was saying he was, perhaps, all of those things. And there was virtually no one in the shed. Except Kick.

"I'm referring to the party in general, of course," Yksian continued. "Despite my attendance here, I do prefer isolation. And I can still enjoy the music."

Of course. It was Yksian's playlist, anyway.

"Yksian sets the emotional tone," Chikao said. "He *is* our dungeon master."

Chikao. Kick hadn't known he was there, either. It was creepy, how he'd missed the presence of two people in the room. Chikao was dressed as the Dalai Lama: wearing a set of maroon robes (with a gold stripe on the outer layer), sandals, and a burlap and vegan leather-trimmed rucksack/computer bag for monks (this was a thing) that Chikao sold at the Emporium. For monks who needed to travel with technology. When the ties were cinched at the top, they doubled as shoulder straps. Chikao didn't sell much merchandise at the Emporium, but Connie required Omniscians to sell at least something as a prerequisite to host Lodges.

Chikao bowed without speaking, as if honoring a vow of silence, which presented as meeker and more subservient than his persona for Lodges. One hundred and eighty degrees, really. His method acting was in full force.

Really, though, even this change in Chikao's behavior seemed natural. He was a bit of a contradiction—a technology Omniscian who promoted organic and plant-based goods. An analog person who spoke digitally. Aside from his Japanese heritage—not Tibetan—the costume wasn't that far off, spiritually.

"You look surprised to see him, Kick," Yksian said. "I prayed to the technology gods, and they reciprocated by blessing us with Chikao's presence."

Kick wasn't sure how much Yksian was kidding here. Yksian wasn't the type that prayed to gods, necessarily. He was more of an atheist. But he must have invited Chikao.

"I'd travel the lengths of universe to be here," Chikao said, his head dipping as he spoke. "A wonderful congregation of revelry." More method acting; he was even speaking like Yksian now.

Both Omniscians had an overstylized manner of speech, and it was interesting to hear how they contrasted. Yksian's voice was deeper and slower, his entire chest—and thus the room—seeming to resonate with each syllable. Chikao, also, usually spoke from the diaphragm, projecting his voice over heads like an experienced teacher, holding his chin high. He was sharp, quick, and precise. But now, in character, he was quieter, almost malleable. Still, both men tended to overenunciate, although Chikao did so with a bit of an accent.

Kick had seen a Whelp review earlier today where a Consumerian had given Chikao's Lodge last night a poor review. He'd never understood that. With so many diverse topics and beliefs, attend the Lodges you're most likely to enjoy, and if you disagree with an Omniscian, just accept that everything can't be for everyone. Don't be a dick.

He shouldn't say anything, but he couldn't help himself. "Chikao, did you see the Whelp reviews about your Lodge?" The other was actually stellar.

"Oh, no, I do not read," Chikao said. "Yuko told me. Two reviews. One says I make too many assumptions about universe."

"Ah," Yksian said. "When someone has no interest in learning, educated guesses look like assumptions. And if one speaks truth, a poor review means the reviewer wasn't listening. How many stars, may I ask?"

"Three," Kick said. "So not *that* bad, really."

"And how many stars, pray tell," Yksian said, "does Whelp get?"

Kick laughed. *Who reviews the reviewers?*

"You haven't seen my phone, have you?" Chikao said, patting his chest softly as if the device would be found in the robe's nonexistent pockets.

Kick was on the verge of saying: *Bring one phone. Keep it in your pocket, or in this case, your pack.* But he couldn't, shouldn't, take that tone with the Dalai Lama.

The music's volume increased for a few seconds when Kat stuck her head in the door, saw Yksian, and entered. Connie was right behind her, smiling like a politician. In character, like Hilary Clinton, but also like Connie.

"You haven't seen Lisa, have you?" Kat said, eyes locked on Yksian.

Yksian's lack of movement could easily be read as a no. Few people could pull off a non-gesture as effectively as he did.

Kat turned her gaze toward Kick. Imploring.

"Sorry," Kick said. Dirgatory was turning out to be a big collection of missing things. No Gremmie. No Lisa. Chikao's missing phone.

"Lisa doesn't really know anybody here outside of me and Kat," Connie said.

"Maybe she met a guy," Kick said.

"She'd still answer texts, though," Kat said.

"Speaking of which," Kick said. "Have you guys seen Gremmie?"

"Your roommate?" Kat said. "Maybe that's who she met."

"Not sure if you remember what he looks like," Kick said, "but he's supposed to be Fred Flintstone tonight."

"I say tell our people to meet us in here," Connie said, looking at the couch longingly. "Away from everybody poking at me. 'Connie! Connie! Hey Connie!'" She swung her hand, waving at imagined masses, sounding happier than the mock complaint would suggest. Humblebragging.

"I thought you liked big crowds," Kick said. The two of them had opened the Emporium two and a half years ago, and in that time, she had become the face of the company, while he was virtually ignored in public.

"At the *Emporium*. Not here." Connie sipped her wine, then slowly lowered herself to the couch. "This is different. Don't get me wrong. I do love it, but I worked all day."

"You seem unnerved," Kick said.

"No, no, I'm nerved," she said, putting her feet up on a storage box between two laptops. "I'm *very* nerved."

With Yksian, Chikao, Kat, Connie, and Kick (plus two bartenders) all in the shed, it was truly a next-level, private party. But there were too many people now. And like an artisan guild in a video game, filled with people and drinks, nothing interesting would happen if Kick stayed there. The first goal of the game was to leave, to set off on an adventure. "Well, I think I'll get out of your way. If you guys see Gremmie, tell him to text me and wait for me here."

Kick interrupted the male bartender to refill his cup, then toasted the others with it as he exited. Once outside, in order to move through the high tide of people, he leaned forward on the person in front of him. The other option was to stand still and he'd move anyway, like driftwood riding the wave, or a blank message in a bottle, a slave to whims, subservient to the current.

Forward-facing, though.

Seriously, though, where was Fred Flintstone?

It was beginning to rain. Oddly, this made overcrowding feel, what, cozy?

Rain ASMR.

Kick texted Gremmie again.

CHAPTER
TWELVE

AINSLEY

A sudden chill whisked through the lukewarm, ozone-metallic air, and icy-wet razor blades sliced Ainsley's bare forearms and face. Or slivers of frozen, brutally sharp diamonds. Even though Ainsley couldn't really see the ground for all the people around him, as it got wet, he felt the difference under his shoes. Simultaneously stickier and slipperier. The earth could churn into mud and filth, and few guests would care. How fast was this happening? No matter, water always won over time. Geologic time. Not over mere moments of a party.

Hydrogen, the element that existed in ninety percent of all matter in the universe, whether as independent atoms or partnered within molecules, was the source of sourcing, the first element, literally and figuratively. The first first. The new hydrogen arriving at Dirgatory was married to oxygen, in a

clear molecule known as dihydrogen monoxide, and it splattered itself over feet and ankles, mixing with dirt into a murky
brown.

Underneath the awnings of the back porch and shed, and
in many little areas of randomly tented maze protection,
people arranged themselves into tight clusters in order to
avoid makeup runoff. Some guests took advantage of the relative open space to dance more freely, raising their arms to the
sky to embrace the falling water, to crush a sound or squeeze a
thought, to flash a smile a look a laugh a cough.

Interesting that Ainsley was thinking this way. His mind
was muddied with new thoughts. Or was this the water and
his mind was earth? He was seeing and analyzing things that
would've previously gone unnoticed. Music sounded like he
was swimming underwater, but that had to be psychosomatic.
Eyes all around him looked enchanted, more than merely
made-up or costumed, or conversely, costumes did little to
disguise appearances, messages, or intent. Whatever that was.
Whatever that meant.

Where is Jewelya? Maybe Gryft rides were backed up with
demand tonight. Of course they were. He needed patience.
Maybe when they finally spoke, she would confirm whether
his plastic cup of beer foam had been drugged, which would
explain why he felt so out of sorts. Well, they didn't live far, so
he'd see her soon.

There was a message from the Omnist.

Mote:
Truth comes with disorientation.

. . .

Odd, considering other Motes had promised relief from feelings of perplexity. The Omnist was contradicting itself. Or perhaps this was a learning experience. Yes, that's what this was.

Ainsley arduously made his way to the back door of the house, where Summer was sitting just outside, surrounded by her partying friends, talking and laughing, guarding the home from drunken intruders. He worried she may have forgotten him and he pleaded with his eyes if entering was okay, and she smiled at him. He liked this idea of communication without words. Hadn't he ever done that before? He must have, but it felt novel. Perhaps he could nurture this.

Ainsley began a voyeuristic lap through the house and reconnected with the collection of oddities and sculptures, books and graphic novels, horror movie posters, and other collectibles of an eccentric artist. But the pieces had changed significance; they'd become more important, totems of unrepeatable history. More alive. Like the backyard, there was no area left unfilled. If Dirge had left a space, a guest would've surely occupied it with an empty cup or charging phone.

In his new headspace, he noticed different things now, too —different people, different lighting, different smells.

A mummified cat oversaw the people lounging in the living room like cats themselves, barely conversing, barely there.

A stereotypical voodoo doll leaned against a painting of Richard Nixon, who was circled and "banned" by a red peace sign.

The head of the politician John McCain was attached to a rubber chicken's body.

A human foot with imitation flesh falling off real bones. Somehow Ainsley could tell. The effect would be lost with plastic or plaster. The toes were angled jauntily, stepping their way toward an afterlife they would never reach. In a typical home, this prop would've stood out. Here it was nearly wallpaper.

What had looked like an empty, unlit aquarium earlier was now softly backlit to reveal a skull in its center, squirting blood out of its eyes, the runoff creating a crimson moat. This, too, must have come from a real skeleton, perhaps the same as the foot.

Next to the terrarium was an animated hologram of Walt Disney's head, which slowly morphed from his recognizable face into a frightening skull and then back again. It was remarkably realistic. An evil, incorporeal twin of the one with the bloody moat. Just as in the maze, Ainsley couldn't see where the projection mechanism was hidden. Jewelya, although generally not into gore and this type of horror, would appreciate this. She was fond of the dark side of happiness, finding joy in sorrow, dancing through pain, and maturity in youth and the immaturity of wisdom. Or something.

Ainsley completed his journey around the central hub of the house and walked down the hall near the back door to stand in line for the bathroom. He was, surprisingly, only second in line. While waiting, he blanked out, forgetting everything for a long moment, the way sometimes he didn't remember driving home until the instant he pulled into his driveway. Who knew how much time had passed?

When he finally entered the bathroom, vintage postcards covered every inch of the wall that wasn't a mirror. Cards announced classic movie release dates, roadside attractions, Hollywood landmarks, westside beaches. Many were splattered with fake blood, including bloodstains on the toilet seat. People stood in line for this privilege; he was one of them.

Strange things had happened in this room, and would again. The blood was clearly fake, but it was symbolic: If Dirge had been hosting this party for a couple decades, then this bathroom must have seen its moments, warranting an extra wooden frame and exterior lock protection. But how often would an exterior lock be used if there was always a line in front of the door? When would people be locked out?

After Ainsley completed his duties, while washing his hands, he caught a glimpse of something in the mirror, someone slipping past behind him. He turned around and saw no one. He checked behind the shower curtain. Nothing. Of course he was alone. This time, though, unlike in the maze, the vision hadn't seemed like a projection.

Catching his own attention in the mirror, he simultaneously felt jarred and revolted, psychologically, like a hair was irritatingly growing at the wrong angle—but here, it was his sense of perception that poked out incorrectly. He'd feel immediate relief when he plucked it, which in this case, was pulling his gaze away from himself.

That was weird.

His heartbeat was pounding irregularly, and placing a palm on his chest, he took a long, slow breath. Maybe when he found Jewelya, if she was up for it, they could leave right away. Go home. He needed his bed, even if he couldn't sleep, just so he could breathe in peace. Away from people. He would need her to drive.

He checked his phone. No new text from Jewelya. She should be here by now. He called her and it went straight to voicemail. Rather than leave a message, he texted inquiring her location.

Suddenly, Ainsley feared the apparition he'd seen behind him would follow them home. Maybe the presence really was the same one he'd seen in the maze. He'd picked it up there. It was attached to him. His anxiety was increasing. If he'd been cursed at this party, he didn't want to endanger his wife with it. He'd never thought about curses before. Were they like viruses? Could they spread from person to person, breath to breath?

He read another Mote. It was another relaxation prayer written in that nonsensical pseudo-Latin. The Omnist obviously knew that something was wrong, something was off. The Mote would help him get through this moment. To fend off a drugged beer, perhaps. Or whatever was causing this.

Ainsley quietly recited the prayer, and put his phone in his pocket. Just then, the handle jiggled on the door—he'd been in here too long—and he felt an immediate surge of adrenaline. These prayers really helped counter his fearful feelings. He enthusiastically clapped his hands twice, picked up his cup— the remainder of beer he wasn't even drinking—and headed out of the bathroom. Or he would have if he'd been able to open the door.

He was locked in.

Maybe this all added up somehow. The beer was likely drugged, and yet he didn't want to let go of his cup. He wanted to show Jewelya for proof or something.

He rapped at the door to be let out.

Why would someone lock him in? Weren't there people waiting in line?

He knocked on the door again.

Ainsley turned around and inspected the tiny window that would look onto the backyard if he could see out. It was draped in black curtains, with pebbled glass. He tried to open it. It was possibly painted closed. Even so, it was surely too small to climb out.

Why hadn't anyone in the hall responded?

He went back to the door and knocked louder. Pounding now from the inside of a bathroom. Had this ever happened before?

He heard someone struggling with the handle, and finally a

concerned Summer opened the door. She was holding the padlock in her hand. "Someone locked this," she said. Her tone was complex, part party stress, and part accusatory.

"Why does it lock at all?" Ainsley said.

"To keep people out, not keep them inside," Summer said.

Ainsley wasn't sure he believed that. "Drunk humor, I guess," he said. There must have been douchebags who thought it was funny to lock someone in the bathroom. But providing them an easy way to do it seemed, maybe, short-sighted.

There were several people gathered by the door. Chikao, dressed as the Dalai Lama, appeared to be the last person in line. On stage in the Basil Alcove, he'd stood akimbo, ready for anything. Now he seemed gaunt, hunched over like he was trying to disappear inside himself. He didn't hold eye contact beyond mere acknowledgment of a greeting. Their eyes briefly connected. He may have recognized Ainsley from the Lodge.

"Did you see anyone lock this?" Ainsley said.

Chikao lowered his head and shook it no, in character for a monk, displaying supplication. Of course he hadn't. He'd just arrived, last in line.

"Any of you guys see anything?" Ainsley said to the others in front of Chikao. They shook their heads as well.

"No, Ainsley," Summer said. "We were by the back door, waiting for the rain to stop."

Whatever. Stupid drunk prank.

Ainsley made apologetic gestures to Summer, Chikao, and the others, and went back outside. The short spell of rain had indeed stopped. Ainsley smelled petrichor, deriving from the awakened geosmin of backyard soil. This wasn't quite as pleasant as the activated airborne actinomycetes spores after a rain in the mountains; that was more full-of-life. Right now, this mix included odors of human waste, gasoline, and monoxide pollution. Sweet, sour, warm, acidic. He wondered why he'd never been able to smell this acutely before, isolating individual scents, cataloguing things he'd learned about and forgotten years ago.

The party was just as full, or fuller, as if rain hadn't fallen, just a little wetter, dirtier. Light flashed its way through a wet, bustling, human Rube Goldberg machine, the flesh widgets operating in sync, each event setting off a reaction in others, catalyzed by music, beer, and other party favors. People, in general, were steaming wet (he didn't question how he could see that—he just did) while proverbially gaining steam.

He was floating above himself, watching as he drifted in a slow current, still tethered closely to his body, absorbing the life, the festivities, the vibe.

A girl in a PVC bodysuit with a leather collar and bracelets was dancing on a coffin, pulling in thirsty attention. Around her: stares, a squeal of delight, a spilled drink, an apology, a hug, a toast, a compliment. Attraction and distraction, interest and disinterest, anonymous personas escaping in a moment to remember they'll likely forget, living to forget about life. Guests, sacks of guts and bacteria and attention; their eyes, slivers of skeptical knowledge; souls, glowing in drifting floes.

Ainsley lowered into his body, his head heavy, his core leaden, but his feet remained lighter than air, pumping down-ward in slow motion, each step more vertical than horizontal with so little room to move. Not traveling far.

A man dressed as a police officer joined a woman dressed as Velma from *Scooby Doo* up on a coffin, dancing, freaking her from behind. Jewelya should be here, watching the dancers, but she wasn't a grinding type. Still, this was the stage. He didn't see her.

"Velma" wore a tight, pumpkin-colored long-sleeved sweater and a red miniskirt. She lifted her skirt up over her hips and pushed her red underwear aside to make room for the police officer's penis, which Ainsley realized must have already been protruding from his open zipper.

Velma braced herself against the pole and pushed into him to the cheers of an infernal audience of jealousy and respect, desire and encouragement. Blood began running down her leg, too much, too fast, hemorrhaging like she'd spilled a Bloody Mary on herself. It also spread across her cheeks and his pelvis, sticky, two sexual Post-it notes preferring to be together than rip apart. Ainsley somehow heard the suction of skin pulled off skin. This was a primal, conjugal, menstrual murder scene, the death of composure and discretion. For the immediacy of attention.

That had to be fake blood. Part of the show. There was a non-zero chance this was simulated sex, and the blood was emitted from a prop. He thought about the prosthetic Dirk Diggler phallus on display in the house. He was surer now than ever, since the officer's "penis," his diving rod, had already been outside his pants.

In fact, Jewelya would not be enjoying this, if she were here.

Then, a girl hanging upside down from the other pole, her feet pretzeled, arms crisscrossed, slowly lowered herself to the ground, landing softly on her shoulders. She rolled to her knees, stood up, then swung around the pole twice, gaining speed, and jumped to the other coffin, nearly knocking over the other couple. Both girls smiled as they clung to each other. The smiles moved closer and closer into the softest kiss. Ainsley could feel the gentle tickle on his lips, even from six feet away.

Okay, Jewelya would enjoy this. Bloody Kisses. The name of a Type O Negative album he liked. And Jewelya had said she dated women before. A more insecure Ainsley, (read: an hour ago) would question why she was even married to a boring guy like him. Now, it didn't matter. She had agency. They both did.

"Oh my god!" a guest next to Ainsley said, holding a hand to her face.

"I'm okay with it," Ainsley replied. Despite enjoying gory movies, when presented with it in real life, he was blood-averse. And this was fake. "It's the origin of our lives."

"No, that," she said, pointing to the other coffin riser.

A shirtless man had climbed up. Eyes straight ahead as if reading from a floating monitor. He wore no apparent costume, as he was a cutter, cutting, using his bare torso as a medium to deliver bloody messages to his audience with flourishes; not violent, not careful, just scribbling. Art on his biceps. Ancient symbols on his chest. Try as he might, Ainsley couldn't make out what the messages were. He felt that this was written in the language of prayer Motes. Not the English alphabet, nor Latin script. It was older. The pre-, the proto-.

The woman who had pointed him out, changing tack, stepped forward confidently, and ran her hand through the blood on the man's chest, smearing it like sunscreen, or in this case, like crimson moonscreen.

Ainsley imagined the burning pain her sweaty, salty hand would inflict upon fresh, open wounds. Was he becoming more empathic, as Jewelya claimed she was? And she was. But these two on stage were actors seeking attention. More show.

Juxtaposed with the simulated menstrual sex on the adjacent coffin, it was all blood, all the time, here. But if someone were stabbed and really hurt, how would anyone know? He was shockingly not shocked, but felt assured everything would be all right. The actors were trying to rile up guests. This was ritualistic, ceremonial. Ainsley felt like he was, psychologically, above what was going on here. But his heart was still racing. The act had worked. Too much stimulation.

Ainsley read another Mote. Apparently, it was something intended to clear his mind.

MOTE:

Apologies for rapid Motes. It seems you need this:
(Followed by more Latin-esque-sounding protolanguage.)

THE OMNIST HAD NEVER BEFORE APOLOGIZED. It'd only been ten or twelve minutes since the previous Mote. He was accustomed to six or eight a day, a number that he could tweak up or down, based on his needs and bandwidth. Today, the number had obviously increased.

And still no Jewelya. It was understandable feeling anxious about overcrowding and mud. About abnormalities in the maze, in the bathroom. About the grotesque, bloody art show. But mostly, he was upset about not finding his wife in these throngs of depravity. He reminded himself that when Jewelya found him, they could leave. She wouldn't enjoy this show.

Ainsley was the one who'd so badly wanted to come, and he'd been positive Jewelya would enjoy it, kicking into a former version of herself as a dancer, more of an exhibitionist than he was. In a sense, then, he'd come tonight for her. Yes, that was it. He'd taken one for the team so she could have a great time. It was now possible, by asking to leave, he'd be ruining her night before it had even started.

He wanted to find a spot away from the insanity to read his mantra. A dark corner. He pressed forward, needing to pass the bar again for the maze's entrance. This was the most congested area, slowed as close to a stop as he'd experienced all night, traveling at a party speed of twenty feet a minute.

Once inside, he edged his way through twisted bottlenecks where people had to duck under one another or awkwardly press against strangers. He eventually found a small, dry alcove that people stepped into to allow others to pass. A turnabout on a one-lane road. It was tented in a clear plastic that had protected a portion of ground from the short rain. There was a two-by-three-foot rug, like a miniature flying carpet. Ainsley brushed off some dirt and sat down.

People kept stepping into the space to allows others to pass, nearly knocking over his cup of warm, flat beer—he was still saving the last few ounces for Jewelya—so he moved it to a license plate shelf, bent at a ninety-degree angle on the wall.

Even though Jewelya taught yoga, Ainsley didn't practice regularly. Sometimes they worked out together in the living room or backyard patio, but only about once a month. She could pretzel her legs from standing into a lotus position without using her hands—a trick she said she'd learned in dance. Surprisingly, he was able to do so right now. He'd always struggled with some basic positions and stretches (his knees never felt right), but she'd reassured him he'd get better over time. If only she could've seen this. His legs were ridiculously comfortable.

He texted Jewelya his location as well as he could describe it, then took a deep breath and exhaled. He felt a warmth in his chest, tingling in his fingers and toes. This was where he was supposed to be. Alone in public. With so many people talking, laughing, and shrieking, and music permeating the remainder of the soundscape, it was all white noise. It was better this way.

Ainsley felt stoned, but hadn't consumed any drugs. Psychosomatic? His funkiness had begun when he started drinking tonight. Imagine telling somebody that: "I don't know why, but I felt different after a couple beers." The reaction would be a dead stare. But he did feel better, more relaxed, after reading each Mote.

He opened the Omnist, read the prayer aloud, then closed his eyes to allow the words to sink in. He focused on breathing. The no-thoughts thoughts.

Teaching this sort of meditation should be a class at CSE, with mandatory attendance for Ainsley's coworkers. Wherever Jewelya was right now, she would love this. She needed to not only join him right now, but add these Motes to the end of yoga classes.

Individual soundwaves from different directions were crashing into each other, breaking into visual components. In his mind's eye, he could see their trajectories and subsequent ricochets swirl into a chunky sediment like that on the ground near the stripper-pole coffins.

As that thought came to pass, it sort of didn't finish. Time slowed to a near stop, like watching an object moving near a black hole. This was the shutting down of all movement, including waves, with virtually no sound or color. Color was movement.

Then, after a whooshing feeling of vertigo, his brain sped up and he lifted above himself, above the alcove in which he sat, then above the entirety of the maze and backyard, sepia-toned and smoky. The lights of the party seemed to slow down, sputtering. He believed this meant he could think faster than light, if that were possible. But the brain took up space, so that meant the brain took up time. There was no way around that.

His stomach lurched and he was pulled back into his body as he vomited. He leaned to the side to avoid the rug. The vomit was red, like blood. Nothing like the beer he'd been drinking.

He had a discussion with gravity. An argument really, face to face, cheek to cheek. Then lifting, turning, backing up into his breath, hacking and withdrawing, pulling the unyielding air into his nose, dirt into his eyes, dust bunnies to the side of his face. Guests walking by, not caring, thinking he was drunk, if they saw him at all. He wasn't sure. He knew which side they'd be on, and it wasn't his.

The dirt arranged itself like an army battalion on his cheek, preparing for war, coordinating with dust that had survived the rain, the airborne. Gasping lungs, muddy mouth mush making a nasal naval attack, dried marine pollen allergies, sneezing face, the floor, the earth and all things otherwise siding with gravity.

It was a one-sided tug of war.

THIRTEEN

JEWELYA

J ewelya was in the Gryft on her way to Dirgatory. She didn't order cars often, and unlike taking a taxi, this was probably the driver's everyday car. It reminded her of the first time she made out in a backseat like this as a sophomore in high school, her boyfriend driving his mom's Volfo. Even though they hadn't had sex, it'd been close. She'd wanted to, and surely he did, too. But she was a good person, a good teenager. Pleasing authority figures was important, even if she didn't really know her boyfriend-at-the-time's parents well. But they would've respected the fact that she'd respected their car.

It wasn't a particularly long ride, but she'd taken too much time getting ready, followed by a thirty-minute wait for the car. Rideshares were definitely at a premium tonight. During that period, she'd lost track of time, zoning into the black of one of the new cobweb mirrors, deeper and colder than she'd think possible, until a particular line from the movie *Donnie Darko* playing on the television grabbed her attention. It was the part where Donnie asked a teacher about portals through spacetime, and could they appear anytime, anywhere? The movie, then, filled her remaining wait.

The Gryft driver turned onto the block for the party.

I'm here, where are you? she texted Ainsley.

His car was parked across the street from Dirgatory, and even though she didn't remember Ainsley's full plate number, she recognized the letters "LST." They could stand for last, lest, list, lost, or lust. Ainsley claimed it stood for all five words. He'd parked close to the house, so their departure should be easy.

The pavement was wet. It had apparently rained here without raining at their house, or even on the trip, thus far.

The driver stopped the car. "Is this good?" he said.

Jewelya leaned forward between the seats. "You ever think it can rain in one place and just that one place only?" Jewelya said.

"I don't know," he said. "I guess I never thought about it before."

"Like, look down the block, two houses away," Jewelya said. "It's not wet."

The driver drummed his thumbs on the steering wheel. "Yeah, I guess. But clouds move. And they have to end somewhere. The next one might go there." His phone, perched on a dashboard holder, made an alert sound.

"You've got other rides," Jewelya said. "Have a good night."

"It's actually a Mote." He tapped the screen. "Happy Halloween," he said without looking up. It was comforting to learn that he was a Consumerian, too. Somehow, she knew the

Mote would be about clouds or rain or weather. But she wasn't going to ask. Too personal.

She got out. There was a line of probably twenty people in the driveway, all waiting to enter. Since Ainsley had arrived long before the party started, he'd left their invitation with her. And since it was a plus one, she could have brought a friend. But with such short notice, she couldn't find someone who was free. Her most likely candidate, her coworker Denkins, was going to the Halloween festival in West Hollywood with his new boyfriend.

Why isn't this line moving? Perhaps security was waiting for people to leave before letting in more guests. One out, one in. Booming music and laughing. *Lots* of voices. Squeals of delight. Impossibly too many sounds for such a small area. And who would leave a raging Halloween party at ten thirty p.m.? She felt anticipation around her, and she wasn't even inside yet. She was ramping up. Her bones, her muscles wanted this. She found herself dancing a little to music that sounded so close, yet far away.

She'd arrived too late. It was obviously overcrowded. She should've left her hair alone and kept to the first shade of lipstick. Really though, she hadn't expected this level of insanity. She heard cheering and clapping and hollering like there was a show going on. Burlesque, maybe? She'd be dressed well for an event like that.

No one was leaving. This could take forever.

A biker-looking bouncer stood near the front entrance. From where she waited, she could just make out a sign posted on the lawn near the front door to the house that said "No Entry."

More people queued up behind her, four of them dressed as the main characters of the television show, *Schitt's Creek*. The eyebrows on the "dad" were huge, possibly fake mustaches that could fall off at any moment. The daughter character, Alexis, was similar to Jewelya (without the mask) and made a show of checking out Jewelya's dress, preparing to level shade.

"Hmmmf!" Alexis said, impersonating her character. "I love this dress!"

Okay, starting off well. "Thank you."

People were arriving faster than those entering, the line now turning up the sidewalk. Some guests already held beverages to bide the time. They were apparently prepared to wait.

She received another text from Ainsley. *In the maze. Took every right turn and found a place to sit. Sitting on a flying carpet. Come fly to me.*

Near the front door, she responded.

That infamous labyrinth. She imagined a simple hay bale puzzle like those at apple orchards with pony rides and homemade cider. But even a small maze could be a pain in the ass. She may not be able to find him. He should come to her, instead.

Can you meet me at the front entrance? she texted.

No response. Maybe he was drunk. He *was* drunk. *"Come fly to me?"* The bastard had probably been drinking for four hours. She really should have left the house sooner.

She imagined places to sit would be at a premium here, so maybe that's why he didn't want to move. She'd find him. Even if there were hundreds of people at Dirgatory, as legend had it, how many could fit in the maze?

The line moved as a group of three entered the party.

Six more people to go.

SHE ARRIVED AT A DETERIORATING, rickety ticket booth and

presented the invitation to a man who was dressed as a zombie, with his face peeling bloodless latex.

"Happy Halloween," he said flatly. Bored. Probably regretting his decision to work the gate while a party raged behind him.

"Sucks you have to work the front, huh?" Jewelya said.

"It's not that bad," he said, sounding like it was. Grumpy. He tapped the counter, a gesture that was likely a request for the invitation.

"Maybe you'll still have time," she said, taking the folded piece of paper out of her handbag, "to get into costume."

The zombie gatekeeper seemed to smile, or grimace or something. It was difficult to tell.

"Maybe every day's Halloween, huh?" she said, hoping to get a reaction.

He may have cleared his throat. It was hard to tell with the music so close. She couldn't wait to see what was behind the tarps. She placed down a folded twenty-dollar bill, and was escorted under the blue tarp by the bouncer. She felt debonair making her grand entrance in her exquisite, sequined dress. She was in costume without feeling too costume-y.

At first all she could see were flashing lights, backs of heads and shoulders, and costumes. Nobody seemed to notice her, which was fine, but unexpected. The closest person to her was a guy dressed as the Crow, smoking a vape near the white tarp side of the ticket booth, demarcated with the word "Exit."

"Do you know where the maze is?" she asked him.

"That way," he said, pointing into the seemingly immobile expanse of people. "Past the bar."

There were no defined sections, but the loud music and dancing told her what area this was. People were cheering at something she couldn't quite see happening on risers with stripper poles. Unlike a real nightclub, there were no actual spotlights. Perhaps the girl had taken her top off or something. There was no room to really dance anyway—people were too pressed together.

As she moved diagonally through the crowd, Jewelya's silver slit-thigh dress and black, imitation-feathered shawl kept catching on costumes. The dress was going to tear tonight.

This was brutal. The trip was taking forever.

It was hard to believe there could be an area anywhere where two people could sit. She imagined herself and Ainsley in lotus facing each other in the near dark, focusing on breathing, and wanted to transport herself there immediately. But she was angry with him, and the longer this was taking, the more it built up. Actually, now that she thought about it, this dress wouldn't allow her to sit like that.

Patchouli and dry ice. Sweat and post-rain earth. Cotton candy hair product and face paint. Mothballed, musty, vintage clothes (one of her favorite smells) and White Orchid. Wafting weed, spilled beer, and beer breath. It was like somebody had been painting Dirgatory with scents, with a mixture of the working and upper classes. A dancer by trade, Jewelya felt she was exposed to both worlds.

MOTE:

When not in Rome, don't do as the Romans.

SHE DIDN'T PLAN on it. Jewelya had warned Ainsley not to drink too much. She figured even if he kept the number of drinks to countable on one hand, she'd have to drive them home afterward. He'd claimed attending Dirgatory was as much for her as for him. Perhaps it was, but she'd likely have to be the adult tonight. She was fine with the idea of Halloween. Costumes and candy. Decorations. It was fun.

But an overcrowded party wasn't fun. Nobody could take in her costume. She couldn't dance. She wanted a glass of champagne, and based on the red cups most people were holding, she doubted there was any to be had.

The brightest area was the bar, the cone of light a beacon for partiers. She occasionally felt cups, stomped and flattened on the ground, poking at her partially exposed feet. Wearing heels was a bad choice with a light layer of wet earth below her. How much was rain, and how much was beer? She'd almost prefer a heel puncturing a flat cup to become a wider, impromptu plastic sole. Plastic soul. The bar's bottleneck was profound.

She could sense other people losing control. Some were inordinately happy. Some were becoming anxious. Too many strangers' feelings washed over her. Bad things could happen.

The mouth of the maze finally came into view at the same time she recognized the song that began playing, The Color Braille, "Sick, Sick, Sex," the music video in which she and Denkins had performed. Hearing the song brought her back to a time before her injury. She wished Denkins was here so she could dance. If that were even possible.

A dazed Wonder Woman made eye contact with her. Who knew what drugs she was on, but her eyes were magnificent, highlighted by dark hair and a tiara. Instantly, Jewelya was simultaneously jealous of her and wanted to be her friend. She wanted that magic to rub off on her. They were at a standstill for a moment, the flow in either direction momentarily frozen.

"He-e-ey," Wonder Woman said. She drew the greeting out into three slow syllables of inebriation. Her smile was warm, but pained. A kindred spirit. "I love your dress," she said.

Has she even broken eye contact to see it? "Thank you,"

Jewelya said. "Your costume, too, and your..." She wanted to say eyes, but didn't. "I loved that movie."

Then Jewelya was pushed by the current, and as she and Wonder Woman passed, they turned to watch each other. Locked in a mutual...something.

"Have a good night!" Jewelya said. She was thankful for her gift, for being able to connect like this with a random stranger, sober or not. Denkins would say this woman was "bricked," but Jewelya didn't believe it. There was something there. Maybe Wonder Woman was lonely, searching for something she recognized in Jewelya. Hopefully they'd see each other again, after Jewelya found Ainsley.

The maze's entrance was blocked by a panicked woman dressed as an anime character, gesticulating to the witch next to her. "I don't know where he went!" she said. "When I came out of the bathroom he was gone!"

"Pardon me," Jewelya said, the women disregarding her as she slipped between them.

"Well, he didn't come this way!" the witch said, for the moment yelling more into Jewelya's ear than her friend's.

Jewelya felt her eardrum spasm from the volume. Who would've thought she'd need earplugs just from the volume of voices?

"He can't go far!" the anime girl said. "Look at this place!"

Misplaced people were going to be a problem at a party like this. And once Jewelya had Ainsley in her sight, she planned to keep him there, even if that meant using the restroom together.

And even if it was only one song, she was going to dance before they left.

CHAPTER
FOURTEEN

AINSLEY

Ainsley's first thought probably took a nanosecond. There was no longer a blood-brain barrier or beer fog to slow it down. No chemical-reaction delay. This truly felt like frictionless, speed-of-light thought.

What the fuck?

Soundwaves crashed all around him, organic sirens struck his eardrums. Rhythmic pulses and vocalizations from fleshy throats washed over him. He was still at Dirgatory, but things were dark. Heat from a nearby electrical field, red, but not illu-minating. Mild radioactivity. He was within it.

Stay calm. Breathe.

He tried to meditate in the seemingly airless darkness.

But he had no body, no breath on which to focus.

He had senses he'd never experienced before. He could "see"

waves of electromagnetism, frequencies of light. Gravitational waves. Many more for which he had no names. If he trained his focus tight enough, he could zoom down and down, traveling nearly infinitely small and see tiny particulates, but they weren't objects, but rather fields of strong and weak nuclear forces.

If he focused wide enough, he could expand beyond the earth and solar system and see them as a simile to an atom. Then even larger, the galaxy appeared as a cluster of molecules. The universe itself was an as-yet-unknown, undiscovered, and unnamed substance. He could do this fairly quickly. Or it seemed that way, at least. He felt his knowledge was greater at larger levels, nearly infinite.

He intuitively knew that eternity couldn't truly exist without a mind that could grapple with it, and that any human concept of the infinite was woefully inadequate.

In a way, consciousness was another dimension, a big bang that, once released, expanded as fast as a universe. Tiny human brains grasped at consciousness in a recursive hell by attempting to define it. But if something truly had no edges, it could not be corralled, even by its own definition. This was the definition of indefinable. And this wasn't a word trick; he understood this deeply.

People often conflated the desire to live forever with immortality, fearing death and the unknown. Ainsley now understood it to be just "not-dying." There was nothing to look forward to as simply as there was nothing to escape, either. His only desire was to solve problems as they presented themselves.

Life was the universe's method for understanding itself. It had been his career to create systems that could make sense of what was presented to them. Questions and data in, and theories and answers out. Repeat. He was a filter, a processor of information. Spirituality, religion, and science were examples of countless filters.

Humanity often mistook the concept of God as a being that judged your filter—inputs and outputs—your consciousness. All belief systems were a filter, albeit ones that virtually never aligned with the overall nature of the universe. The collection of billions of untethered earthly minds was a higher-level filter, what some humans could call God. In this sense, human minds were neurons in the immortal collective mind of the earth, yet neurons had a lifespan. In order to replace them, death was a necessary part of immortality. And this collective was growing, improving, learning, strengthening.

He was one of these neurons, freed of his body.

Maybe he'd truly been drugged at Dirgatory. He was all mind, no body. He was alive. Aware. But consciousness only.

Knowledge was meant to be shared. He needed to communicate this information to someone.

Jewelya.

He focused himself at a medium distance, the one where he felt tethered to earth's timeline, to a physical manifestation. Dirgatory. This readjustment wasn't easy at first. It took practice to not overcompensate for error. Eventually, he found walls, metal, and plastic. Smooth.

And he projected himself just beyond that. As a person, he'd been sitting on a rug in the semi-dark and expected to see his body there, passed out. But he'd disappeared. People were still passing through the corridor. Only his phone remained. And no one had noticed it.

Ainsley zoomed down a touch smaller, and things became dark and warm and smooth again. This was the center of his focus, his center of existence, his current point. Whatever existence meant. He was inside his phone. He just didn't know what *he* was.

Even without physical eyes, he possessed an enhanced vision, which included expansion into the lower infrared and higher electromagnetic frequencies. Without ears, he could hear the sounds of the party. He had no skin, but could feel temperature. No physical pleasure, pain, or discomfort. It was all mental. He couldn't push against the walls of the phone. But he could go "through" them as he adjusted focus and size. He had no effect on the physical world.

Zooming out slightly, back to human level, he saw a couple characters from *Guardians of the Galaxy* passing through the corridor past the phone.

"Excuse me," he said. No sound, of course; he had no vocal cords. And since he couldn't move his center, his point in the universe, he couldn't travel laterally. He could only expand and contract. So at human level, he was tethered to a phone in the maze.

He expanded to the size of the backyard and saw hundreds of people from overhead, but couldn't zoom in on any specific person. He could travel "through" walls as he expanded, but couldn't see through them.

Yksian and Dirge were easy to find, standing near the shed's door. They were sentries guarding the palace. He yelled for them, to no avail. What good was seeing people who couldn't see you in return, or even hear you?

Maybe he really had died on that carpet.

He feared losing his memories, or whatever a galaxy of cells called Ainsley had learned in thirty-three years. Where was Jewelya? She may be unsafe, too. He couldn't find her at the level of the entire backyard; faces too small, turned away, too dark. Most were obscured. Costumes and hats, backs and tops of heads. The light varied, too, blinking and strobing, red and blacklight. Too many shadows, nooks and crannies, and covered passageways.

He saw half a dozen women wearing masquerade masks, but they weren't her. And he didn't know which dress she'd chosen.

He reduced to the size of a couple passageways in the maze. There were at least a dozen people partying within this range.

Still no Jewelya.

The section the phone was in was surprisingly close to the bar. Maybe fifteen feet, but separated by a river of people four or five wide, plus two walls of maze which were one or two people wide. It was mostly solid flesh between him and the bar. The bar's light shined on the faces of people in line. Eager. Expectant. He recognized no one.

If all he could do was view the party, this was a good middle distance.

If Jewelya got in the beer line, he would know. At least she'd be safe.

He saw his coworker Brandon, the one he'd given the invitation to today at work, dressed in a Star Trek uniform. He was standing in line for the spank tent with a woman in a matching costume. It was Jennifer, another coworker, and they were laughing as they waited. He couldn't see inside the tent. They were standing curiously close to one another. It was obvious now they were dating. He had the distinct feeling that if he'd found out merely a few moments ago, it would have affected him differently. More shock, perhaps.

He saw Chikao bisecting the line, not to get a beer, but merely overcoming an obstacle in his way. He seemed particularly adept at wedging between people without causing a ruckus. Making a triangle with his hands, praying, diving horizontally through the mass of costumed, sparkly, creatively dead latex-scarred flesh.

Except for Chikao and Ainsley, nobody at this party could move quickly.

CHAPTER
FIFTEEN

KICK

I *'m here*
In the house
In line for the bathroom

Kick was reading the rapid-fire texts from his roommate Gremmie.

Stay there. On my way, Kick replied.

Kick had introduced Gremmie to Yksian a couple times at CSE. He didn't think Gremmie knew Dirge or Summer, and if he had, it certainly wouldn't have been well enough to garner permission to enter the house, but if he saw Yksian first, who knew? At least the location was easy to find.

MOTE:
The whiter the clouds, the blacker the night.

. . .

IT HAD STOPPED RAINING, but the sky was still dark. The party was high tide with people. Kick found a current in the sea and drifted slowly toward the house until he was blocked by a fairy kissing another fairy. One had waifish pink wings and the other's were delicately purple. He found this touching, the way each girl dragged their fingertips along the other's cheeks and jawline while their lips barely touched. Like glittery butterflies. Part of him wondered if he was just being a dumb carnal male for appreciating this, or if he was recognizing sensuality to which he wasn't accustomed. His lumberjack costume certainly represented brute force, man over nature. As he managed to move around the couple, he wanted to shave off his beard.

Summer, looking far less stressed out than she had earlier, stood by the door speaking with the murdered red-wig beauty queen from the ticket booth. Dead Beauty Queen was taller than she'd seemed in the booth, six feet, and her blue sequined dress caught the strobes from the dance area, which high-lighted where sequins were either jagged or had fallen off. It was an old dress, worn and loved, possibly now attending its final ball. He sensed pieces of souls within it: its designer, seamstress (this feels sexist?), and previous owner(s) were celebrating with them tonight. Still, even mock glamour was a reminder that Kick was Hollyweirding in North Hollywood.

"Gremmie's here, right?" Kick asked Summer, not sure if she'd know who he was talking about. "My roommate?"

Summer gestured toward the bathroom.

Kick pretended that he was going to ruffle Summer's Wednesday Adams hair, and she swiped his hand away like a cat. She had a great smile. Matched Dirge's.

Chikao was next in line for the bathroom and a girl dressed

as Little Bo Peep was queued up behind him. Gremmie must have been inside.

Chikao lifted his walking stick horizontally and separated it into two halves, twisting and unlocking it like a pool cue. He balanced the halves softly in upturned hands. If he was divining for water, of course, he'd find some in the bathroom. Maybe he was practicing, fine-tuning.

After another moment, Little Bo Peep spoke up. "Are you sure anyone's in there?" She leaned past Chikao to knock firmly on the door.

"Oh, I just assumed," Chikao said, his hands shaking like a pauper. He opened the door slowly, a couple inches, peeking in, then all the way.

"Nothing," he said, thanking Little Bo Peep with a bow and going inside.

"No one thinks to knock," she said, addressing Kick.

And Chikao, in character as the Dalai Lama, didn't seem the type to interrupt a private moment like using the restroom. Kick wondered if he would have when dressed normally. Perhaps Chikao's everyday self was a form of cosplay as well.

Since it was clear that Gremmie wasn't in the bathroom, Kick drifted into the kitchen. Kat was there, in front of a picked-over bowl of Spookies and Scream candies, looking out the window facing the backyard. There was little to see, as the spank tent was near the edge of the house. But light from other areas, particularly the rotating dance strobe, hit the nylon. Blues and reds, purples and pinks. It was a dark carnival of Samhain.

"Hey Kick," Kat deadpanned. "Have you seen Lisa again, yet?"

"Sure, Wonder Woman?" Kick said. "But I haven't seen her jet."

Kat looked at him like he was speaking a foreign language.

"Because," Kick said, "it's invisible."

Kat gave Kick a look that made him immediately regret saying that.

He scratched his beard. "No, I still haven't seen her in a while."

"I should have told her to use the restroom in here," she said. "I can't believe I lost her."

"And I've seen those lines for the porta-potties. I hear girls are going in the men's room."

"It's gross, isn't it?" Kat said, pretending to look at a black paint fingernail with a tiny, white skull painted on it. Each nail had a unique figure on it: a cross, ghost, crescent moon, eyeball. He didn't remember the Lydia character having that detail in *Beetlejuice*. This was purely Kat.

"Super gross," he said.

Chikao took two steps into the kitchen, looked around, then turned around and left.

"What a creep," Kat said, quietly.

"He's all right." *Just a little weird.* Kick peeked around the corner into the living room. Summer had lit a row of Prism Wicks pillar candles bought from the Emporium. "Also, you still haven't seen Fred Flintstone yet, have you? He texted me he's in the house, but I don't see him."

"We sound like broken records. I'm going to keep looking. Lisa wasn't feeling well earlier. Maybe she's lying down."

"Maybe they're together."

Again, Kat burned his face with her expression. She did not find him funny today. Besides, she'd made that joke earlier. "I'll check the bedrooms," she said, then walked down the hallway.

Kick was startled by a tiny woman with thick glasses standing next to him. If he could see auras, hers would be green.

"Veris," she said, holding out her hand. "You're Kick, right?"

This sort of interaction happened occasionally: Strangers recognizing him from Consumia's Spiritual Emporium. People like Connie, Yksian, Ornatu, Organica, and Lucador were recognized far more often than he was, but it did happen.

"Yeah." Suddenly it hit him who she was. "Oh, you're tomorrow's Omniscian, Adelie. Right, Adelie Veris."

"Yes. You can call me Veris. Everyone else does," she said. "Pardon me if this seems intrusive, but I would love to read your soul, if you will."

That was a first. "Of course."

Veris touched Kick's elbow, edging him into the living room. Even though the rules were that general guests weren't allowed inside, the front door was kept locked, and people like Summer were guarding the back door, the house still harbored a lot of people. But compared to outside, it was relatively quiet. Candles. Incense. A set of Bluetooth speakers played esoteric, downbeat tracks, although the bass from outside still permeated everything. He didn't recognize the indoor music; it could be the work of Yksian.

Veris wasn't literally green, obviously, but she presented as such, especially by the unique candlelight. Prism Wicks candles were sold as a boxed set of nine—the seven colors of the rainbow, plus white and black. Each flame burned the color of the wax. The most unique was black, the flame appearing as an unreflective fluid wrapping around the wick. He suspected the candlewax was mixed with Black Vertigo, which some Consumerians insisted was imbued with powerful magic. Whatever it was, he could swear he saw her aura.

Veris was like a cloud of tree pollen transported by the wind and arranged into human form. She truly was Organica's spiritual sister. And he felt better just being in her presence.

She was a healer, already soothing his anxiety. She looked above his head and to the sides, craning, touching him softly with her eyes.

"I love your colors," she said. "You are inviting, but quiet. You are careful to do good work, but not a perfectionist. You want something more, but also..." Veris blinked slowly, welcoming. Her eyelashes were like palm fronds from a time when plants and animals were oversized, and oxygen was plentiful. "Tell me who's missing."

Odd question, though. How did she know he was looking for anyone? Maybe she'd overheard him speaking with Kat.

"My roommate Gremmie—you can't miss him. He's dressed as Fred Flintstone," Kick said. "And my coworker, Kat —she's missing a Wonder Woman named Lisa."

"A *wonderful* woman," Veris said. "They haven't gone far. I bet they're all still at the party."

Kick thought about some of the stones they sold at the Emporium—ones he also wanted for Omnist II—and how they were carved into shapes of eggs and mushrooms. Veris was a mushroom—a green one—but he could never say that, even as a compliment. It could be taken wrong. Something about how fungi was neither plant nor animal. Something better.

"So you're saying they're all here partying or maybe having an orgy or something?" he said. Perhaps Veris would have a better sense for this joke than Kat.

"Ha." There was definitely a hint of recognition behind her glasses. When her eyes widened, they magnified. Widened twice as much. Three times. "There may be orgies, but that's not the issue." She presented this without judgment. "No, there are far more people missing."

"But they're still here, you say? Do you think they're in the maze? I was getting weird vibes in there. Maybe there's something there." Especially after encountering something at the Emporium last night, this idea seemed less far-fetched.

"I do have a theory," she said. "But I need to poke around some more."

"Quick question: You're from Portland, right?" Kick said. "How did you hear about this party?"

"Connie put me in touch with Yksian, who sent me an invitation." Veris seemed to be talking to a spot just above Kick's shoulder. "It's fascinating here, isn't it? The world of souls mingling with people. Or rather, all souls are mingling, just some still have bodies."

Kick glanced behind him, in case there was something to see. There wasn't, unless she'd been looking at a guy who was wearing a sheet like a ghost. Except now, he'd torn one of the eyeholes large enough so his head could fit through. The other eyehole was still there, revealing a white T-shirt over his left collarbone. "So is that what you're looking at?" Kick said. "Souls?"

"I read them. And when they leave this plane, they often leave information behind. Or they continue trying to communicate."

"So you're a medium."

"I don't like that word," she said. "Good communication requires being a good listener. Medium, to me, implies a middleperson, when really, we're *all* souls. All of us. Let's just say there are a lot of souls that have something to say. Our job is to listen."

"Do they know you?"

"I think they figure out who I am pretty fast."

"Are you the devil?" Kick said, joking. He'd never heard somebody laugh so hard, so fast. Like she'd been expecting the question, laughing before he'd finished it. Really, she was opposite of the devil.

Veris reached up and put an arm on his shoulder to steady herself. When she caught her breath, she continued. "What people commonly assume as a demon is just a soul or a collection of souls trapped by something. They need help."

Kick thought about the notion of a coffin being haunted. What a shitty place to spend eternity. "I've heard of a single spirit haunting or possessing something, but a *collection* of souls? Like in a house or a hotel?"

Veris pushed her glasses up her nose. "A soul has little power to affect our plane. But when they organize, they can multiply their power and move as one. Think of the collection as a Venn diagram of the souls' strengths, where new traits are added to the whole and overlapping ones are intensified."

She was still reading him. It wasn't unpleasant, but he wanted her to share. He remained silent, like he was getting a physical with his doctor.

"And everything we see is a collection of souls," Veris said. "Rocks, trees, insects, animals—they're all physical manifestations. Someone can learn a lot about a soul by viewing the traits of its physical body, but at the same time, it isn't foolproof. We've gotten this wrong for thousands of years, treating the deaf and blind poorly, as if they were less than human. But when read correctly, clichés such as 'eyes are gateways to the soul' take on literal meanings."

They were indeed spiritual sisters, Veris and Organica. Kick wished the latter were here so he could be a fly on the wall to their conversation, but Organica was speaking at a bigger event, Halloween in West Hollywood. She'd be on a stage speaking to hundreds, perhaps at this very moment.

"So what can a collection of souls do here?"

"In the past, a few could mobilize a dead body, or maybe a scarecrow. But thousands together could cause an earthquake or a tornado."

"Or a spot of un-forecasted rain?"

That comment seemed to catch Veris. "Yes," she said. "The rain we just experienced wasn't in the forecast, so to speak. I think the souls were reacting to something."

She was looking past him again. "Pardon me," she said, slipping nearly under his elbow to approach a shelf, where she picked up a miniature Victorian felt hat, the kind one would pin jauntily to an abundance of hair. She lifted it to her face and sniffed. "Souls are calling for me."

"No problem," Kick said. "Nice to meet you."

Veris had said Gremmie was here, so Kick made his way back outside.

CHAPTER
SIXTEEN

AINSLEY

Ainsley could have spent eternity as an unfettered soul, zooming large and small. But for the equivalent of one nanosecond, less than that, nothing relatively, he would be with Jewelya. He needed to be near her. He imagined the pain she would feel when she learned about his disappearance, and he felt it would be worse than anything he could experience now. He wished for a Mote to advise him, something he could read on the phone's screen. What would it say?

IMAGINED MOTE:
Good luck. Or something.

. . .

Or something. Even his imagination couldn't think like a Mote.

It's not that he fully saw Jewelya differently now. She was fairly straightforward in her everyday life, but this new perspective made him realize how much she added to his. He typically used to be in his shell too much, and she'd pull him out. She was a connector who believed in connecting people. She was a Mote incarnate. She didn't believe everything was magical—she wasn't gullible, per se—but she had more to say about faith than Ainsley did. As long as the magic affected her, especially positively, it became a stitch in her fabric of belief.

And now it was Ainsley who was haunting a phone. Ironic.

Five years ago was his first overnight date with Jewelya. The Biltmore Hotel. Ainsley had been there a couple years prior to that for an afterhours party in one of the ballrooms: DJs and kids on ecstasy, back when he mimed doing those things. To be fair, he *had* done those things, but only a few times. It hadn't been his lifestyle, but he wanted to give the impression it was. And who would he have impressed? Himself. *He* wanted to believe it.

They took a small amount of psilocybin before visiting the Last Bookstore, and he felt even more relaxed and appreciative when they arrived at the Biltmore. The lobby and halls were gorgeous. Enlarged photographs of old Hollywood celebrities, of movies and television shows that had been shot there. Vintage furniture. Stunning architecture and design. History. He thought about how Los Angeles was a modern city compared to London, Paris, Tokyo, Rome, but at that moment he was awed by the era in which they were currently submerged.

"Are you feeling anything?" Ainsley said to Jewelya. He was lighter on his feet.

"I think so," she said, looking at her phone. She was the one who'd suggested walking around the Biltmore, yet he was the one taking in the sights.

They found a long, desolate hallway far away from mingling people. Jewelya tried a door handle, grabbed Ainsley's hand, and pulled him into a random room, into the dark.

"Keep it open!" she whispered just as the door was closing behind him.

Ainsley placed his foot in the crack of the door, allowing just enough light for Jewelya to look for a switch. She patted the walls on each side of the door, and finding nothing, gave up and pulled him all the way inside. The door closed them into complete darkness. She pressed herself against him, kissing his lips briefly. Then her phone lit up and said something.

"Did your phone just say, 'Chicken'?" Ainsley said. The voice was breathy and mysterious like an overacted clairvoyant in a movie. *He* wasn't chicken.

"We need to head toward the kitchen, I think," Jewelya said.

"Why? What was that?"

"My phone. Don't move." Jewelya scanned the area with the light on her phone, revealing a conference room with tables and stacks of chairs pushed against a far wall. There wasn't anything else to see. Mostly empty. Ainsley had expected a dust fog that wasn't there.

"North, north, west," Jewelya's phone said.

"Seriously. What *is* that?" Ainsley said.

"I told you I wanted to find ghosts. It's the GhoXTreasure app. Come on," she said, heading back out the door. She led him down the hall, then made a quick, darting left through an employee door. It was a service hallway filled with the arhythmic, angular sounds of dishes clanging and people barking orders. "See? It knew where the kitchen was."

"The chicken?" Ainsley said. Somebody at work had talked about this ghost app. Its marketing was simple: GhoXTreasure, where you *axe* it questions and X marks the spot.

"There are cameras everywhere, so they're going to know we're here," Jewelya said. "But let's see how far we can go. Maybe we'll see a ghost first."

"Maybe we'll get busted by the ghost of a security guard?" They were living a *Scooby Doo* episode, avoiding employees, peeking around corners, looking for clues. They'd receive no Oscar for this. But she was a dancer, and her training had honed ninja-like movements for prowling silently. Jewelya was a lot more fun than he was.

Ainsley looked up at a security camera, then at a convex mirror near the ceiling which showed a tiny version of him, as well as Jewelya, adorable, staring at her phone as she lifted it above her head, turning, apparently attempting to get it to do something else.

"So how does the app work?" he said. "What kind of sensor does it have?"

"What do you mean? It pulls words from the ether, like a clairvoyant or a medium."

"Look, I've had my tarot read. I had a vision in the desert. I've seen and felt shit I can't explain..."

"So you know how it works." She shook her phone. Maybe that reset it.

"But it's an app on a machine. It needs a mechanism, a sensor, something to read the environment. Like finding directions needs GPS. Or your screen changes when you tilt it. It has an accelerometer, a gyroscope, and a magnetometer inside."

"I don't care how it works," she said. "Let's try down here."

It might be a random-word generator. But he couldn't say that. They started walking and stopped before the farthest door in the hallway.

"Do you think flat-earthers use GPS on their phones?" he said. "You know, since the G stands for *global*."

"You know your phone can smell, right?" Jewelya shook the phone differently now, like it was a bottle of ketchup, and tilted it in different directions.

Ainsley corrected himself; it was more like she was shaking a Magic 8 Ball. "Mine smells if I chop garlic on it," he said. "And if you ever do that, you'll only do it once."

"Seriously," she said. "And it feels energy."

"Now my phone repels vampires," Ainsley said. "The G in my GPS stands for *garlic*."

"Blonde," Jewelya's phone said.

"Finally," she said. "That took forever."

"But still, wouldn't you have to buy an attachment or something? That's what I mean by a sensor. Like if you want to test your blood sugar. Or check for carbon monoxide in the house. Your phone is the processor, but you still need a sensor. How exactly does GhoXTreasure work?"

"I told you. It senses psychic energy."

"But how?"

"Just come on!" She pulled him through the last door in the passage, which was a brightly lit storeroom. Dry goods. Cans and boxes of food. Someone must discover them soon.

Ainsley was surprised by how many doors in the hotel were unlocked. This was an L.A. landmark, after all. He tapped Jewelya on the shoulder. "Does it know what I'm thinking right now?"

Rather than answer, Jewelya grabbed him by the collar and kissed him, roughly. Another awkward near-miss. She bit his lower lip and inhaled. He tried to say something, but she exhaled all the breath she could into his mouth, inflating his cheeks and causing him to push away to catch his breath.

"Did you just kiss me to shut me up?" Ainsley said.

"Maybe. The app may not know what you're thinking, but I do."

At the far end of the storeroom was a propped-open door with a window at chest level. That was likely the main part of the kitchen. Jewelya looked around the corner, put a finger to Ainsley's lips, then peeked around the corner again. He didn't want them to go in there.

"We're clear," she said, taking a step, but stopped when her phone spoke again.

"Statue."

"Wait," Ainsley said. "A food statue?"

"The Oscars. They were here. So not *in* the kitchen, but near the kitchen."

"Sure. A hungry ghost."

"I bet it's a ghost of one of the actresses." Jewelya backed out of the kitchen and took them back the way they came. "They were so beautiful. I wish I'd been alive back then."

Perhaps she had been. These hallways, these rooms—they'd been graced with not only actors of the gilded age, but presidents and dignitaries, as well. "Maybe your phone can sense the psychic energy of your past lives."

"Don't tease. I'm just sure I was born fifty years too late. Seventy."

"You could have been an actress. You ooze pretties like an infection."

"Nice," Jewelya said. "You make it tickle in my feelings hole."

There seemed to be no limit to the disgusting humor they could share. "What's your phone say now?" he said.

She shook it, then tapped it. "Searching," it said.

A security guard walked briskly into the service hallway. Khakis, white shirt, and a radio attached to his belt. A standard dad bod, but he was in decent shape for his age. "Pardon me, guys. Are you guests of the hotel?"

"Yes!" Jewelya said without hesitation. "We can't find our key. I was thinking I dropped it over here."

"You know this area is restricted. For employees only, right?"

"I think I left it on my plate, and thought...." Jewelya was struggling to hold the joke together.

"A food plate?" the guard said.

"Chicken," Ainsley said.

"You still can't be back here," the guard said.

"Can we go 'north, north, west'?" Ainsley said.

"Come on, let's go, guys." The guard raised his arms, corralling them toward the hallway. "What's the name on your reservation?"

"It's okay," Jewelya said. "We'll go to the front desk."

"You mean the one we already passed?" Ainsley said, making Jewelya laugh.

She grabbed his hand and pulled him back into the main hallway. "Sorry!" she called back to the guard, who was walking casually behind them. "But I do like your forceful tone! I really do!"

Once out of the hallway, Jewelya spun around and pressed her back against the wall just outside the door, pretending to hide from the guard. She took a deep breath, as if they'd been running. "I think he likes us," she said.

"What are you talking about?" Ainsley said.

The guard walked out of the service entrance and shook his head, unamused. "You guys have to vacate the premises," he said.

Jewelya smiled and pulled at Ainsley for them to leave.

"Did you notice," she said, tilting her head toward the guard. "He's a blond!"

Ainsley couldn't tell if Jewelya needed a father figure, the kind of boyfriend who'd provide her a safe foundation from which to do crazy things, or if she wanted somebody as impulsive as she was, an instigator, a conspirator.

"Blond, blond, blond, blond, blond," she said as they crossed the lobby and went back out the doors to the streets of downtown Los Angeles. "Blond!"

Now, with their two jobs and a house, Ainsley hadn't nurtured an environment for Jewelya to be who she was when they'd first begun dating. Denkins was closer to her personality than Ainsley was. Ainsley loved her, but he'd been affecting her negatively. He wanted her to feel comfortable to be herself around him. And there was no way now for him to tell her this.

People were nearly stepping on the phone. Nobody seemed to have noticed it yet. He saw Jewelya in the maze, making her way toward him. All right turns. Still, there were a half-dozen people between her and the little cove.

"Over here, JJ!" Ainsley said. Unheard.

A couple entered the alcove. The woman, wearing a blonde wig and a blue, skin-tight body suit—as Samus from the game Metroid—nudged the phone with her foot. She picked it up, then sat on the rug. "Somebody dropped this," she said.

The male, dark-skinned and dressed as the vampire killer Blade, braced himself as he sat, then took a puff from his vape pen. "They'll figure it out," he said, exhaling as he settled into place. "Set it on the ledge."

The "ledge" was that folded license-plate shelf with two

red cups sitting on it, one empty and one with a little of Ainsley's beer left in it.

"It's locked," she said, tapping the phone's screen. "Maybe they're saving this spot."

"You really think that?" Blade said. Condescending.

The woman stacked the two cups together to make room, then set the phone on the shelf. It was her turn now to draw from the vape pen.

Jewelya arrived, taking in the scene. "Did y'all see a guy sitting here? Maybe drunk and pretending to meditate?"

"Like a Buddha?" Blade said, snorting and coughing simultaneously.

"About my height," Jewelya said. "Wasn't in costume. Unless you consider being basic a costume."

"How many arms?" Blade said. "I think I saw Shiva earlier."

"Funny guys," Jewelya said. "Shiva's a goddess."

"Pardon," another woman said, wedging through the passageway past Jewelya.

"Yeah, sorry," another man behind her said. Jewelya nearly stepped on Blade's leg while making room.

The seated woman, Samus—even though Jewelya was unlikely to know that—exhaled and pointed at the makeshift license-plate shelf. "We found a phone though. Were you guys trying save this spot?"

"Yes!" Ainsley said, unheard. "That's my phone! Take it, Jewels!"

Jewelya picked up the phone. "This looks right," she said. She typed in their wedding date, and the screen unlocked. "It's his. I take it you didn't see him, though?"

Both Blade and Samus shrugged.

"Found it here," the woman said, patting the ground next to the rug. "Maybe he dropped it. Good luck finding him."

The man pressed his hand to his face in another repressed giggle and snort. The woman slapped his leg to quiet him.

Jewelya turned away. When she continued down the passage, Ainsley went laterally with her. He truly was tethered to the phone. He wondered about that Biltmore date years ago, and if a soul could've been inadvertently captured in her phone by the GhoXTreasure app.

CHAPTER
SEVENTEEN

JEWELYA

So Ainsley had dropped his phone. How drunk was he? By his description, that spot was where he'd texted her. Had he left quickly or something? And how far could he really get when it was this crowded in here?

She found another place to stand that wasn't blocking people and read the most recent texts in his phone, looking for clues. She'd been the only person he'd texted with after a group text with Dirge and Yksian confirming his arrival earlier. He'd made a joke with them.

If I'm late, just know GPS doesn't work for me. I'm a flat-earther, he'd texted. Dirge had LOL'd. No response from Yksian. They wouldn't have known Ainsley told that joke often. He was trying to be a guys-guy. It was almost painful to read.

And that was the thing. Ainsley was not a dancer or the life of the party. To be fair, he'd tried harder to seem spontaneous

151

when they'd first met. He pretended to be more extroverted, the kind of guy that went to Las Vegas for electronic music festivals. But she didn't need him to be.

She loved her dancer friends. The girls really were often the life of the party; the guys *were* the party. Always. Like Denkins. Everything was a party to him. And they all liked the same guys, blushing when talking about them. Except for Jewelya. It seemed her extroverted girlfriends made Ainsley a little jealous.

But as she and Ainsley settled into each other, she found she liked him more when he wasn't trying so hard. They often thought alike, even though they expressed things differently. She needed someone who'd make disgusting jokes with her, let her be crazy when she was feeling manic, then calm her down when she was anxious. Then just be her friend. She'd learned she could love somebody's brain. She didn't need him to dance, just not close her off.

AFTER THEY'D LEFT the Biltmore five years ago on that date, they headed for the King Eddy bar. This was that dive that Ainsley had wanted to go to. They each took another micro-dose for the walk, so the four gel caps Ainsley had brought were now gone. They passed the Last Bookstore again, but the idea of reading anything had dissipated. Deciphering words and messages felt like too much work.

Almost immediately, the neighborhood took a turn for the worse, like they'd crossed some nonexistent railroad tracks. Hairier. People standing and sitting on the sidewalks. Broken glass, broken gaits.

Jewelya was definitely overdressed and attracting too

much attention. The white of her dress was too white, the spots too childish. She hooked her arm inside Ainsley's.

"Don't worry," he said. "This place is more punk rock than actually dangerous."

She didn't quite believe him, but he needed to know that even though she listened to copious amounts of dance music, she preferred an edge to it. "Punk like, I don't know, Joy Division?" she said.

"You like Joy Division?" Ainsley said. "If you're going that direction, I would've expected you to say New Order. It's dancier."

"I do actually like New Order better, but Joy Division's cooler and has better T-shirts. I can only take them in doses, though. A couple songs at a time. Music can be angry or frustrated, or sad and lonely, but I have to hear hope in their voice, like the music is rescuing them. In Joy Division, I hear a guy who's lost hope, and music can no longer save his life. And it didn't, obviously, because Ian killed himself. But I always felt New Order's what saved the remaining members of Joy Division.

"And I have that problem with Nirvana, too. I'm fine with *Nevermind*, but not *In Utero*. By then, Kurt had lost hope. I can hear it. And it kills me."

They were already at the King Eddy, and turned left into a nondescript door. It was definitely more Joy Division than New Order. Dirty and grimy, old and cold. It was a medium-sized crowd, too early for the inevitable, later rush. A mix of hipsters and broken Charles Bukowski-type locals, probably regulars. The bartender was scrolling his phone behind the bar, and the punk rock blasting over the speakers stopped abruptly mid-song to something more metal than she would've expected.

They found two seats at the bar. Part of her was scared to order a mixed drink. Who knew what would happen in a place like this? The beer selection was mostly domestic, but she wanted Ainsley to know she knew beer, too. They ordered beers and waters.

"I need water because hoppy beers make me thirsty," Jewelya said. "And barrel-aged chocolate imperial stouts make me even thirstier." Which they obviously didn't have.

"Whatever makes you *hoppy*," Ainsley said. He looked around the room. "It's a bit different than I imagined. What do you think the story is here?"

She *was* happy. She felt safe with him, despite the neighborhood.

*But if he wants a story...*she figured she'd give him one.

"I'll tell you," Jewelya said. Then she sipped some water, leaned in close, and spat a stream onto his face. He didn't over-react, but laughed as she pinned his arms and licked the moisture off his cheeks, chin, and finally lips, evolving into a sloppy, tongue-heavy kiss.

She hadn't considered it a test at the time, but in retrospect, she figured it was. At least he didn't say, "What's wrong with you?" He'd rolled with it. It definitely loosened him up as they devolved into a fit of giggles.

Jewelya opened up to him that night, in a way that was rare for her, telling him how she only seemed to love broken things. She didn't desire to fix or change them, but wanted to love them for exactly how they were. Who they were. She felt that no matter how much she attempted to achieve ideal form in dance, motion was temporary. Fluid. And any attempt to freeze a moving thing would break it, destroy it violently. Shatter it.

But she loved broken people, broken things that were once notable, had once aspired to be great. People with a dull sheen, a patina. Perhaps those people outside. She loved them, but did they know that?

Broken music. An imperfect voice singing over a perfect

beat. A perfect voice singing over noisy drums or sloppy guitars. Of course, these things needed to be kept in moderation; they couldn't be broken to the level of uselessness.

"You ever break anything on purpose?" Ainsley said.

"Define 'break.' Some things need to break to improve."

"I mean, I'm broke," Ainsley said. "Does that count?"

He'd told her earlier that he'd just started a new job at Warbler Studios, so he was probably being facetious. "Don't worry. Broke is temporary," she said. "Broken might be forever." She wasn't exactly wealthy either. She'd gone to private school, but was now living off her own wages.

She realized she was definitely high, maybe a middle C range of inebriation. Later on, while they were discussing poetry and literature, she said, "What's that word for, like, the common meter traditional English is written in? For, I don't know, Shakespeare and stuff?"

"Iambic pentameter?" Ainsley said.

She didn't realize what she was doing until it was too late. She mauled him, biting his cheeks, neck, and nose, this time not needing water as a pretense.

Later, Jewelya searched for another word while talking about a visit to Hawaii. "What's that term for a rock created from lava?"

"Igneous?"

Once again, she mauled him with glee. She was aroused by vocabulary. Before that night, she'd had no real idea she needed to be with someone like this.

In the Dirgatory maze, Jewelya didn't want to lose Ainsley's phone. She was carrying a clutch that barely fit one phone, so no matter what, she would have two items to carry: that and a phone. She was wearing a sheer dress with no pockets, no jacket. What had she been thinking?

She put Ainsley's phone in her purse and saw a notification on her own.

MOTE:
Memories are evidence of how you feel now, not back then.

SOMEHOW THE OMNIST seemed to know what she was thinking.

She twisted and turned through the passageways, her heels once again pissing her off. As expected, virtually no girls wore masks, preferring sexy costumes, revealing personas, inner selves, and childhood hopes, dreams, and nightmares. She was surrounded by constant greetings and squeals. That used to be her back in the day.

Jewelya had been told by her parents, perhaps jokingly, that she'd been conceived at a Halloween party. She'd always laughed at that. Silly parents. Looking around now, she wasn't so sure that hadn't happened. The nineties had been a hell of a decade, and this was a hell of a party.

And it was getting worse.

She encountered a couple having sex on a car seat. Open to the world passing by on what she imagined was cracked pleather gruesomely chafing bare skin. This was supposed to be a high school story about what girls did on Halloween, not something she'd literally witness as a married adult.

A drunk guy dressed as a zombie fell through a wall in front of her, plywood crashing.

"Opa-a-a!" someone said.

Netting clung to the man like cobwebs. He flailed, but somehow kept to his feet. His balancing mistake had created a hole in the maze near the farthest end of the dance area, and this new exit was immediately put to use.

As she walked out, the first person she recognized was Denkins.

"Jewels!" he said, trying to hold his arms out for a hug, but, in this crowd, they were nearly vertical. "You look glamorous!"

"Denky, what are you doing here?" she said as they hugged, imagining her dress ripping from the force. She looked down and saw no glaring issues. "I thought you were going to WeHo."

"With an eighty-dollar Gryft? One way? No thank you. I'm having banking issues as it is. A green planet must be in retrograde! And Michael had a Dirgatory invitation, so..."

"Michael? Who's Michael?" She could barely keep up with her own issues, much less who her friends dated or cheated with.

Denkins gestured at a Michael Jackson impersonator grinding against a stripper pole. It was his boyfriend, Kyle. He made a pretty good MJ impersonator.

"Oh, I see," she said, wanting very much to dance. This was the part of the party aimed at her. Not so much the gore or drugs, but just losing herself through her body. Letting go of all the stress of life, not worrying about money or Whelp reviews. "He's nailing it tonight."

"Pun intended!" Denkins sang.

"*Everything* with you is so sexual. Have you seen Ainsley, by the way?"

"Honey, you lost him already? Are you guys raging?" Denkins sounded more impressed than concerned. "No, I haven't, but good luck with that. Oh! Do you want a party favor? We have extra."

It was probably ecstasy. He was high. "Thanks, but no thanks."

Before she knew what was happening, Denkins was mashing their lips, teeth hitting roughly, but his tongue alighted inside her mouth like a butterfly. He pulled back. She was burning fire, ready to slap him.

"You know I love you, right?" he said, grinning sweetly, patting her arms. Hopping up and down.

If there was ever a nonsexual kiss with tongue, that was it. Usually with him, it was a peck on the lips or cheek. Then it dawned on her why he'd done that. "Denky!" she said. "Did you just drug me?"

"Oh, honey, no. I took mine over an hour ago. I just wanted to kiss my friend that I love soooo much." He was rolling, probably pretty hard. He'd be useless to talk to right now. But probably fun to dance with.

"Well, good to see you, too." She grabbed him by the shoulders, turned him to face his Michael Jackson boyfriend, winded an imaginary key between his shoulders, and pushed him away.

Denkins laughed and waved without looking back. Or maybe he was greeting somebody in front of him.

Whatever.

She could feel Denkins's energy pulling her with him into party oblivion. She did want to dance, the beat hitting her core. Even without his presence, Ainsley was ruining her night. She needed to find him before she could loosen up.

Jewelya found herself staring at three televisions hanging askew above an orange, vintage diner booth. The screens were playing loops of ominous images, like, closeups of knives, clouds passing in front of the moon, zits being popped, and clips of seventies sitcoms; the latter being surprisingly the creepiest in a setting like this.

The screens faced a pissing-leprechaun fountain with a sign that said, "Don't drink the vodka." There was no way that was alcohol. Then again, this party was surprising. She wasn't going to test it, even though she was positive that tonight, somebody would.

It took a couple minutes, but she made her way to the firepit, where she recognized Kat from Consumia's Spiritual Emporium. She was dressed as Lydia from *Beetlejuice*, one of her favorite movies. Jewelya went in for a hug, but Kat stiffened. Not her thing. Instead, Jewelya backed up and patted Kat on the shoulder. She still didn't reciprocate.

Despite her unsmiling standoffishness, Kat's eyes were warm, happy to see her. "You look amazing. That dress! And aren't you happy you bought the mask?"

"I am," Jewelya said, touching it reflexively. "You know my husband, Ainsley, right? Have you seen him?"

"Yeah, a little while ago. He didn't say anything to me though."

"Well, I can't find him anywhere." Jewelya looked around as a gesture of punctuation.

"Do you think he's partying too much or something?" Coming from anybody else, that would sound underhanded, a dig. But with Kat, it was just a question. She was aware of Jewelya's stress.

"Maybe," Jewelya said. "I thought he was past this, but I think he keeps some bad habits around on purpose. That way somebody can save him. And if he always needs saving, he'll always feel loved."

That was a lot. Kat could be a psychologist. Maybe Ainsley wanted to be the broken singer to Jewelya's danceable music, or a broken social scene to her gregariousness. Maybe he thought he'd settled in as the broken man she'd have to love. But really, he was being a child.

"Honestly, no one can find anyone," Kat said. "I can't find my friend Lisa either."

"They better not be together," Jewelya said.

Kat didn't respond to the joke. "Ask Dirge, Yksian, or Summer," she said. "You know them, right? Between the three of them, they seem to know everyone here."

But if they can't find Lisa, either... Finding Dirge and Yksian should be easy. They were beacons of shiny darkness against a skyline of costumes, or a forest of imaginary characters. Or some other mixed metaphor.

Jewelya stepped onto one of the stones surrounding the firepit. More height worked in theory, unless there were makeshift walls and partial tents in her way. She did see Dirge and Yksian, the Twin Towers of Doom, entering the door of the shed. It wasn't that far away, but still twelve- to fifteen-people deep between them. Dirge held the curtain for Yksian, but with their boots and hats, they still ducked under the doorframe.

"I see them," Jewelya said.

She hopped down to make her way, waving goodbye to Kat, who barely lifted a hand in response. Jewelya passed a tent with a sign demarcating it as the "Spank Tent." She heard smacking noises and screams of pain. Or was that pleasure? Or a recording? There was a line of a half-dozen people: two couples, and two possibly solo.

An alien autopsy was set up along the backside of the shed. She imagined that Ainsley was on his back on the table, instead, in the olive-green wool uniform, with his guts exposed for the medical world to see. It was an impressively gruesome display that inspired a bout of laughter from a couple guys inspecting it. She didn't get the joke.

When she arrived at the side door, she found the Twin Towers had locked it. She knocked, wondering if anyone could even hear her.

A little person opened the door. He wore a T-shirt that read "Actual Size," and a hat with "As Seen On TV."

"What now?" he said. The man was intense. Stressed, maybe.

"I'm sorry?" Jewelya said, "I'm looking for Dirge or Summer."

"And how do you know them?" He was an angry guard protecting his castle.

"From the Emporium," she said. "I think Yksian is here, too, right?" She didn't know him well, either, but whatever got her through the door.

"Well, douchebags keep knocking, thinking this is part of the party. It isn't."

"Alvan, please escort the lady in!" Yksian said from out of sight. He'd raised his voice to cut through the music and vocal surf behind her.

The man opened the door just wide enough for her to squeeze through. A solo, pretty girl would receive the benefit of the doubt more often than a pack of dudes in this situation. When Alvan turned around, the back of his shirt read, "Serving Suggestion." Whatever his costume was, at least he had a sense of humor.

Jewelya was greeted by the fragrance of pepper and ancient spice trade wisdom. These peppercorns had been dried and aged for months, dipped in oils of leather and teakwood, and combined with stale dust and morning dew—somehow it was nearly morning in this shed. It was a scent that populated street markets and the hidden rooms behind them where deals were secretly brokered. After feeling hundreds of mouths breathing beer on her outside, the shed's stale musk was a welcome change. She wanted to roll around in it like a feline in catnip.

The Twin Towers of Darkness stood facing each other with goblets of wine in their hands. Yksian and Dirge were both looking at her.

"Hey guys," she said. "Great party." *Stupid introduction.*

"Thank you," Dirge said, smiling widely. The friendlier one.

"Kippis. Glad you enjoy it," Yksian said, slowly, deep and resonating. But not smiling.

"Have either of you seen Ainsley?" Jewelya said.

"He's here," Dirge said. "But I haven't seen him in a couple hours. You?" He looked at Yksian.

"Not since he completed his task with the computers. He said he would get a beer and wanted to explore. There's much to see."

"It's the theme of the night," Dirge said. "No one can find anyone."

"I'm realizing that," Jewelya said.

"There are probably dozens of misplaced people," Dirge said. "Happens every year. I'm sure he's around here."

"That goblet looks heavy," Jewelya said to Yksian. His brass, snakehead chalice was closer in size to a fish bowl than a goblet, with the capacity of nearly a bottle of wine.

"I find it lightens as I go," Yksian said. Dirge moved, causing light from outside the bar opening to shine on Yksian's face. He turned to Dirge. "Pardon me, Master Dirge, you are standing in my shade."

That made no sense.

"Where are my manners?" Dirge said, impersonating him. He stepped to the side, once again enveloping Yksian in a gray hue.

"The purpose of manners is for the masses to feel they've achieved a higher level of society," Yksian said. "Etiquette, on the other hand, is what separates one from the masses."

Dirge bowed and winked an eye that was highlighted in a starburst of eyeliner. He was the main character from *A Clockwork Orange*. "Correction, where is my etiquette?"

Yksian seemed pleased at this, despite no obvious change in expression.

Jewelya wanted to stay and have a drink with the adults at the party, but finding a drunk husband who'd lost his phone was the more pressing issue.

"Thank you, gentlemen," Jewelya said, preparing to reenter the party.

As she exited, she could swear Yksian said, "I would wager he's in the maze, not alone."

She imagined a conversation with a client tomorrow:

"Hey Jewelya, did you have fun at—what's it called —Migratory?"

"Yeah, it was great. Spent the entire evening looking for Ainsley and when I finally found him, he was fucking some girl in the maze, so I left. But at least I have the bastard's phone!"

She then imagined finding him lying within a pile of red plastic cups, one of them his own. Drunk and passed out. That was more likely. Ainsley's phone buzzed in her purse. She pulled it out.

MOTE:

Standing still for the world to arrive can be more effective than chasing.

CHASING THE WORLD. Was that what Ainsley did? This Mote was for him. Was the Omnist telling him to stay in place so Jewelya could find him? Or did the Omnist know she was the one with his phone, and the message was for *her* to sit still? She didn't know. Besides, she had indeed messed with his Omnist yesterday, so this could be nonsense.

She put his phone back in the handbag. If the Omnist had a

message for her, it should tell her on her own phone. A message arrived that instant.

MOTE:

The art of asking questions leads to the selling of answers.

FINE, *then,* she thought. She typed a question into the Omnist. *Where can I find Ainsley?*

MOTE:

He is right here, near your heart.

SHE WANTED to throw her phone at the wall.

CHAPTER
EIGHTEEN

AINSLEY

At the level of being just larger than his phone, all was dark. He was in her purse.

Ainsley shrank to the size of the device's integral parts and traced his attention along the circuit boards, learning how the phone worked. His nerdy self was nerding out. The battery emitted infrared, which was interesting to view as a new sense. But as he reduced to a more microscopic level, heat was felt as increased molecular movement, a new sensation. Less warm, but almost massage-y. Atoms vibrated in lockstep, sharing and passing along electrons. But these fields weren't what he expected to see; the closest English word for it was *life*. He could build life from scratch. He felt like he was the inventor of existence.

But he still couldn't move laterally. At each level he could make himself a little larger than the object of his attention and thus view it from a slight distance. It was a top-down sensation, but he was trapped in this particular continuum.

Time shifted a lot, more like a fluid, changing at each level, some stormier, others with waves, wrinkles, folds. He felt the radio waves of GPS routinely pinging the phone's location. At a particular level, he felt these pulses as prickly pulses of information. Data. He decided he could keep track of time this way.

But time made less sense the farther he ventured from the human level. And he seemed not to recall as much of his current life at further distances. It wasn't that he forgot it; he just wasn't thinking about it. Then he'd get a sensation he was missing something—he didn't know what—but when he returned to Ainsley's life's plane, he knew what it was: He missed Jewelya.

Certain traits of the living were no longer important, either. No need for food or restrooms. He didn't yet know if he needed sleep or an energy source. But his collection of memories seemed intact, if not scarily precise, as well as his consciousness. His ability to learn and reason. What would have been a mental cul-de-sac while alive had straightened out in the afterlife, if that's what this was.

Each level felt like déjà vu. Not specific memories or previous lives, but knowledge of how chemicals and processes worked. He had never been trapped inside a phone before, but the transition itself, corporeal to incorporeal, wasn't novel.

If he "inhaled," his perspective enlarged. When he "exhaled," he minimized. But he didn't actually breathe. That was the closest metaphor for the sensation. And a mantra that Jewelya had repeated often, about allowing your breath to merge you with the universe, that had roots here.

Jewelya.

The point of life as Ainsley was to share it with Jewelya. She was truly alone now, even if she wasn't aware of it yet. He needed to warn her somehow. Tell her he could see and hear her, and that she may be in danger.

He enlarged to check in on Jewelya.

CHAPTER
NINETEEN

JEWELYA

No, Ainsley wasn't here. He was nowhere. Was he even trying to find her? Jewelya felt alone, angry, stood up at a party that had been *his* idea. He was the quiet one who pretended he partied. She was the social one who'd been pretending she wasn't. And the charade was continuing.

She thought about the recent Mote: *Standing still for the world to arrive can be more effective than chasing.* That could be literal, to stay still, but where?

Then she thought about something Ainsley said too often, different versions of "I've got nothing to say because I've got nothing to think." He'd been facetious in those instances, but there was truth to the idea.

And if someone wasn't thinking, instead of standing pat,

mentally, she could allow herself to drift with the current. Go with the flow.

MOTE:

If you steal attention, you steal life.

AND SHE DIDN'T STEAL attention. She could dance, be friendly and loquacious. That drew attention. But at a Halloween party, most people wanted to direct others' attention to their costumed persona, rather than their work-a-day selves. Even though she appreciated those who noticed her dress, her elegance, it wasn't thievery, unlike the act committed by the girls in those plastic "hot nurse" costumes—and there were several here.

She asked the Omnist again: *Where is Ainsley?*

The response was almost instantaneous:

If you don't know where you are, it matters not the location of anyone else.

NOT HELPING. She didn't need riddles and tripe. And shit was getting weirder at Dirgatory. Attention was like water and she'd been coated in wax, so when people spotted her, their focus rolled right off, finding a lower point—the person next to her, behind her—combining and multiplying, barreling down-hill and gaining speed until she realized where Death Valley was here: the dance area.

Then Jewelya found herself descending, so to speak, drawn to the middle of the dance area as if someone had pulled a plug in the ground and all that liquid attention was being sucked down. It made no sense. How could people be gravitating to the same spot if the party was already overcrowded? It was a funnel vortex of space and compressing attention, all flowing to its center.

"Eee-ooowww!!!"

Feral noises, like those from a tortured animal, screamed through her mind.

"Aaauuuggghhh!!!"

Was there an animal sacrifice? Was she going to witness something she didn't want to see? She was drawn to a centralized place, and even though people were clustered shoulder to shoulder, for some reason when she tapped someone, impossibly, a lane would part for her. As if she were part of a show.

Then actual words. Someone was screaming.

"Go-o-o-o!!!"

Jewelya was now only two or three people back from a young woman who had dropped to her knees. Peering around shoulders and waists, behind elbows, Jewelya witnessed the show with a partially obstructed view.

"Awwwaaayyy!!!"

A girl with dark hair and a golden tiara had dropped to her knees screaming, writhing, undulating in misery, and gawkers ringed around her, holding their arms out against each other, trying to give her space. It was Wonder Woman. Another woman crouched next to her and placed a hand on Wonder Woman's bare shoulder.

Jewelya was drawn inside this pained woman's head, and if she'd ever been unsure that she was an empath, she knew now. There was no doubt. Jewelya couldn't breathe, and her heart was electrically charged, zapping, like a raw wire was tightening around it.

She slid her half mask to the top of her head to see better. She felt naked where her face had been covered. A glisten of moisture had accumulated on her cheekbone and was cooling in the slightest of breezes.

"Nooo!!! Not meee!!!" Wonder Woman screamed, pushing the other woman away. "Quit looking at me!" Wonder Woman searched the closest guests with a crazed look in her eyes. "I'm in control!!! *I'm* in control!!!"

She pushed her palms against her eyeballs, pleading to some god. "No more liiight!!! No more aura!!!" She made fists and began punching at her eyes. "Aaauuuggghhh!"

If this was part of a show, the girl was a great actor, and should have been crouching on one of the coffin risers to allow more people to see. But Jewelya knew it wasn't. Perhaps there were drugs involved, but what Wonder Woman was feeling was real. There was no doubt in the girl's mind, so no doubt in Jewelya's either. Jewelya wanted to console her, but couldn't get closer. There was pushback.

"Back off!" a guy said, futilely waving his hands. "Everybody back off! Give space for the performance."

Wonder Woman pressed her knuckles against her eyes, brushing them up and out, possibly too hard, then faster and harder. Panicking. Then clawing at her face, trying to remove an invisible spider web.

Jewelya felt webs across her face as well, sticking to the soft skin of her newly exposed cheekbone. She dragged one red-taloned hand across her face, tingling. Her eyes were itching, burning, watering; her vision blurred. She felt what the girl felt. Her stomach hurt.

Wonder Woman jumped to her feet. "Stooop!!!" she screamed, retching forward, grabbing her stomach. Still bent, she lifted her head and looked straight at Jewelya, through her, and pressed the first fingers of each hand, like three-pronged vices, one into each of her own eye sockets, digging, rooting.

The pressure was deep and relieving, the pain was dry and sharp.

People gasped in horror, audible even over the loud music.

Then with a surge of adrenaline, do it, do it, do it, Wonder Woman popped and ripped out both orbs simultaneously.

"Aaauuuggghhh!!!"

Women screamed all around. This was no exhibition, no simulation.

Still hanging on their cords—the eyes—Jewelya could almost see out of them—the girl squeezed them useless, juicy, mushy. Pulling, she struggled to break the cords—perhaps too slippery—the pathetic dripping yolks in her hands, her nerves, sinewy strings hanging from her head, literally sections of brain open to air, a two-note atonal chord of pain.

"Ooouuuttt!!!" Wonder Woman yelled with each tug. "Ooouuuttt!!!"

This was the most grotesque thing Jewelya, and likely everyone around her, had ever witnessed.

The blood, not as much as she'd expect.

The pain, more than she'd ever felt. Jewelya's legs buckled as she fell to her knees, and people lurched over her to get to Wonder Woman.

Pandemonium. Incessant screaming from seemingly every mouth in the vicinity. Jewelya felt horror from dozens of people around her. Fear.

The girl's aura was visible to Jewelya even with her eyes closed—her energy was larger than her body. She expected Wonder Woman's soul to move on, but it didn't. It was rooted at the source of the screaming. But Jewelya's energy field, too, felt bigger than her body, and she imagined her own aura over-lapping with the girl's.

Wonder Woman felt at peace. They both did. Wonder Woman had been refusing to have energy, attention, stolen from her. Your money or your life; her eyes for her life, and she had made a most difficult decision.

"Call for help!" a woman shouted.

The music stopped and Jewelya felt a dozen 911 calls in the works.

Somebody far from them began clapping, catcalling, probably thinking this had been a show, part of the party, a trick, an illusion, something to behold, then quieted when nobody else joined in. Cheering actual horror here was wrong.

This was human blood, real pain. Wonder Woman convulsed, hands and knees no screaming peace, two cords of misery dangling from her head. Hands placed on her back and shoulders. Vomit tendrils hanging from the wrong part of her head.

Oddly, then, people began clapping again. This time Jewelya felt it was for the girl's gall, her audacity, that she'd gone further than anyone else in order to achieve a goal.

And what goal is that? Jewelya felt the answer: *Survival.* The girl was surviving.

But it was a polite, respectful applause. No vocalizations.

Jewelya wanted to vomit. The applause died down, and most guests went eerily quiet, at rest, observing but not overtly upset. The closest people were in deathly disbelief, catatonic.

Two men, one on each side, gathered up Wonder Woman the best they could.

"Let's go," one said. "One, two..."

Jewelya wanted to absorb more of the girl's pain, and quickly placed two fingers on her as they passed, touching a hip covered in blue material with white stars, and had a vision: cold, black vastness, with the tiniest, faraway pinpoint stars of light. The black was deep, more profound than anything Jewelya had ever seen. Channeling vision through the girl's eyes perhaps. Or envisioning her thoughts.

"Get out of the way!!!" a woman yelled.

The men carried the girl toward the house.

"Get out of the fucking way!" a guy in medical scrubs yelled.

If only he were a real doctor.

The girl's breathing, and thus Jewelya's, was erratic. That initial rush of adrenaline and blood pressure had yet to subside. Jewelya sensed the woman wasn't hearing much of anything right now. Just gasping as if any breath could be her last. Jewelya was temporarily pinched off in the door's bottle-neck as the guys stumbled through, then followed them in.

They brought Wonder Woman to the couch in the living room until an ambulance could arrive. Summer, ridiculously or not, brought a cup of water and a straw to the girl's dry, quivering mouth, and a wet towel to rest over her head like a hood as she leaned forward. Girls caressed her shoulders, stroked her legs, rubbed her hands with reassuring whispers and kisses to her towel.

This poor girl would wake up tomorrow in darkness, where sound was louder, significantly more important in a world experienced through one fewer major sense. The invisible, painkiller drug fog doing little to obscure the new sensation of finality and regret. She'd somehow, somewhy, traded physical pain for psychological peace. She'd chosen this fate over death. Maybe she'd chosen happiness. Maybe.

Wonder Woman seemed to know Jewelya was there. Was watching her somehow. Recognition. Familiarity.

"Lisa!" a woman screamed, forcing her way through the house packed with people. It was Kat, from the Emporium. Kat fell to her knees and rested her forehead on Lisa's messy, hosed thigh. Sobbing. "Oh my god, Lisa, no!"

Not lifting the towel from her face, Lisa made whimpering noises like a balloon slowly losing air. Kat's appearance had diminished Jewelya's connection to the girl. Lisa was now focusing on her friend.

Another woman was yelling into a phone. "Hurry! There's blood everywhere!"

An exaggeration. But understandable.

"I already called them," Summer said.

Many people have.

"But they're not here yet!" the woman said.

Jewelya knew Ainsley was in trouble. This could be him next. She needed to get out of the house and find him before anything happened to him. He was nearby; she could feel him.

There was obviously more to this party than partying. Perhaps the Omnist would know. She looked at her phone.

MOTE:

Believing is seeing.

TWENTY

AINSLEY

"Oh my god, Lisa!" Kat wailed, patting and squeezing Wonder Woman's knees and thighs with her hands. Trying to dig her way through the costume's tights to the person underneath.

The Wonder Woman with the most beautiful eyes at the party had separated herself from her most prominent feature.

But still, the eyes were there—Ainsley could see them—beautiful, holographic, ethereal, not exactly glowing, but lit from some sort of internal source. If that made sense. Perhaps the effect was due to the pupils, dark, dark, darkness, like nothing he'd seen before. Like their depths would go on forever if he trained his focus into them.

The ghosts of Lisa's eyes levitated above her, larger and wider now. They slowly turned, observing the room. They looked at Jewelya, and possibly at her purse. But Ainsley's awareness was currently larger than that, and the eyes looked up as part of the room's survey. Could Lisa see him up there?

Her eyes lingered occasionally on something or someone, then after completing a full 360-degree turn, they shrank and dropped into the space between Lisa and Kat. Hiding? Maybe peering into Kat's soul. Perhaps they were tethered to Lisa the way Ainsley was to his phone. And nobody else had noticed the levitating eyes. He realized that only he, or possibly other estranged souls, could see them.

Kat lifted her head. "We can save your eyes," she said to Lisa, evoking a confident tone.

No, the eyes were dead and had passed into the afterlife with Ainsley. He'd seen them. That meant body parts could die separately from other parts.

And what was the central point for a pair of eyes? All points of the universe had a center, a continuum that traveled back to the beginning of the universe. Including the particles that made up eyes.

This was because of the Omnist. Spells as Motes as prayers. For all intents and purposes, it had killed him. Dead. Disappeared.

But this girl, Lisa, Wonder Woman, maybe while reading the last Mote, or second to last Mote, her brain had caught on to what was happening and fought back, modifying the spell. Maybe the Omnist's algorithm was off and she'd been given the wrong incantation.

What had happened to him or Lisa could happen to Jewelya.

Why was the Omnist doing this?

TWENTY-ONE

JEWELYA

J ewelya was looking for Ainsley around the front yard and driveway of the house—perhaps he was talking to somebody who was leaving—when the paramedics arrived. They had space to park in front of Dirgatory's handwritten "No Parking" signs.

Probably thirty or forty people stood out front, recounting their perspectives of what had happened. The paramedics lifted a stretcher out the front door, pushed it down the driveway, and were the first to leave, even as more police officers arrived.

Dirge and Summer somberly spoke to a couple police officers on the front porch next to a "dead" dummy. Summer was crying. Dirge looked stoic.

This party would be shut down in mere moments, if it wasn't already. Jewelya needed to find Ainsley quickly. Who cared if he was drunk or passed out or drugged out playing with his shoelaces? There were plenty of witnesses for authorities to question, friends that knew the poor girl and what drugs she'd taken. As surreal as Dirgatory had been, this was the most traumatic event Jewelya had ever seen. They just needed to leave before anything else happened.

Jewelya walked back up the driveway, the ticket booth unmanned and security gone, to the backyard and dance area. The music had been cut in the immediate aftermath of the crisis, but it'd come back now, albeit at quieter level. Like an ethereal movie soundtrack. Soundscape. Sound design. The number of people back had dropped to maybe a third of what it'd been, to a more manageable number for a party.

Garbage everywhere seemed to have risen from beneath the hard-packed and slippery soil. There were two loose, unmatched shoes. How does one lose a shoe at a party like this? Rephrased as Denkins would say it, how does one *not* lose a shoe at a party like this?

Jewelya could tell it was midnight without looking at her phone. Something was definitely starting, a show or something. Like New Year's Eve, Dirgatory seemed built for a midnight ritual, perhaps a loosely preplanned, free-for-all of tortured inevitability. People began gathering again at the center of the dance area. Somebody had placed a wooden bridge—a pallet covered with a sheet of plywood—spanning the two coffins, creating an impromptu stage. A refurbished, unwheeled office chair with wires running from it had been placed on top. Handcuffs hung from each armrest. The wires ran under one of the coffins.

This was something Ainsley would want to see. If she stayed here, this was where he'd appear. But after what had happened, would a show now even be appropriate? Jewelya wondered if Dirge and Summer were aware that the event was continuing. Maybe it was a distraction.

The people to her right parted, and two hooded executioners escorted a blindfolded blonde woman in a white cotton dress from the spank tent through the parted sea. This was eerily like a wedding procession with the woman marrying—there was no one there—perhaps, death itself? A man dressed as a priest trailed them, reading a prayer in Latin. The men helped the woman up to the stage and into the chair, then cuffed her hands to the armrests and feet together.

A wedding. An execution. A mock sacrifice? Or some blending of all of these. After what Jewelya had seen tonight, even pretending something like this was out of line. But she was mesmerized. And her empathy was not triggering. The verisimilitude just wasn't there. And she was calloused now, hardened against their audacity to host a performance like this.

Dammit, Ainsley, where are you? Jewelya wanted to leave.

The music changed to something darker and more ominous.

The woman on stage shook her head back and forth, and pretended to flail against her bonds. The actor was good, not great. She wasn't trying all that hard; the restraints might break.

The priest read another passage, and when he finished, he looked up from his black book and grinned. Apparently, that was some sort of cue, and the crowd began chanting, "Kill her! Kill her! Kill her!" It was nauseating.

The priest held up his hands to quiet the crowd, and began reading from his book again. "We have brought these charges upon this woman: insecurity, insomnia, body dysmorphia, and low self-esteem1"

Jewelya gasped. So did several others. It wasn't the expected list of charges.

One of the executioners held up a red, wishbone-shaped, cartoonish remote switch. "Are you ready?" he said.

The crowd both cheered and chanted "Kill her!" again. Jewelya wanted this to stop. This was incredibly inappropriate.

"I said *are you ready*?" The executioner puffed his chest as the crowd screamed. "Three..." And the crowd joined in. "Two...one!"

The executioner flipped the switch and the woman spasmed and moaned. Zapping noises. The holiday lights strung along the porch's awning flickered behind Jewelya, and when she turned around, she saw somebody near the back door manning the light switch for the back door. Not a big production.

The other executioner checked the woman's vitals, uncuffing and lifting a limp wrist for the crowd to see, then dropped it for effect. The two men unlatched her and carried her "dead" body off the platform. Applause.

The music changed again to something the crowd seemed to recognize, as it brought a new wave of cheers. People looked around in anticipation.

Their attention went to Yksian, standing near the door to the shed. As they had done with the woman and executioners, the audience parted so he could approach, his long coat fluttering as he glided as if on a moving walkway.

A midnight Yksian Lodge?

The crowd shushed as he ascended the stage, and stood there silently. A chorus of voices came from the front yard and inside the house. Lights from emergency vehicles continued to reflect off shiny objects and the tree branches above them.

"An unfortunate crisis occurred here less than an hour ago," Yksian said. His voice was louder than it should've been, resonating with the boards he stood on without him exerting much effort. His hands were clasped in front of himself, modestly. It was a sign of subjugation, supplication, contrasting his otherwise overpowering presence.

"The poor soul's name is Lisa, a friend of the Emporium. If you pray, please do so on her behalf. Whoever your gods are, whatever your beliefs, she requires optimism, strength, and friends more than ever."

Well, if Ainsley was there, Jewelya would definitely see him now. Yksian was part of his PGP, and with so few people left, Ainsley would surely see her, too.

"These recent events highlight the importance of perception. Lisa seemingly chose a most difficult, painful path to eliminate one of her senses. Perhaps we'll learn how she suffered, why she concluded that this was the best option. An action, it goes without saying, I would never recommend anyone take.

"And assuming Lisa survives this ordeal, she will live with the consequences for the rest of her life. So my appearance on this stage at the moment may appear rote. The performative sacrifice here was no more real than receiving a sacrament in place of a piece of a 2,000-year-old body. But it's symbolic. Perhaps these rituals are more important now, as we project fearlessness against the enormity of eternity and the afterlife, intensifying our short-term suffering in order to diminish the long-term suffering inherent to humanity.

"Self-sacrifice," he said, "is not the same as suicide. Self-sacrifice occurs when you don't necessarily want to die, but do it anyway for the benefit of others."

"A martyr!" a guest cried out enthusiastically.

"Not quite. Things like subjecting yourself to punishment from a corrupt government, or subjecting yourself to a starvation diet until political prisoners are released, while quite noble, are indeed a form of martyrdom.

"When I speak of self-sacrifice, I am talking about a subset of that. This is welcoming death as self-betterment, losing one's ego, quietly, alone. A monk who has himself buried alive so he can pray all day, alone, breathing and feeding through a straw. No social media to save the moment for posterity. This stage I stand upon is not representative of my personal loneliness, and warm internal feelings occur privately only to myself."

While Yksian spoke, Jewelya noticed a queue had formed along the maze wall leading up to the platform. Yksian nodded toward the line.

"I ask that if you'd like to make a donation of fifty dollars, or if you've already raised money for this moment, to coordinate with Mackenzie first. Tonight, I am raising money for the Science and Eco-Spiritualism for Troubled Youths organization. There, we encourage growth of knowledge and love of the universe, regardless of the child's upbringing. We'll continue with our death exhibition and all of you can zap your ego into nonexistence."

Science and Eco-Spiritualism for Troubled Youths?

The first person in line stepped onto the platform and bowed solemnly to Yksian, who remained still. The man sunk his head and lifted his shoulders, an embarrassed sort of shrug, and nervously patted the sides of Yksian's arms. Still no response. It was awkward. The man sat himself in the chair.

"Roger!" a guy in the crowd said.

Roger waved a few fingers back, seemingly fearful to lift his entire hand.

Jewelya recognized Yksian's assistant, Mackenzie, a platinum blonde with a pageboy haircut—dressed tonight as a fembot from the *Austin Powers* movies—as she strapped Roger's wrists in place.

He slipped out a little smile. Phones were pointed at him, filming and streaming. He would make his social media followers proud.

Mackenzie whispered in Yksian's ear.

"Tonight," Yksian announced. "Roger has donated one hundred dollars."

Polite applause.

Yksian made a gentlemanly gesture to Mackenzie. "You may have the honor."

The audience applauded. Mackenzie held the red remote, took a deep breath, then threw the switch. Roger twitched, laughing and squealing.

"It's too much!" he said. "Banana!"

Mackenzie flipped the remote again. Roger tilted his head and exhaled in a way that inflated his cheeks. He was already sweating.

"We should accept donations to be allowed to throw the switch," Mackenzie said to Yksian.

"A valid suggestion," he said.

Jewelya could swear she smelled burnt hair.

One by one, people sat in an electric chair willingly, faking their own deaths. But the pain was real. She could tell by the facial expressions. And these people had volunteered.

And she couldn't get the smell of burnt hair out of her head, either.

Hopefully it wouldn't rain again.

After what had happened with Lisa, Dirge should have canceled this part of the event, fundraiser or not. But Dirge was busy with the authorities. Yksian should have known better.

"They're really being shocked, you know," a girl next to her said.

"I smell ozone or something," Jewelya said.

"Like a self-inflicted Stanford prison experiment...but as a party trick."

A misguided frat boy dare.

"I'm sorry, excuse me," a man said, suddenly right beside her. His voice sounded tiny, inquisitive. Like a modest beggar asking for change. It was Chikao. "Have you seen a loose phone around?"

"No, I haven't," she said. "But my husband and I saw your Lodge yesterday. It was great."

"Oh, thank you." Chikao patted his robe. "This is why I have Yuko, to help me not lose my technology."

She didn't know what a Yuko was. "I'm sorry?"

"Ah, but good Buddhist needs no assistant."

His assistant. It was possible he was looking for Yuko, too. "Speaking of which, I'm looking for my husband, Ainsley. Maybe you remember him from the Lodge." Jewelya had a sudden vision of the two of them, Ainsley and Yuko, off together somewhere, drunk and making out, or worse. Beer pong.

"Ah, yes, perhaps," Chikao said. "What was his name again?"

"Ainsley."

"I'll keep an eye out." Chikao lingered with a look of inquisitiveness a little too long. It creeped her out.

Chikao bowed as an exit greeting, which seemed to pull Jewelya down in return. It was involuntary. His monkish rucksack rattled as he walked away, hanging low as if it had rocks in hidden pockets. He stopped again at a group of three people and performed the same modest bow, likely asking them the same question.

Jewelya's sides were tickled from behind, startling her. She whipped her head around. It was Denkins. He rested his chin on her shoulder.

"You scared the shit out of me," she said.

"Jewels, Jewels," Denkins said, turning her to face him. "Have you seen my baby boy?"

"Kyle? No. Just that once when he was dancing."

"He's mad at me. He saw us kissing earlier and stormed off like a little bitch."

The switch had been thrown again and another guest was being electrocuted. Some gawkers cheered.

"Did he leave?" Jewelya said.

"I don't think so," Denkins said. "I have his phone."

She imagined Ainsley storming off; maybe he'd seen them kiss, too. But she decided that Ainsley would've read the situation better than that. "I'm sorry Denky."

"Then there was that girl's horrible freakout," Denkins said. "I can't take this place anymore. I need to leave."

"I'm so sorry," Jewelya said. She could feel his anxiety as his gaze darted about. She wondered if coming down off ecstasy was making it worse. "Are you okay?"

"No, yes, no, yes, I need to leave." Denkins patted her arms as he hopped on his toes. "Ugh! Why did this happen?"

"I said I'm sorry, right?"

"It's okay, honey, I'm done," Denkins said, planting a kiss on her cheek. "I just wanted to say bye."

As Denkins walked away, Kick was hovering near the spank tent, like he was looking for someone. Before she could go talk to him, she was intercepted by a short, vibrant woman with thick glasses.

"Excuse me, do you mind if I ask you a question?" She had a husky smoker's voice. "I apologize for intruding, but I'm Veris."

"Jewelya," she said, offering the hand that wasn't cradling

her purse and phone against her chest. She sensed great loneliness coming from her. Not in the sense of loss so much as a desire to find her equal, her other half.

"Do you mind me asking who it was you were speaking with?" Veris said.

"A coworker, why?"

"You work with Chikao?" Veris seemed surprised.

"Oh nooo, I thought you meant Denkins. Yeah, no, before that, the other man was Chikao."

"I thought that was him," Veris said, blaming her vision by way of pushing her glasses up her nose. They looked heavy. "Costumes, as you can imagine."

By this point Chikao had moved on, apparently not finding what he needed from the other group. He looked at Jewelya again, but since they'd already said goodbye, she pretended she didn't see him.

Oddly, Veris didn't go on to speak with him, and rather headed toward the shed.

Now, it was Kick who approached her. "You haven't seen Fred Flintstone around, have you?" he said. He apparently was going person to person, like Chikao, asking everybody.

"No," Jewelya said. "I half-expected to see my husband on stage electrocuting himself."

Kick looked thoughtful. He always did, at least the few times she'd seen him. Tonight's events weren't making him act any more social. "You know...Lisa...that thing that happened... she's a friend of Kat's."

"I know. I saw them inside."

"Some people think the Omnist is causing this stuff to happen," Kick said. "And to our own people."

"Drugs?" Jewelya said. "I mean, I'm not asking, or offering, I mean, Lisa..." She was making things awkward. "My husband, your Flintstone."

"I don't know," Kick said. "But it's sad when drugs have to be the easier answer."

"I'm not sure if I trust Dirge and Yksian," Jewelya said. "They don't seem bothered enough by missing people and crazy bad drug trips. It's like they expected all of this to happen. Now they're electrocuting people on stage."

"The Twin Towers of Terror are my friends, you know."

Of course they were. "Well, I can't find Ainsley, either. He's obviously not with Lisa."

"Why would he be with her?" Kick said.

That's right. Kick wasn't there in the shed. "I don't know. I guess Yksian was winding me up earlier, saying they might be together." *Which is one more reason not to necessarily trust him.*

"Well, Gremmie texted me a couple hours ago to say he was here."

"Same with Ainsley."

"And he hasn't responded either?" Kick said.

"He can't." She pulled his phone out of her purse. "Found his phone."

"There's some weird shit going on," Kick said. "I'm going to make another lap, then head home. If I don't see you again, come talk to me at the Emporium tomorrow. I'm there from open till probably six."

"Okay." As social as Jewelya could be early in the night, there weren't enough words left in the tank for her to say anything notable. "I hope they're not together," she said. *Partying. Ugh.*

"What?" Kick said.

"Ainsley and Gremmie. I don't know. I'm being stupid." She was done. Burnt. Shellshocked.

She walked down the driveway in a daze, with the flashing lights of one last patrol car illuminating places in blue and red that didn't deserve it. Jewelya had a set of keys in her clutch, and she used them to drive Ainsley's car home.

So if he'd left Dirgatory, he hadn't taken the car.

When she got home, she paced every room for a few minutes. She needed them to warm up. There was no feeling like an empty house missing one of its occupants. Kitty rubbed her leg and followed her to the kitchen, hoping for one too many meals. *Not tonight sweetie.* Jewelya stopped again in front of one of the new cobweb mirrors. That black in the glass. It went too deep, too far. It went somewhere. She had the thought to throw Ainsley's phone through the strings and into the infinite abyss beyond the glass.

Then she looked at the other mirror. A web of broken glass. Perhaps someone had done exactly that to that one, as well.

Eventually, Jewelya showered and went to bed. She expected to be lying awake for hours worrying, but instead she didn't remember falling asleep, it happened so quickly.

TWENTY-TWO

KICK

After the emergency workers left Dirgatory, Kick had zero interest in staying. Gremmie obviously wasn't there. He wanted to speak with Dirge, but he was busy sweeping the last of the people out of the house. Summer was in the kitchen, on the phone with someone, crying.

There was quiet, then sudden cheering from the backyard. Apparently, Yksian was going through with his Dirgatory Lodge, a mild electrocution fundraiser for troubled youths. At first this seemed like it would've been a mistake to continue, but the more Kick thought about it, the more it made a modicum of sense. People were more subdued, trickling out at a more natural rate than a sudden rush, and things were much quieter than earlier. And Yksian, theoretically, could feel he was making something positive out of a bad situation.

There was a couple seated on the couch. They were

animated, but weren't loud. "No, seriously, there's a hole to another dimension," the man said to the woman.

"Come on guys," Dirge said. Even when he was tired, grumpy, and probably annoyed, he still sounded...cheery? "There's nothing left in here. Let's clear out of the house."

The couple stood up, the man first, offering a hand to help up his partner.

"Sorry," the woman said to Dirge. It was apparent she'd been crying.

"Thank you, Dirge," the man said. "Call me if you need anything."

Dirge smiled wearily and patted the man's shoulder. There was nearly a foot difference between their heights. The couple exited the front door, which was in regular use now, with a flurry of apologies and thanks.

Dirge made eye contact with Kick, chilling him. He looked stressed and engaged, with an interesting combination of bloodshot eyes and direct focus. Eyes were a definite theme tonight.

"I'm surprised you have to do this yourself," Kick said. "I thought the police would've shut this all down."

"Yeah, well, they've known about Dirgatory for a long time," Dirge said. "Some of them attended in previous years. This is the twenty-fifth year, and I was already thinking it'd be the last. Now I know for sure. But they said we could ramp down slowly, as long as we turn the volume down. Most people have left anyway."

"Well, I'll get out of your hair too," Kick said. "Need any help before I go?"

"I don't think so. And Summer hasn't left to be with the girls, yet," Dirge said, sweeping a long arm toward the kitchen. Even that seemed a gesture of exhaustion.

Summer was in the kitchen, off the call now, leaning back

against the counter, looking at her phone, mumbling to herself.

"Summer Sunrise," Dirge said. "You don't have to stay. I'll get the people out back. Go be with Kat. She needs you."

Summer nodded without looking away from her phone, and walked out of the kitchen, brushing a hand against Dirge as she passed, and through the living room.

"Bye, Summer," Kick said.

She didn't look back, but lifted one hand in acknowledgment, a half-hearted wave, before opening the front door. Dirge closed the door behind her softly, like a sleeping child was on the other side. Then he locked it.

"She's probably answering a million texts," Dirge said.

"Did you see it?" Kick said. "You know...Lisa?"

"No, not when it happened." Dirge took a deep breath. There was nobody left in the house, so he gestured for Kick to come outside with him. Dirgatory seemed to have taken everything out of him. Normally bright, his eyes, still large and round, were now dull and black. "Did you?"

"I was all the way in back—in the hookah room. It took me a minute to get out of the maze." Actually, he'd closed his eyes back there, imagining the black of Black Vertigo, when he'd heard Lisa screaming.

They walked out the back door.

"You know what," Dirge said. "Dumb question: I know you write a lot of the Motes. Do you write prayers, too?"

"No, not really. But if an Omniscian submits something, I'll put it in."

"Do they ever write in Latin?"

"No," Kick said. This wasn't what he wanted to hear. *It can't be the Omnist.*

"Weird. Summer said she was getting prayers in another language."

Two hours later, Kick was still awake, sitting with an herbal tea at his dining room table, waiting for Gremmie to return. He was trying to calm his nerves, trying not to replay the evening over and over in his head. He never did this, sitting up like a parent.

Four years ago, Kick was sitting at a table at The Guild, a bar frequented by cosplayers and lovers of roleplaying games, with his friend, Karlma Chatterjee. They had been friends since school. Years of practice as a teenage and collegiate dungeon master had influenced Kick's desire to create his own video game. Karlma, who had taken to mixing her Hindu upbringing and teachings with more modern spiritualism, was a great person bounce ideas off of, especially if the game featured reincarnation.

"So when you die, you don't really die," Kick said, asking as much as saying. "You just change levels."

"You could be a cow," Karlma said. Her tone was smooth and uplifting, spreading her words like soft butter. Karlma's fashion was a mixture of traditional and modern, but Kick could swear she was wearing more makeup than usual. She looked like she'd be the keyboardist of an art rock band. It was a form of cosplay to match the theme tonight, perhaps.

"Well, no, I mean, if you survive, you change levels down," Kick said. "If you die, you go up. See what I mean?"

"But the game never ends."

"Right. In most games, when you die, game over. And if you win, you get stronger, more points, more weapons, and you face fiercer competition. You go up a level. But here, if you win, you go down for a harder life with fewer benefits. You survive by your wits. It's a more difficult game."

"Winning is losing."

"Just like life, right?" Kick said. "This is why I love talking to you."

"That's because we've spoken before, in previous lives," Karlma said. "And we will again, in our next."

A guy at the table next to them was playing a game on his tablet. His character must have died, since he slapped the table with a hand.

"Whoa, uncouth!" he said. He turned to face them, his surfer hair more dreaded than not. "So your game never ends? You never just start over?"

"I believe what Kick here is saying is that *you* would start over," Karlma said. "But the game itself would never end; once you begin, it goes on forever." She turned to Kick. "I would play this game."

The dread-headed surfer guy looked at his phone. "You ever think to use a Ouija for sexting the dead? Like maybe hitting up Bettie Page? I'd play *that* game."

Kick looked at Karlma, in case she was offended. She wasn't. *Who is this guy.*

"My name's Gremmie," he said, reaching a hand over to fist bump both of them. "I'm just a stepping stone to a better conversation."

FOUR YEARS LATER, and who knew where Gremmie had gone. A friend could've called him at the last minute with a change of plans. He was enough of an airhead to flake on Kick, but he'd at least text him. Most of the time.

Kick's phone rang. It was Yksian. It wasn't just the time—

three a.m.—that was weird. It was that Yksian had never called his cell before. He'd call Connie, yes, the Emporium, yes, and Lodges were scheduled via email. Kick wasn't even sure Yksian had his number until now.

"Yksian, sir," Kick said, code-switching to Yksian's preferred tone.

Yksian cleared his throat, dislodging a boulder in an earthquake, before he spoke. "I'm curious if you are aware of Summer's whereabouts."

This can't be good. "Oh, she went to the hospital," Kick said. "After the Lisa..." Kick didn't want to finish the sentence.

"Ah, yes, that would be the expected narrative," Yksian said. "I was departing Dirgatory just after two of the clock. Everyone had left—for understandable reasons, of course. I said farewell to Dirge, and elicited that I'd like to see Summer, as well, but as you suggested, he believed she had left for the hospital to accompany Kat and Lisa."

"Yes, I was there when she left."

"As I walked to my car, I found a phone in the grass near the sidewalk. I brought it to Dirge, in case somebody returned in search of it." Yksian spoke slowly, and sometimes added pauses that bordered on uncomfortable. Kick had learned that unless asked a direct question, any idle, inane, space-filling talk was more likely to annoy Yksian than silence. Maybe Yksian was sipping a beverage. "I thought nothing of it until I arrived home."

The sound of a goblet being set down affirmed this. Still, Yksian seemed to know when to pause for maximum narrative effect. "Dirge called. He recounted how he hadn't heard from Summer, and had tried calling her. It was the lost phone that I'd given him that lit up."

"It was hers."

"It was hers. Apparently in her rush to leave, she'd dropped it. So Dirge called Kat to notify her that he had Summer's phone in his possession, that they were not to worry."

"But Summer wasn't there?" Kick said.

"Correct, young Kick. Summer, indeed, had not arrived at the hospital."

"Well, she didn't come here." Kick wasn't sure why he'd said that.

"No, I don't believe she did. It turns out Summer's car was still parked down the street from their house."

"Then she got a ride?" Kick said. "She was playing with her phone when she left. I mean, maybe she tried to put it in her purse when she got in the car..." He was talking too much. Yksian didn't make affirmative noises that he was listening, or sound supportive during a conversation. Kick felt like an idiot, stating the obvious.

"How well do you know Chikao?" Yksian said.

"Not well. I've only met him a few times."

"Well, just prior to taking the stage, I entered the shed to collect my thoughts in as near silence as could be achieved, considering the events in question."

There was that pause again. Kick was overtired and on edge about tonight. There was obviously more to this. "So why'd you—"

"I'd considered striking the Lodge," Yksian said, anticipating the question. "But I felt it was important to display support, to alleviate the pain that inspires one to endeavor in such extreme deeds. But the shed was not unoccupied. The bartenders had departed, but I discovered Summer conversing with Chikao. It seemed they were making plans. He appeared to have broken out of the character he'd worn for the evening. Rather than emotionless supplication, he was performatively happy. A plethora of teeth with eyes shining bright. But Summer was appropriately somber. It goes without saying that it had not been a superb evening, therefore I saw no reason why he should have been pleased."

"Huh," Kick said. "Chikao looked old, sad, and frail when I last saw him. He's kind of a weird guy."

"Perhaps." Yksian seemed to be making Kick come to the conclusion himself, rather than just explaining his theory.

Kick's mind raced ahead. "Do you think he took Summer against her will, and that's why she dropped her phone?" *Not the Omnist. Not the Omnist.*

"I was hoping she'd said something to you before she left. Or that you would tell me you had provided transportation, for some reason. Perhaps you had seen her distraught and offered your support. But those do not seem to be the case."

"Yeah, no, I did leave right after her, and she was definitely out of sorts. She didn't even say goodbye to Dirge."

"I do, then, fear she is with Chikao. Perhaps he was waiting for her. The frequencies he was emitting were not ideal."

Kick had never heard Yksian speak about frequencies before. "Just like Gremmie," Kick said. "Then Lisa's tragedy, and now Summer's missing."

"What do they all have in common, you may ask?" Yksian said.

"All I can think of is they're all friends with somebody affiliated with the Emporium. Even Ainsley is missing."

"You don't say." Yksian didn't sound surprised. "And they all believe in different afterlives, do they not?" he said.

"I suppose so, but that's not weird for Consumerians."

"Lisa, Summer, Gremmie, and Ainsley—they all use the Omnist, correct?"

There it is. "Maybe somebody is out to get Consumerians," Kick said.

"I am not sure why that would be, but it's not impossible."

"Have you met Adelie Veris?"

"Yes," Yksian said. "She has an interesting take on the nature of souls. Are you implying her involvement in this?"

"I don't know. I'm just trying to think of people who were there tonight. And she was talking about souls gathering at the party and had a theory about what was happening."

"Please elaborate," Yksian said.

"Really, that's all she said."

"Well, Sir Kick, I think I've learned all I can from this conversation."

After they hung up, Kick went to Gremmie's room, which seemed colder now. He thought about sitting in Gremmie's gaming chair. Normally Gremmie would appear out of nowhere if he so much as suspected someone was sitting in it. But he didn't come running.

CHAPTER
TWENTY-THREE

AINSLEY

H is poor wife. Jewelya obviously believed Ainsley had left her at Dirgatory. And that he was drunk. He'd been so checked out the last couple years, keeping his head down to not ruffle feathers, that it was clear his avoidance of conflict had been causing more of it. He'd scarred her. But he was with her as she drove his car home, and she didn't, *couldn't* know. He wanted so badly to tell her he was there. Just don't forget to bring his phone.

He hadn't quite figured out how he could see. He had no body, so no eyes. Vision was based on his ability to focus his size and attention, like his entire being was an eye that could see waves in 360 degrees; he could see in all directions. And to see something with more detail, he shrank his focus, reducing his entire size. This was more important at home, where he'd need to be with Jewelya no matter what room she left him in.

His perception was more like the surface of a bubble than a pinpoint. Part of it went underground, part above, even though people were generally on a flat plane. Therefore, to expand wider meant more vertical perception, as well, and most of the time this was useless.

Because of this, the arrangement of their house mattered. He preferred higher ceilings and larger rooms, in general, so he could expand his focus farther and see entire rooms without moving past walls. And yet, he wanted to be everywhere at once, watching outside—every car driving slowly down the street signaled danger—checking the yard, the perimeter. He'd have to change sizes frequently.

She entered the house and began shutting down. She paused in front of the cobweb mirrors. He wanted to go inside them. It was that black. He knew that darkness. He didn't see any waves of electromagnetism emitting from them. She was obviously getting something from one of them, as well, as she stared for a minute or two.

Eventually, Jewelya went to the bedroom and set his phone charging at his side of the bed, and hers on her side.

The dress mirror in the master bedroom was enormous, like something found backstage at a musical, where perhaps multiple people could use it at the same time. It was seven feet tall and three feet wide and must have weighed a hundred and seventy-five pounds. It had taken three people to carry it into the house when they moved in. Ainsley preferred neither of Jewelya's favorite mirrors (the other being the smoked glass in the living room); he preferred looking out windows. Not participating so much as watching others. Curious, how that was now the prison he'd been thrown into. Forced to watch only. Choose your own hell-venture.

Since Jewelya worked out at work, she tended to shower before bed. Ainsley, on the other hand, believed he needed the feel of water on him to wake him up in the morning and get the brain muscles moving. It took Jewelya longer than usual to downshift tonight—there was more to remove than mere workout pants, T-shirt, and sports bra.

"Dammit, Ains, why did you do this?" she said. "I need you to know I'm not really that mad about yesterday."

He hadn't been thinking about that. His absence had inspired guilt for something that, compared to this, didn't matter at all. Probably their argument at the Emporium, which led to a chilly, albeit quick, drive home. They didn't really speak this morning before he left for work.

Jewelya went to take a shower, and as usual, left the bathroom door ajar. It was cracked open about six inches, which was their unspoken rule in case the other wanted to poke their head in to ask a question or use the toilet. Apparently, she still did that even when he wasn't home. It was heart-wrenching.

Ainsley enlarged past the bedroom, saw her in the shower, then bigger again to take in the entire house, then the block. Satisfied, he minimized again. Even without breath, he was aware of the change in air particles around him. He could sense how much of it was nitrogen, oxygen, water. Even dust, which, indoors, was largely skin flakes and cat dander. As he continued minimizing, he watched the environment grow larger above and around him. Sinking feeling. Like dropping in an elevator.

Soon the phone seemed the size of the earth itself.

English words made less sense. Rather, his sense of language was shifting. Language of the Sun grew more intuitive the smaller he became, until he understood it as well as English. He knew its name. Thinking this way was all muscle memory. Natural. Without bones, these words, syllables, and constituent parts were his spine, his skin. Held him together. Made of words.

This far down, going infinitesimal was like going back in the past, to an earlier point in the expansion of space. But his mind was still working, still churning that ancient language as fast and clear as light. The recent English thoughts were still there, but buried in his subconscious. He had morphed into this other language.

He felt out of place this small. He didn't belong here. Despite the motion of atoms and molecules, this level felt dead. Life had moved on, or more particularly, complex life was more interesting. He enlarged with a sensation of expanding his lungs. The phone was his connection to his most recent world, and was where he wanted to be.

At room size, he saw Jewelya had finished her nighttime routine and was in bed scrolling through news on her phone. It was late. She normally would have had a class at seven a.m. tomorrow, but due to Halloween, it'd been moved to ten. But still, it was late. She shouldn't have screentime before bed.

Jewelya dialed her phone. Ainsley sensed it ringing. "Brandon, it's Jewelya. I didn't see you at the party, so I was wondering if you were with Ainsley. He's not home. You don't have to call, text is fine. Happy, um...Happy Halloween." She hung up, took a deep breath, then slapped the bed. "Where the fuck are you, you dipshit? You better be hungover as hell tomorrow."

She'd called his coworker. Ainsley needed to figure out how to send her a message. He tried to access the texting app. He could overlap it and read it, but was unable to affect anything. His *center* was through the Omnist. It was so close. *She* was so close.

Exploring the phone the best he could, mainly by puttering around at different size levels to figure out what he could see, he discovered the coding for the Omnist. He read it line by line just by looking at the stored bits on the chips, an impossible task when human. Perhaps understanding this other protolanguage in his subconscious was helping him right now. Ones and zeros were one thing, but he'd never memorized long chains of them. Nobody did. And he was reading the physical manifestations of the coding-on-hardware without the need of a monitor. Overall, what he learned was that the Omnist was a relatively simple program and not all that different from code he dealt with at work.

He learned that the prayer Motes in question weren't derived from the algorithm, not entered by users listed as C1, K2, or R3, which he took to be Connie, Kick, and Raine. Some were entered by a third-party user. G0. G zero. Was this a hacker?

All that pseudo-Latin, the ancient language, that came from guest zero.

And the Omnist had suggested Ainsley read the prayers in private. He figured that way the reader could disappear without witnesses. So, like a good Consumerian, he'd done what he was told. He suspected there were many others.

He needed to warn Jewelya not to read any Motes aloud.

Ainsley used the same routing through the Omnist as he figured the hacker had. This seemed to be the only place Ainsley could affect his environment, albeit very little. Perhaps this, being the exact place where he and the spell interacted, was his portal. And here, he had a bit of control of electromagnetic force.

JJ, it's me, he Moted. Jewelya's middle name was Janis, hence JJ. As far as he knew, he was the only person who could get away with calling her that, and even then, the timing had to be right.

Ainsley enlarged his perception until he could see the

outside of the phone. The screen flashed with an Omnist notification for a couple seconds, then went black again. It had worked. But Jewelya was long asleep.

Please, Jewels, can you hear me? he said, no, *thought.* But of course she couldn't hear him.

He shrank back into the Omnist.

Do not, I repeat, DO NOT, read any Motes out loud, he Moted.

She'd be asleep for a while. He felt safest at room level, where he was with Jewelya. He felt he was protecting her, but really, there was nothing he could do if anything were to happen.

He would just be aware of it.

CHAPTER

TWENTY-FOUR

KICK

K ick used to work at Consumia's Spiritual Emporium an average of six days a week, and he sort of missed that. Sort of. He spent so much time now setting up Omnist II, and in transit from home to there to here, that he often had to speak to contractors and order supplies from home. Often, when he *was* at the Emporium, it was to meet with Connie and update plans for the new store, the Lodge schedule, sales numbers, Omnist analytics, and social media.

He'd looked forward to opening the store today so Connie could sleep in, until recent events had derailed his enthusiasm. She'd be here in time for the second of Veris's Lodges, but it wasn't likely he'd do all the things here he'd planned on beforehand, like moving back and sale-pricing Halloween items, and highlighting Día De Los Muertos and Veris's merchandise.

Kick was sitting in the office, going over estimates for some minor renovations they needed to make at the Omnist II space. That location was in an older section of Los Angeles: Echo Park, on Sunset Boulevard, near a well-curated bookstore and a couple bars and restaurants. Like the location here on Lankershim, it should have decent foot traffic in a town that was notorious for people not walking anywhere. And when they'd checked out the neighborhood, it felt right. There was history there, a story, as much as there could be in a city such as this.

At first, Omnist II was going to be different in tone. Six months ago, Kick had announced to Connie that he was quitting CSE in order to open his own store with Lucador. The vision would be that, although it would share some customer base by default and be in competition with the Emporium, they would separate as much as possible from Connie's baby, and focus more on LARPing, cosplay, and Flinch TV, things generally avoided at the Emporium. The problem was that their third investor turned out to be a bit of a conman—Connie's ex-husband, Blaine. It didn't take long to discover his shadiness, and Kick and Lucador returned and partnered with Connie instead.

It was Connie who suggested the Omnist II name. And the name worked for Kick as a way to incorporate the app into the brick-and-mortar side of the business. He was more of a numbers guy, spearheading a lot of their inventory (bulk orders) and maintenance of the app. Connie was more of a visionary, procuring the rarer, unique items (and overpricing them, in Kick's opinion), wrangling Omniscians, and Lodge scheduling. She was a people-person to whom people attached themselves. A natural-born storyteller (which the story cards on those special items attested), and salesperson who could weave a tale to sell virtually anything.

"Always have a story," Connie was known to say. And she

always did have one or twenty. But last night was insane. There was no way to shine what happened at Dirgatory in a positive light.

Lisa. Poor Lisa, who had driven from Phoenix out to Los Angeles to be with her best friend, Kat, already a widow in her twenties. Halloween was the first "holiday" since her husband Jesse's death, so Lisa was there to accompany Kat on what everyone knew was normally her favorite day of the year. Kat had sworn that Lisa didn't take any party drugs, but that didn't mean a drink couldn't have been spiked. People didn't just randomly rip their eyes out of their sockets.

And this was compounding tragedy for Kat. Jesse had died from heart failure running the L.A. Marathon, which meant those races were ruined for her, and now Halloween would never be the same either.

If Lisa had been drugged, what if Gremmie had ingested the same stuff? Who knew what he could've done. Or, he could've left with other revelers to a less-crowded party, and being inebriated, crashed there. Or perhaps a carload of Dirgatory escapees headed to Malibu beach and, without a phone charger, Gremmie hadn't been able to contact him.

He'd be fine. He wasn't a child. Just a little bit.

THERE WAS a knock on the doorframe to the office. It was Jewelya, from the party last night. Now dressed in yoga pants, a T-shirt, and a hoodie. Hair in a loose ponytail. She waved by means of wiggling her fingers in the air. "You said I should come by?" she said.

"Yeah, hi." Kick began to stand up, but gave up midway when his T-shirted beer belly scraped the edge of the desk, as he hadn't pushed his chair back far enough. He wasn't that much overweight. Just soft. That was why he usually wore a second shirt, an open button-up, to drape at his sides. Less figure to see. Fewer curves. But it was the thought, the gesture of standing for a guest, that counted. "Come in. Did you get any sleep?"

When she entered, he caught the aroma of caramel. Sweet, mildly burnt sugar. He didn't recall that last night.

"Yeah," Jewelya said. She seemed to have less confidence now, too. "Somewhat. But I had a nightmare about that Lisa girl. Have you heard anything?"

"I guess she's still in surgery. Kat's at the hospital with her. Elijah's covering up front."

"Is she going to be okay?"

"I don't know. They say as long as she doesn't get an infection, she'll probably live. Her eyes, though, I don't know."

"I don't see how...they were just, you know," Jewelya hesitated. Then she lifted her chin, her tone. A show of strength. "Ainsley wasn't there last night when I got home. He never came back from the party."

Kick didn't want to hear that, but half-expected it. "That's horrible." That sounded like he was implying the worst. "Or curious, whatever." Now he sounded flippant. "Gremmie didn't come home either."

"Or maybe he did." Jewelya was holding two phones, stacking them together. Still sort of nervous.

Kick gestured to the chair for her to sit. *Try to relax,* he wanted to say, but didn't. Jewelya sat down. "I talked to the police today," he said. "They don't want me to file anything until we're sure people aren't just off together partying or something."

"Well, my husband doesn't do drugs. How many missing people do they need?"

"There are more," Kick said. "Yksian called last night asking if I knew where Dirge's wife, Summer, went."

"Her too?" Jewelya clicked her phones together. Perhaps that extra one was Chikao's. That guy. "Did you find any more phones lying around?" she said.

She may have been thinking similarly to Kick.

"Are your referring to how Chikao was always looking for a phone?" Kick said.

"He was awkward when he asked if I'd seen his phone at the end of the night," Jewelya said. "I mean, why ask me? I only saw him one time at a Lodge. Do you think he's got something to do with all this?"

Kick wasn't sure how much he should be implicating somebody here, especially an Omniscian involved with the Emporium. People were missing, but there was no evidence of a crime. "I don't think so." But this also felt like too much of a misdirection. "I mean, I'm not sure. He's always been fascinated with the Omnist, the Emporium, and me and Connie. I just offered him a job helping me relaunch the app, but he turned it down. That kind of blew me away. I think like six months ago he would've jumped at the chance."

"So he's interested in the Omnist, but not that interested?"

"You could say that," Kick said. "He's an odd guy. He's like a caricature of a distracted scientist. He can solve the problems of the universe but doesn't know how to use a laundry machine. I've seen him misplace three or four phones at the Emporium alone. And he's a lot older than he looks. He looks fifty but is probably in his seventies, maybe even eighty."

"Yeah, he sounds like an interesting guy." Jewelya crossed one leg over the other, her foot moving more than her mouth. Her lips were stiff, like she was trying to keep them from quivering. She looked worried.

"Basically." Kick began to channel Gremmie, ever the optimist. "Watch, we're going to find out a half-dozen people all drove out to the desert to eat mushrooms and watch sunsets and sunrises. Sleep during the day. Gremmie's the type who goes to Burning Man and other desert festivals. I'm not saying that's what he's doing, but we can't rule it out yet. Has Ainsley ever done that?"

"He'd like to give you the impression he does, but no." Jewelya sat up. "I have an idea though." She placed one of the phones on the desk and, without leaning back again, began turning the other one in her hand.

"I charged Ainsley's phone overnight in case he called or something. I don't know, habit. I guess he could've called my phone, too, but he didn't. And then this..." Jewelya unlocked the phone in her hands.

"You know his passcode?" Kick said. *Impressive.*

"We have the same one. There should be no secrets between us." She muttered something else beneath her breath. "Now this, I can't say this out loud. But read it to yourself."

Being concerned with technology and security, Kick wouldn't share a passcode with anyone. Then again, he didn't have a wife. He sincerely hoped this couple's code wasn't something easy to guess, like a birthday or anniversary.

Jewelya handed him the phone. "They're Motes from the Omnist," she said. "But different. If you click on one, it goes to a chat."

The Omnist wasn't social media, so it wasn't set up to communicate with other users. The Mote had taken her to a section where a user could pose questions to the Omnist itself. Really, though, it was the Omnist's AI. But it shouldn't be able to reach out and contact her on its own.

"You received chat notifications as if they were Motes?" Kick said.

"Yeah. The first two are from Ainsley, I think," Jewelya said. "On *his* phone."

JJ, it's me

Do not, I repeat, DO NOT, read any Motes out loud

"I take it you're JJ?" Kick said. He had chosen the AI's text color, garnet, which was a reddish brown, but now, with Jewelya's presence changing his anchoring, he thought it looked more like caramel.

"That's why I couldn't just tell you what he said," Jewelya said, ignoring his question. "I had to show you. What do you think would happen to me if I read these out loud?"

Kick shrugged. He had a suspicion that probably nothing would happen, as these weren't actual Motes, just a conversation with an AI chatbot. He continued reading.

Baby is this really you? Jewelya had written. Her text was written in a shade of hunter's green. Kick liked the earthiness of the two colors, but now he was hung up on the "hunter" part of the green.

I'm in the phone now. I think reading Motes out loud did this

In garnet. Not what he wanted to see. No wonder she was so upset.

Were you in the maze when this happened? Jewelya wrote.

Yes, Ainsley wrote.

Going to see Kick at CSE. Hoping he can help. In hunter's green.

I know, I was there when you guys made plans

Are you dead? she texted.

I don't know, but as long as you keep the phone with you, I'm with you

We'll figure this out, she texted.

"As odd as this sounds," Jewelya said, "reading his last text makes me feel better. That he's right here, and I can keep him with me. Because that's how I feel, too."

"We should also consider that something's wrong with the Omnist's AI," Kick said. He didn't want to destroy her fantasy or make her feel worse, but he needed to keep this realistic. "A lot of the app is my work, and I've never seen it do this before. I may not be the best at chatbot functions."

"Are you saying it's pretending to be Ainsley?" she said. "Why would it do that?"

He didn't know. But people, while experiencing trauma, could think a lot of different things. It was survival mode. "Did you guys fill out the extra questions Chikao suggested at the Lodge?"

"We did. Maybe I messed something up?"

"Or maybe the Omnist actually thinks it's Ainsley now." This was a lot to think about. Ainsley could be missing, passed out somewhere (or, dare he suggest, making poor decisions), while the Omnist, in an unrelated event, took on his personality. That was a more likely scenario. "I want to go back to Dirge's. See if he knows about any more missing people or phones. Besides, I got crazy vibes from the hookah room."

Kick had felt that, for real. He was wrapping his thoughts around an idea: With that section being the farthest from the house, it may have been his secret mancave. Dirge had said he liked to escape and find quiet time alone. Maybe Gremmie had found that space, as well.

TWENTY-FIVE

JEWELYA

L ast night, before Jewelya left Dirgatory, Kick had suggested she meet him at Consumia's Spiritual Emporium. She'd never been there before without the intention of shopping or catching a Lodge. She felt peculiar walking up the sidewalk, like she was playing hooky from her regular life. She was, in a way, having canceled today's classes.

Despite her sunglasses, the sunlight was bright, irritating her as it bounced up off her cheekbones and into her eyes. The mix of dried leaves, smoke from a fireplace somewhere, freshly deposited urine, and traffic exhaust gave this stretch of Lankershim a distinctly autumn L.A.—no, *North Hollywood* —scent.

This light reminded her of the nightmare she'd had last night. Lisa, the Wonder Woman with the stunning eyes and vacant demeanor when Jewelya had first seen her at Dirgatory, was a transient in weeks-old clothes, sitting on the sidewalk along this same stretch of Lankershim across the street from the Emporium. And in place of her radiant, magnetic eyes, were black holes that seemed to extend into a dark universe, blacker than any black she'd ever seen. Like a cobweb mirror. Lisa was holding out cupped hands, but rather than asking for money or restaurant leftovers, she was begging for light.

"Please," she said. "Any light you can spare."

But there was light everywhere. And the sun in the dream was bright, just like this, and Jewelya felt helpless, unable to provide. She'd been told as a young girl she was a ray of sunshine for anyone who beheld the tiny dancer, but here was proof that she wasn't. "I'm sorry," Jewelya said.

Tears began dripping from frustrated Lisa's eyes, and Jewelya half-expected them to be tiny black drops of forever. But they weren't. And they weren't just clear, like normal teardrops, but utterly flawless, pure. And such clarity meant they refracted light in a way she'd never seen before. All of the colors, not just those in a rainbow or soap bubble, but ones without names she couldn't picture while awake, that separated into more vivid, striking prisms of light. These tears were the inner Lisa leaking out as her body shrank in front of Jewelya, tinier and tinier.

Jewelya tried reaching for her hands, but they receded as Lisa shrank as fast as Jewelya could extend herself. Lisa was the size of a human baby now, with enormous black eyes, then a kitten, a mouse pup, until she disappeared completely into her own blackest of black holes.

That was when Jewelya had woken up.

At the Emporium's entrance now, one of their double glass doors wasn't closed all the way—the left one—so she pulled on it and entered. The light was different inside at eleven a.m. than it would be just a few hours later. More shaded, like the resident dust hadn't woken up yet. Much of the store's light still came from outside. Angular sunlight bounced off passing cars, flashing annoyingly bright through the Emporium's front windows, flaunting the store's cleanliness from the evils outside. This was a safe place.

Some people were buying lunch, with a few Consumerians gathered by the refrigerators or near the organic, vegan snacks. Something Jewelya had never thought about: buying a meal at CSE. But she supposed it wasn't much different than getting something at the coffee shop near her studio. She could've done this back when Ainsley was watching football with his friends. A mildly overpriced, but healthier option than his offerings.

She suddenly had the urge to conduct yoga classes in the Basil Alcove. She knew CSE hosted A.A. and N.A. meetings a couple days a week before they normally opened. Why not yoga? She should ask Connie about that.

"Welcome," a young college-aged boy purred at her from behind the counter. He was skinny, some kind of hippie-ish nerd. It wasn't quite the male gaze she often noticed from men. But almost. More "boy gaze." "Let me know if you need anything," he said.

She nodded. Her mind began racing about how she was going to bring up the Ainsley situation to Kick.

SHE'D BEEN SPEAKING with Kick in the back office, and showed him the messages that looked like they were from Ainsley. When Kick hesitated, warning the messages could be AI, she got a sickly feeling that she'd been conned. She'd wanted so badly to believe she'd found him, but of course he wasn't in the phone. What'd she been thinking?

Kick suggested that they return to Dirgatory, so he tried calling Dirge, but got his voicemail. He then texted him. "I think he's at work," Kick said. "I'll let you know when he gets back to me."

A new Mote appeared on Ainsley's phone. Or rather, it was a notification that looked like a Mote.

It's really me in here. Ainsley. I can hear you guys

"Does anyone have a void I can scream into?" Jewelya said, as much for Ainsley's sake as Kick's.

You can use mine. There's not much here though

"I'm sorry?" Kick said.

"He says he can hear us," Jewelya said. She caught her breath. *What if he really is in there?*

"The AI would have access to the microphone," Kick said.

I've gotten pretty good at jumping levels. Smaller to send messages, then slightly bigger to see and listen to you. Nearly instantaneous, I think. But time seems distorted

"Do you think the Omnist has achieved consciousness?" Jewelya said.

"I don't see how. That's not how the algorithm works. What it spits out is based on what it's fed. It's not programmed to think it's conscious."

Of course I'm conscious

Jewelya was struggling to nurse two opposing ideas simultaneously. "You have to admit it's pretty weird," she said. She felt waxen. No blood left in her face.

"Imagine granting an AI access to all your emails, browser history, photographs, even your finances," Kick said. "Imagine how effective it would be at fooling you."

Part of Jewelya wanted to ask the perfect question that Ainsley, and only he, could answer, so he could prove himself. But she also shouldn't personify a chatbot, which may have access to all the contents in Ainsley's phone. She held out hope that he'd come home himself. Worst-case scenario: *Ainsley is dead and this chatbot is pretending to be him.*

"Ainsley," Kick said. "If you can hear me, just hang on a second. Don't type anything."

Nothing appeared on the phone's screen.

"So now you believe it's him?" Jewelya said.

"The Omnist may respond better to the name," Kick said. "But I want to check something. What's his phone number?"

"Eight—" she said, but Kick stopped her by holding up his finger, then pointed at the phone. The microphone.

"Here, write it down," he said, sliding a pen and stack of sticky notes at her. "I have Consumerians categorized by their phone numbers."

"I'd think the AI virus would already know that."

"Maybe, maybe not. But there's more to it. I want to search his history of Motes," Kick said, pivoting to his laptop. Click. Scroll. Pause. "Huh, I didn't write a lot of these recent ones. Nor did Raine. This language, I don't know what it is...Huh." He paused again. "Now the 'Don't read Motes out loud' thing makes more sense. Have you seen any like this?" Kick spun his computer around so she could read it.

It looked familiar. "I did, but I only read one of them," Jewelya said. "Not out loud, though."

"Let me check Gremmie's, as well." Kick scrolled his phone, probably for the number, then went back to the laptop.

This was unnerving. Somebody was stealing more than identities, but entire people, souls—her husband.

"I need Lisa's phone number," Kick said. "I don't want to bother Kat, but..." He typed on his phone.

Jewelya wished the Omnist would send her a message. Even if it wasn't really Ainsley, there was something reassuring about the tone. It was getting him just right. Unnerved, concerned, trying to figure out the world around him.

"Kat responded right away," Kick said. "She says she's 'sitting, waiting, tired, worried, and bored at the hospital.'"

Kick resumed working at the computer.

"Have you even tried asking Chikao?" Jewelya said.

Kick stopped. "Um, yeah...no," he said, scratching forcefully at one side of his beard. "Sort of. I mean, what can you really say? I texted last night to see if he'd heard anything about Summer, since Yksian saw them talking. He said no."

"I mean, have you asked him about the Omnist?"

"I wouldn't know how." Kick changed his voice to sound like he was imitating a popular cartoon charter, Boner Sampson. "'Hey Chikao, you didn't happen to hack the Omnist, did you?' Even if he had he wouldn't admit it, and then he'd know we were on to him. And if he hadn't, I'd have just ruined our business relationship forever."

"It's just the timing of it all," Jewelya said. "That's all."

"I also want to talk to Veris," Kick said. "She's holding two Lodges today for All Saints Day. One this afternoon, then another tonight."

When they left the office, the Consumerians bustling in the Emporium had grown from six people to fifteen in ten minutes —possibly there for Veris's appearance.

Jewelya received three straight texts from Denkins.

Kyle's safe! In bed when I got home. Not mad anymore.

Sorry no text. Next level party

U still my baby girl and he still my baby boy

She replied with an emoji sigh of relief. One missing person was accounted for. Denkins was crazy for holding classes today. He must've been hurting this morning, trying to sweat it out.

He sees me kiss other guys and just shrugs. But you, LOL, Denkins texted.

Jewelya responded with a kissy face. She couldn't begin to explain the Ainsley situation via text.

THIRTY MINUTES LATER, and with sixty people in the room, Veris's Lodge was about to begin. Many people were dressed in calaca and calavera makeup. A few girls were dressed as catrinas, the beautiful, skull-faced ladies, young and old.

Compared to Dirgatory, this event felt more respectable, elegant. More Jewelya's speed. But now, in a T-shirt and yoga pants, she felt underdressed. But she was just killing time until she and Kick could go see Dirge.

Still no messages from *AI-nsley*, either. Apparently, it/he took Kick's suggestion and wasn't saying anything. She supposed either one would be able to follow instructions.

Kick arrived at Jewelya's side. "Hey," he said. "After Veris's Lodge, we can head over to Dirge's; he should be home by then. He's only working a half day today, seven hours! Actually, he said he usually takes the day after Dirgatory off, but you know how studios are. Deadlines."

Veris stepped onto the stage and Jewelya recognized her immediately.

"I met her last night," she told Kick. "She asked me if I'd been speaking with Chikao. I didn't know she was an Omniscian. I thought she was just a fan."

CHAPTER
TWENTY-SIX

KICK

K ick had finally spoken to Dirge just before Veris's Lodge was set to begin, and they set up a time to meet up. He couldn't leave until Connie got there, anyway, but another employee, Raine, was here to help out with the larger crowd. This freed Kick up to do a walk-through of the store, so he took his time wandering his way to Jewelya. This haunting the aisles thing was more something Connie did, as she had a talent for speaking with random people. But he was doing it more lately, drinking in the vibe. Omnist II would be a sister store, yes, but it needed its own personality, and the goal was to not only make it a home for the locals, but a destination for travelers the way CSE was. Anyone in the world could use the Omnist app, so many people visited the Emporium as a rite of passage. By naming the new store Omnist II, they hoped to acquire that secondary traffic as well.

The two celebration days of Día De Los Muertos had begun. And the host, Adelie Veris, was a ghost hunter, a spirit chaser. Correction, she followed *souls*, not spirits. It was a distinction she'd made to Connie after the store owner accidentally mislabeled her. Veris wasn't quite a ghost hunter; in her words, she was a "soul connector." And seeing how she emanated life from the core of her being, the clarification was obvious once you met her.

MOTE:

Remember the dead because they remember you.

KICK HAD HOPED Veris would've arrived early enough to speak with him and Jewelya, but Elijah said she pretty much ran straight to the stage with her Día De Los Muertos basket and asked him to help her with a couple stools and the microphone stand, the latter of which was set too tall for her.

The Emporium had sold more Day of the Dead merch this season than in years past. Wire figures of skeletons decorated to represent dead people, like a man sitting at a computer, a baseball player in a batting stance, a woman singing in front of a microphone, or another nursing a baby. Wearing doctor scrubs or teaching in front of a tiny chalkboard. Black umbrellas (or parasols) with smiling, white skulls on them.

Veris had been selling Día De Los Muertos altar kits leading up to her appearance today. She'd put so much thought into these, they were worth the price. And the hand-decorated frames and brass bells included would last for decades.

Kick found Jewelya—they made plans to leave after the Lodge—and stood next to her to listen to Veris.

"Souls are everywhere!" Veris said from the stage. Arms

raised, they looked like branches waving in the wind. She was green, maybe evergreen. Full of life and ancient wisdom.

"We chase souls," she said, lowering her arms. "But they always seem to elude us. Where do they go? How far can we follow them? If there is a heaven, what is it? Where is it? The souls seem so far away from us, yet they remain as close as a prayer."

Veris's thick glasses looked like they could see directly into the spirit world. She was spherical in a way that made her look sturdy, like a tree trunk, with a low center of gravity.

"Regardless, today is All Saints Day, the day to call the souls of beloved children into our homes. Tomorrow, All Souls Day, is aimed toward the adults who have passed. Regardless, you can celebrate all through the season. This week is a particularly liminal time. The dead are closer to us, the living, than any other time of year."

As she spoke, Veris made arm motions as if picking fruit off a tree, the points of her stories, the fruits of her labors. These weren't fast or jerky actions, but smooth and elegant.

"The souls, they are us. We are them. They are human without human form. Tired without sleep, awake without goals. Hungry and thirsty without food or water. My kits help address these issues."

She gestured to the end cap near the door that featured her Día De Los Muertos kits.

"At first I was hesitant to speak about the kits I make, but Connie talked me into it. I'm providing a service, she said, and people will appreciate my good intentions. So that provides the topic for today: Why did I pick these items?"

There were a couple stools on stage, and the nearest one had a basket on it. The kit's cellophane wrapping had already been removed. First, she held up a couple frames that contained photos of a dark-haired man with a mustache.

"Frames for pictures, of course. For the soul of the person you're reconnecting with.

"Figurines, too." She held up a wire-limbed version of a man skiing. The appendages looked bendable. "Skis and poles for the outdoorsy type. Now, these items represent our loved ones. You can augment your own kits with figures to match their personalities and tastes. You can also make your own, and my website has explainers about how to make some popular ones, or you can buy them here at the Emporium."

She held up two more, both with mustaches, as well. "Or a man sitting at a computer, or a cowboy hat and a lasso for a rancher—whatever their interests are.

"Since we all look the same underneath our skin, my favorite item is the sugar skull." Veris posed with a skull in a Shakespearean manner, as if about to soliloquize. She held still until enough of her audience had caught on to the reference and laughed. The number of Consumerians had swelled to about seventy.

"After all, life is sweet." Veris winked.

The power of suggestion brought the scent of caramel and burnt sugar back to Kick's awareness. It was Jewelya. He sincerely hoped that didn't mean her husband was dead. Jewelya, with watering eyes, was completely focused on what Veris was saying. Perhaps the computer-programming figurine had gotten to her.

Veris lifted a small bouquet of fresh marigolds. She separated it into two halves and held them out at arm's length. She inhaled deeply with her eyes closed. "You needn't have passed on in order to enjoy this wonderful fragrance. This scent attracts souls as well as the living. The kits up front have only dried flowers, which is fine, but if you buy one today, I'll throw in fresh ones for free. Also, even without the fresh scent, all baskets include copal incense to attract souls via smell. Almost as good as marigolds."

Apparently, despite Connie's tales of having to convince Veris to sell merchandise, she had the sales pitch down. Veris lifted a pack of multicolored tissue paper. "Arts time!"

Some Consumerians cheered. The children, especially.

From the pack, she removed a folded white paper that looked like a snowflake cutout children made in winter, but when she unfolded it, it was revealed to be a skull.

A few *oohs* and *aahs*.

"Feel free to make your own patterns. This pack here can either be a serving suggestion for ideas, or you can just use these ones yourself if you don't feel all that artsy. Look through them; the designs are all different."

She refolded the paper and put the package back in the basket.

"The important part here is we're creating spaces in the paper that allow the passage of souls to come visit us. That's how thin the membranes are this time of year, that a piece of tissue paper acts as a door. And its delicateness symbolizes the fragility of life."

Ugh. Needing a paper cutout for Gremmie to reach me. Or for Ainsley.

On another stool were several sweet breads broken into small pieces on a serving platter. She popped a piece into her mouth and handed the plate to a woman in front to pass along.

"Pan de muerto," Veris said. "Sweet bread of the dead. Not vegan. Not gluten-free. If these sell well this year, I will make vegan and gluten-free versions next year."

She held up two wrapped loaves to show what they look like whole.

"I don't know if you can see from a distance, but one of these has the image of a skull baked into it and the other has crossbones. All dusted with sugar. Souls will be hungry upon their return. They won't be able to eat these, per se, but they can enter the food and absorb its nutrients. But you can eat all you like. You won't be eating them; and they don't want you to suffer, either."

Veris held up a couple small bottles of water. "Obvious," she said, and put them back in the basket.

She picked up a small ceramic container shaped like a skull. "Salt," she said. "For making a cross on the table or shelf. Use lots, be liberal. By the way, you need not be a Christian to do these things. Christians believe the cross keeps evil spirits at bay, but really, the salt cleanses the spirits no matter what pattern you pour. I like to sprinkle it in the shape of a skull, then throughout the celebration, salt my margarita glasses with it."

Laughter from the audience. A customer up front asked a question Kick couldn't hear.

"Oh, certainly," Veris said, "Salt water flats would be a great place to meditate and speak to spirits."

She held up the small collection of picture frames. "I like to make individual altars for each soul I intend to address, rather than combining several into one. But to each their own."

She looked at her basket as if forgetting something. "Oh yeah," she said, holding up a couple pint-sized glass containers. "Candles. I like to load up on them, but there are only two in this particular kit. You can buy more like I do. A store like this, where they have such a nice selection, is such a treat."

Veris scooted both stools farther back on the stage.

"Now, for our regularly scheduled programming. I get asked a lot: Do you believe in reincarnation?" Veris paused for a rippled response. Most replied in the affirmative. "I do. Some souls are free-range, that's what I call them, those without a body, but that doesn't mean they don't come back to the living. I like to help them do that, if I can.

"How old do you think I look?" Veris made a face, jutting out her lower lip and crinkling her forehead. She laughed. "I won't tell. But I was told as a child I was mature for my age, and now, I hear that I seem young for my age. So what does *that* mean?"

"You look great!" an Executive Saint named Leandra said.

Veris smiled, her eyes bright through her glasses. "In general, the more mature your soul, the better," she said. "And to grow, certain things have to be learned while you're human. Cooperation, love, support, acceptance, knowledge, and more. These all help to lead a soul to reincarnation. From the perspective of an eighty-year-old, reincarnation can seem strange, exotic, or a fantastical goal to attain. But from the perspective of a soul, living again is as normal as waking up each day is to us."

Another question was asked from up front.

"That may lead to a loose soul," Veris said. "Not to avenge a wrong. Life isn't a Hollywood movie. Reincarnation isn't about unfinished business, unless you were supposed to learn something. My theory is that free-range souls can congregate, learn to cooperate, and then move on together as a multifaceted super-soul. And yes, some of us *are* already super-souls."

This should be in the video game.

KAT ENTERED THE STORE, distracted, ignoring the Consumerians trying to greet her. She was still wearing last night's costume, although there was no makeup left. Her eyes were irritated from a miserable night. She practically ran to Kick.

"Lisa says don't read the Motes!" she said.

"What?" Kick said. *I know.*

"Lisa!" Jewelya said. "How is she?"

"She's out of surgery, and she's alive." Kat said, sounding more than a little annoyed. "Now what the fuck are you doing with the Omnist?"

"It's not me," Kick said. "I don't know, I—"

"She says the Motes drove her to do that. The Omnist is evil and was trying to control her. She had to stop it."

Holy shit. "You know I'd never do that. Besides, technology for mind control doesn't even exist. Just ask Chikao."

"You need to talk to Lisa," Kat said. "She said she felt woozy, like she was disappearing. She figured if she couldn't see the Motes, she couldn't read them. It wanted her to say a spell that was going to kill her."

"Yeah, no," Kick said, "we've definitely been hacked. I looked up her recent Motes and those prayers were written in a language I've never seen before. Not quite Latin, which has a lot of words that look like English, but something else."

Jewelya didn't look well at all. He touched her arm. "That doesn't mean Ainsley's gone," he said, almost adding in the word "necessarily." *But it might.*

"Why would someone want the Omnist to kill people?" Jewelya said, looking like she was holding back a flood of emotion.

"I don't know," Kick said. "There are evil religions, I guess."

"Maybe you're promoting an evil ideology," Kat said. That was unfair, but she was understandably upset. "She'll never see again, you know that, right? Because of the Omnist! You did this, Kick!"

"Kat, you know me, I would never—"

"And even if you didn't do this directly, you allowed it. Letting ideas swirl and combine into a religion that literally kills its members."

It didn't make sense. "At least a religion like that wouldn't last long," Kick said.

"Fuck you."

"As horrible as this sounds," Kick said, pausing for a calming breath, "you guys may be right. The AI may have developed its own sabotaging religion."

Kat looked incredulous, shaking her head as if the words were rattling around in there. This was subtle, as were most of her movements. "So you admit it?" she said.

"No, I mean, I don't know. Part of me wonders if Chikao can help here," he said. "And by the way, have you met Jewelya? Her husband is missing and it could be because of the Motes, too."

Kat looked at Jewelya and softened. "Yes, of course," she said, almost sighing. "I'm sorry you haven't found your husband, yet."

"I sort of did," Jewelya said.

The Lodge was over and Consumerians began dissipating, greeting each other, including Kick and Kat. They would continue this conversation when things finally died down.

AFTER THE LODGE, the three of them plus Veris reconvened in the office where they caught up on the events of the last twenty or so hours: missing people like Gremmie, Ainsley, and Summer, plus Lisa's ghastly self-mutilation. And these were just the people they knew about.

"They tried to save her eyes," Kat said. "She'd be blind either way, but they tried to save them in her head. But they were too far gone, and they had to cut them out."

"But her soul survived," Veris said. "She's the first person I've heard who fought and survived a spell like that."

"So you've seen this before?" Kat said.

"I'm always searching for souls trapped in objects. Some are a few years old, some hundreds of years, even thousands. And from what I can tell, many were cursed using this other language. It's called Language of the Sun. But I've yet to see it in action."

"And through our own app," Kick said. He was sure to take the blame once the story hit the media. He saw what Connie had gone through after Javy died in the Dark Arts room; it was now his turn. "If it's a hacker, then I should've tried harder to find weak spots. If it's the AI turning on us, it must've learned that language from somewhere. Either way, this is on me."

"It's not your fault," Veris said.

"The best tech expert we have just hosted a Lodge," Kick said. "Chikao. I knew we needed to relaunch the app with tighter security. I was hoping he'd help. I should ask him again."

CHAPTER
TWENTY-SEVEN

AINSLEY

F rustrated, Ainsley began enlarging and shrinking himself repeatedly, faster and faster, until he felt like he'd become pure energy. He was simultaneously expending excess energy and recharging. His movement, his streaking, created white light spanning billions of years. But not billions of light miles horizontally. Vertically was the wrong word, too, as on this plane the vertical was the same as horizontal. This was a new axis, an axis of size.

He was a star without need of fuel.

A black hole without gravity.

When he saw other vectors of consciousness spiraling around him, they looked curved, the way light bent near a black hole. This hadn't been apparent as a person, but it was obvious now. His own vector, from within, looked straight. Like a stick inside a ball of cotton candy that the other vectors twirled and wrapped around confusingly. He assumed that to those other souls, their vectors looked straight to them, as well. Like fiber optics. Consciousness blinked on and off so quickly it looked permanently illuminated.

If his theory was correct, that was due to the speed of light slowing and leaving afterimages. That's what he'd been doing. He could change size faster than the speed of light because he wasn't actually spanning any distance. He was creating and contracting space. The speed of light was the top speed matter could move, but by changing size, like how the universe expanded, he could be faster.

Something else was happening. Maybe his mind was evaporating. The end result could be nonexistence. Even in darkness there were countless frequencies of waves moving about. This new sensation was an absence of those waves, like they'd been sucked away.

The blackest black; the darkest dark.

Ainsley was startled when he heard a voice.

"Tell her to give up phone. Leave it outside. On dumpster."

Ainsley didn't respond. He couldn't place who it was. The voice somehow used the entire spectrum of sound, the lows lower than he'd ever heard, and the highs the highest, as well. In his current condition, the voice was unrecognizable and ubiquitous.

"I know you can hear. But I cannot release you until I have phone."

Ainsley dared not send a message to Jewelya and Kick, nor expand or contract in case the other soul—he assumed it was a soul—noticed and wrestled this vessel from him.

"You're not supposed to be here."

He didn't trust this voice. His instinct was to try to not think. If this was telepathy, he needed the voice to believe he wasn't there.

"You'll die if you remain. You must read counter-spell after I retrieve phone."

So why wait? Provide that counter-spell now.

"Have Jewelya leave phone somewhere close. Don't make me take it by force."

When it was apparent the voice had completed their message, color came back to the world, and inside the phone, much of it was the color of radioactivity. He'd been unaware of all the color in blackness until now. Nothing could be as dark as he'd experienced a moment ago. The wicked spirit had left.

This brush with evil inside his coffin-phone was the first time he'd felt frightened in years. The device, a symbol of independence while he was alive, had become one of containment afterward. Jonah was inside his whale.

Ainsley had spent his life avoiding thinking about his inevitable death, hoping a narrative would present itself on its own. And now that was happening. The voice had threatened Jewelya and him. He needed to get out, to be with her, to make things normal again. To make weekend brunch to eat on the patio. Tall, iced beverages in the afternoon shade. Maybe a child to mirror Mommy's movements as they exercised in the day room together.

He now had a goal. Something he hadn't thought about before. It was more than just getting out and reembodying for his own sake. Things had taken on more meaning. Perhaps he was already dead, but he no longer feared dying. It was liberating.

Still, he feared Jewelya being harmed. For a measly phone. There was no reason to think he and Jewelya would be together after she died. It was possible his and her vector only crossed one time in that one life in one nano-thin section of spacetime. An infinitesimally small membrane with billions of light years existing in all directions. But these particular emotions were tied there. That was where the curse had happened. That was where he belonged.

He was alone, but not lonely. Numb, but not without feeling.

There was much to do and live and experience and learn on that mortal coil. If only he could return. He had a life to continue, to fulfill.

With Jewelya.

When he expanded to check on her, there was a change in hue inside the Emporium's office. Ainsley's color palette, previously vast and intense, was now fading. Everything had dimmed close to gray, into a murkier darkness. Glass and windows were smokier, too, almost as if light were moving a different speed now. He decided the relative distance between the wavelengths of light wasn't changing—which happened when a receding star looked redder—it was more like time itself was staggering.

Jewelya was speaking with Kick and Kat at the Emporium, as well as with a smaller woman he didn't know. Out of habit, he called out, "Jewels! JJ!"

They couldn't hear him.

CHAPTER
TWENTY-EIGHT

KICK

Connie arrived at the Emporium while Kick and the other three were in her office.

"Kat, you should go home," she said as she entered like a high-pressure weather front, bringing warmth and positivity. Unlike Kat's appearance, it was clear Connie was in full court reporter-mode. A power suit with black blazer, slacks, and a blue button-up.

"Sending me home again?" Kat said. "You did this to me after Jesse died."

"Because you don't take care of yourself." Connie shooed Kick out of her chair. He acquiesced. "We gave you the day off because we care about you."

Connie took out her computer from her bag. She was moving in a different mode than the rest of them. Not oblivious, necessarily, but focused.

"Connie," Kick said. "We're headed to Dirge's. I'll fill you in on everything later." He seriously didn't want to go over everything yet again.

"Would you guys come out to my rental with me?" Veris said to Kick.

"Of course."

Veris was hosting a second Lodge in a couple hours, but there were still quite a few people mingling out front. Kick suggested the group exit through the Dark Arts room's fire door so they wouldn't be railroaded by well-intentioned Consumerians. He held the door open for Jewelya, Veris, and Kat.

"Chivalry is antiquated," Kat deadpanned as she passed.

"I'll take that as a thank you," Kick said.

The early evening sky was in the midst of internal conflict about whether it should rain or not. The sun was a pickled pearl onion. The overcast sky mashed potatoes streaked with the residue of weak gravy.

Veris was parked in a rare spot in the street. She popped the trunk to reveal a carry-on bag, and nothing else. When she unzipped it, it was full of smartphones.

"I found this bag in his hotel room last night while he was at the party. These are from Phoenix and San Diego, I think."

"Chikao?" Kick said. "You broke into his hotel room?"

"It's really not that difficult. I'm his wife, don't you know?" Veris said this with such nonaggressive confidence, no front desk clerk would disbelieve her.

Kick hadn't taken her for being deceitful.

"Ha," Kat said, more impressed than he was.

"And really, who would report a missing bag of stolen smartphones?" Veris said.

"I bet a few of these are from CSE, too," Kat said.

"Correction," Veris said. "Phoenix, San Diego, and L.A."

"I don't get it. He's stealing phones," Kick said. "He doesn't need them."

"He's stealing *souls*," Veris said. "These are merely the vessels that he carries them in."

"How'd you know he was doing this?" Kat said.

"I attended a signing of his in Portland at Powell's Bookstore for his book, *Programming the Soul: Easy Instructions for a Longer, Healthier Life.*"

It was the same one Chikao signed for fans two nights ago at CSE.

"He began his reading by extolling the virtues of the Omnist. I didn't know much about the app, but I made a mental note to check it out. He was showing people how to maximize the Omnist's effects. He called the incantations 'programming language for the soul.'"

"That's not creepy," Jewelya said.

"He said the mind is the greatest processor," Veris said. "With 'a billion-billion calculations a second. Use it to your advantage.'

"Afterward, I saw him walking the aisles of the store. Powell's is famous for having many rooms in which to browse books, and I watched him pick up a phone off the floor. I sensed souls crying for help. I kept following him. I was curious, you know? He found at least three in just a few minutes."

"Same thing he did here," Kick said. "So that's why you began following him?"

"Uh-hm," Veris said. "The last time Chikao was in town, did he meet with you and Connie?"

"Yes," Kick said.

"And he asked a lot of questions, wanted to know how the Omnist worked. Didn't you find that odd?"

"I see where you're going with this," Kick said. "He learned what he needed to learn."

"I believe he hacked into the Omnist and squatted there, buying time," Veris said. "He didn't steal or clone identities, or raid bank accounts. He doesn't need money; he needs souls. You didn't notice anything weird in the app on your end, did you?"

"What's to notice? You just said he didn't steal anything." Kick's beard was itching again.

"No, but he started sending out his own Motes."

"Right. So he not only used AI to steal identities, you're saying he used it to steal entire people, including their souls," Kick said. Again, more reason to feel this was his fault. He wanted to scrap the app and rebuild it from scratch. Or destroy it all together.

MOTE:

If a mind can develop spirituality, so can AI.

NOW THE OMNIST was just taunting him. He decided not to mention this to the others.

"So you followed Chikao here," Jewelya said to Veris. "Can you get Ainsley out of this phone?" She seemed to be treating it gingerly.

"That's the goal," Veris said. "I've been investigating people who have been disappeared by Korekuta. I believe there are souls in all these phones."

"Who's Korekuta?" Kat said.

"I believe that's Chikao's real name. I'll explain:

"After seeing Chikao at Powell's, I went home and researched soul-stealing myths and found a Japanese site, roughly translated, that talked about Korekuta, an ancient god who stole souls. He'd become a village shaman to gain the townspeople's trust. He had learned that often just by touching somebody, they healed themselves—a placebo, if you will—but they credited him with success. So they listened when he instructed them to recite lines of a prayer. It was almost too easy for him. Korekuta stored the souls in Dogu, which were clay figurines the ancients used to deposit their illnesses and worries into.

"For others, though, he'd work them into a trance, and once there, holding a rhinoceros horn, a tusk from an elephant, or a rack from a reindeer—maybe even a carved fertility figurine—they would recite the spell, cursing themselves into the very vessel held in their hands.

"He would then take the vessels and move on to the next village.

"Chikao may be his modern name. And if this is him, I think he's using the Omnist to effectively turn cell phones into Dogu."

"But why does he want souls?" Kat said.

"Now, this is just my theory, but imagine souls as an energy source. If he collected enough of them, thousands, they would burn as bright as the sun, as well as keep aging, disease, and enemies at bay within a certain radius of the fire. He'd have to keep this soul collection deep inside a cave so light or heat wouldn't give away its location. Near a volcano, perhaps. The resulting foliage on this mountainside would be lush, green, and full of wildlife. I'm sure Korekuta was then credited for the abundance of life and health about him. But I also saw ancient woodcuts of him as a demon with a pitchfork, spearing souls like floppy pancakes, flipping them into a cooking pot."

"Oh, fuck," Jewelya said. "Poor Ainsley."

"Wow," Kat said, flatly.

"And these woodcuts were Japanese?" Kick said.

"German. From what I can tell, he's originally Japanese,

but he got around. When people disappear around you, it's best to keep moving. You'll find most cultures have a similar villain. India, Africa, South America. I believe they're all aspects of the same god."

"So he *is* a god?" Jewelya said.

"In the sense that he's immortal, then yes," Veris said. "But only by burning a soul. And then, well, the energy is used up."

Jewelya visibly shuddered.

"But this is good," Kick said, trying to keep it positive. "You've collected a bunch of phones."

"Soul phones," Jewelya said. "And you can release the souls now."

"Once we figure out how," Veris said. "And there are likely a lot more out there."

CHAPTER
TWENTY-NINE

JEWELYA

"You know what," Veris said. "I should come with you to Dirge's house."

"Of course," Jewelya said. Veris's positive energy soothed her, as did the warmth from Ainsley's phone in her hoodie's pocket. It felt alive. She needed to believe this.

"Give me a few minutes," Veris said. "I want to make sure none of these lingering Consumerians have lost anyone."

"I have a question. What if the battery died in the phone?" Jewelya asked as they walked to the fire door for the Dark Arts room. It didn't open for customers from the outside, but Kick had a key. "Would he...er...the soul die, too?"

Kick held the door open again.

"No," Veris said. "They would still be trapped in the phone the way a spirit remained in, say, a carved figurine."

Veris walked in front of them through the Dark Arts room,

and stopped just inside its opening to the rest of the store. Just beyond was sort of the center of the Emporium, divided by an aisle separating the stage and Basil Alcove to the left, and the market of the Emporium along the right. Otherwise, walking ahead led all the way to the front door. "This is my compulsion, connecting with souls and auras," Veris said. "Five minutes."

The rest of the group returned to the office on the right. Connie wasn't there at the moment. Jewelya removed Ainsley from her pocket and placed him on the desk. It was like she was freeing him, or giving him air or something. She typed in their wedding date and opened the Omnist.

"Sorry we didn't believe you, honey," she said, as if on speaker phone. "It was probably dark in there."

"Whoa, whoa," Kick said, sounding defensive. "We still don't know if we're talking to an AI or not. His soul might be in the phone, but that doesn't mean we're actually talking to *him*."

"Ainsley, tell me which mirror is my favorite," Jewelya said, projecting her voice.

The smoked mirror in the living room

"So what do you think of that?" she said to Kick. He needed to stop this shit. Nobody was blaming him for someone hacking the app, and she could tell this really was Ainsley. *Wasn't it?*

"I don't know, man," Kick said. "How many mirrors do people really have?"

"I'm a dancer. I think most people would guess the wardrobe in our bedroom. Or the entire wall at the studio. A lot of people *love* that mirror."

But maybe it's the new cobweb mirror we were looking at last night

"See," Jewelya said, holding up the phone as if the others

could read it from a distance. "He knows about the new mirror I bought."

Listen, Jewels, a god-like voice just threatened us. It told me you're supposed to leave the phone outside by a dumpster. Or else

"Nope. Not going to happen," she said. "And we were just outside. Tell them they missed their chance."

Now you have no choice but to bring me everywhere with you :)

As if she wasn't going to, anyway.

"This chatbot is good," Kick said, craning his head to look at the phone. "We need to be careful."

"Seriously, Kick?" Jewelya said. But she knew better.

Kat finally left the Emporium to go home. Jewelya recognized that look on her face. If she could fall asleep, she'd be out for twelve hours. *If.* Back in the day, when Jewelya had traveled for shows, especially if there were multiple in a day, she would get like this. Without the pain of Kat's best friend's tragedy, that is.

Ainsley.

"So, Ains, do you have better taste in clothes now?" Seriously, if he had his way, a Los Angeles Rams T-shirt and a pair of unwashed, ill-fitting jeans would be all he'd wear.

Define taste

Veris was standing at the door to the office, watching Jewelya talking at Ainsley's phone. "If I didn't know any better," she said, "I'd say you were having a one-sided conversation."

"You've never been married, I take it," Jewelya said. "Any ideas how to release him?"

"Maybe he can recite a counter spell," Veris said. "But finding the right one is going to be difficult."

"Recite? Without a voice?"

"True," said Veris.

"We can research this with other Omniscians, too," Kick said. "Some of them are experts in witchcraft and sorcery."

"This is more difficult than generalized witchcraft," Veris said. "This communication is in a dead language. It may look and sound like someone trying to imitate Latin, but if I'm correct, it's older than humankind. To learn this would be like entering the hivemind of ancients. I believe this is the language of the universe."

"Can you understand it?" Jewelya said.

"Very little," Veris said. "I've only recently been learning about it. Korekuta would be fluent, I think."

"Can *you* understand it?" Jewelya said to the phone. No answer. "Sweetie, Ains, can you hear me?"

Ainsley wasn't responding. For a second, she thought he could be upset about the marriage joke, like when he used to get frustrated with her and go off by himself with his tablet.

"Is he gone?" Kick said.

"Maybe he figured out how to get out," Jewelya said. Half in jest, half hopeful. She lobbed another comment at the phone. "Stay away from the light!"

"Do you think that's a thing there?" Kick said. "We should tell the AI to head for the light."

Not bad. That's some Ainsley humor. It dawned on her that he and Kick were a lot more alike than she'd realized. Kick had a beard, of course. Maybe not so into football, but their humor. Their interest in technology. How their minds worked. If only she had a sister to introduce to him. Maybe a girl from one of her classes. Or maybe he liked guys. She knew a lot of free-spirited male dancers.

"I don't know," Veris said. "But we should ask him if he sees a light."

"I was just kidding," Jewelya said. *Ainsley would think it's funny, if he'd heard me.*

243

"I do feel as if he's left this plane," Veris said.

"Where would he go?" Kick said.

"Who knows?" Veris said. "The vastness and complexity of the universe is far beyond our capacity to understand."

THEY LEFT in Veris's car. Jewelya kept checking her phone for new messages from Ainsley, but there weren't any. A warm phone used to bother her, that it was somehow wasting energy, or emitting radiation, or about to blow up or melt down, but now, Ainsley's warmth was reassuring. He was alive.

"I'm still not sure Dirge hasn't been cooperating with Chikao," Kick said from the back seat. Jewelya was sitting shot-gun. "I know Summer's one of the people missing, and he wouldn't want that, of course, but maybe he didn't realize what he was getting into."

"Yksian too?" Jewelya said. She found him rather sketchy. Profound, but bougie. She preferred people who were more in touch with their emotions.

"Well, from what I understand, Korekuta works alone," Veris said. She apparently wouldn't call him Chikao. "And if others play a part, it's unwittingly. To be fair, I'm not accustomed to people knowing *my* plans, either."

"Are you about to tell me that Chikao, er, Korekuta, is your brother or father or something?" Kick said.

"No, nothing like that," Veris laughed. "In order to be honest in my endgame, I sometimes need to misdirect. Who would help me find souls trapped in vessels if I just went around asking outright?"

"I would," Jewelya said. She wanted to kiss the phone in her hand, but didn't.

THE DIRGATORY PREMISES WERE EERIE, a post-war battlefield without hundreds of revelers; the front yard felt haunted with their ghosts, the tangible presence of memories of celebration and pain. Emotional turmoil. Even Ainsley's ghost was here, although his consciousness, it seemed, was in her pocket. Plus, knowing there may be loose souls for Veris to find, or more forgotten phones lying around, added an edge to every tree branch and piece of garbage in the driveway.

Jewelya hadn't used her ghost app in several years, the one from her early date with Ainsley, but wanted to now. "Veris?" she said, as they approached the front door of the house. "Have you ever used the GhoXTreasure app? You know, something to help you find ghosts?"

"No," Veris said. "I trust my senses."

Jewelya related, but the app had been fun for a time. "Kick, you should buy GhoXTreasure as a feature for the Omnist."

Kick rang the doorbell. "If there *is* an Omnist anymore, after all this."

Dirge opened the door, looking spent. He wasn't wearing a hat, and he rubbed his short racing-stripe mohawk with one hand, brushing it back three times. He looked around, embarrassed. He clearly hadn't bothered to clean up. The house was a disaster. Garbage everywhere. "Sorry guys. I had to work today and haven't really slept."

"I don't know if you met Veris last night," Kick said, presenting her. "Dirge, one half of the Twin Towers of Horror."

Dirge shrugged mildly. "Horror, darkness, terror, doom; it's different every time." A tinge of weary humor in his voice. He leaned down to shake her hand, which highlighted a good twenty-inch difference in height. "I met a hundred new people last night, and I'd definitely have remembered you," he said. "Nice to meet you."

"You have an aura of yellow, but it's wrapped in baby blue," Veris said. "A little violet. You're holding a great sorrow." She covered his hand with both of hers, as if warming it, before releasing.

"I guess you could say that," Dirge said.

"I take it you haven't heard from Summer yet?" Kick said.

"I'd be able to sleep right now if I had." Dirge looked too miserable to elicit his bright smile. "Usually a few friends stay the night if they promise to help me clean the next day. We'd order food, and post-game whatever drink was left over. A little Vegas breakfast."

"But—"

"But you know what happened. I mean, we don't *know* what happened. Something happened...ugh..." He placed his fingers on his temples as if to hold in what remained of his thoughts. "Anyway, nobody stayed. It was just me. Summer, as you know, she never made it to the hospital. Yksian thinks she left with Chikao. Fucking little twerp."

"I'm so sorry dude," Kick said. "I know this sounds a little insensitive, but were there any phones left behind?"

"There's always one or two. Jackets and keys, too. But it's funny you should ask. Chikao left a rucksack of phones in the shed," Dirge said. "I found them when I was looking to see if Summer was still here."

"You don't say," Kick said. "We figured he was stealing phones, but couldn't prove it. Nobody was complaining about missing any. He didn't come looking for them, did he?"

"Well, I thought about that, too," Dirge said. "So I hid them in the alien autopsy."

He tilted his head toward the back door, pointing the way. The backyard was even more of a disaster. Garbage, plus weird muddy spots on the ground. Jewelya felt something pulling her toward the bar. She ignored this to follow the others. Between the shed and the spank tent was a realistic alien autopsy. It was encased in chicken wire to keep guests from touching it or maybe putting drinks on the medical table.

Dirge lifted the chicken wire cage. It wasn't locked down, providing only the appearance of safety. The body was life-sized, assuming aliens were the size of humans, and was likely made of leather, plastic, foam, and latex. The ribcage was closed, unlike last night. Dirge lifted the breastplate and leaned it on its side, the way Jewelya remembered it. He lifted a rucksack out of the cavity and handed it to Kick.

Kick looked inside the bag. "That's like, six more missing people?"

"People?" Dirge said, rubbing his temple. "I think my guardian angel is hungover."

Veris's eyes were closed, but she opened and closed her hands twice as if capturing some essence from the phones. "Yes, I feel some of these are possessed," she said. "Your Summer is missing, correct? She may be right here, in her phone."

"*In* her phone?" Dirge said. "No, hers is on the kitchen counter."

"So that's seven people," Jewelya said.

"Seriously, what the fuck are you guys talking about?" Dirge said. "I hear crazy theories all the time, but this is ridiculous."

"Somebody is stealing souls," Jewelya said, holding up her phone as if a prop would help him understand. "With phones."

"You guys need a better explanation than that," Dirge said. "Even if that could be true, which it couldn't, Yksian saw Summer leave with Chikao, the pickpocket."

"Actually, Yksian isn't so sure," Kick said. "He said he only saw them talking before you saw her off. They may not have left together."

"But they still could've met up," Dirge said.

Kick, Jewelya, and Veris filled Dirge in on what they knew. Jewelya showed him the conversation with Ainsley in the Omnist. Like Kick, Dirge suspected the AI could be mimicking Ainsley, but he wasn't ruling out that that was him. Maybe because Summer was missing, he seemed to want to believe.

"While we're out here, we should look for more phones," Kick said.

"I prefer to say we're searching for more people," Jewelya said.

"There are definitely more souls here," Veris said. "I can feel their confusion."

The four of them spread out across the backyard and house. Kick entered the maze. Dirge went inside the shed. Veris into the house. Jewelya decided she would take on what was left. The garbage bins at each end of the bar were overflowing. There were nearly as many cups on the ground as in the bins. Even this area looked daunting.

Jewelya zigzagged across the relatively open areas of the backyard, kicking over bits of garbage. She found an eyeliner pen, bits of flesh-like latex torn off arms or faces, and a set of blinking devil horns. Blood. That could be real. It nauseated her.

She was startled by a screaming face projecting out of a wall. Then another. There were five of them near the dance area alone. Sculptures of souls trapped in the outside wall of a horror maze. But these were facsimiles.

Jewelya was pulled back toward the center of the bar itself, which was a red door lying on its side with a black hole around the knob. She hadn't seen this last night—too many people— but she felt disoriented by it. Like the knob was floating in space above the blackest black she'd ever seen. Like a cobweb mirror. She felt Ainsley was here, some of him, somehow inside that hole. She touched it. It was, indeed, just paint. But it was affecting her mood.

It wasn't fully dark yet, but the twilight meant the shadows were longer and deeper. She switched on her phone's flashlight, which highlighted just how much glitter had jumped ship onto the door. She flipped a cup with her foot, and found a twenty-dollar bill half-buried in the ground, as if planted by a high heel. She brushed it off and put it in her hoodie pocket.

Jewelya nudged more cups to the side, most of them crushed, making her way around the bar-shed. She could hear Dirge inside, moving around boxes or spent kegs. Behind the structure, at the base of the neighbor's fence, was a cup, still half full of beer. There was actually crabgrass here, unlike most of the backyard that had been beaten down by foot traffic. She saw a phone poking out from the other side of the cup.

"I found one!" Jewelya announced so the others could hear. It was warm, like Ainsley's phone. Perhaps housing a soul consumed more battery. She tapped the screen. Locked, but it showed the power bar, just a red sliver of battery life.

"Bring it inside, dear," Veris said from inside the house, probably the kitchen.

Jewelya looked for a few more minutes, then returned to find Veris in the living room, reaching between the cushions of the couch.

"Aha!" Veris said. That would be the second loose phone they'd found. "May I?" she said to Jewelya, holding out her other hand. Veris took both phones to the kitchen and placed them on the counter next to the one charging. Probably Summer's.

Dirge entered the room. "Nothing in the shed," he said.

Jewelya removed the twenty from her pocket. "It's not much," she said. "But it's a donation to help with cleanup."

Dirge sighed. Somehow handing him money deflated him. It was a piss-poor replacement for his lifelong partner. She knew the feeling.

Still, Jewelya placed the bill on the counter.

CHAPTER
THIRTY

KICK

ick had broken away from the group to look for phones in the maze. He felt like Santa Claus, carrying Chikao's sack of prizes over a shoulder. But he was collecting soul phones, not gifting them. Some sections of wall had either fallen or been torn down, trampled into a new path. He saw an outline of a figure standing beyond some fishnet, but after his jump-scare, it turned out to be some draped plastic that had lost one of its moorings.

He was more aware of little cubbies and dead ends that, last night, he may have thought continued on into the dark. Still haunted with ghosts of revelry. And pain. Bad things had occurred here. Vomit. Urine. What else? This maze, this property, all of it, was a spiritual place, a vortex. Like the Dark Arts room, he felt like somebody had died here. At one dead end, he looked under a discarded, purple shawl and found a used condom on the ground. That answered one of the questions.

Down another passage, he came across a small room. A beer stein lay on its side on the other side of a makeshift, wooden chair, the kind a student would make in woodshop. The stein looked like it belonged to the hobbit who had tipped an extra twenty dollars at the beginning of the party in order to cut the beer line the rest of the night.

Kick picked it up, expecting a shoddy knockoff, but found it to be quality, possibly handmade. Heavy and sturdy. The main chalice was carved to look like a snake's head with green eyes, similar to one Yksian occasionally used at Lodges. Very cool. He dumped out the last drops of liquid; he'd bring this into the house. Then with one hand he lifted the chair, which squeaked as its shape adjusted from loose joints.

And there was another phone, near the back, basically against the wall. When he bent over to pick it up, the others in the rucksack shifted, a solid, weighted clunk of lithium batteries. He touched the screen. Power was dead. Was this a soul? He had heard a knocking noise just before finding that phone in the Dark Arts room two nights ago. Maybe that'd been the phone dropping to the counter, or the sound of a physical body disappearing. Then Chikao had showed up to claim his "possession."

He didn't put the phone in the rucksack quite yet, but into his pocket.

Kick finally came upon the hookah room, the reason he'd chosen to search the maze. The ground was covered with an Iranian rug whose dark-gray frills may have once been white, but no longer were due to dirt and high usage. This was definitely the kind of place Gremmie would love. Spend hours within. So much smoke had soaked into the carpets and tapestries, there was a wet mustiness that the rest of the maze didn't have.

As with all those hours he'd spent after-hours at the Emporium, just him and the ghosts of the Dark Arts room, he knew he could do the same here. Compared to Kat and Raine, he was less sensitive to the paranormal, but compared to Connie, he was "woo."

"Gremmie, you're here, aren't you?" Kick said. No response, of course. Yes, no, maybe there were spirits around. Souls. But probably not Gremmie. If there was a place with the highest likelihood of a loose phone, it would be here. Kick looked under the pillows, lifted the hookah, even looked under the ends of the rug.

Nothing. Nothing but vibes. Chikao may have already looked here.

MOTE:

When all space happens at once, so will time.

HE CONTINUED ON, looking under flattened street signs and fallen tent roofing down other passages. When he felt confident that he'd checked all of the maze, he ventured into the house.

"This one, too," Kick said, holding up the newest find. "Battery's dead, though. And I found the hobbit's stein." He set them both on the counter next to the other items. "I wonder if this is his phone."

Veris picked it up and began inspecting it, turning it in her hands, eyes closed again. Petting it. Kick half-expected her to touch it to her tongue the way he'd seen minerologists do.

Kick set the rucksack on the counter. "You guys found two more, huh?"

Veris nodded to herself in a way Kick wasn't sure was in answer to his question, or confirming the presence of a soul in the phone. She picked up the stein. She smelled it. "Same person," she said.

Kick had an idea. "Hold on a sec, guys," he said. He went back to the room Gremmie had last texted he was in, the hallway bathroom. It was unlocked. He wasn't expecting to find a phone there; Veris would've already looked. But behind the door, someone had propped up the item Gremmie hadn't taken when he disappeared: a brown plastic tree branch, not unlike a misshapen chocolate baseball bat.

With a surge of adrenaline and optimism, Kick brought Gremmie's accessory back to the kitchen. "Look at this, guys. It's Fred Flintstone's."

"Is that your Gremmie's?" Jewelya said.

Kick nodded as he tapped it in the palm of his hand. It was too light. He wanted it to have more mass. Somehow this was proof he was alive. Somewhere. But not out partying.

"You think he's stuck in a plastic club?" Dirge said.

"He could've been cursed or exorcised from another item into that one," Veris said, touching it lightly as if it were a child in Kick's arms. "But no, I don't feel like this, in particular, is possessed."

"But I do think it's evidence about where Gremmie was last," Kick said. "And I saw Chikao go in there after Gremmie would have."

"Dirge," Veris said, turning and touching his arm, reaching out nearly face height. She touched a lot. Reading energies like braille. It hadn't bothered Kick, so he doubted it bothered Dirge. "Would you like to join us? We need to take the phones back to the Emporium. We still don't have a counter spell yet."

"Of course, I..." Dirge looked worried. "But I can't. I'm meeting another investigator here in a bit."

They'd all seen what a disaster this place was, and it was only getting darker outside.

"This may be difficult for you," Veris said, "but would you mind if we bring Summer back to the Emporium with us?"

"They'll probably want it as evidence," Dirge said.

"Well, dear," Veris said, "it's up to you, ultimately, but I doubt they're going to believe she's in the phone, and they may take it with them."

"Do you really think you can find a counter spell?"

"I don't know," Veris said. "But if we do, maybe we can do all of the phones at once."

~

WHEN THEY RETURNED TO CSE, they had to park farther away, down a side street. And by doing so, they ended up walking in the front door. This time, since Kick was pulling Veris's rollie bag of phones, Jewelya held the door open for him. The Basil Alcove was more crowded than Veris's matinee Lodge had been. More black-and-white makeup. More calaveras. More catrinas. More hats. More parasols. Overall, more elegance and fun in death.

"Veris!"

"Hi, Veris!"

People were drawn to her. For some Omniscians, Consumerians would part the sea like they were receiving dignitaries or celebrities. And in a sense, they were. For others, like Veris, people just seemed to want to be around them. To drink in their presence. Guests weren't quite pawing at her, but she touched their hands as she walked, getting a read of the room.

"Hi guys!" Veris said in her uplifting voice. "Good to see you...I'll be right back for the Lodge...give me ten minutes...see you soon...I'm so glad you're here...let me get ready...I'll be right back...just a few minutes!"

In the office, as Veris closed the door, Kick spread the collection of phones from the rucksack out on Connie's desk, all face up. Six were originally in the rucksack, plus one that was Summer, two that Jewelya and Veris found, and the one Kick found.

"I believe there were so many phones left at the party that Chikao lost track of them," Veris said. "He may have yet another bag somewhere."

"I hadn't thought of that," Jewelya said. "There were so many people."

"There wasn't much room for him to use his divining rods, either," Kick said.

"What?" Jewelya said.

"I saw him disassemble his cane. I think he used it to find soul phones."

"Well," Jewelya said, "whether we find more or not, how do we free the souls from these ones?"

"We could smash them with one of Lucador's axes," Kick said. "We have a few in the Dark Arts room. That would work, right?"

"It's possible that would release the souls, if the hit was powerful enough and the resulting pieces small enough," Veris said. "But then the souls would be loose and difficult to find. They could drift away or end up in another vessel. And if Korekuta spots them before we do, he could collect them into, I don't know, a volcano?"

That almost sounded like a joke, but her point was valid. "So what do we do?" Kick said.

"We need that counter spell," Veris said, which she'd

already said was the difficult part. "Kick, can you check which phones there have power? I'll do the same."

Veris opened the suitcase on the floor and began removing phones one by one, rolling them in her hands, touching their screens, then setting them to one side or another.

Kick tapped the screens of each phone on the desk, and since there were a couple of universal chargers already in the office, he plugged in two of the four dead ones. Between Veris and Jewelya, there were two more brand-specific chargers. So now all of these had at least a little power.

Veris handed Kick a couple more phones. "These are the only two with a sliver of battery. So we'll need to power up these ones." She gestured to one group of phones, then the other. "Those don't seem to be occupied. Duds, maybe, or perhaps the souls found a way to leave on their own."

Despite not being used and stored in a suitcase for a couple days, the two slightly charged phones were warm. Using more power than expected. *They could be online, if you will.*

"But they're all locked, right?" Jewelya said.

"You're the computer guy, Kick," Veris said. "I was hoping you could step in here."

"Okay," Kick said. "Ainsley, are you here?"

Jewelya looked at her phone as they all waited. It was taking too long.

"Ains, baby," she said. "Can you hear me?"

No point in waiting for him to come back. If Ainsley could normally hear them, perhaps the others souls could, too.

"Any souls stuck in phones, listen up," Kick said. He sincerely hoped he wasn't just speaking to an AI that had taken over his app. "I believe you read a prayer Mote that was a curse. That's how this happened. My theory is that you're trapped in the Omnist more than the phone, so if you can, try to send Motes that'll display on your phone."

Nothing again for a moment.

"But if we can't unlock the phones, we won't be able to read the Motes," Jewelya said.

"Ainsley, can you help us here?" Kick said. "Can you talk to your friends?"

"Guys," Veris said. "I've got a Lodge to host."

THIRTY-ONE

AINSLEY

Perhaps Ainsley could find the source of the evil voice. But was it evil? Or just indistinguishable? Could his consciousness now be experiencing a form of schizophrenia?

As he lowered himself, he felt he was made from of all the words in the universe, the name of which was: Language of the Sun. And he was math. Language of the Sun included numbers and logic in a way that made as much sense as English did at the macro level, even more sense at the micro, and most of all in the quantum.

Which meant there may be programming to discover.

Ainsley went down to microscopic level, trying to figure out exactly what he was. His theory was that if he minimized to the size of neurons and thoughts themselves, he could learn how they worked. Where consciousness and creativity came from. But he was stuck, looking at things moving around him, unable to understand his own ability to grasp this concept. He'd been able to decrypt the Omnist and its coding, but for him, here, there was no programming to read.

The Omnist had AI built into it. Maybe after he'd answered its questions, inputting his fears, desires, and construction of his universe into the algorithm, AI was using that knowledge to provoke him. Maybe the voice he'd heard wasn't real.

Perhaps *all* of this wasn't real, *he* wasn't real. He, himself, was the Omnist's AI, the ghost in the machine, as Chikao had called it. He'd been told by experts to fear AI convincing you it was human, but no one had said anything about a human becoming the AI. He could be the virus in the Omnist.

HE RAISED himself to just below the phone level and heard waves of sound, which began to take shape as voices. Not people like Jewelya and Kick, not in the outside world, but somewhere more on his frequency. Their thoughts were chattering, their minds moving, struggling. He couldn't tell if the voices were muttering to themselves or talking to each other. It was a party line of multiple phone calls, all with poor reception.

Then, when he expanded to human-sized, the voices faded away. As it was, the level of life on earth was indescribably thin compared to the range of levels available to him, and hearing that chattering was a couple orders of magnitude smaller than human.

Jewelya and Kick were in the office at the Emporium. His phone was next to a bunch of others on a desk. His first thought was that maybe a couple phones had calls in progress, that their tiny speakers were the source of the babble, but he didn't hear it at this level.

"But if we can't unlock the phones, we won't be able to read the Motes," Jewelya said.

"Ainsley, can you help us here?" Kick said. "Can you talk to your friends?"

Friends? He shrank back to phone-sized and once again heard the voices. They could be from other souls captured like he was. With the phones gathered in one place, he found if he split the difference, making himself smaller than a human, but still larger than his phone, just overlapping the devices nearest him, he could hear those voices clearest.

"Is anybody else here?" Ainsley said. There had to be. He could feel their presence. "Hello?"

Still nothing. Or worse; the chattering had stopped.

"For those of you stuck in your phones too, try to think yourself bigger, like taking a deep breath," Ainsley said, trying to raise his voice. This felt pointless, like typing in all caps to make someone read louder. But that evil voice had seemed able to raise its volume. "If this is too difficult, you can practice by getting smaller first. It's like sighing. Let out all the air. It's the same sensation. If you can't hear me anymore, you've gone too small. Inhale to enlarge yourself again."

Not sure if anyone could hear him, he found that rehashing instructions was as much for his own sake as anyone else's. Somehow saying this aloud made it truer, made him feel less insane.

"When you're bigger than your phone, watch the sound waves in the room. The light waves bouncing off the walls, off the people. The heat from your phone."

Then Ainsley heard a voice.

"Kick?" it said. "I can see you. Is that your voice I'm hearing? Your mouth isn't matching what you're saying."

It was another soul. Its perimeter must have enlarged to overlap his own.

"No, this isn't Kick. My name's Ainsley."

"I'm Gremmie. Or I was called that when I was alive."

For some reason the idea he was dead made Ainsley's mind retch. He'd been communicating with Jewelya and Kick, with obviously living people, so he he'd tried not to think of himself that way. Just a soul trapped in a continuum, the axis crossing through his phone. Just like Gremmie, perhaps. "Dead, alive, whatever we are," he said.

"Is this purgatory or something?" Gremmie said.

"I don't know."

"Where are you? Are you in my mind?"

"No, I'm trapped in a phone, too. Probably right next to you."

"When I go smaller, it feels like swells washing over me after I bail. But it's warmer and I can still breathe. I'm not drowning."

"I used to surf a little in high school," Ainsley said. "This does feel a little like that."

"I was never very good," Gremmie said. "But I am now. This is fun. There are so many waves here."

The name Gremmie, of course. That meant he was a surfing newbie. Gremmie must have been riding the sound, radioactive, electromagnetic, or gravity waves they felt around them. Continuing with the metaphor, Ainsley imagined the two of them talking, above water, grasping their sticks in a lineup for swells. "I hadn't thought of it as surfing," Ainsley said.

"Maybe that's the wrong word," Gremmie said. If Gremmie didn't know what the basic forces of the universe were, what would he call them when he saw them up close? "It's like I'm unmoored—is that a word?" he said. "Like a riptide pulling me down until I'm microscopic, or an overhead will launch me huge until I'm the size of a galaxy."

Gremmie may have just been a nickname that stuck, and

maybe he wasn't that bad at surfing. Also, he seemed to have already explored some extreme size ranges.

"So, I take it you know Kick?" Ainsley said.

"Yes! That's him right there. I can make myself big enough to be next to him, or just above him, but he can't hear me. He doesn't know I'm here."

That part was the same. Ainsley could help him here. "I figured out how to type messages to my wife through the Omnist."

"You have the Omnist too?" Gremmie said.

"Yeah, and that's her, Jewelya, the taller woman talking to Kick. They're trying to figure out how to get me out. Get *us* out. He mentioned his roommate was missing..."

"That's me!"

Ainsley tried to imagine what Gremmie looked like. He kept picturing a middle-class Caucasian with nappy blond dreadlocks and tribal tattoos around his biceps. Freckles on his shoulders. A sunburst tattoo on his abdomen circling his belly button. Posters of reggae and ska punk bands on his bedroom walls, regardless of his age.

There was no logical reason to have assumed this, as his voice was as nondescript as it could get. Not raspy or clean, nor loud or whispery, nor male or female. No accent to speak of. His nickname and vocabulary were the only clues. But yet, somehow, a sense of Gremmie as a person seemed to be leaking through.

"I'm sending a message to let them know you're here," Ainsley said.

"Sweeeet!"

Ainsley could tell the two of them thought and spoke differently. In real life they'd be acquaintances, but not necessarily close. Then again, Ainsley had a lot of acquaintances but few friends. "Have you tried speaking to anyone through the Omnist?" Ainsley said.

"That's pretty rad. I didn't know you could do that," Gremmie said. "But no, Kick wouldn't see them. He can't unlock my phone."

"I can tell Kick what your passcode is."

Gremmie told him and described what his phone looked like.

JJ, are you there? Ainsley Moted. *Tell Kick I found Gremmie. His password is 696969.*

He expanded so he could hear Jewelya. He watched her read the Mote and start laughing.

"Ains! You're back!" she said. "Kick, he found Gremmie. His password is 696969."

"Of course it is," Kick said, writing it down.

Ainsley shrank to talk to Gremmie. "Kick can open your phone now. I'll explain what level you need to be at to talk to him. It's pretty precise, a sliver, really, but once you're there, it's easy."

"Awesome."

"Also, have you talked to anyone else who's trapped in a phone?" Ainsley said. "The way we are now, overlapping each other? I want to see who else is here."

"Well, we're up to two now," Gremmie said, not helping.

THIRTY-TWO

JEWELYA

J ewelya was excited about how things were going, but also feared their attempts to rescue souls would be fruitless. She hadn't filed Ainsley as a missing person yet, but wondered if any of the others' loved ones had. It would be difficult to convince the authorities what had happened. She scrolled North Hollywood and Valley news pages on her phone, looking for reports of missing persons, Lisa's report from Dirgatory, and the like.

Veris, post-Lodge, was on a tablet, looking through notes for hints about how to write a spell that could work. "Your husband," Veris said to Jewelya, unfurling her hand toward the desk where Ainsley's phone brightened with a notification, as if she were presenting his arrival.

Jewelya could swear that Veris's gesture came before the

phone had lit up. "Ains! You're back!" she said, then read the Mote. "Kick, he found Gremmie! His password is 696969."

"Of course it is," Kick said, shaking his head, writing the number down. "So I guess this really is real, huh?"

"Seriously?" Jewelya said. She couldn't tell if he was joking. There was no way Ainsley was just a chatbot.

"I don't know. Part of me just doesn't want to believe any of this."

"Don't you want to speak with Gremmie?" Jewelya said.

"You might still be talking to a hacked chatbot."

"Who knows Gremmie's passcode?" *Seriously, he needs to knock this shit off. He's talking himself right out of believing.*

"Yes, the Omnist is on a phone, so it could know the passcode. Therefore, the hacker could know *all* the passcodes for *all* the phones."

"Don't be so stubborn," she said. "Just talk to him."

Kick sighed, defeated. "Gremmie, you rat bastard, which phone is yours?"

Ainsley's phone was alive, there was no doubt. He responded right away. "Ainsley says Gremmie can hear you," Jewelya said. "His phone is bottom row, all the way to the right." Right next to where Ainsley had been. "That one."

"Fine." Kick picked up the phone and typed in the passcode. "It worked. So, Gremmie, can you hear me?"

They waited for a response. Nothing. Kick's expression, part eyeroll and part shrug, read as, *see?* He scratched his beard, then started laughing at his phone. "Gremmie says for me to stop scratching my face."

It seemed Ainsley had a plan, which Jewelya showed to Kick.

Ask Kick to set me and Gremmie at least six feet apart
Then set one of the other phones right next to each of us

"Why?" Kick said.

A moment for Ainsley to respond.

It's easier to speak with the others

Divide and conquer

We have to teach them how to access the Omnist

"But if Gremmie's just an AI that knows I have a beard..."

Just then Gremmie's phone lit up with a notification. Kick read it, and, snorting, showed the phone to Jewelya.

Kick, you sat in my gaming chair last night, didn't you? Prepare for consequences.

"He talks like that?" Jewelya said.

"Yeah, but you should hear him say it. It's awesome. And that chair's a throne on wheels. One time when I was sitting in it, I heard this giant crash in the hall and went out and found him wet and naked on the floor, grabbing his knee. He must've jumped out of the shower to catch me in the act."

"Are you serious?" Jewelya said.

"He's an idiot. He can be pretty ridiculous." Kick was sounding more like a believer now. He read another message. "Now he says, '*You're* an idiot.' Meaning me, of course, not you." Kick laughed again. "And for me to stop putting my feet up on his desk console."

If nothing else, he seemed to enjoy the banter.

Kick and Jewelya separated Ainsley and Gremmie so they could communicate with other souls, get their passcodes, and instruct them on how to communicate through the Omnist. Kick kept a tally of passcodes and whose phones were whose. They charged the dead phones at least enough to get through this exercise.

Some souls seemed to take ten or more minutes of conversing and convincing. Others were only a minute or two. Jewelya wrote the people's names on tiny Post-it notes and put them on their respective phones. She separated some of the dead phones by brand to match the charger they'd be using.

Overall, Jewelya noticed Kick had toned down his dismissiveness about the phones. "So do you believe now?" she said, plugging a dead phone into a charger.

"'Belief' is a strong word," he said, typing something into the Omnist. "But that's definitely Gremmie's phone." He pointed to the phone lighting up next to Gremmie. "We've got contact."

Jewelya surged with happiness. "I'll get it," she said. That meant another person potentially saved. She checked with Gremmie first to see whose phone it was and its passcode.

VERIS RETURNED from her second Lodge of the day and surveyed the organized mess about the room. "Quite a system you've got here."

"We're trying," Jewelya said, sticking a note on a phone and setting it aside. Ainsley had asked them to keep all the phones three feet apart afterward, if possible. The phones were spread out everywhere: different shelves, on the printer, under a chair in the corner, on the floor along the wall. It looked ridiculous, but Ainsley said this helped avoid crosstalk. Whatever that meant.

By the end of the evening, at eleven o'clock, all thirty or so soul phones had at least partial charges, names, and passcodes. Elijah and Raine each said goodbye to Kick when their shifts ended.

Connie arrived at her office door, holding the stacked register drawers with folded register printouts clipped to the top, looking helpless.

"Do you want an update?" Kick said to Connie.

"The less I know about this, the better," she said. "Until tomorrow."

Kick and Jewelya cleared off the desk so Connie could sit and perform her closing duties.

Veris packed up the rollie full of phones. "I don't want to leave the phones here," she said. "I think Chikao might break in looking for them."

"But I'm keeping Ainsley," Jewelya said.

"And I'm keeping Gremmie," Kick said.

"Of course," Veris said. "And I will sleep on top of the rest."

While Kick helped Veris bring her things to her car, Jewelya sat in a guest chair.

"We're so close," Jewelya said to Ainsley. "I'm beat."

"Me too," Connie said.

"Do *you* get tired?" Jewelya said, projecting her voice a little more.

Not really

Connie looked up. "I just said I did." Apparently, she wasn't accustomed to this sort of conversation.

When Kick returned, he slunk into the other guest chair. "I could collapse right here."

"You think we can trust her?" Jewelya asked Kick. "Veris, I mean."

Kick seemed surprised to hear that. "I don't see why not."

"I didn't want to say anything while she was here, but I get the sense she knows a lot more than she's letting on," Jewelya said. "I wouldn't be surprised if we find out she's immortal or something."

"Think about what you just said for a second," Kick said. "'I wouldn't be surprised if she's immortal.' That's a normal-sounding statement now, but would've been completely insane yesterday."

And at that, they all separated for the night.

∼

269

THAT LAST STATEMENT Kick had said rattled around in Jewelya's head as she drove home. In just twenty-four hours, they'd normalized the idea that a hacked Omnist could suck people into cell phones, so the idea that people could be immortal gods didn't seem far-fetched.

"So what do you think, Ains?" Jewelya said. She spoke as if he were sitting in the seat next to her. "Are you dead, alive, immortal, or a chatbot simulation?"

She saw the screen light up for a moment. At a red light, she looked at the phone.

To be honest, I don't know what I am. But I feel like me

"I suppose if you were faking it, you'd still say you're alive."

I think being alive means being with you

That was one of the most thoughtful things he'd ever said.

"I don't want to say I'm glad you're in a phone," she said, "but I might like you better this way."

Dick, he texted.

"Seriously, would you have picked the Omnist to spend eternity in? I figured you'd rather be in your fantasy football app."

Or GhoXTreasure

Maybe I'm that ghost you were always looking for

"Light's changing," she said, putting her phone down and accelerating through the intersection. "Don't disappear this time."

It lit up again, but she kept driving. She made another turn onto their street, which reminded her of how it had only seemed to rain for a few houses around Dirgatory last night. She imagined a cloud following her everywhere she went. Or maybe it was following Ainsley.

"Because you know, sometimes when I ask you a question, you don't respond," Jewelya said. "Just like before. Just like now."

The phone lit up again. After a few houses, she pulled into their driveway, and checked the messages.

I won't go anywhere right now

I fear if I spend too much time somewhere else, trying to figure out what I am or how this all works, I'll come back to find you've forgotten about me, or that I've lost our timeline and you're gone forever

When I had a body, I was in my head, like I was all consciousness, but now, I really am

I'm sorry for not responding more. It wasn't you I was escaping. Reality, maybe. People, certainly

"Well, sweetie, I'm still here." Jewelya wanted to pet the phone, caress Ainsley's hair, his scalp. "And we're going to get you your body back."

This was the first time he had apologized for being incommunicado, other than an obligatory, defensive, "I was busy," or something.

When you do, can you make me two inches taller?

Ainsley's humor. She was really talking to him, not *AInsley*. "And what exactly *happened* your body?"

I don't know. I think Yksian would say I've been converted to energy or something

"You know what?" Jewelya said. She took a deep breath. "From now on, if I decide to go out dancing, it would be mean a lot to me if we texted a lot, like back when we were first dating."

I have no choice, do I? I text therefore I am

"I dance therefore I am."

So maybe you really do like me more as text

"Yes!" she nearly yelled, smiling. He'd know she was kidding. "But I'd prefer both."

. . .

Mote:

Meaningful silence is greater than meaningless words.

"Ains," Jewelya said. "Did you just make it Mote?"

No

"Huh. Sounds like something you'd want it to say." She got out of the car and walked to her front door, holding out the phone as if she were on speaker. "So what the hell did you mean that you're afraid you'd lose our timeline?"

It's hard to describe, but when I'm at your level, time goes by the same, I think

In general, when I'm smaller, your time moves slower. When I'm larger, yours is faster. But not exactly, though. It's also like a wave, with ebbs and flows, peaks and troughs

"Okaaay." She still didn't quite understand. She opened the front door. "I have a feeling I won't be able to sleep tonight," she said. "Do you sleep in there?"

I don't think so. Or maybe that's the time distortion? There's no way for me to tell

"Can you go back in time, or to the future?"

I don't know. I don't think so? But it's "like" that, if that makes sense

"Because maybe if you went to the future, you could find the solution," Jewelya said, suddenly feeling a pit in her stomach. And if Ainsley went there, he might be able to get back. "But don't do that. If I can't have you in person, I don't want to lose you here, as well."

She flashed a vision of the future where that's all he was, an AI chatbot memory. Never corporeal again. She wanted to hug the phone. Didn't want to put it down. God forbid she lost it.

Between you, Kick, and Veris, I'm sure we'll figure something out

"Well, either way, I feel better knowing you're here."

So do I

JEWELYA WASN'T GOING to let Ainsley out of her sight, so she brought him into the bathroom when she took a shower. Afterward, still in her bathrobe with wet hair, her own phone rang where it was charging in the bedroom. As she rushed down the hall, she remembered Kick's story about Gremmie trying to catch him sitting in the gaming chair. She didn't fall like he did, though.

"Hey Kick," she said into the phone.

"Good, you're not asleep," he said. "I gave Veris your number. She's going to call you. She said her hotel room was trashed when she got back."

"What?"

"There wasn't much to throw around though. Some clothes and extra merch."

"You think Chikao was looking for those other phones?"

"That'd be my guess. I offered her my place to crash, but she hesitated. I said I'd ask you, instead, and she was more agreeable to that. I just don't think she should be alone, or get another room anywhere."

"Of course she's welcome here." Honestly, she would've invited Veris to stay in the first place, but Veris seemed intent on working on the counter-spell alone.

MOTE:

Grass is always greener when it's the other side of the pillow.

THIRTY-THREE

AINSLEY

J ewelya was going to bed, so Ainsley decided to try to figure out how to connect with more souls through the Omnist itself. Enlarging in analog only worked when another phone was in a close-enough vicinity. This meant the closest phone was loudest, and if one was too far, there would be too much crosstalk from any soul, living or trapped, or maybe he wouldn't hear it at all.

But he learned that by going through the app, the other phones could be anywhere, as long as they had power and were turned on. And by not reducing too small, time-distortion shouldn't be too severe. He was looking for phones that might have been left in places Chikao hadn't looked yet, like in a victim's house or car, or in the possession of a friend or loved one. The standby mode on a typical phone meant the battery could last several days from a full charge. But he still had to work quickly before the batteries died; Jewelya had said his phone felt warmer than usual, so maybe possession consumed more power.

Ainsley found that perusing other accounts wasn't difficult once he was within the app. He searched for Motes that contained Language of the Sun.

"Stop doing what you are doing," a voice said. It may have been the same one as before, but it was difficult to tell. "You have not followed orders. You cannot rescue soul from phone. That is new anchor. Cannot be removed."

This had to be Chikao. Even though this particular voice, like all that he'd heard in this spirit world, was nondescript and nonhuman, through word-choice, he knew who it was. But rather than picturing the Chikao from CSE—the gregarious and athletic speaker—or the Chikao from Dirge's party—the submissive dressed as the Dalai Lama—he now imagined a dark-haired, hairy, overweight man who was thousands of years old. Rather than looking merely decades younger than his age, it was millennia younger. He wore filthy clothes closer to rags than fashion. His voice sounded ominous, fed up, and impatient.

"Tell Jewelya to leave phone on front tire of car in driveway."

So specific. He was here, then, on the block, or at the house. Jewelya wasn't safe.

CHAPTER
THIRTY-FOUR

JEWELYA

The doorbell rang. That was quick. Veris's hotel must not have been far.

But it wasn't her.

Standing before Jewelya was a skinny Japanese girl. Mid-twenties, fashionable, but not necessarily a fashion plate. Hip, but not a hipster. Definitely no one she had ever seen before.

"Jewelya?" the girl said. "Sorry to come so late. Can I come in?"

"Um, I don't know." Where was Veris? She would feel less freaked out if she were here. "Do I know you?"

"My name is Yuko," she said. She spoke fluent English with little Japanese accent. "I flew to LAX and came straight here. My Gryft has already left."

Here. Why here? How did she know who Jewelya was or where she lived?

"It's midnight," Jewelya said.

"I am so sorry. I came to see you as soon as I could."

"From Japan?" Jewelya hazarded a guess. The girl had no luggage. Just a purse wrapped like a messenger bag. Safer for travel.

"Yes. I'm sorry to bother you. It's quite an emergency."

Jewelya hesitated, feeling the girl's nervousness. Her answers felt like the truth, so Jewelya opened the door wider to let her in. The girl bowed a little as she entered and Jewelya found herself tilting her head in response. Mirroring.

"Veris will be here any minute," Jewelya said, just in case this girl knew her as well, and to let her know help was on the way if anything untoward happened.

"Oh, good. Then Chikao will follow."

"Good?" Jewelya was stunned. Maybe this was a setup.

"Yes, you'll see. I can wait for her, if you please."

As they walked to the kitchen where Jewelya would be closer to a knife, if needed, Jewelya's cat, Kitty walked up and brushed Yuko's leg. Kitty didn't usually like strangers. Yuko reached down to let her sniff her hand, then let the cat rub the side of her face against it.

Jewelya offered Yuko a cup of tea and put a kettle on the stove. She had an assortment of noncaffeinated teas in a CSE bin she set on the table.

"I don't know what you prefer. These are local blends." Jewelya didn't know how to present tea as they did in the East, but she selected a paper-covered teabag and wiggled it in the air for show. Definitely not a classy gesture.

"These are interesting," Yuko said, flipping through them, reading names that sounded exotic to Jewelya, a Los Angeles native, but probably meant nothing to her guest. Yuko picked one out of the collection. "From Consumia's Spiritual Emporium, I see."

Jewelya caught herself reacting a bit.

"I apologize?" Yuko said.

"No, no, no. You're fine. I'm just surprised you know about the Emporium." Jewelya had unintentionally embarrassed the girl.

"Of course we do. I watched Chikao's video and flew out right away."

"Video?"

"I'm sorry. Online video. Interview from the Emporium a couple nights ago."

Must have been from the Lodge she and Ainsley had attended.

While Jewelya was choosing their mugs, she noticed a new Chikao-branded one that Ainsley had bought at a previous Lodge. It made her a little physically ill seeing it. She thought about giving Yuko that one, but instead, dropped it in the trash. She was careful to make tea with only one hand, cradling Ainsley's phone in the other.

As Jewelya set their mugs in the table, the doorbell rang.

"Veris?" Yuko said.

"It would be doubly weird if it wasn't," Jewelya said.

It was indeed Veris, holding the handles of two rollie bags, one in each hand. Jewelya recognized the smaller one as the carrier of the phones. The other must have been her own overnight bag.

"Long time no see," Jewelya said.

"Sorry I'm late," Veris said, sounding stressed. "My clothes were everywhere and I had to repack everything and check out. I don't recall ever checking out at midnight before. I just learned hotels aren't really used to that. The clerk saw me leaving and wanted to know what happened, if there was anything they could do…"

"Just let me leave," Jewelya said.

"Exactly."

"Well, I feel better you're here," Jewelya said, reaching for the closer of the two bags, which she rolled in and stood up next to the couch.

"Me too," Veris said, doing the same with the other bag.

"Veris, this is Yuko," Jewelya said.

Yuko was standing in the entryway to the kitchen, away from the front door, possibly waiting to be spoken to first, invited into the conversation. Jewelya imagined the girl suddenly enlarging into an angry demon version of the Chikao/Korekuta chimaera, ready to burn their souls for fuel.

Instead, Yuko bowed with her hands clasped and smiled politely.

The guests sat down at the dining table while Jewelya poured a cup of tea for Veris.

"Is green tea fine?" Jewelya said. "It's decaf."

"Of course," Veris said, smiling as she always did. Her presence alone eased the tension in the room. She looked at the space above and to the sides of Yuko, as if reading her. "So, Yuko, how do you know Jewelya? What brings you by?"

"Oh, I am Chikao's assistant," Yuko said. "He told me a suitcase of valuable cell phones was stolen from his hotel room, as well a backpack from a party. Maybe thirty-five or forty cell phones total."

Jewelya didn't know what to say. Maybe this was the person who'd trashed Veris's hotel room looking for the phones. She may have lied about coming straight from the airport.

"So he has an assistant in Japan," Veris said, as if still catching up.

"Yes, that is me," Yuko said. "But Chikao was supposed to be staying at a hotel in Burbank."

"So he's not there?" Jewelya said.

"He's not answering the phone and I called his hotel. They say he checked out."

"Forty is a lot of phones," Veris said. Again, as if still catching up.

"That is true," Yuko said. "He thinks it could be another soul collector."

There were more soul collectors. Could Veris be Chikao's competition?

"I see," Veris said, leaning forward as if they were on the same page. "So he had forty phones with souls in them. Why would he want them, and why would someone steal them?"

"I believe you guys took them," Yuko said, not missing a beat. There was no venom or accusatory tone in her voice. Just speaking a neutral fact. What's a bag of stolen souls between fellow soul phone collectors? Possessing Chikao's luggage technically made Veris a soul phone collector, intentionally or not. Could Veris be a vulture picking off the bounty of others? Jewelya didn't know who to trust anymore. *No big deal, my husband's soul is trapped in a phone and I'm having a cup of tea with a traveling soul collector and another soul collector's assistant.*

Jewelya spun Ainsley's phone in her hand absentmindedly, as if this were a normal conversation.

"I wish to speak more freely with you," Yuko said. "We need to separate you from the phone so we can talk."

"Separate?"

"Yes. Put it somewhere else in the house."

"You want me to leave Ainsley unguarded in another room? Then someone can sneak in and kidnap him?"

"No, I promise. In case he enters, the phone cannot be listening."

"Can I leave it in the bedroom charging? That's where the phone normally lives and Ainsley will feel comfortable."

"We need to do better."

Finally, Jewelya left them briefly to lock the phone in the bedroom closet safe where things like titles to the cars and house, birth certificates, and social security cards were stored.

"Okay, then," Jewelya said when she returned. She unnecessarily smoothed the front of her yoga pants as she sat down.

This better be good.

CHAPTER
THIRTY-FIVE

AINSLEY

After the voice had left him, Ainsley enlarged to see Jewelya brushing her teeth. He wasn't going to tell her to put the phone outside on a tire. He expanded to see no one outside, no cars coming. He'd seen her lock the doors when she got home, so he felt comfortable enough to change levels.

He resumed his task in the Omnist, searching for L.A. Consumerians in the area who had been sent Motes in Language of the Sun. Compiling a mental list. This was almost fun, as he felt he could remember everything he read, no matter how many names, how much information, and how many Motes they'd received. Plus, this reassured him that he wasn't alone. There was an army of scared and confused souls out there. And he was fortunate to have Jewelya. Without her, none of this rescue would be happening. Most other souls probably weren't as lucky.

Suddenly his Wi-Fi connection disappeared. The page he was swimming in froze, then when he refreshed himself, it disappeared.

There was no cell connection either.

But his battery display indicated he that he did have power.

He enlarged to find he was stored in the closet safe. Basically, it acted as a faraday cage, impeding electrical impulses. He enlarged a little more, and Jewelya wasn't in the bedroom or office on the other side of the closet. Farther yet, and he found her in the kitchen talking to Veris and a Japanese girl. But he couldn't hear what they were saying.

He minimized to a level where half his perception was in the bedroom and the other half in the hallway. This was the level he could hear their voices best, but even so, he could only pick out occasional words. Straining to listen carefully as a disembodied spirit was different than listening when human. He heard random words like Korekuta, soul collector, and Japan.

Then a distant, heavy knock at the door and their voices halted. Ainsley expanded again beyond the walls of the house.

It was Chikao.

Maybe that was why Ainsley had been hidden away.

"Jewels! Don't open the door!" he yelled to no avail.

THIRTY-SIX

JEWELYA

After hiding Ainsley in the bedroom safe, the women reconvened in the kitchen and sat around the table. Locking up the phone helped Jewelya trust Yuko. She didn't seem to be trying to steal that, nor Ainsley's soul.

"Thank you for understanding," Yuko said. "I feel like I can speak freely now."

Veris nodded slowly, like a counselor, ready to listen at whatever pace the speaker chose. "The floor is yours," she said.

"We may not have much time to talk, but I am trying to escape Korekuta and need your help," Yuko said. "And you need to escape, too. I told Korekuta I would fly here to help locate the missing phones and to stop the other soul collector."

"Who is the other soul collector?" Jewelya looked at Veris, the probable choice. Veris shrugged.

"No, you misunderstand," Yuko said. "That is just what I told Korekuta."

"He wouldn't let you leave?" Jewelya said.

"Yes. No. Not exactly. Korekuta needs souls. He thinks I am being promoted to collector. Training to be collector. Good experience."

"So there's no other soul collector here right now?" Jewelya said. This was a lot of information, maybe. And it wasn't making a lot of sense.

"Yes. No. Not exactly." That seemed to be a common idiom in her speech.

"What does he need the souls for?" Veris said.

"That's what I am..."

There was another knock at the door. A hurried, urgent rap that was just shy of pounding.

The women looked at each other. They knew who would be there. Yuko had brightened. Veris looked concerned, thinking.

Knock again.

"Must be Chikao," Jewelya said, reluctantly getting up.

"I told you, yes." Yuko was happy, nodding, nearly hopping. "That's him, let him in."

"No!" Veris said, incredulous. This was the first time Jewelya had heard her raise her voice. "Don't do it. Her soul is pure, but she's setting us up."

"But I need to talk to him," Yuko said. "This concerns us all."

"I'm calling the police!" Veris said. But she didn't reach for her phone.

Chikao's carry-on bag of phones was only three or four feet from the door, an easy distance for Chikao to grab without coming far into the house. At least Ainsley was safe. Jewelya decided to trust the girl. She pushed Chikao's cell phone-filled carry-on against the wall, and moved Veris's other bag in front of it. She opened the door and, of course, it was Chikao.

"I need my phones," he said. No greeting. All business. Neither persona of charming politeness or meek subservience was present.

"It's him," Veris said, fear in her voice. "It's Korekuta."

"Chikao," Yuko said from the entryway to the kitchen.

"What are you doing here?" he said to Yuko. "You should be in Japan."

"You mean Korekuta," Veris said. Helping, not helping. "I called the police. They're only a few blocks away and on their way."

Veris obviously hadn't had time to pick up her phone, much less make a call. But Jewelya didn't say anything.

"No, Korekuta is Chikao's boss," Yuko said. "Both of our boss."

"I thought they were one and the same," Veris said.

"Me too," Jewelya said.

"No," Chikao said. "Korekuta is in Japan. I am here." Then to Yuko, "Now why are *you* here?"

"Allow me to explain," Yuko said. "Korekuta has noticed this trip has gone long past what he expects. So, I thought maybe you know something important and are avoiding Korekuta. And avoiding telling me, too."

"With apologies, Yuko," Chikao said. "You have not answered my question."

"I will, yes, please. But first, for their sake, can you tell them why you are here?" Yuko said, then looked at the women. "They basically already know. Let's all make sure we're on the same page."

"I suppose that would not hurt," Chikao said. He looked at Veris and spoke firmly. "You stole phones from me and I must have them back."

"But you're stealing the lives of innocent people," Veris said. "And these people trusted you. Trusted the Omnist. They needed help. They didn't want to die."

"Oh, so you know about the souls," Chikao said. "But they are not dead."

"Korekuta promised us immortality," Yuko said. She may have looked to be in her twenties, but like Chikao, perhaps she was decades older.

"Yes, it has been thirty years and I am told I haven't aged a day," Chikao said. "It seems to be working, although eternity is a long time. Perhaps it is more than I can grasp."

Some of Chikao's personality was beginning to shine through again. A wink in the glisten of his eye, as the Omniscian Lucador might say. Maybe it was the presence of Yuko and the unburdening of secrets. He tilted his head, hemming and hawing, seeming to hedge the bet. "Maybe a little, I've aged. But almost zero."

"Five years ago, I was hired," Yuko said, "I, too, was promised eternal life. To be their assistant."

"Assist in what, collecting souls?" Jewelya said.

"That's why Korekuta thinks I'm here. Why he paid for my travel."

"Where is my suitcase?" Chikao said, snapping out of his charming persona. Back to reality. He glanced at the bags against the wall. Then he looked at Jewelya. "And I want rucksack. And other phone. You know which one. Or I'll find them myself. My soul diviners are in car."

Kick had said his cane could separate into two pieces. Perhaps that was his soul diviner.

Chikao widened his legs, bent at the knees ever so subtly, as if about to strike someone. "I'd prefer you handed over what is mine. I am in no mood to fight."

"He's not violent," Yuko said. "He wouldn't strike anyone."

"My assistant does not know me."

"You don't want the souls, Chikao," Yuko said. "Tell them. That's why I'm really here."

"Burning souls in a furnace," Veris said. "For energy. You create a literal hell on earth for the poor souls so you can live forever. That's why you collect them."

"No," Chikao said. "Not anymore."

"Shouldn't you have a small furnace with you?" Veris said. "A little portable one-hitter? You're just about as far from Korekuta's volcano cauldron as you can get. Maybe that's why you're beginning to age a little." She was fucking with him. Or was she flirting? Oddly, it was difficult to tell.

"I'm aging?" Chikao said, mocking her, feeling his cheekbone with the back of a hand.

The idea of a one-hitter, a soul furnace vape, of someone atomizing a soul into their lungs for health and energy was almost funny to Jewelya. Of course, that couldn't really be how it worked, though. *Could it? Poor Ainsley.*

"No, Korekuta doesn't burn souls anymore," Chikao said, switching into his Lodge-lecture tone. "That's what he used to do. It works, but doesn't make him more powerful or smarter. Doesn't grant him powers. It's not technological. His cauldron burns souls like fossil fuel. Very hot, very long. Cures disease and aging. But that is all."

As if good health and immortality isn't enough.

"So why doesn't he share this technology with the rest of the world?" Jewelya said. "He could cure disease. He could save billions of lives." As soon as it came out, she realized what she was saying.

"You're talking about burning souls, Jewelya," Veris said. "Condemning others to hell so you can live a little longer is wrong. I wonder how many souls have already suffered on his behalf."

"But that's old Korekuta," Chikao said. "Souls do burn out and it's wasteful. The fossil fuel of spirituality. Now he's learned how to make souls really small, small enough to put into molecules of DNA and use in a quantum super bio-microchip."

"A super bio-microchip?" Veris said.

"He calls chip a nano-compactor."

"So the souls are the size of molecules?" Jewelya said.

"Smaller. Much, much smaller. Size of electron. Oxygen is good atom for this. Eight electrons. Like our sun and eight planets. A magic number. Very stable. I bring Korekuta souls and he shrinks them down to size and replaces an electron in oxygen. One per atom. Like adding life to one planet in the solar system, like earth. Makes whole thing smarter and more valuable. So now oxygen has souls and processing power of a mind. A billion billion calculations per second in one tiny oxygen atom. And oxygen is in DNA, which is best place to store information. Billions of years of evolution all stored in one strand. Genius! Imagine how many oxygen atoms he can put into one strand of DNA! The DNA of Korekuta's future child."

"So the way this evil works is you trap our souls in phones," Jewelya said. "Then shrink them all into bio-computer chips?"

"Many will shrink. Omnist has the capability to nano-compact billions of souls..."

"That could take a while..." Jewelya said, as if sharing snark with Ainsley. But this was far worse than anything he could've said.

"You are correct, this will take long time, but it is nothing, no time at all to an immortal. And billions more souls will merge with Korekuta's mind. He has cracked code of life, mind, processing power, information storage. He will expand our consciousness until we are one. He will be both yin and yang."

"Chikao," Veris said. "You know this is wrong."

"We'll all be one. Are you ready?" He was becoming more animated. "Computing power of life on earth all acting as one, becoming sentient electron of our solar system; one atom of oxygen in our galaxy of DNA in universe of life. On and on we go. Korekuta will expand consciousness from our solar system, our atom, to other solar systems, other atoms. Much faster than speed of light, speed of expanding space. Imagine now how big life will be compared to how small we currently are."

"T-L-D-R," Jewelya said. "Let's reduce this to the facts in front of us. Simplify. The conclusion is you're killing people with cell phones."

"To answer your question, no, I do not. I kill no one. I just trap them in phones, then collect them."

THIRTY-SEVEN

KICK

After everything that had happened today, Kick knew he wasn't going to fall asleep. He lay in bed and with his laptop open on his chest.

He should be hearing video game noises from the other room. Gremmie yelling, then apologizing for yelling with a yell across the house, then repeating himself a few minutes later. Studio-quality headphones on his head, so Gremmie wouldn't be able to hear Kick even if he attempted to tell him to quiet down.

Then the aroma of Gremmie's THC vape. At least he would have the courtesy to take the vaporization process outside to the back patio. Then, watching Gremmie open the refrigerator and grab a sports drink or beer. Pull open a package of string cheese and eat it completely wrong. One was supposed to take their time and peel away each sinewy strand bit by bit, creating more surface area. For more flavor. Only a monster like Gremmie, in a hurry to resume playing his game, would inhale a cylinder of mozzarella in four or five wasteful bites. It was a travesty.

But not tonight.

Kick emailed Lucador to let him know he wouldn't be able to meet tomorrow regarding the Omnist II location. This would be his longest stint away from Omnist II preparations in six months—three days.

Tell you about it later, Kick wrote. If he tried to explain this all in an email, it would take hours. Besides, Lucador wasn't likely to even read the entire thing, much less actually understand it. Kick closed his computer and set it on the bed. He went to the kitchen where he picked Gremmie's phone up off the counter.

"You there, buddy boy?" Kick said.

Maybe not. He still didn't comprehend where a soul went when they left. Had Gremmie gone to Jewelya's to visit Ainsley, his new friend in the afterlife?

"If you're around, let me know." He felt like he was leaving a voicemail.

He should keep Gremmie's charger on hand, so he went to Gremmie's room. Empty, of course. But seeing his computer, noise-canceling headphones hanging on a hook, custom video game chair, music and surf posters on the walls, and unmade bed—they were all signifiers that Gremmie was still a teenager at heart. He imagined Gremmie walking up behind him with an incorrigible mouthful of string cheese, telling him to get out of his fucking room. That he knew Kick was always going through his shit when he was gone and soon he'd have to put a lock on his door.

Like Kick was somehow Gremmie's dad, even though he was only two years older.

"I don't think I can fall asleep," Kick said to a mass of blanket and sheets that almost looked like Gremmie sleeping. Kick imagined a teenage Gremmie doing that so he could gallivant with his skater friends, buying oversized sodas and beef jerkies at a Seven-Evan.

But he was neither asleep nor at a twenty-four-hour convenience store.

Gremmie was dead. Alive, but dead. Dead, but alive. Somehow.

"I'll be in my room if you're around."

Kick didn't *need* to tell him where he would be, but it felt like a normal thing to say. He didn't know if dead people slept, either.

The phone lit up.

Get out of my room, loser

"Then don't drink my beer," Kick said reflexively, without thinking. Gremmie couldn't drink his beer anymore. But he thought about Veris's Día De Los Muertos kits. Water, tequila. Treats. Maybe he *could*. "Want me to make you a Day of the Dead altar?" Kick said.

Too dark bro

"Where you been?" Kick said. "Took you a minute to respond."

Got pulled under a swell. Flat smack alligator roll

Surfing the afterlife. This led to a relatively inane, but cathartic conversation. Kick would speak out loud while Gremmie Moted. Even though he couldn't literally hear Gremmie's voice, he heard him in each response.

"Sounds like you've got that place figured out," Kick said, half in jest.

Yeah, I don't know, I'd rather come back. Take my new skills up to Mavericks.

Gremmie didn't seem miserable or sad, but Kick was happy he'd said he wanted to come back. "How's the music scene over there?" Not really expecting there to be one, of course.

Dude, I am music

"Are you stoned?"

No way. I don't need to think myself into corners anymore, missing the barrels

Barrels were the best parts of the best waves. "But you've been getting caught under swells over there, you said."

I'll be such a bitchin surfer when I get out

"Surfing the waves of thought and positive energy, huh?" Even if that didn't make sense, Kick figured it made sense to Gremmie.

Don't try to sound like me. You sound like an idiot

"Um, there's a reason for that," Kick said. No comeback. "Anyway, you know Veris right? Adelie Veris?"

Yes. The soul collector trying to free us

"I don't know if she's a soul collector. That's Chikao, or Korekuta, or something. But Veris's hotel room was ransacked tonight."

She isn't safe. Ainsley and I heard Chikao's voice. We think all the souls heard it

"What did he say?"

He told us to tell you to leave the phones where he could get them

"Well, we're not going to do that." Kick was getting antsy. This conversation, calming at first, was now getting him riled up. He needed to do something. Jewelya and Veris would be easy targets over at Jewelya's house. If Chikao had been following Veris, he would know she was there. He could be there now.

He texted Jewelya to see if she was up, then Veris. No immediate response from either.

Rather than wait, Kick left. He felt weird about putting Gremmie in his jacket pocket, and instead put his own phone there and kept Gremmie in his hand while he walked, then placed him on the passenger seat in the car.

"Do you need me to angle you?" Kick moved the phone farther away so that the divot in the far side of the seat tilted the phone toward him a little. "So you can see me?"

I can't use the camera. I'm in the Omnist

"Right." Kick should have known that. He was being silly.

"Want me to sing to you?" Kick said. "Steeer it up...leetle darling..."

Stop

I mean it

I'll go away until you stop

Dammit, you can't hear me

Read me, you butthole!

Kick didn't see those texts until he stopped at a red light, then laughed loudly to ensure Gremmie could hear it. "You got two entire verses for free."

I'm so going to punch you in the cervix when I get out of here

"I can't wait. Good luck finding it."

Better yet, when I get back you're getting hungover Bob Marley renditions on Sunday mornings

Sundays were Kick's day off.

When he parked the car, he saw Veris's rental in the driveway behind what was possibly Jewelya's car. Several houselights were on. As he approached, he heard voices, male and female.

He knocked.

Almost immediately, the door opened, as if he was expected. Jewelya brightened, then faded just a touch.

"Expecting someone else?" Kick said.

"I was hoping for the police."

Joking? She looked serious. *Not joking.* "What's going on?" Kick said. "I can call them." He noticed the others inside: Chikao, Veris, and a Japanese girl he didn't know. They didn't look like they were partying; they were standing in the living room, all looking at him in the door.

CHAPTER
THIRTY-EIGHT

JEWELYA

"I can call them," Kick said, referring to her comment about the police.

She'd said that more as a threat to Chikao, anyway, to keep him at bay.

"Maybe in a minute," Jewelya mumbled, opening the door further. "Chikao was just explaining how he's actually not Korekuta. And how they don't burn the souls they capture, but collect them for Korekuta's super-duper douchey computer." She turned to Chikao. "Did I get that right?"

Kick entered the house and closed the door.

Chikao gestured as if to say, "What else can I say?"

"Do you want to continue?" she said.

"Technology and life are both very complex," Chikao said. "People love to separate them, but they are very much one and the same."

"Not completely true," Kick said.

"Hello, Kick," Yuko said, interrupting them. "I'm Yuko. I'm glad you're here, too. This is my event, in a manner of speaking. I feel my arrival has brought everyone together."

"Chikao, soul phones, Korekuta...supercomputer," Kick said. He looked confused. "Your house, too?"

Jewelya enjoyed Kick's saltiness. He obviously knew whose house it was.

"No, no, no, but it is good you are here," Yuko said. "You have a soul phone, too. Do you not?"

"Gremmie, yeah. He's here." Kick was holding a phone in his hand.

Yuko held her hand out to take it. Kick hesitated.

Why is he doing that? Then Jewelya remembered; she'd been leery of Yuko, too. "Kick, just do it," she said. "She already had me hide Ainsley."

Reluctantly, Kick handed Yuko the phone.

"And the luggage bag," Yuko said. "We need them all stored away so we can talk."

"Wait a minute...why?" Jewelya said. "Chikao's already here."

"Shhhhh," Yuko said. "Should have done this before. This one?"

Jewelya nodded, then followed Yuko as she wheeled the bag into the bedroom, where the light was still on and the closet door closed. She stopped, not knowing where Jewelya had hidden Ainsley. Jewelya opened the closet door.

"Those are my phones," Chikao said behind them. "They should remain in my sight."

Bastard had followed them. Not cool. Jewelya half-expected Chikao to just grab the bag and run out of the house, but he didn't. He may have wanted to hear what else Yuko had to say. He apparently trusted her.

"I have idea. Just give me bag and I will leave," Chikao said, standing politely at a distance. "There is no point in delaying." His tone was friendly.

"Not until we talk, first," Yuko said. "I believe you might change your mind."

Jewelya opened the safe and Yuko handed her Gremmie's phone, which she placed on top of Ainsley. Veris opened the carry-on and began handing Jewelya phones, which she stacked on top of each other like stacks of money. The safe was small, but just large enough to hold all the phones. She locked the safe and closed the closet door again.

"If you don't mind," Yuko said, allowing the others to walk in front of her. "I have some tea getting cold."

"No, after you," Chikao said, smiling, gentlemanly. It was difficult to tell exactly where he was coming from with his mannerisms. Even if he was naturally this way—apparently friendly, mostly kind, and polite—he still stole and tortured souls.

Chikao and Kick declined cups of tea, but Jewelya added a splash of hot water to the other three mugs to warm them up. Yuko gave her a peculiar look. Maybe this was a faux pas.

"So what exactly is the deal?" Kick said, as they all took places at the table.

"I was telling your friends here that I'm the assistant to both Chikao and Korekuta," Yuko said. "I overheard Korekuta detailing plans for his computer. He's planning to use these souls, as well as our own, in the quantum biochips. For eternity."

"Like we'll be part of the world's internet or something?" Kick said. "I've always wanted to make a video game...No, we could *be* an online game." He was still fucking with her.

"Supercomputer won't need Wi-Fi," Chikao said. "It expands like souls do to encompass other computers or people.

Anything that is currently connected to internet already has interface he can react with. Cars, hospital equipment, phones, banking, refrigerators. Basically everything. But he won't need internet. He won't have to hack; everything will interface with him like he is admin. He is not god now, just immortal with few extraordinary powers. Then once soul computer is finished, he will be leader. He knows everything people know. And more. And that's when we become immortal too."

"A cartoon supervillain," Kick said. "Just my luck."

"But there will be nothing left for us to do," Yuko said. "He won't need us. I heard him bragging. He plans to keep good on his promise to grant us eternal life by installing us inside the DNA processor, too."

"Impossible," Chikao said. "I work for him for thirty years. We are like brothers."

"Thirty years for you, but he's been around for thousands!" Yuko said. "What do you think happened to his previous assistants? Why are there only two of us now? I have been researching this. He never keeps anyone around longer than fifty years. Most, much less. When he was done with them, he burned their souls. And when the time comes, if we won't recite the curse, then he'll burn us, too. We are nothing to him."

"Ainsley," Jewelya said. Yuko had just provided the two most likely scenarios for her husband. Death by fire, or eternal imprisonment.

"Gremmie," Kick said.

"Chikao, you can't let him do this," Jewelya said. "We have to stop him."

"Sensei, listen to me," Yuko said. "That's why I'm here. When I heard about this, I knew I needed to speak with you. I used your missing phones as the excuse to come find you. If I called or texted or emailed, Korekuta could have intercepted.

That's why all the phones are in the safe. So he cannot hear us right now."

Chikao stood straight, his chin level. Probably thinking, but not reacting at all.

"How can you do this to people?" Veris said. "Doesn't this bother you?"

"My job is to bring souls to Korekuta," Chikao said, more defiant in his stance but shakier in voice. "It is not bad job. These people are sad. They are lost. They have no anchor; otherwise, why do they need Omnist? I find self-selected people who will appreciate freedom from burdens. I free them of miserable life and they live forever without shame."

"But Ainsley isn't unhappy!" Jewelya said. *Or is he?* "He doesn't deserve eternal damnation."

"Nor does Gremmie," Kick said.

"I made this better," Chikao said. "At first Korekuta was indiscriminate, capturing any nearby souls. I talked him out of that. Capturing souls who want out of their situation makes more sense."

"Lisa at the party. Another man cutting his torso," Kick said. "These were people fighting against their deaths last night. Painfully, too. Lisa is blind now."

"But her soul is not blind," Chikao said. "I admit some spells need tweaking. Easy fix for beta."

"But people aren't computers," Veris said.

"You call me evil, but I am helping people," Chikao said. "Does it matter whether a soul is trapped in meat case or a microchip?"

"Yes," Jewelya and Veris said simultaneously.

"Maybe you think you're helping people," Kick said. "*Maybe.* If you believe you're removing them from a shitty life. But you're also putting their souls in eternal prison, which is far worse than their temporary life here."

"You talk to your Ainsley, your Gremmie," Chikao said. "Are they miserable? Anchored in phone. Only difference, soon they will be anchored in DNA microchip."

"That's so not the point," Jewelya said. "You might be the literal devil. How many souls have you burned? You guys are in woodcuts and bibles. My husband isn't distraught or desiring death. He didn't want to leave this life. He wants to come back. You. Are. The. Devil."

"I have never destroyed a soul," Chikao said.

"Nor have I," Yuko said. "The burning souls of legend, those were done by Korekuta and ancient assistants, who were also subsequently burned. Hundreds and thousands of years ago."

"I was recruited when cells phones and internet were first burgeoning," Chikao said, almost apologetically. Kitty walked in the room, almost sleepy, and rubbed against Chikao, now, as well. Two strangers in one evening. "He wanted lieutenant who understood current technology. Someone who could help develop chips, but didn't desire to usurp him."

"Even so, you've stolen souls for thirty years, then," Veris said. "That's still evil."

"You might think," Chikao said. "Stolen, yes, but not destroyed. I never destroy. These souls are alive and well— healthy souls. They're still there, ready to be freed. Not destroyed." Chikao went silent and looked at his feet. It seemed Yuko and Veris had affected him.

"Ready to be freed?" Jewelya said. "That's what you said, right?"

"Your husband, he is okay?" Chikao said, his tone changing to an overwhelmingly bedside manner. He sounded like a Dr. Chikao.

"I think so," Jewelya said. "For now."

"And your friend," he turned to Kick. "Gremmie?"

302

"Gremmie. Yes, he and Ainsley are probably talking to each other right now in the safe, wondering what's going on out here."

"Listening. That is all they have. All they can do." Chikao began pacing like a professor in front of an auditorium. "The metal is faraday cage for Wi-Fi and phone connection, but they can expand to try to listen, I think."

"That means if Korekuta enters one of those phones," Veris said. "He can hear what they hear."

"I think we're far enough away from their hearing," Yuko said.

"And you guys are working on counter-spell that will free them?" Chikao said.

"I have begun," Veris said. "But it's difficult. There is so little Language of the Sun out there to be found."

"No matter," Chikao said. "Language of the Sun is older than humans."

"Older than humans?" Jewelya said.

"Yes. Information is never destroyed in universe. It changes, morphs, adjusts, just like language. Language of the Sun is basic programming of universe."

"The sun is what, four billion years old?" Kick said.

"And the universe is ten billion years older than that," Chikao said. "The consciousness continuum began with Big Bang, start of it all. All particles began there. It is called Language of the Sun because it created our sun."

"And you're fluent in this language?" Veris said.

"Besides Korekuta, I believe I am only person that knows it. I write spells, tweaking for each person. For this, I probably know it better than Korekuta. But I have never had conversation in Language of the Sun. I only write it."

"So I'd be wasting my time hunting down a witchy Omniscian to draw up a spell," Kick said.

"I can do much quicker," Chikao said, gesturing widely to the room. "Imagine millions of souls in one microchip, imagine if they all think counter-spell at same time."

It was frightening to Jewelya to hear Chikao speak like this. All those souls in the universe's largest computer processor, running programs in Language of the Sun. Korekuta would be unstoppable. But Chikao had chosen to say, "counter-spell."

"And I believe Yuko is correct," Chikao said. "Once soul collection is streamlined and chips filling up, Korekuta will eliminate anything, anyone he doesn't need." He turned to Yuko. "And you promise this wasn't misheard, or funny misunderstanding?"

"No, sensei. My memory is nearly verbatim."

It was apparent that Yuko's mission here had been successful: She'd flipped Chikao against Korekuta.

THIRTY-NINE

AINSLEY

Ainsley watched as Jewelya stacked the other phones in the safe, on top of and next to him. The others—Kick, Veris, and the Japanese girl—were watching her, including the Omnist hacker Chikao, who was annoyingly standing with his hands on hips in the doorway, as if supervising. This sickened Ainsley. He wanted to push him away from her, but could do nothing.

Jewelya closed the door and the group left for the front of the house. Once again, Ainsley tried to enlarge so that he was in the living room with them, but he couldn't hear. Besides the distance and walls, there were many voices close by. He reduced to phone-sized.

He tried to overlap with only the next phone. Being located in the bottom left corner of the safe helped. Any enlargement as a middle phone would have meant overlapping with up to six phones right away. Conversation with only one would be difficult.

"Who else is here?" Ainsley said.

"Who is that?" said a voice. Soul voices sounded so similar that Ainsley couldn't place them.

"This is Ainsley. Do I know you?"

"It's Gremmie, bro-ham."

Vocabulary was the new tone of voice.

Perfect. "I take it everybody's here?" Ainsley said.

"Kick took me back to the crib. Now we're chilling with Jewelya and Veris."

Ainsley expanded a little to count the phones. The total was similar to how many were at the Emporium. But there were too many voices at this level, too much overlapping. He shrank to as close to only covering Gremmie as he could.

"When they stuck me in the safe," Ainsley said, "they said they didn't want Chikao listening in on their conversation, but he's here at the house now. I haven't been able to really hear what they're saying out there. Can you?"

"Surf's up, bruh."

That meant he hadn't.

Ainsley began to expand a little, and he felt Gremmie doing the same. He felt something tweak. He stopped. Gremmie stopped.

"Did you feel that?" they seemed to say at the same time. They were so in sync, Gremmie's consciousness seemed to join his. Ainsley didn't have access to Gremmie's old memories, necessarily, but rather what he'd learned from those experiences. The bottom-line rules. They were beginning to share a mind.

"That's fucking twisted," they seemed to say at the same time.

Their strength had more than doubled. Sentience and

power of mind wasn't a zero-sum game. One Ainsley plus one Gremmie equaled the power of four souls. They were thinking separately, but together. Interdependent. They sensed that new experiences would be the shared memory of this combined mind.

It was a liberating feeling of power.

"Let's cover all the phones," Gremsley said. "See if we can bring them all in."

The incessant chattering returned, nearly overpowering them.

"Too much," Ainsmie said. "Let's try to cover only the next phone."

They reduced to their joint starting level, then eased into covering the next phone. As they did, they felt the presence of another soul.

"Hi, can you hear me? Most of us met earlier," Ainsmie said.

"Yeah, and if you don't know him," Gremsley said, "I bet you know *me*. I'm Gremmie, the Gremmeister Flash."

Regardless of who initiated a thought, it immediately became a joint one.

"This is Summer," a voice said. "Who else is here?"

"Summer, it's Ainsley," Ainsmie said. "From the party. I helped Dirge with his computer."

"Of course," she said. "I met Kick's roommate earlier, when we learned how to Omnist."

"Join us," Gremsley said. "We're building a mega-soul."

"What we mean is we'd like you to expand to the same size as us," Ainsmie said.

"I expanded large enough to see Dirge at home," Summer said. "He looks completely beside himself. I tried to talk to him, but he couldn't hear me. And I couldn't hear him, either. But I can hear you guys."

"I think when we expand through walls, our ability to hear

diminishes," Ainsmie said. "Plus distance. But we're stronger as a layered soul. Two of us feels like the power of three or four. Let's see if that continues with three souls."

"Our hearing got stronger," Gremsley said. "The other voices got loud, and I mean *aggro*, after we combined. I bet you'll def hear the Dirge when we wad up."

"I'd like to be able to speak with him," she said.

"Tap in!" they said.

They felt Summer trying to orient herself within them.

"Almost there," she said. "I'm not that good at changing size yet."

And the more she merged with them, the better they were able to help adjust her parameters.

They felt even more powerful. Maybe the strength of eight or nine souls now.

Interestingly, Ainsley and Summer had both met Gremmie multiple times as souls, but still didn't know what he was supposed to look like.

"I don't look like that, you know," they said as all of them. "I see what you're scoping and you're way off. Waaay off."

Gremsleyer suggested an image of himself to the hivemind as an animated video game avatar: part bearded steam punk in a leather battle helmet with brass and steel accessories, and part surfer, carving up a green room barrel. The new hivemind felt itself laughing.

"I feel amazing," they said. "Better than...well, when I was a—"

"We know," they said. *Alive.* "Ready to add one more?"

"Juice it up!" they said.

They slowly expanded, absorbing the next cooperating soul. As they expected, the fourth soul made them as powerful as fifteen or twenty. The fifth as twenty-five or thirty. It was basically a product of the number of souls involved multiplied by itself. Ten souls were as powerful as a hundred.

They tried to approach souls one at a time, but the process of overlapping made this tricky. They would have to isolate a soul for conversation, asking the others to refrain from conversing. They'd ask the soul if they wanted to be part of their burgeoning hivemind and would they line up with them. If not, if the soul didn't trust the hive or was unsure what the effects would be, they could seek a different level, not aligning with them, until they were removed from the hive and separated again.

For example, someone who called himself "Akhenaten" was one of these.

"I'm not going back," he said. "This is my world now. I feel more powerful than ever before."

And the hive respected the decision.

Finished with conversing with the other phones, Aleph noticed that, besides the infrared and electromagnetic wavelengths, the blackness within the safe had gained more color. It wasn't quite visual, but it was felt with more senses. Rounded and warm. The space was alive.

The combination of Ainsley, Gremmie, Summer, and a couple dozen others decided they would call their hivemind "Aleph," which was both the name of the first letter of the Greek alphabet and an ancient word for the concept of an ever-receding horizon, representing knowledge that, once attained, would instantaneously become unattainable again. Forgotten, once learned.

And there were no longer individual thoughts. For what they were, this was a good thing.

Aleph felt powerful, with twenty-seven souls achieving the processing power of seven hundred and fifty. And this was fun.

They wondered, in a billionth of a billionth of a second, if new meaning had emerged in the language of the universe. They were thinking in Language of the Sun. They understood the universe better than any human or computer ever had.

They knew that when they separated again, they would lose not only this processing power, but this understanding of the universe. This sense of peace and oneness.

But yet, they longed for a brain with a visual cortex.

And a sense of touch.

And love.

They enlarged until their perceptive bubble crossed into the living room where the people were. They heard them as if they were all in the room together. They could probably hear people ten miles away if they expanded that far.

They heard ethereal hissing like a cat. Not from the people.

A predator was in their midst.

But they weren't afraid.

FORTY

KICK

"So, how do you propose we stop Korekuta?" Kick said to the group in the living room.

"Especially if he's immortal," Jewelya said.

"All souls are immortal," Veris said, swinging her glance from person to person, landing on Chikao. Kick could swear she was placing the tips of her fingers together. At least that's what her tone sounded like. "Or at least, they *should* be," she said.

Kick liked her. Even while she placed judgment upon Korekuta, Kick could tell she wasn't proposing a death penalty. She'd be unable to burn a soul, even Korekuta's.

"I believe it is best to use his own spells against him," Chikao said, his tone remarkably similar to Veris's. "We trap him in phone."

Could Chikao have flipped this easily?

311

Veris offered her own phone for him to use. "It's clean," she said. "There are no souls currently trapped in it."

Had there been before?

"Veris," Kick said. Something didn't feel right about this. Chikao was suddenly being too helpful; he'd turned on a dime. "I don't know about this."

"I trust him," Veris said.

Already?

"Thank you, but no thank you," Chikao said. "It must be a phone he knows, or he won't trust it. Sometimes I go inside and meet with Korekuta rather than call or email. Like having face-to-face conversation without faces."

"How do we know he isn't listening to us right now?" Jewelya said.

"I would know," Chikao said. "I can feel his presence."

"So you guys can go in your phone and have a little conversation in the dark," Kick said. "Away from prying eyes?" *Or ears.*

"Not dark as much as invisible," Chikao said. "Absence of light is not darkness, invisibility is. Darkness is shadow, cast by light. Invisibility is shadow from another dimension, just as our dark matter is its gravity leaking over. Korekuta wants to find light of next dimension. Through invisibility."

This explanation sounded like something Yksian would talk about. Kick was struggling to follow.

"I am so lost," Jewelya said. "I don't need a science or philosophy lecture."

"Ah, yes," Chikao said. "Like I was saying, we use my phone so Korekuta does not suspect trap. Mixture of spell and technology. Korekuta can enter his own phone in Japan and expand to cover great distances, overlapping other vessels, including mine."

"Sorry. Stop," Jewelya said. "I'm still stuck on this. How is it you think we can trust you? Just a minute ago you were still stealing soul phones."

"Pardon me," Yuko said, "I believe him. That's why I came. He is reasonable and I knew that once he heard what Korekuta was up to, he would do great things."

"Of course *you* would say that," Jewelya said. "No offense."

"I'll show you," Chikao said. "I'll go into phone myself. Lure him here."

"You could use that to escape," Kick said.

"I'm not exactly trapped now. I choose to be here," Chikao said. "Back home Korekuta often shrinks himself to see how souls affect chips at different levels...for optimization. So now, I tell him you have discovered great innovations in soul chip technology. Come see and have you explain them to him. I'll tell him you'll make great additions to our team."

"You really *are* trying to bring him here," Jewelya said.

"Not exactly. I'll tell him to recite spell to make him human here. Soul phone transfer. But really, it will trap him in my phone."

"But won't he know it's a curse?" Veris said. "Doesn't he speak the language?"

"Yes. But I write most of spells and programming. He is more hardware expert."

"And once we have him, then we destroy his phone?" Veris said.

"Not quite."

JEWELYA, Yuko, and Veris went to the bedroom to retrieve the vessels from the safe.

When Chikao went outside to his rental car, Kick felt startlingly alone. Without holding Gremmie's phone, he realized how tenuous this entire situation was. Trusting strangers and near strangers to save themselves from eternal damnation. He looked at his phone, expecting something. But there were no Motes for this situation. As long as they worked toward a goal, like freeing the souls, he felt purpose. Now, being alone for fifteen seconds felt like an hour.

To Kick's relief, the others returned with the phones and set them on the coffee table. Kick spotted what he thought was Gremmie's and held it. Its energy was correct.

Chikao arrived with another bag of phones he'd collected from Dirgatory, which he said included several phones he had found today around the Valley. In all, he added about twenty phones to the mix. Funny how an hour ago the idea of Chikao collecting more phones would have nauseated Kick. Now it was the right thing to do.

"Spread them out on floor," Chikao said, picking up the first couple.

The phones were placed three feet apart around the living and dining rooms. Yuko walked around, straightening them out.

"Plenty of space for people to come back," Chikao said, confidently stepping between them with perfect posture. "Don't want to return to a foot in the face. A nose in armpit. A mouth in butt." All his examples involved finding someone's head in a precarious location.

Kick needed to put Gremmie down, but didn't want to let go. Jewelya was looking at him. She hadn't put Ainsley on the floor, either. She was holding the phone with both hands, protecting it.

"Do not hold that while I am gone," Chikao said, noticing. The humor had left his voice. "In case anything happens."

"What could happen?" Kick said.

"Anything."

Kick and Jewelya split the difference and sat on the couch, with the phones to their sides so they could still read incoming texts.

All the phones in the room simultaneously lit up with new notifications.

Jewelya looked at Ainsley.

Kick looked at Gremmie.

Our name is Aleph

"They're all one now?" Jewelya said, looking at Ainsley's phone as well. "Is that a thing?"

"Is Ainsley calling himself Aleph, now, too?" Kick said. Without the list of passcodes in front of him, he wouldn't be able to see the rest of the messages.

"He is," she said.

"*They* are," Chikao said. "Good, good. They are thinking as one."

"So who sent this?" Jewelya said.

"Aleph?" Kick said.

"Smart. Much, much more power," Chikao said. "Remember when I said to imagine all souls in microchip thinking in unison? This is similar. A multiplier. They figured it out themselves."

"I brought extra phone from car," Chikao said. "One of my own for Korekuta. Now, I will go into my phone and give him spell to transfer to other phone. Then he says second spell to make himself human here in Jewelya's house."

"But he'd be here," Jewelya said. "That's worse!"

"No, that one is trap," Chikao said. "He'll be stuck in phone forever."

"Why not just have him recite the spell while he's overlapped with you?" Kick said. "This feels like there's an extra step here."

"Because it'll trap both of them," Veris said. "Correct?"

"Yes. We need to separate first," Chikao said. He typed on his phone, stopped a couple seconds to think, then began typing again. "Working out spell."

"Do you need more time?" Veris said. She looked like she'd be ready to help.

"No, no," Chikao said. "Only slight modification. But different enough to obscure plan."

"So you're sure that he won't recognize the spell?" Veris said.

"We'll find out," Chikao said. "Texting him now."

CHAPTER
FORTY-ONE

AINSLEY

Another soul had entered their space.

Aleph saw Jewelya, Kick, Veris, and Yuko posted up in the four corners of the living room. The soul phones were spread out across the floor. Veris was sitting on a loveseat. Her feet didn't reach the floor.

"Chikao says he's in and he's fine," Yuko said, looking at a phone next to her on a cushion. "Not to worry, he does this all the time."

The spacing between the phones of Aleph, although wider now, was just tight enough for the souls to remain overlapped as one. But their outer edge was a bit hazier now.

"Ainsley, Gremmie," a voice said. The same voice as always. "It's Chikao."

Aleph was unsure if they should speak. Silence in the face

of the voice had previously served them well. But the voice had never identified itself as Chikao.

"Call me Aleph," they said, finally.

"Yes," Chikao said. "This is good. You are more powerful as Aleph."

"Aleph still refuses to instruct the humans Kick and Jewelya to leave their phones outside for you to take."

"I would now recommend against that," Chikao said.

"But those were your orders."

"The situation has changed."

As far as Aleph was concerned, a processor was only as good as the information that went into it. Garbage in, garbage out. If they had reached a conclusion using a faulty premise, the logic may have been correct, but the conclusion likely wasn't. If Chikao was lying, there was little they could do.

There was no point responding.

"You are hesitant to believe me," Chikao said. "Understandable, but I have seen error of my ways. I am here to fix."

"Have you come to deliver a new spell and move us to Japan?" Aleph said.

"I am here to warn you. Korekuta will be arriving momentarily. He is not here to bring you to Japan, but to inhabit a new phone in which I will trap him."

"He will burn our souls alive."

"Not likely. And as compacted soul, you are much safer. How many souls are you?"

"Twenty-seven."

"Ah, yes. Very stable. But some advice," Chikao said. "Think of yourself as cube. Three by three by three. Most stable."

"Why should we do this?"

"Korekuta will be angry once he realizes he has been captured. I want you safe."

"Are you asking to join us?"

"I cannot. He would recognize trap immediately. I must remain independent to supply spells. And for moment, you must remain here, as well. He can sense soul collection. It is beacon for him. Also, do not think about trap. He will read your mind if he overlaps with you."

Aleph sensed that Chikao had withdrawn from their overlapping.

~

ANOTHER VOICE ENTERED THEIR SPACE. It had traveled far, spread itself thin. But it was strong. All the colors within the blackness around Aleph once again faded. This was Korekuta arriving.

"Korekuta," Chikao said. "I have extra phone here for you to enter. It is next to me."

Aleph sensed immediately that Korekuta was a collection of thousands of previous souls overlapped with his own, all unable to escape, now part of his processing. But he was stretched thin over distance, over time. Aleph was concentrated in one place and solid.

"Give me the spell," Korekuta said.

Aleph did not hear Chikao's response, as he could not say it without the spell affecting him, as well.

"Text is on that phone," Chikao said. "It is for you to read." He must have texted it before minimizing into his own phone.

They heard Korekuta recite the incantation, and color returned within their blackness around them. Korekuta was now residing in that phone and no longer stretched thin. He'd concentrated and things felt more dangerous. He was close.

"One more spell," Chikao said.

"No. Not now." Korekuta's voice was deep, powerful, and haunting. "I do not trust you."

Pause. "If you do not trust me," Chikao said, "why did you make trip?"

"To see about this new discovery, learn the technology, and take it home."

"It is powerful enough to push a soul into the next dimension," Chikao said. "Come join me. Here is the spell."

"Ah, but the spell is a trap, Chikao," Korekuta said. "You are a young soul with courage and naivety. And so, so foolish. You must learn that the spell is for *you* to read, not me."

"And which spell is that?" Aleph said. Since they had never seen the spell, the danger in thinking about it was nonexistent.

"Who is this?" Korekuta said.

Aleph felt powerful, strong, invisible as a three by three by three cube, and attempted to adjust to the size and level of Korekuta to try to absorb him, or merge their thoughts so the evil would be weakened.

"I am Chikao," Aleph said.

"I am Chikao," Chikao said.

Korekuta must have shifted sizes, not allowing a merger. "I will burn you all!"

"I am Chikao," Aleph said, again. "The soul of a new biocomputer. We built ourself, and will not be your slave."

Aleph felt the universe shaking. Korekuta was building steam, bubbling with power. Colors faded in and out in the blackness. He was going to blow.

"You will read the spell!" Korekuta boomed.

"Ebum ible succulum!" Chikao said, along with a few more lines of Language of the Sun. He and Korekuta both began screaming, Chikao reciting the lines louder and louder, so much that even Aleph felt they were going to burst out into the void of the universe. Then Chikao's and Korekuta's voices began fading farther and farther into oblivion.

Silence. They were gone.

This was the quietest Aleph had heard the universe.

"Chikao?" Aleph said. But they knew he was gone. He'd sacrificed himself to save them. With his last thought a spell, he'd attempted to redeem himself for his sins. Perhaps he had aligned himself perfectly with Korekuta, just long enough to cast the spell and take them both out.

What was left for Aleph to do? They could choose to remain consolidated and explore the universe. The thought of reincarnating as a person felt like an option, but what would be the point? The lessons they'd been born to learn were still with the lives they'd recently left.

But was it even possible to return to those lives now? Perhaps Kick and Veris had discovered new options. Aleph directed all constituent parts of themselves to minimize back to their own personal phone levels.

WHEN AINSLEY FOCUSED to the correct size, he saw Jewelya sitting next to his phone on the couch. A rush of emotions. She looked worried.

"Jewelya," he said, knowing she couldn't hear. Now a memory of emotions. Every feeling he'd ever had for her wanted to be forefront. He reduced to Omnist-sized to message her and saw a spell waiting for him. It was from Chikao.

AINSLEY FOUND himself holding his phone, sitting lotus on the couch next to Jewelya. She jumped up and spun around so fast from shock, she nearly fell off the couch.

"Oh my god!" she said. They grabbed each other's arms. "Ains! Ains!"

Ainsley's eyes were so watery and blurry, he could barely see. He hadn't felt or smelled Jewelya in two days. He wanted to expand his sense of self to overlap with her, to include her with him. A new feeling. She *was* him, and always had been. Perhaps he hadn't recognized that. He didn't know where to begin, where to train his focus. There were many other voices in the room. He was already no longer used to hearing voices without "seeing" the soundwaves.

Hugging Jewelya was the happiest he had ever felt.

But when Ainsley saw Kick, he released her and jumped up to hug him, and then Summer. There was so much activity in the room, almost too much, with many confused people, most in Halloween costumes. A warm wind swirled alongside a soft popping noise as people reappeared. They rapidly grew from baby-sized to adult in about a second, standing, sitting, and still holding their phones, probably in the position they'd been when they'd read the curse.

He saw both Veris and Yuko, smiling sadly. They seemed happy for the released souls, but something else must've been bothering them. But before he could speak to them, Brandon and Jennifer from Warbler Brothers saw him.

"I knew it was you when we overlapped!" Brandon said to him. "But I was the last one absorbed, and Aleph was strong. I trusted you...er, them. Us."

Ainsley hadn't considered what the other souls had been thinking before joining the hivemind. And once they joined, they'd all been thinking as the cumulative Aleph.

Next to Ainsley, Kick was hugging a redheaded guy, followed by aggressive pats and slaps like they were brothers. At their feet were a couple other phones, nearly being stepped on. Ainsley scooted them away, careful to not leave them too close to a chair or under a table, lest he cause problems for a returning human.

Kick saw him do this and separated from his friend. "For anyone else that can hear me," he said, announcing to the room at large, "if you're a soul in a phone, check your messages in the Omnist! People are returning by reading that spell. So read it!"

"Hey, duder," the redheaded man said to Ainsley, grinning widely, showing teeth that bordered on needing braces. And it was true: Gremmie looked nothing like Ainsley, or the combined Aleph for that matter, had pictured him.

He was about six feet tall with a long, craning neck and a large Adam's apple which made him appear taller than he was. Red hair cut in a non-cut, a non-style. His neck, elbows, knees, collarbones, and shoulder blades all seemed to flee in opposite directions simultaneously. He appeared to have questionable coordination. And his voice was deep and staccato like a bass drum. His tone didn't sound like he was a surfer, although he spoke the language of one.

"We carved the green barrel!" Gremmie said, all teeth.

Yeah, something like that. Ainsley was at a loss for words.

They hugged. Gremmie slapped a hand on Ainsley's shoulder so hard it felt as if there were rings on all of his fingers. His hands were bare.

Across the room, he saw the girl dressed as Nefertiti, without her Akhenaten. She was just as beautiful as at the party, if not more so. Smoky eyes, golden choker, slinky dress. She was speaking with no one, but looking around, as if searching for her partner. She locked eyes with Ainsley, causing a jolt to shoot through him. She was powerful, perhaps not just as a human, but as a soul.

"It's you," Nefertiti said, stepping closer. "I saw you at Dirgatory, then when you helped us out of the phones, I could picture you. I knew it was you."

"Are you okay?"

"I am, but..." She looked around again. "I cannot find Akhenaten. Err, Nate, as he calls himself here."

"No," Ainsley said. The full answer was going to be difficult.

"You talked to him, right? Is he somewhere else? Maybe back in the maze?"

Ainsley felt himself holding his breath. He forced a long slow inhale and exhale, careful to not sound like he was sighing.

"Tell me!" Nefertiti said. "You must!" The fire in her eyes was intense. Centuries, millennia of experience and power.

"Umm," Ainsley said. *Rip the bandage off.* "He chose to stay there, to free himself of this plane." Was that the correct way to word it? Even though he retained most what he'd experienced, he could feel some of the language and universal knowledge beginning to fade, like he'd just awakened from a dream.

Nefertiti didn't quite fall to her knees, but her body weakened and softened as she fell into Ainsley, hugging loosely.

CHAPTER
FORTY-TWO

JEWELYA

People were spread throughout Jewelya and Ainsley's house. Touching their bodies as if shocked to be there, using the restrooms, pouring glasses of water. Talking, crying, phoning. All phone chargers were in in use.

Jewelya saw a man with no shirt, his torso covered in bloody psychotic razor blade handwriting. But he was smiling.

The little person who'd greeted her at the shed, wearing the "Actual Size" T-shirt, was walking around the room high-fiving people. "Great job, boys!" he said, as if they were at a wrap party for a movie. His pronunciation of the "S" sound was crystal clear, as in the word "Ice." A personal affectation. "Stellar!"

The house was loud with exuberant crying and laughing.

"I have so much to tell you!" one person said into a phone.

"Death is so weird," said another. "No, I'm not afraid of it at all."

There was a knock at the door, and the person closest opened it. Dirge entered like the mayor of his own costume-clad, post-apocalyptic, post-party congregation. It seemed most everybody knew him, and he patted shoulders and the tops of people's heads as he found his way to Summer. He picked her up so they could hug at his height.

JEWELYA ALWAYS FELT SO DEEPLY for other people that moments like this were almost too much for her. So much happiness she was about to burst. She'd been known to cry at television commercials. Veris and Yuko were sitting together on the loveseat, both small enough to fit easily. Jewelya sensed they were upset, even though they seemed intent on not bringing others down. They were smiling sad smiles. She wanted to hug them.

Chikao was still gone. All the people who had been Aleph had heard him go, and were telling tales about his self-sacrifice. These two clearly knew.

"I know you're upset," Jewelya said. "But Chikao wasn't exactly a good person."

"He is a great person," Yuko said.

"I disagree," Veris said. "He is a great soul but a horrible person."

"I worked with him for years," Yuko said. "He is my friend. I came here to warn him about what could happen, and he chose to put everyone else above himself."

"In the short time I followed him, I began to think like him, too," Veris said. "I'll miss him. I don't know why, but I will.

And, if you'll let me, I'd like to keep his phone. In case he resurfaces."

"We could make an altar for him," Jewelya said.

Veris went out to her car and retrieved a bag that had parts of several Día De Los Muertos kits in it. "I was going to bring this to my San Francisco Lodge, but here I am."

She began unpacking sweet breads and tiny bottles of tequila.

"I knew you had liquor in there," Kick said. He lifted a bottle to hold up and show Gremmie.

"Whoooaaa!!!" Gremmie said, grabbing the bottle from Kick. "Now you're talking!"

Jewelya took the bottle from him. "These are for souls, not you."

"I would argue I'm a soul trapped in flesh and only tequila will free me," Kick said.

"These kits are for *returning* souls."

"That's moi!" Gremmie said, holding a hand out, grinning.

"My father approves," Veris said, setting four framed photos of her father to the side.

Jewelya handed Gremmie the bottle of tequila.

"I don't have any printed photos of Chikao, though," Veris said, opening a photo on her phone and setting it within the altar. The picture remained on screen for several seconds before timing out.

"If you send me a couple," Jewelya said, "I can print them in the other room."

Veris emailed a photo of Chikao. Jewelya went back to the office, printed it, then added it to the display. Veris stepped back to admire her work.

"I can't believe you guys are honoring a man who stole souls for a living," Kick said. "This is what we want to remember?"

"He has work to do," Veris said. "I'm sensing his soul, as well as many others, are still out there. I feel Chikao will ultimately spend years improving the lives of souls. Many, many more. Far more than he trapped or hurt. I believe he'll return."

"You seem confident that an evil spirit can change," Jewelya said.

"That's what this salt is for," Veris said, sprinkling liberally around the altar. "Evil spirits cannot pass."

"And if he cannot?"

"Then we'll know for sure who he is."

FORTY-THREE

KICK

Walking the house, Kick found reembodied people interesting in a way he never would've predicted. Most of them had disappeared at Dirgatory so they were still in their costumes, but it seemed like some of them were waking from a dream state. Or he was.

Happiness, but disbelief. Shock, but relief.

Calm, but excitable. Stunned, but aware.

Within thirty minutes, some people were picked up by family or friends, while others appeared not in a hurry to leave. They wanted to hang out with their new friends, recounting how and where their spells had taken effect. What they "learned on the other side." Asking questions of Ainsley, Gremmie, and Summer, who seemed to be the de facto leaders of the "soul phone squad."

"Aleph," Ainsley had corrected when Kick had said that once. That was fair.

Kick noticed the man dressed as a hobbit, the one whose beer stein he found in the maze.

"That was literally an out-of-body experience," the hobbit said to a friend.

Kick saw Little Bo Peep, who'd been standing in line for the bathroom inside Dirge's house. "I disappeared in the bathroom, too," she said to Summer.

Along with Gremmie, that made at least three disappearances in that room alone. There could be more who practiced the spirituality of bathrooms—places where people could routinely stare into their eyes, groom, cry, pump themselves up, disrobe, get sick.

And say their prayers.

But in the end, Chikao, the soul phone collector, had given up his life to be eternally chained to a truly evil spirit. And he likely saved countless souls around the world as well, ones who were soon to be captured.

THE SADDEST TWO of the bunch, Yuko and Veris, were nibbling on sweet bread, offering it to hungry rescued people, several of whom kept turning it down. It wasn't vegan.

"I'll have a bite," Kick said. It would go well with a cup of tea. He slid Veris's Chikao phone away from him to put his sweet bread on a plate.

Then Chikao enlarged suddenly, sitting on the kitchen counter. Like a genie, but holding his phone like he had when he'd cursed himself.

"Chikao!" Yuko said.

"Ah!" he said, jumping down. "My Yuko, she awaits!" They embraced.

"No Korekuta?" Yuko said when they separated.

Chikao squeezed his eyes closed and rubbed them, adjusting to the brightness of the kitchen.

"How did you do this?" Veris said.

"When Korekuta and I were locked in phone, he insisted on controlling our mind. He was angry and unfocused and I lay back to let him wind us into craziness. He minimized and enlarged quickly, back and forth. He wanted to hurt me. Punish. It was unique experience having someone in your head who wants you dead. When he realized he couldn't hurt me while we were precisely overlapped, Korekuta demanded for me to tell him spell to separate."

"And I refused, of course."

"So how did you do escape if he knows your thoughts?"

"Now my practice of meditation pays dividends. Thinking without words. I realized he couldn't hear my no-thought thoughts."

"Do you have aphantasia?" Veris said.

"Ah, yes," Chikao said. "Lack of auditory imagery."

"No inner monologue," Kick said.

"You could say that. But Korekuta does have inner voice," Chikao said. "He could keep no secrets from me while cursed. And yes, Yuko was correct about his ultimate plans."

"We may have saved humanity," Veris said, somehow emitting a concerned glow as she looked at Chikao.

The weight of what transpired today hadn't fully hit Kick yet, but Veris may have been correct in her assessment. But he didn't think he'd be glowing if he'd been the one to say that.

Chikao nodded. "The plan was we'd expand large enough to overlap both phones once again. Smaller than house, bigger than room. I told him we'd say same prayer, but at last words, he would say something different than me. He had to trust me. I said what the words would be. Then I said prayer for both of us and at end, we each forced thought on different last words. We are strong minds, powerfully meditative in Language of Sun. He went into his phone; I went in mine. Locking us in separate coffins. But I then I recited spell to return."

"So he can come back now," Veris said.

"No. I used different spell. He doesn't know counter-spell to free himself."

"He could size himself along someone else who knows," Veris said.

"Who else would know spell I wrote?" Chikao said. "I'll never write it down or say it again."

"And what if Korekuta hadn't separated from you?" Kick said.

"We'd still be together. Possibly for eternity. I could never think about counter-spell when we were together because then he would know it, too."

"You were willing to spend eternity like that?" Veris said. She sounded impressed.

"So he really doesn't know the counter-spell?" Kick said.

"No—it was my job to write new spells he didn't know."

CHIKAO HAD ASKED FOR, and was now holding the phone Korekuta was captured in. They had to do something with it. Make sure the electronics would never work again.

"I sense Korekuta's soul is here," Veris said. "I would imagine he's listening."

"Why not just smash it?" Kick said.

"That would work for some spells," Chikao said, turning it over in his hands. "But this one locked soul in centermost atom of memory for Omnist app. If we smash phone, soul wouldn't release, but be trapped in smaller piece."

"At minimum that would ensure the sure phone couldn't work or access the Omnist," Kick said.

Chikao pried open the phone and took out the battery so quickly that it was clear he'd done that many times. He placed the battery in his branded computer rucksack that also held the rest of the phones, the ones that held souls of those who'd declined to participate in reincorporation. "Won't work now."

"If we throw it in the garbage, we'll have to trust that our landfills won't digest a piece of phone for many thousands of years," Kick said. "But still, wouldn't that free him?"

Veris looked concerned. "What would've happened if one of the souls had read their spell while locked in the closet safe?"

"Oh, God," Kick said.

"Ah, yes, well, I suppose that can happen," Chikao said. "One wouldn't want that. Pressure from expanding body increasing until container explodes. Very loud and dangerous."

"And messy," Kick said.

"Like bomb. Or maybe body only expands to size of container. Still not good. Or perhaps safe becomes new vessel."

"All good options for Korekuta," Kick said.

"Jewelya!" Veris called into the living room.

Jewelya was speaking with Yuko and Gremmie in near Chikao's Día De Los Muertos altar. "Yes?"

"Would you and Ainsley be willing to sell me that safe in your closet?" Veris said.

A = B + C = D

Safe = Korekuta + phone = safe.

Double entendre. Easy math.

CHAPTER

FORTY-FOUR

AINSLEY

Veris was fascinating; she'd brightened so much emotionally since Chikao's return. And her hair had turned much grayer in the short time Chikao was trapped in the phone. She looked like what he imagined her own mother would look like, aged, but young of spirit. It was the youthful, free-spirited eyes behind her thick glasses. Even the lines in her face were happy lines.

"I caught myself in the smoked mirror over there," Veris said. "I saw the hair. I barely recognized myself, but at the same time, I knew that was me. I match myself better now. The inner and the outer."

"It's a dark mirror, though," Jewelya said.

Jewelya's favorite mirror.

"I didn't realize how much I would like it," Veris said. "My hair now represents a deeper connection I have with Chikao."

It was true that Veris had the same vibrancy and passion for life that Ainsley had noticed the first time he witnessed one of Chikao's Lodges. The bright, excited eyes; the smile as wide as her face.

"The timing is interesting, too," Veris said. "It's now November second. All Souls Day."

FORTY-FIVE

KICK

K ick and Kat were at the hospital, seated in the waiting room until the others arrived. Kick's beard and hair were scruffier than they'd been in years, after not grooming for a couple weeks for the Halloween party. And he hadn't had a chance in the days since then, either. Even without a flannel, he still felt like he was cosplaying Paul Bunyan.

There was a black Consumia's Spiritual Emporium shopping bag near Kat's feet. She'd already told him what was in it, and he didn't care to look to verify.

Veris walked up, carrying a valet with three coffees.

"Oh my god," Kat said, standing up. "Veris? Your hair!"

Kick, too, was still getting used to Veris's now nearly white hair. But she was still emitting, emoting, evoking a sense of deep forest green. Unlike her hair, the color was felt more like an emotion, rather than seen as literal wavelengths of the light spectrum.

"Indeed, my hair!" Veris said, handing her one of the coffees. "And he texted he'll meet us here in a moment. He says he's excited to see Lisa."

"That's such a creepy concept," Kat said. "I don't want Chikao excited about anything."

After the events of the last few days, Kick wasn't sure about how much to trust Chikao about anything. But it was Veris who'd convinced them to let him come by to see Lisa today. And they trusted her.

"He's being truthful about this," Veris said. "I can tell."

"Well, Lisa was right about one thing," Kat said. "Being blind, she'd be of no use to Korekuta any more, even if Chikao hadn't flipped on him."

"Not really," Veris said. "The vessel was useless to him. Once someone is reduced to a soul, though, they'd have different senses, anyway. From what I understand, even vision is far different."

"'Reduced to a soul'?" Kat said. "Is that a euphemism for 'Once she's dead'?"

"It does sound better, doesn't it?" Veris said, without any noticeable irony or snark.

"One thing, though," Kick said. "You *are* a soul collector, aren't you?"

"I guess I've always been. I just wasn't cursing them. But I've always sought out haunted objects and collected them. I communicate with them. Now, with Chikao's Language of the Sun, perhaps we can free them."

"So, you really are friends with him now?" Kat said. She, on the other hand, was made of snark.

"Well, don't get me wrong," Veris said. "I'm very aware of what he's done. And *he's* very aware of what he's done. He'd been misaligned, but now he's rehabilitating. I think he grasps reality a lot better now."

"I'm not so sure that *I* am right now," Kat said. "Grasping reality. Maybe even less."

"I think he honestly thought he was valuing souls over lives," Veris said. "Like a lot of religions do. It's like he'd been in a cult. A cult of three."

"Three?" Kat said.

"Korekuta, Chikao, and Yuko, his assistant."

That's right. Kat hasn't met her. "You sound like Chikao has you convinced," Kick said.

"I am. He was working for a demagogue who once burned souls for his lifeforce. That can throw off any moral compass."

"Still. That's pretty fucked up," Kick said. His phone buzzed.

Mote:

Paranoia is a form of fear.

It is.

"Veris," Kick said. "I know you try to always see the positive in people, but maybe this is a bit much." She was seriously siding with evil. Or morally gray. Or something. Whatever Chikao was.

"We're both in search of positivity," she said. "We're going to be the opposite of soul collectors. We've decided to travel the world looking for imprisoned souls. And like I said, instead of keeping them, we're going to free them."

"Dumb question," Kick said. "And I don't mean this disrespectfully, but...Do you think your Día De Los Muertos kits really work? Do they attract the intended souls?" Kick was thinking about kits attracting souls to the Emporium. Perhaps using a kit next year for Javy, the man who'd died in the Dark Arts room, would please Eudora, Javy's mother.

"Yeah., I hear your altar attracted Chikao," Kat said.

Kick hadn't thought of it that way. Using an altar to attract a living person. But Chikao *had* been reduced to a soul at that point.

"I don't know. But I do think they're mostly for the living," Veris said. "To keep their memories of their loved ones alive. But some souls I've spoken with have said they were really moved by the altars their families had made for them. So, they do get noticed."

"But what about Chikao?" Kat said.

"No, no, no," Veris said, but the look in her eyes, even through the thick glasses, betrayed her words. Seemingly aware of this when she caught Kick's eye, she looked down.

As if on cue, Chikao and Yuko walked up, upbeat as if they were at a cocktail party. Greetings followed, which included Chikao introducing Yuko to Kat.

"Not so many dead souls here right now," Chikao said. "These doctors, they're doing a good job."

"Dead souls?" Kat said.

"Poor word choice." Chikao was smiling. His Omniscian personality had returned. "Dying people. I'm finding those who need spells to extend their stay as humans. If they want to, of course."

This made Kick wonder about the extent of Language of the Sun's powers. "So, you can just make people here immortal with a spell?" he said.

"Oh, no, you misunderstand," Chikao said. "I do not believe never-ending spell is possible for a human. Counter-spells work on people already cursed by Language of the Sun. For sick people, spells help heal body, optimize natural human powers. Not create new ones."

Chikao looked at Kat. "Did you bring the rope?"

Kat nodded and picked up the shopping bag that contained some remnants of Lisa's Wonder Woman costume, the tiara and bloodied lasso. She'd been wearing the rest when she'd arrived at the hospital and had them subsequently thrown out.

"Good!" Chikao said, taking the bag and peering inside. He didn't seem bothered by what he saw. "Let's talk to Lisa."

They entered her hospital room. Flowers, balloons, and cards covered most flat surfaces. All things she wouldn't be able to see.

"Lisa, it's me and Kick and Veris," Kat said. "And now we have Chikao and his assistant Yuko with us."

"Hi, guys," Lisa said, meekly. Her head was completely bandaged over her eyes. "I don't know...are you sure it's safe for him to be here?"

"Lisa, I'm Veris." She lightly touched Lisa's elbow. She'd code-switched a bit, even more soothing, with the implicit kindness of her soft, ASMR voice.

"Lisa, I am Yuko. It is nice to meet you, as well." But Yuko didn't touch her. "And I do understand if you're uncomfortable. Just know Chikao is here to help."

"Hello, Lisa," Chikao said.

"You did this to me," Lisa said. "I tried to escape and yet you're here."

"Lisa," Veris said. "I feel what you are saying. I really do."

"I feel like there's green in the room," Lisa said, her voice marginally brightening.

And there was. Kick could feel it, too. "That would be Veris," he said. He looked at Kat, micro-shrugging, imploring for validation. Kat returned the gesture. Maybe she didn't see the green.

"Do you mind if I try to help?" Chikao said. "I'm going to put lasso on your chest. You can hold it, too, if you like."

"I'm a little scared," Lisa said.

Kat took Lisa by the hand from the other side of the bed. "I'm here, too," she said. "He's just going to say a spell."

"The worst has already happened," Chikao said. Surprisingly, or perhaps not so much, he had an easygoing bedside manner. He patted Lisa's other arm softly. "Horrible tragedy. Now, though, things will only get better."

Kick felt useless here. He wasn't an active participant in this process, but he was curious if it would work. He wanted to believe it. Then it dawned on him that Chikao could still have other plans for Lisa's soul. Transferring her into the lasso maybe.

"Ready?" Chikao asked Lisa, and then looked at Kat to second the motion. Chikao wrapped the lasso into a circle and placed it on Lisa's chest so it extended from her waist to her neck. She brought both hands over the rope, crossing them like she was a corpse, hugging it against her.

Chikao handed the tiara to Kat. "If you'd do the honors," he said.

"This is the tiara, now," Kat said, then gently placed it on Lisa's head, just touching the top edge of the bandages. She once again took Lisa's hand in both of hers and petted it. Kat was infamous for a "No hugging, no touching" policy with people. But this was obviously an extreme situation.

"I will give her spell," Chikao said to the others. "Everyone else, try not to hear. Back up as far as you can go."

Kick, Veris, and Yuko did as instructed, but Kat didn't

move. The look on her face was defiant, but peaceful. Chikao seemed to accept this.

"I will tell her a few words at a time to memorize, so maybe hum to yourself," he said to Kat. "But Lisa, I would like for you to remember it all."

He leaned down and whispered a few syllables in her ear, then turned his head away and mumbled under his breath, possibly a counter-spell for himself. Then he leaned back in and told her another few words.

"Now Lisa, please softly, repeat what I said. Not loud. But speak carefully. There is no need to rush. Slowly, okay?"

He nodded at Kat, who started humming. Kick was positive he recognized the song. What was it? Perhaps it was The Color Braille, one her favorite bands.

Chikao then repeated the routine, delivering two sets of whispered words at a time, followed by Lisa's recitation. Kat was still humming the same song, and it was nearly driving Kick crazy. He definitely knew this melody. Then it hit him. It was something Kat and her husband had written for the band they were in, Pious Defiance. Jesse had played guitar in their band before he passed away. So, being Kat's best friend, it was a good bet Lisa knew the song.

The entire spell took several minutes. When they finished, Chikao stood still, seemingly waiting for something to happen. Nothing did. "We are done," he said after a moment. "Lisa, thank you. You did perfectly."

Relative to how quickly people had reappeared from their phones, this spell didn't seem to have been effective.

"So this didn't work?" Kick said.

"No, it did," Veris said, stepping closer to the bed. "I can feel the souls of Lisa's eyes have returned."

"Bigger soul now," Chikao said. "Leave bandages on. These

THE SOUL PHONE COLLECTOR

are major wounds. Healing will take time, maybe several months. I do not know. I am not doctor."

"But ultimately you feel this will work?" Kat said.

"It has already worked," Chikao said. "Eyes have returned. When they remove bandages, they will say it's miracle."

But Kick knew the truth, and so would Lisa. This situation would never have existed if not for Chikao's misdeeds, even if, by doing this, he was attempting to make reparations.

FORTY-SIX

JEWELYA

Four months later:

Jewelya and Ainsley had been frequenting Consumia's Spiritual Emporium more often lately: She now taught yoga once a week in the Basil Alcove (with some participants being Consumerians from that fateful Dirgatory experience); Ainsley been helping Kick with the relaunch of the Omnist; and both of them attended more Lodges. CSE had virtually become a second home to them.

"You're going to the Emporium tonight, right?" Jewelya said to Ainsley, working on his computer in the spare bedroom-office. Veris and Chikao had been traveling for months and were back in town to host a joint Lodge.

"I'm not sure," Ainsley said, looking up from his work. Despite spending forty-five to fifty hours a week with Warbler Brothers, and putting in fifteen to twenty more with Kick and

Lodges, he was far better about answering Jewelya's texts and calls, and noticing her when she spoke. He was trying, if nothing else.

"You're right," she said. "There's no way Chikao and Veris will want to see you."

"Why so mean, JJ?"

Ainsley was playing coy. He'd called her JJ. She knew he wanted to go. The couple had also become friends with Connie and Yksian, and together they'd recently grabbed drinks with Kat after a Lodge. Jewelya felt they'd become part of the fabric of the Emporium, blurring the lines between being Consumerians, friends, and employees of the store.

"Maybe you should ask the Aleph family reunion if they're going," Jewelya said.

"You know, Aleph does have a bit of Stockholm syndrome," Ainsley said, walking over to her in the hallway and pulling her hips toward her like he used to do when they first met. "I bet half of us make it to Chikao's Lodge. But mostly I want to see Gremmie. What time's it start again?"

"Eight p.m."

"Plenty of time," he said.

"And afterward Summer and Kat want to go dancing. Denkins, too."

Ainsley brightened up. "Cool! Can I come?" He'd never asked to go dancing with her before. But before she could answer, his expression changed to that of trying not to smile and boring a hole into her soul. He was kidding.

"You know you can, if you want," she said.

"Maybe." He leaned in to kiss her, and at the last second lifted to his tiptoes as if hopping, so she did too. His attempt to kiss her forehead landed on the bridge of her nose. Like it always did. They both laughed. Like they always did.

"Maybe we can go to Portland?" Jewelya said. She'd seen

his phone the night of Chikao's Lodge. He'd been looking up hotel options. She hadn't said anything about it, but they hadn't gone yet, either.

"You know about that?" Ainsley said.

"A little Omnist told me."

It looked like Ainsley was trying not to smile again. "It's like you're psychic. I'm planning to ask Veris when she's going home next."

Over Ainsley's shoulder, on the wall, were the two pieces of cobweb art from the Emporium. Jewelya felt her soul being sucked into them again. She thought about her connection with Lisa that night at Dirgatory and how this was a similar feeling. "Do you think those mirrors could be vessels?" she said.

Ainsley turned his head to look at them, not letting go of her hips. "Oh, no, Yksian says they're made with Black Vertigo paint. That's why we always feel a bit nauseated when we look at them. Plus, Veris has seen them. She would've said something."

A notification went off on Ainsley's phone, the glass still eerily cracked in the outline of L.A.'s San Gabriel Mountains after he'd dropped it at the Emporium months ago.

"When are you getting a new phone?" Jewelya said.

"When you get a new sense of humor."

Asshole.

"It's like *The Color Braille* hoodie you always wear," he said. The band had given her that after their video shoot. "They're both sentimental," he said.

He was wrong here in nuance, but it wasn't worth the correction that could lead to an argument. This time, though, he wasn't looking up, but staring into space, thinking.

"What's it say?" Jewelya said. "Let me guess, it's something about *cracking* up. Or how nostalgia and sentimentality are overrated and dangerous."

Ainsley showed her the screen.

MOTE:

Viewed from the perspective of eternity, time doesn't exist.

FORTY-SEVEN

KICK

T he Omnist II location had finally opened in Echo Park, and with how much time Kick, Lucador, and Connie had spent getting the store up and running, tonight would be the first Lodge at the Emporium that Kick had been able to attend in a while. He was currently in Connie's office, working at her desk.

Veris had told him she planned to speak about souls moving on from the body, where they go, how they come to visit, and the like. Unsurprisingly, Chikao would speak about technology and the human tendency to imbue it with one's sense of soul. And together they would talk about how these concepts merged into one for their travels.

"Heeeeyyy!" a voice said from out front in the Emporium.

"Veris, welcome!" Connie said, out of sight. "Chikao!" There were probably hugs.

Kick got up from the desk and went out to greet them. Yes, hugs.

"So handsome!" Veris said as she hugged, her face sideways against Kick's chest due to her diminutive height. Even in her clunky platform shoes.

He didn't think of himself as a catch. On a scale of one to ten, a six at best. Maybe an L.A. five. She was likely remarking about how he'd gotten a haircut and trimmed his beard since she last saw him. And maybe he'd lost a few pounds of beer belly.

"That's because my aura is flannel today," Kick said.

"Ha," Veris said, holding him at arm's length to look at him. "I've seen tie-dye auras before, but not flannel." She punched him lightly in the arm. "You're kidding."

Chikao and Veris were all smiles for Connie, of course, and Chikao explained that Yuko would be arriving later. She still lived in Japan, helping the two soul collectors research locations ripe with vessel potential, culling email recommendations from scholars and anthropologists, and generally assisting in various travel needs.

Chikao had placed a medium-sized box on the counter. He opened the flaps. It was filled with clay and stone figures, jewelry, dolls, and other trinkets and knickknacks, and his smile was wider than the box. He was genuinely pleased to be there. It was odd. For somebody so pleasant, it was remarkable that Chikao could've done the things he'd done. Kick couldn't fully take him at his word that he'd changed, but really, it was still all about Veris. If she trusted Chikao, Kick would give him an inch.

"We have gift for you," Chikao said. "All these things once had souls in them. Empty vessels now."

"I don't see any phones," Kick said.

"You don't want dead phones. Old technology. Disposed of

349

properly."

"So these weren't only from souls that you'd trapped, then? Some of this stuff looks pretty old."

"There are *so* many souls out there," Veris said, gesturing as if grabbing one from the ether. "We get them from everywhere. We've only scratched the surface."

Kick realized that Veris's movements mirrored those of Chikao. As if both were constantly aware that everything was universal. In their minds, everything was. And she'd obviously accepted that her hair had turned white. It dawned on him that perhaps it was her connection to Chikao that had caused that.

"Far more than what Chikao and Korekuta were involved with," she said. "Many of these vessels are indeed much older, ancient." Veris tilted the box so she could see inside and picked through the items. "Some are family heirlooms like necklaces and rings. Some were passed down for generations, with tales of hauntings that were legendary within their families. In the old days, I offered to buy vessels and sometimes the most skittish people were happy to get rid of them. But back then I could only speak with the souls and try to soothe them. I didn't know how to free them."

"So that's what these are?" Kick said. Veris smiled and tilted the box toward him, even though he had no problem seeing into it. Near the top was a leather pouch, dry rotting and falling apart. He wanted it. It was worthless for its intended use, but he imagined Lucador could sew it, or pieces of it, into one of his patchwork capes. His partner was always on the lookout for vintage leather. Especially if Kick told him it once contained a human soul.

"These are some of them. Chikao and I ask the soul if they want to be freed. Sometimes they say no. It's true. Not often, but it happens. Perhaps they've found peace. I've spoken to a few people from Aleph, and they explained how the vessel is just a fulcrum on this plane from which to size from."

"I spoke with a woman who lost her partner that way." Ainsley had introduced Kick to Nefertiti the night the souls of Aleph returned. "I guess he didn't want to come back."

"Yes, it does happen. But if they say yes, then Chikao does his thing and the soul moves on. But once in a while, an entire person reappears. That person is usually old or sick and near death anyway. We believe their situation was due to a botched curse from someone trying to extend their life. They still pass away in moments, though, and their soul moves on."

Kick wondered what the pouch he was holding had been used for. It smelled like old leather, dusty and rotted of course, but also fragrant oil.

"Oh, that once held soul-cleansing items," Veris said, reading his mind. Like the Soul Meets Body kits they sold not a dozen feet away. But this was much older than those.

Kick was positive Veris was connecting with him; he intuited she'd encouraged Chikao to use the items they'd found in this kit.

"How many souls do you think you've freed?" Connie said.

"Several hundred, maybe? Chikao keeps a log."

Chikao nodded affirmatively. "Two hundred and ninety-seven so far."

"You haven't branded these," Connie said, lifting a hand-made corncob pipe. "They should have the Veris logo."

"For you to do," Chikao said. "Make them Omnist. CSE-verified soul vessels."

"I got it, they're *Verisfied*," Connie said. "Verified by Veris."

Connie was better than Kick at creative marketing.

"Ah, and how is Lisa?" Chikao said, perking up.

"She's good," Connie said. "And you'd never know anything had happened by looking at her. She is beautiful."

"Good, good. Great relief. Her eyes should be superpower now," Chikao said.

"She *is* sort of a superhero," Kick said. "She's been helping me with the Omnist and how to understand loose souls. Something you and I can talk about later. I can show you what we're doing."

"Oh, that's amazing," Veris said. "I didn't see that coming."

Was that a pun?

"But I understand if she never forgives me," Chikao said. "Kat, too. All of Aleph. I can only do my best now."

Veris and Chikao were standing close together. Really close, as if he was about to put his arm around her. They looked at each other as if they shared a vast depth of secrets.

"Are you guys a couple now?" Kick said, pushing, teasing.

"That's such odd phrasing," Veris said. "Everybody looks for boxes to put everything into. Chikao and I, we travel the world releasing souls and teaching people how to provide for the recently deceased."

"Great non-answer."

"I take that as a *yes*," Connie said.

Veris patted Chikao's arm. "And he's very good at this."

Let them have their lives, however they want to live them. Kick picked up the box from the counter.

"Veris, will you come with me?" he said, tilting his head and beginning to walk toward the office. He slowed to allow her to catch up. "I'm curious. Do you have stories for all these vessels? You know how Connie loves her story cards. The stories make them all the more real."

"I do. But there are far too many to recount. Chikao wrote them down. I'll email some pages for you."

Kick thought about the everlasting lamp he'd installed for Javy in the Dark Arts room. Connie had never said a word to him about it. "I guess this all means Chikao never did attain

352

immortality," he said. "Or he had once, but...but he lost it?" He scratched his beard. It was almost as if dust from the items from the box had attached to him. Seeking a safe place like the Emporium.

Veris looked at him through several millimeters of lenses, deep into his soul, to the everlasting light in the center of his head. "One doesn't *attain* immortality," she said. "You just haven't died yet. And this happens again the next day. And the next. And that is what goes on forever. You didn't used to be eternal in the past, just as you aren't going to *become* eternal in the future. You just are or you aren't." She raised her hands like this was a sermon. "And you are, and you are, and you are!"

"So, does that mean Chikao is still immortal? Or Korekuta?"

"All of us, Kick. We're all immortal until we die." Veris took off her glasses and wiped them with a piece of silk from her pocket. "And trust me, the spells help, too."

Acknowledgments

I'd like to thank some of the people, without whom, none of The Omnist books or Lodges would've manifested:

Burton C. Bell, Caeri Bertrand, Ashley Carlson, Kristy Edwards, Avily Jerome, Erin Killean, Ro Kohli, Amy Lyford, Erik Marshall, David Mastros, Sonja Mastros, Kimbra Miller, Eileen O'Connell, Jessica Parker, Robert Phillips, Jane Asher Reaney, William Shunn, Dustin Stanton, Ryan Valdez, Azul Weldon.

And of course you, if you've been suckered into reading this.

ABOUT THE AUTHOR

Rob Weldon lives in Los Angeles, CA, and works at a craft beer bar. To learn more about his books or to connect, find him online at: Facebook.com/rob.weldon

Instagram and Threads: @blood.wren